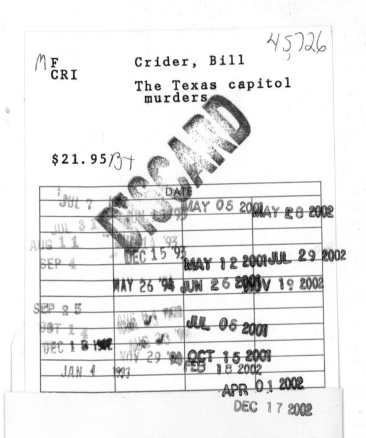

☑ **W9-AGX-700**

M F
CRI

Crider, Bill

The Texas capitol
murders

45726

$21.95 BT

DISCARD

DATE		
JUL 7		MAY 05 2001	MAY 28 2002
JUL 31			
AUG 11	NOV 14 '93		
SEP 4	DEC 15 '93	MAY 12 2001	JUL 29 2002
	MAY 26 '94	JUN 26 2001	NOV 19 2002
SEP 25			
OCT 14	AUG 25 '94	JUL 05 2001	
DEC 18 1992	AUG 29 '94		
JAN 4 1993	NOV 29 '94	OCT 15 2001	
		FEB 18 2002	
		APR 01 2002	
		DEC 17 2002	

Austin Memorial Library
220 S. Bonham St.
Cleveland, TX 77327

101877

BAKER & TAYLOR BOOKS

A GIFT FROM THE
ESTATE OF
SELAURA HALLUM FALVEY

THE TEXAS CAPITOL MURDERS

ALSO BY BILL CRIDER

Blood Marks

SHERIFF DAN RHODES MYSTERIES

Evil at the Root
Death on the Move
Cursed to Death
Shotgun Saturday Night
Too Late to Die

PROFESSOR CARL BURNS MYSTERIES

Dying Voices
One Dead Dean

Bill Crider

THE TEXAS CAPITOL MURDERS

ST. MARTIN'S PRESS   NEW YORK

The following is a work of fiction, but while the characters are not
intended to represent real persons, the Texas Capitol building is
obviously quite real. I have tinkered with some details of its appearance and architecture, but otherwise it exists very much as I have
described it.

There is no chief administrator of the Texas Capitol. Like all the
characters and situations in this novel, this position and the duties it
entails are the inventions of the author.

THE TEXAS CAPITOL MURDERS. Copyright © 1992 by Bill Crider. All
rights reserved. Printed in the United States of America. No part of
this book may be used or reproduced in any manner whatsoever
without written permission except in the case of brief quotations
embodied in critical articles or reviews. For information, address St.
Martin's Press, 175 Fifth Avenue, New York, N.Y. 10010

Production Editor: David Stanford Burr
Design by Judith A. Stagnitto

Library of Congress Cataloging-in-Publication Data

Crider, Bill.
      The Texas capitol murders / Bill Crider.
            p.   cm.
      "A Thomas Dunne book."
      ISBN 0-312-07093-4
      I. Title.
PS3553.R497T48   1992
813'.54—dc20   91-33409
                                        CIP

10 9 8 7 6 5 4 3 2

This one's for the cousins:
Michelle, Scott, Sunday, Sarah, and Lauren

PART ONE

ONE

It was cool and quiet in the basement of the Texas Capitol building, where Wayne the Wagger was sleeping soundly in a blue trash hamper, covered by layers of crumpled newspaper.

When Wayne slept, he slept like a rock, and this was the most comfortable bed he'd found in quite some time, a hell of a lot better than the alley pavement that he usually slept on, though the fact that it didn't smell of urine and grease and exhaust fumes kept him awake for a short while.

Wayne's brain had long ago been fried by a wide variety of bad street drugs whose names he could no longer even remember. He had gulped them, smoked them, popped them, snorted them—hell, he would've taken them in through his ears if he could have. Now he merely dreamed about them, recalling in his sleep their colors and seeing in his frazzled mind a kaleidoscope of red and blue and yellow and white as he flew like a slightly crazed bird into a turquoise sky and then swooped and dived through a crowd of long-haired men and women who smoked hand-rolled marijuana cigarettes and talked about making the world a better place to live, a place filled with peace and love and understanding.

The gentle, decent ones of those distant days had somehow disappeared. The ones who were left, like Wayne, shared a dazed, confused existence in which they drifted around the city, often gravitating to the Capitol where the pretty girls and boys, the ashtrays full of cigarette butts, and the lack of any energetic law enforcement created a virtual paradise for the "drag worms," as the locals called them.

The paradise was not what it had once been, however, because the man in charge of the tour desk watched the kids like a hawk, and the people running the tourist desk were now middle-aged and professional. The number of tourists had also increased, making things much less fun all around. There were older people who came in on big buses, did not smoke, and pushed Wayne when he got in their way. There were lots of young families, too, whose older members eyed Wayne with wariness and suspicion.

Much of the time Wayne sat half hidden in some nook, looking at cute messengers and tour guides, bouncy young tourists in shorts. At other times Wayne wandered the halls, playing with himself under his dirty clothes, getting his satisfaction out of irritating the people he associated with. He was scared of the Capitol cops, but they had long ago decided that he was harmless and for the most part left him alone in order to spend their time drinking coffee and gossiping, though they didn't mind rousting him late in the evenings if they could find him.

Tonight they hadn't caught him, and he slept in relative peace until something, some noise or other, drew him out of the depths of his dreaming and brought him back to a kind of fuzzy awareness, which was about the only kind of awareness he ever managed to achieve these days.

He lay in the hamper and didn't stir. He'd learned over the years that it was best never to make a move until you knew where you were and what was going on. Otherwise, somebody might kick the shit out of you.

Since it usually took Wayne awhile to figure out where he was, much less what was going on, he lay still and quiet and listened to the voices.

One belonged to a man. "Oh, yes. Those are nice. Very nice. Really very nice."

There was a sound of heavy breathing, grunting, and smacking kisses. Then, "I've got something nice for you, too. Can you feel it?"

A woman's voice answered tentatively. "*Sí.* I can feel it."

"I bet you can. Here."

There was the sound of a zipper.

Shit, Wayne thought, catching on to what he was hearing. *He's gonna screw her right here.* He thought about taking a peek out over the top of the trash hamper, but he decided against it. No use getting in trouble. He might lose his comfortable bed.

He wanted to watch, though. He liked watching as much as anything. Maybe more. He didn't like to admit it even to himself, but looking and wagging were about all he could do, all he had been able to do for a long time.

"Let's lie down and get comfortable," the man said.

"But the window," the woman said.

"Screw the window," the man said.

The woman giggled, as if she knew very well the man wasn't going to screw the window.

There was more kissing. Wayne figured they were going to start doing it any second now. He wanted to look, but he was too scared. There was no way he could get out of the hamper quickly if they saw him, and he didn't know what the man might do to him if he were caught watching.

Then he noticed a little hole in the canvas of the hamper. Very carefully, he started enlarging it with his finger.

"Yes," the man said. "Right there. Yes."

5

Wayne got his eye to the hole. The light in the hall was still on, and he could see them lying on the floor not more than a couple of feet from his hamper.

He knew the woman at once. She was one of the custodial staff, and he'd seen her pushing a mop around the place every now and then. She was a young Hispanic, not bad looking. Wayne had wagged at her a couple of times, but she hadn't paid him any mind.

He thought he knew the man, too. He knew him pretty well, in fact, but somehow he couldn't quite place him. His memory didn't always work like it should. Both of them were breathing heavily now, and then the man started to move between the woman's legs.

They were quiet and intense, and Wayne knew why they weren't making any noise. They didn't want the cops to hear them.

It didn't take long. The man collapsed on the woman's breasts and lay there panting for a minute. Then he shoved himself up with the palms of his hands and looked down at her.

"You're a very pretty girl, Mona. You date a lot of men besides me, don't you?"

"No," the woman said. "Not many."

The man got off her and sat back on his heels. "That's not true. You know it's not. Have you told anyone about you and me?"

The woman looked up at him, but she didn't answer. Wayne thought she looked a little afraid.

"I'm afraid you have," the man said.

"No," the woman said. "No, I have not told anyone."

"You have a tendency to talk, though. Everyone knows that. But that's all right. I hope you haven't talked to the wrong people." He got up and began fixing his pants. He straightened himself and pulled up the zipper.

The woman was standing now, too, and Wayne couldn't

see their faces. He could tell that she had her back to the man and was buttoning her blouse, apparently relaxed.

"No," she said. "I have not talked to anyone at all."

"Good," the man said. He sounded pleased.

The show was over. Wayne settled back to go to sleep, careful not to move too much and rattle the newspapers that covered him.

That was when he heard the woman choking. It was a terrible sound, as if she were trying to say something or maybe there was something stuck in her throat that she was trying to get out and couldn't.

Wayne put his eye to the hole again. He didn't want to, this time, but he did. When he saw what was happening, he felt his scrotum tighten with fear, but at the same time he felt an awful fascination, a need to see more. He wasn't so worried about noise now, and he swiftly enlarged the hole in the hamper.

The man held the two ends of something in his hands. It might have been a scarf or a just a big handkerchief; Wayne couldn't really tell. Whatever it was, it was around the woman's neck, and the ends were crossed behind as the man choked the life out of her. She wasn't very big, and he had lifted her completely off the floor. She kicked her feet backward at his shins and clawed frantically at her throat with her hands, but nothing did any good. The man was far too strong for her.

She became still very quickly. The man didn't let her slump to the floor. He took a step and dumped her into an empty trash hamper that was sitting end to end with the one Wayne was in.

Then the man started pulling newspapers from Wayne's hamper to cover the dead woman.

Oh, Jesus, Wayne thought. Sweat slicked over his body and poured from his hair. He was holding his breath now, trying to make himself as small as Sniffles. *Oh, Jesus. He's going to kill me, too. He's going to find me here and kill me.*

But to conceal himself, Wayne had used several days' editions of the Austin *American-Statesman,* and the man was in a hurry. He used only the want ads and the sports section, and then he was gone.

Wayne thought for a minute about what he had seen, and then he decided that maybe he hadn't seen anything at all. He had some pretty weird dreams, and this was probably all just a part of one of his dreams.

That was it. Just one of his crazy dreams. Sure. Had to be. He looked at the hole he had made in the blue duck hamper and wondered why he had done a thing like that. Oh, well, he would just go on back to sleep. He probably wouldn't remember a thing in the morning.

He hardly ever did.

Wayne the Wagger wouldn't have been sleeping in the basement that night if he had not eluded the Capitol cops for once. The building was supposed to close at 11:00 P.M., and the cops had usually rousted all the transients by then. But this time Wayne had been too smart for them.

He generally looked for a place to crash on the upper floors, and he knew every closet and unused room in the building. The trouble was that the cops knew about all those places, too, and they usually checked them out. It wasn't just Wayne they were looking for. There were plenty of transients in the Capitol, and people didn't like the idea of that at all. There wasn't much the cops could do about the transients during the day. But night was a different story, and they could force everyone to leave when the building closed.

If you had a pencil and a piece of paper that you wrote on now and then, you could claim you were "doing research," at least during the day. Then nobody could bother you. All the transients knew that trick and went from place to place bumming pencils. Wayne had tried it when he first started hanging out in the Capitol, but he had never been good at it. Then the wagging urge had gotten too strong. He started going on the tours with the pretty guides too often, and their director got him thrown out of the building. When he came back, he avoided the guides and the tours, and the cops pretty much left him alone until late evening, when they would chase him outside—if they could find him.

They had the spy cameras, too, and used them to watch people with. Wayne could feel the electric rays zapping his brain every time he passed one. He had stopped the rays by putting a piece of aluminum foil inside his greasy Houston Astros cap, but he knew the cops could still see him. The foil stopped the rays, all right, but it didn't make him invisible.

This time, though, he'd fooled them good. He'd gone down in the basement to the snack area late in the afternoon to try to cadge a quarter or two from the tourists, but no one had given him a damn thing. So he'd wandered off down the east hallway, slipping quietly under the spy camera, not that slipping quietly did any good, and turned off down a cul-de-sac that bent around into a space the size of a large closet.

The space contained two trash hampers, their blue canvas suspended from wheeled steel frames, and a window.

There was no spy camera.

Wayne had stood there for a long time, looking out the window. Mainly he could see the cement wall of some kind of narrow shaft, but every now and then someone would walk by and he could see their legs silhouetted against the sky through the top of the window. He kept hoping that a good-looking woman would come by, wearing a skirt maybe, and that the wind would blow the skirt and give him a glimpse of her panties, but it never happened. Most of the women he saw were wearing either pants or those plain straight skirts that didn't blow. Most of the tourist women wore shorts, even in the Capitol, and it depressed Wayne just to look at them. He might be a drag worm, but he still had certain standards.

Finally he glanced into the trash hampers. They were empty, and that was when he got his idea. He had not had an idea lately, and he was pretty pleased with himself for having this one.

He walked back down the hall, past the camera, resisting the urge to flip the cops the bird, and into the snack area. He went up the wide stairs to the first floor, stopping in front of the tour-guide desk to grab his crotch and shake it for the benefit of the two pretty young guides who were leaving the desk to change into their regular clothes and go home for the day.

They were talking and laughing and ignored him completely, but that was all right. He'd gotten used to that. Too bad they didn't know what he had for them. They wouldn't ignore him if they did. This notion was the only weapon he had left to use against the increasingly retreating world.

The hall on the first floor was much wider than the one in the basement, and the ceilings were very high. That was all to the good as far as the tourists and workers were concerned. It meant that they could give Wayne a wide berth.

It wasn't so much his looks that bothered them. It was his smell.

Wayne wasn't given to bathing, and he wore several layers of clothing even in the summer. On the outside he was wearing an orange and white University of Texas sweatshirt portraying the head of Bevo, the school mascot. The shirt was streaked with grease, dirt, and other unidentifiable substances. Wayne also wore fleece-lined gray warm-up pants at least as dirty as the shirt, and a pair of ragged and dirty Keds high tops that had been white long before Wayne found them but were now almost black, along with his Astros cap. It was hard to tell what he might be wearing underneath the sweatshirt, though the collar of a red-and-black flannel shirt protruded above the neck of it.

Wayne's hair was long and black and greasy, and he had a thick, matted beard in which a close inspection, should anyone be crazy enough to attempt one, would have revealed a few hard flecks of catsup, residue of Kentucky Fried Chicken batter (Extra Crispy), a minute portion of a French fry, fragments of a hamburger bun, bits of scrambled egg, and other things less easy to identify. These things along with Wayne's general aversion to soap and water caused him to have a definite air about him. People edged to the sides of the hall as he approached.

He didn't care. He hardly noticed them. He was looking for a newspaper.

He found a whole pile laying outside the door of some senator's office and took it, not even caring if anyone saw him. Now all he had to do was wait. Tonight, he'd be sleeping in solid comfort. Those stupid cops would never find him.

Wayne woke up the next day feeling much refreshed. He climbed out of the trash hamper, hoping it would still be there that night. He couldn't think ahead much further than that. In fact, even as he thought it, he was afraid he might forget where his bed was. He didn't remember things as well as he once had. At least he didn't think he could. He couldn't remember whether he could or not.

He glanced at the other hamper, saw the crumpled newspapers, but didn't give it another thought. If there was anything in there, he didn't want to know. It didn't have anything to do with him.

He walked back to the main hall and headed for the snack area. He had sixty-five cents, enough to get himself a Dr Pepper for breakfast and have a little something left over.

Out of habit, he glanced up at the security camera. There

11

was a piece of masking tape stuck over the lens. Now there was a good idea. Wayne was sorry he hadn't thought of it himself, and he hoped he could remember it for later, though he knew he probably wouldn't.

He raised an index finger to the blind camera, something he would never normally have done, not liking to draw attention to himself. It looked as if it might be a pretty good day.

TWO

There had been a time when Jane Kettler had enjoyed driving toward the Capitol down Congress Avenue from south Austin. Of course, that had been thirty years ago, when her name had been Jane Warren and she had been a freshman at the University of Texas.

In those days before the proliferation of banks and office buildings, the street had not been lined with high rise after high rise. The view of the Capitol had been unobstructed and impressive. It was still impressive, she supposed, but now that disease and old age had wiped out a number of the spreading shade trees that had once grown on the grounds, the newly planted American elms looked scrawny and disappointing, as if the building itself had somehow suffered.

There hadn't been a traffic problem in her college days, either, but now she was surrounded by cars, and there were one-way streets, buses galore, horns being honked by impatient drivers, women putting on makeup as they waited at the interminable traffic lights—all the things that were common sights and sounds in Houston or Dallas but that she never would have thought she would see or hear in Austin.

She entered the grounds, driving past the red-on-white sign that said NO BUSES BEYOND THIS POINT. The sight of the sign irritated her. It was a result of the new renovation and expansion project, and it meant that tour buses now had to park quite a distance from the Capitol. That in itself wasn't bad, but it worked a hardship on visitors in wheelchairs and on those with any kind of difficulty in walking.

She drove her gray Cutlass Cierra to her parking place opposite the east entrance. It was five minutes before eight. As chief administrator of the Texas Capitol, her job was to make sure that the right hand knew what the left hand was doing, or to put it more accurately, to make sure that the activities of the House and Senate, the west side of the Capitol and the east, did not conflict with one another or with the plans of the governor and his staff when the legislature was in session.

For years, every department had handled its own business pretty well. Then everything had begun to grow and get complicated. Agencies moved out and the legislature needed new departments. People still came to the Capitol when they wanted information or action—usually both—and tourism had increased exponentially.

Jane's main duties recently had been to referee the arguments over the renovation and expansion, a job that was no fun at all and was filled with political tension. Parking, always at a premium, had to be changed constantly, and the situation with the buses was only a small part of the problem. In one of the nastier battles, Jane had been forced to mediate an especially unpleasant argument between the lieutenant governor and the secretary of state over a parking space. These two men were ordinarily polite gentlemen of the old school, but the conflict over the parking space had barely stopped short of bloodshed.

Jane went up the steps and through the massive high doors, almost bumping into a fat woman wearing black polyester pants, a loose-fitting cotton top printed with an indescribable pattern, and dirty white canvas shoes. Her graying hair was drawn tight and pulled into a bun at the back. She was carrying an armload of boxes.

Shit, Jane Kettler thought, remembering who the woman was. "Hello, Mrs. Stanton," she said, forcing a smile. "You're getting an early start today."

"It's never too early to do the Lord's work," Mrs. Stanton said, moving by Jane and out the door. "Me and Miz Tolbert and Mr. Easton have a new exhibit to put up today. It'll save a lot of babies that people are murdering now all the time."

Jane looked down the hall. Near the rotunda, there was another woman, this one almost Mrs. Stanton's opposite, dressed for success in a navy blue suit. She was setting up a card table in front of the secretary of state's office. There were four tables already sitting in the hall, starting near the tour-guide desk and extending eastward down the hallway.

Jane walked down the hall, her royal blue Nikes with the white swoosh carrying her silently along the art-deco tile floor that had been installed in the state's centennial year of 1936. She stopped when she got to the second woman, who was grunting as she struggled with a balky table leg.

"Good morning, Mrs. Tolbert," Jane said.

"Good morning," the woman said, grunting again as the leg snapped into place. She set the table on the floor with a satisfied smile and looked down the hall to where Mrs. Stanton and a clean-cut man in his early thirties were coming through the automatic door with two more tables. The east entrance was the only one with an automatic door for deliveries, though Jane never used it herself.

"Just two more after these," Mrs. Stanton said as she got to where Jane was standing. "Then we can get the exhibits."

"I don't believe you mentioned 'exhibits' in your request for permission to set up here," Jane said.

"Humph. I told the senator it was a right-to-life exhibit.

15

Who do you think owns this place, anyway?" Mrs. Stanton didn't wait for Jane to answer. "I'll tell you who. We the people. The taxpayers of the state of Texas, that's who, and I'm one of 'em."

Jane had learned that any statement that included the words "I'm a taxpayer" meant trouble. She wondered if these ignoramouses used it on highway patrolmen or White House guards. She suspected that they did.

In the past, she had tried to get the cops to eject Mrs. Stanton and her more offensive displays from the building, but the cops hadn't wanted to get involved. The two women and the man with them could be almost violently aggressive, and no one was willing to mess with them. There was the possibility of bad publicity, and nobody wanted that. Besides the women had the support of Senator Wilkins, who was leading the push for an anti-abortion bill in the upcoming legislative session. Wilkins was a powerful man, and no one wanted to risk crossing him, no matter what his feelings on the subject.

Jane left the women setting up yet another table and went into her office, located in the south foyer of the Capitol, just across from the governor's appointment office. She had been given the office, formerly that of a representative, when they created her job. It was unsatisfactorily small, having once been part of another office. However, when the new addition to the Capitol was completed, she was to have a new room with plenty of space, along with as much staff as she needed. For now, it was enough to have the messengers to answer the phone and run errands.

As soon as she was inside she kicked off her Nikes and slipped into the heels that she kept under her desk. She would have preferred to wear the running shoes all day, but it was the rule that members of her staff wear heels. Sometimes she forgot and rushed out of the office in the Nikes. That was why she had chosen the blue and white ones.

She had good taste and dressed beautifully, a feat that required careful shopping on her part, since state salaries did not encourage extravagance. Today her skirt was navy blue pleated silk, and she wore a tailored blue and white plaid jacket buttoned with heavy gold buttons. Her jewelry was always either gold or pearls.

Zach Venner wasn't in the office yet. He was nearly always late, but never outrageously so. He was a college student who worked as a Senate sergeant. The sergeants had been alternating as her office help since her secretary, Margaret Sanders, had married a lobbyist. Eventually the position would be filled with a full-time person again, but for now, Jane was having to make do. The sergeants, like the students who worked as tour guides, varied in dependability and personality—she never knew what one of them might do or say—but they could be trained to be surprisingly competent.

Zach was one of the better ones. He was quiet and funny, and Jane enjoyed his stories about the Senate as long as he used his head about what he told. His uncle had once been speaker of the house, however, so Zach had grown up in politics and was generally discreet.

She turned on the computer that crouched on her desk and called up the calendar. Senator Wilkins, already in town for the session that would begin next week, had scheduled a press conference at eleven o'clock, but that was the only time the press room would be in use. No problem there, but she hoped there wouldn't be any trouble from Stanton and Tolbert during the news briefing. Those women were capable of anything. She got depressed just wondering what kind of "exhibit" they were even now setting up in the hallway.

There would be tours coming in all day, busloads of children from day-care centers, high school students on class trips, senior citizens on tour. She had arranged a reception in the governor's reception room for one group and a coffee in the lieutenant governor's reception room for another. Media had to be reminded of all the photographs to be taken. Thank God the Capitol caterers were efficient. She never had to tell them anything.

There wasn't a single hour free from activity. Jane hoped that Stan Donald, the tour-guide director, was ready, but in fact he always seemed to have things well in hand. Maybe they would get through the day without a major crisis.

If they did, she thought, it would be the first time.

Claude Hebert, who was reasonably proud of his Louisiana Coonass heritage, but who got damn good and tired of telling people that his last name was pronounced "A-bare," was on the security monitors in the north wing office used by the Capitol police. It said something about his alertness that it took him over an hour to notice that one monitor was blank.

That was because Claude was generally interested in looking at pretty women, and there never were any of those on the monitors between seven o'clock, when he came on duty, and eight. So he didn't really look too hard.

When he finally did look, he thought at first that something was wrong with the monitor, but then he noticed that he could see just a tiny bit of the hallway, or something, in the monitor's upper right-hand corner.

"Damn," he said aloud. "Somebody's been messin' with the camera."

"Who you think'd do a thing like that?" Darrel Prince said. He was drinking coffee from a white Styrofoam cup, and Hebert could smell it as Prince looked over his shoulder at the nearly blank screen.

"Fuck if I know," Hebert said. "Somebody's gotta check it out, though. Guess that'd be you."

He shifted in his chair with a creaking of leather as he turned to grin at Prince, whom Hebert thought of as a little dried-up fart. On the other hand, Hebert thought of himself as a fine figure of a man. So what if he had a little gut on him?

18

Showed a man knew how to live, showed he appreciated good food, and there was nothing wrong with that.

Prince, for his part, thought Hebert was a fat, lazy, obnoxious asshole, who liked being a cop mainly because it let him carry a gun, a nightstick, and a five-cell flashlight. The Capitol police were not affiliated with any other police agency, and Prince was pretty sure that Hebert couldn't have gotten on with a *real* police force. He didn't say anything about that to Hebert as he left the office, however.

He glanced down at the souvenir stand as he went out, but there was no one there. It was too early for it to be open yet. He went into the rotunda and turned left into the east hall.

Mrs. Tolbert and Mrs. Stanton were putting their exhibits on the card tables. Prince knew who they were, and he wondered vaguely what kind of weirdness they were up to today. He remembered that only a few weeks previously they had set up the same nine tables in the LBJ Building and placed on each one graphic photos of abortions in progress. They got thrown out of there, but the Capitol was more tolerant.

This time their display looked to be even better than the photos, or maybe worse, depending on your point of view. There were nine model uteruses, each one sectioned to show the growth of the fetus inside during each month of pregnancy, and laying on the table in front of each model was a tiny doll representing what the fetus would look like if it were ripped from the womb during that particular month.

All they needed was a little fake blood, Prince thought. Like that rubber puke you could buy. Make little puddles of it on the tables.

A youngish man Prince didn't know was talking to the women, making them giggle. He looked at Prince with a smile, and Prince turned to go down the wide black stairs. He passed Wayne the Wagger, who was coming up from the basement, Dr Pepper in hand.

"Mornin', Wayne," Prince said. He knew most of the

transients by name, though in most cases, as in Wayne's, he knew only the names they were called by those who worked in the Capitol rather than their real names. Hardly anyone knew what those were.

Wayne said nothing. It was his policy never to speak to or make eye contact with a cop, and he slid by Prince, effluvium trailing after him. He just wanted to get outside and drink his Dr Pepper in peace under the trees. Then he would come back inside and spend the day wandering the halls of the Capitol.

Prince went on down the stairs, turned right at the landing, and descended to the basement. He passed through the snack area and walked down the hall to the camera. Someone had stuck masking tape over the lens.

Prince ripped it off, wondering just how long the tape had been there and thinking briefly of Wayne.

"Nahhhh," he said, shaking his head. Wayne wouldn't be that smart. Someone was, however, and as Prince idly wadded up the masking tape, never thinking that it might be evidence of something, he wondered vaguely who might have done it, and why.

He looked around for a trash can to toss the tape in, but he didn't see one, so he carried the tape back to the snack bar area and threw it away there.

"Well?" Hebert said when Prince came back to the office.

"Well, what?" Prince said. "Is it working or not?"

"Yeah, it's working. It's a little blurry, but it's working."

Prince looked at the screen. It wasn't really blurry, but the tape had left a sticky residue that someone would have to clean off the camera lens. It was the residue that was affecting the picture.

"Masking tape," Prince said.

"What the fuck?" Hebert said.

"Beats me," Prince said, shrugging. He picked up his coffee cup and took a sip. The coffee had gotten cold and tasted like mud. He went to the Mr. Coffee and refilled his cup. Then he sat down, picked up an old issue of *People,* and devoted his attention to a pictorial on the Princesses Di and Fergie as he awaited the day's next big excitement.

THREE

The morning's first busload was from Arkansas, a bunch of old fogies who would find fault with everything, or at least that was Chrissy Allen's experience. Still, old people were better than high schoolers. The football players were always trying to make time with her, and the girls talked behind her back about her hair and her tacky dark skirt. Preschoolers were sometimes worse. You could never tell when one of them would throw up on your shoes.

Chrissy was a junior communications major at the University of Texas and had been working as a Capitol tour guide for about a year. She was the kind of tour guide that most people wanted. With lots of long blond hair and twinkly blue eyes, she had a way with people, no matter what her private opinions of them were. Young children, old people, high schoolers—she fussed over, flirted with, and petted them all. Not as knowledgeable about the historical material as some of the other guides, she was more popular because she captivated even the scholars.

Stan Donald knew she had limitations and was glad his

entire staff of twenty-five wasn't so bubbly. But she loved her job and never caused trouble, which wasn't always the case with tour guides. Stan was the kind of boss who kept a close watch on his workers, especially the friendly, flirty ones like Chrissy because in the past there had been people around the Capitol who thought of flirting with the guides as part of the routine. The only real scandals were in the past, but Stan was careful to avoid even the appearance of impropriety. Appearances were important to him. Maybe, Chrissy often thought, too important.

"Ready, Chrissy?" he said.

Chrissy looked at him. She thought he was cute in an elderly kind of way. After all, he must have been at least thirty-one or two. Still, whenever he took off those old-fashioned glasses with their thick plastic tortoiseshell rims and rested his dark brown eyes, he looked pretty good. He was tall and lean and probably in good shape, too. She knew that he ran five miles on the jogging trail beside Town Lake every evening before work. She could see why he might appeal to a woman, even someone as young as she was, though of course he didn't appeal to her.

"I'm ready," she said.

"Good," he said. "How do you think they'll feel about the Weird sisters down the hall?" The guides had been giggling about the two women setting up the abortion display; although they were divided on the question of abortion, they were united in their opinion of intrusive displays and bossy, loud-mouthed people.

Chrissy smiled at Stan. She had read *Macbeth* in one of her required English classes. "I thought there were supposed to be three of them," she said.

Stan Donald looked down the hallway at the card tables. Stanton and Tolbert were walking along behind them like border guards.

23

"I don't think I could handle another one like those two," he said.

Chrissy didn't think she could, either. And she thought the displays they had set up were disgusting. It was probably true that the inside of a person's body wasn't very attractive, but that was no reason to put models of it out where everyone could see. Besides, Chrissy was pro choice. She knew someone who had gotten pregnant by a married man. She had wanted to have the baby, but the man had insisted on an abortion. Chrissy was sure the man had been right. Babies were whiny and demanding and really, really messy.

"Here they are," Stan said, referring to the Arkansans. The bus had unloaded its passengers a long way from the east entrance, but the first wave had now arrived at the door. There would probably be at least one or two trailing along far behind, thanks to the new parking rules.

"They'll all have to go to the bathroom first," Chrissy predicted. She didn't blame them. The bathrooms on buses were probably too small and dirty for use by anyone with any refinement at all, not that Chrissy knew for sure. She would never be caught dead on a bus herself.

"Never mind that," Stan said. "Better get out in the rotunda."

"All right," Chrissy said. She went to stand beside the wooden sign that announced the starting time of the next tour. She was already smiling and ready to welcome the group.

When the first ones reached her, she could hear the women whispering among themselves. She picked up words and phrases like "disgusting," "disgraceful," and "never in Arkansas." Apparently they had not been impressed with the Weird sisters' exhibits.

After everyone arrived, there was a bit of milling around before the tour began. It took people a minute to get used to their surroundings, and most of them had to spend a second or two looking up from the floor where they stood to the top of the Capitol dome, 260 feet above them. Then they looked down at the floor on which there was a huge star representing the Lone Star State.

There was a crack running across the star.

"Say, what made that crack?" someone asked. It was a man's voice. "Somebody fall from up there?"

There was uneasy laughter. Everyone could see the winding spiral staircase high above that led to the outside of the Capitol dome. The stairway seemed to tilt slightly, and it looked as if it might be easy to fall all the way from there to the hard tile floor.

Chrissy didn't bother to look up. She had seen it all before. She'd heard the question before, too, hundreds of times. Someone in every group invariably asked it.

"No," Chrissy said, her voice echoing in the rotunda. "The crack was caused by a foundation shift, not by someone falling. The interior of the dome is repainted every seven years, but the crack wasn't made by a falling man."

She didn't bother to tell them that a painter or a carpenter or someone like that *had* fallen, years before the tile floor had been installed in 1936. The floor had been glass brick in those long-gone days, and the man had crashed through the brick and gone right on down to the basement. Chrissy knew that a lot of people, the kids especially, would like the story, but Stan wouldn't let the tour guides tell it.

When the rest of the group arrived, she began her talk. "Welcome to the Texas Capitol," she said, beginning the explanation that Stan had written so carefully. "The Capitol was completed in 1888. Instead of being paid for with public funds, it was paid for with public land." She went on with her description and began to point out the portraits of former governors that lined the rotunda's wall.

"What about your Miss Americas?" someone said. "We got pictures of our Miss Americas in the Arkansas Capitol."

How tacky, Chrissy thought. "I guess no one in Texas ever thought of that," she said.

Stan, listening in, knew that it was going to be a long day.

Wayne the Wagger thought it was a wonderful day for January. The sun was shining through the leaves of the trees, the humidity was low so that the grass was dry, and the squirrels were running all over the place, chattering at one another and at Wayne, who was sitting and leaning against the largest remaining oak tree at the Capitol. He had finished his Dr Pepper and was ready to go back inside. He took his can with him so that he could throw it in a trash container. He might be a wagger, but he was not a litterbug.

He went in through the east doors and walked past the anti-abortion exhibits without paying them any attention. Today he was looking at the Corinthian columns that lined the hallway. They were made of cast iron and painted white. Their leafed capitals fascinated him, and he might have simply stopped and stared if he hadn't heard Chrissy's voice in the rotunda.

Though he didn't know her name, Chrissy was his favorite tour guide. He thought she was quite beautiful, and he felt an old familiar urge take hold of him. He shoved the Dr Pepper can inside his sweatshirt and picked up his pace.

Chrissy was leading her group out of the rotunda and back past the tour desk when Wayne got there. She was about to take the Arkansans up to the second floor.

When she saw Wayne, a look of disgust marred her pretty face. She knew what was about to happen as surely as if it had happened ten or fifteen times before, which it had.

Stan Donald was already coming out from behind the desk, but he was not going to be in time.

Wayne spread his legs, planted his feet, and grabbed his crotch with his left hand. He waggled his hand and whatever it contained slowly and suggestively up and down while a wide grin split his beard, exposing a mouth that was lacking a couple of incisors and several molars, which was just as well, since the ones he had left were nothing to brag about.

Stan got in front of him just as the first shocked gasps from the blue-haired Arkansas matrons were being uttered.

"Goddamn white trash," a man said.

Chrissy was blushing furiously, but she carried on. "Right up these stairs," she said, leading the way without looking back.

The Arkansans followed her, but several of them, especially the men, glanced back over their shoulders to see what was happening.

Stan Donald was dressing Wayne down in a stage whisper. "I've told you at least ten times that I was going to have you arrested if you did that again," he said. "This time, I mean it. You've humiliated one of my guides and tour groups for the last time."

He was standing less that a foot away from Wayne, and the transient's odor was almost overpowering. Stan backed up and reached over the high desk top for his phone.

Wayne just stood there clutching himself, as if he were not aware that Chrissy had gone. Then he turned slowly, becoming aware of the Dynamic Duo for the first time. Their young man had left, and they were watching from behind their tables with a questioning interest. They certainly were not as pretty as Chrissy, at least not to Wayne, but they were nevertheless an audience. He rubbed himself gently, and his smile grew even wider.

Mrs. Stanton and Mrs. Tolbert's interest turned to horror. It was their worst nightmare come true. What if this dreadful man sexually assaulted them? Because of their beliefs, they would be forced to bear his unspeakable progeny.

He took a step closer to their tables. Mrs. Stanton's eyes bugged. Sweat ran from her tightly controlled hair and stained the armpits of her indescribable blouse.

"Go away, you . . . you animal," Mrs. Tolbert said, picking up a model uterus and taking a quarterback's stance. "Don't you dare touch us."

"You'd better get around here quick," Stan said into the phone. "I think there's going to be real trouble this time."

"If you take another step, I'll scream," Mrs. Stanton said.

Wayne either didn't hear her or didn't care. He took another step.

Mrs. Stanton screamed.

Mrs. Tolbert heaved the uterus, not seeming to care that she was risking the life of the model fetus inside.

Wayne let go of his crotch and snatched the flying womb out of the air while the two women scrambled for safety. In the process they knocked over one of the tables and a uterus banged to the floor.

Jane Kettler, who had been speaking to someone outside her office when she heard the ruckus, rounded the corner. "What's going on here?" she said.

"Nothing, Jane," Stan said. "It's just Wayne again."

Wayne was looking at the womb he held as if studying for a biology exam. It was red and yellow and pink, and the colors momentarily captivated him.

Mrs. Stanton and Mrs. Tolbert, meanwhile, had huddled together like a pair of affectionate bears in one of the doorways leading to the secretary of state's office.

"Have you called the police?" Jane said.

"Yes," Stan told her. "But you know how that goes."

Jane knew. Though the Capitol police were only a few steps away, it might take a half hour for them to get there. You could expect a better response time from the local police, and they would have to drive from the downtown station while more or less obeying the traffic laws.

Wayne was tired of looking at the uterus, but he must have liked what he saw. He started to put it under his sweatshirt. When he did, the Dr Pepper can fell out, rattling

28

on the floor like hail on a tin roof. He set the womb down and picked up the can. Then he picked the fetus up again.

"You can't have that!" Mrs. Tolbert yelled without leaving the safety of the doorway. "That's our exhibit."

Jane couldn't help wishing that Wayne would take all the wombs, but she said, "She's right, Wayne. You can't take the display materials."

Wayne looked disappointed. "Hey," he said. "She gave it to me."

"She didn't mean to," Jane said. "You'd better put it back. The police will be here in a minute."

Wayne walked over to one of the tables and laid the womb on it reluctantly. He wasn't a thief.

At that moment, Darrel Prince rounded the corner. *He had a face like a prune,* Jane thought, but he was the best of the cops. Unfortunately, that wasn't saying a hell of a lot.

"Well, well," Prince said. "At it again, are we, Wayne?"

Wayne just looked away, studying the columns again, staring at the leaves that topped them. It was as if he hadn't heard a word.

"He tried to attack us," Mrs. Stanton said. "He was going to rape us."

"That's a very serious charge," Prince said. "I advise you to think about what you're saying. There are witnesses."

"That's right," Stan said. "I saw the whole thing. Wayne didn't do anything other than what he normally does, did you, Wayne?"

Wayne didn't say anything. He wondered if that was a lizard he saw peeking from among the leaves that topped the column.

"You wanta tell me about it?" Prince asked Stan.

Stan explained. The story was familiar to both Jane and Prince. Similar things had happened again and again.

"I've told you before, there's nothing we can do to him," Prince said. "He didn't actually expose himself. He's a nuisance, but we can't just have him hauled away to jail for grabbing his di—" Prince glanced at Jane "—his sexual organ."

"Isn't there a law against being a public nuisance?" Stan said. He wanted Wayne out of there. "How about vagrancy?"

"You gotta be kidding," Prince said. "You want the ACLU down on us? We got enough troubles around here without a bunch of liberal lawyers on our case."

"You can at least get him out of the building," Jane said. "He's disrupting our tours, and the senators won't like that."

Prince knew she was right, and he had overused that ACLU bit. He also knew it was almost as bad to get the senators upset as it would be to rile the ACLU. "OK," he said to Wayne. "You're gonna have to spend the rest of the day outside, big boy. Let's go." He motioned for Wayne to follow him, but he didn't touch him.

Wayne didn't move.

"Now, Wayne, don't make this any harder than it has to be," Prince said, his fingers playing with the highly polished black nightstick that hung from his black leather belt.

Wayne was insulted. He hadn't done a thing, and now this cop was threatening to hit him. Wayne decided that he wasn't going anywhere. He crossed his arms and looked stubbornly at the top of the column.

A walkie-talkie, also attached to Prince's belt, squawked.

He took it in his right hand and held it to his mouth. "Prince here," he said.

The walkie-talkie squawked.

"Yeah," Prince said. "It's Wayne. He's actin' up. You wanta come help me?"

The walkie-talkie squawked again and then Prince signed off.

"You're gonna be sorry you didn't cooperate," he told Wayne. "Now old Claude's gonna be on your ass."

30

Jane and Stan looked at one another and sighed. They had the same opinion of Claude that Prince did, that he was an obnoxious asshole.

"Maybe I could help," Jane said. "Let me talk to Wayne."

"No need for that," Prince told her. "Here comes Claude."

Claude flabbed into the hallway, three hundred pounds of cop on the hoof, and hardly an ounce of it muscle. Rolls of fat bounced up and down under his uniform shirt.

"Trouble?" he said.

"That man tried to rape us," Mrs. Stanton said. Now that she was used to the idea, it seemed a bit exciting, and she wanted to repeat it.

"Who was gonna help him?" Claude said.

"Humph!" Mrs. Stanton said. "I suppose you think it's funny."

"Damn right, I do," Claude said, who thought of his own girth as being more of a sign of his excessive virility than anything else, while Stanton's was clearly a sign of an inability to control a massive appetite. "You need help gettin' this bastard outta here, Darrel?"

"He don't want to go," Darrel admitted.

"Well, let's help him along then," Claude said.

They closed in on Wayne, and each grabbed one of the transient's arms.

"Jesus," Claude said. "You smell like you been bathin' in a septic tank, Wayne."

The two cops started pulling Wayne along the hall. He didn't help them any, locking his knees and planting his feet, but the slick floor made their job easy. The soles of Wayne's Keds squeaked on the tile as they pulled him along through the rotunda and out the south entrance.

Stan followed to see what would happen. He didn't much care what happened to Wayne, but he didn't want any of the blame for it if they hurt him.

Claude and Darrel released Wayne on the south porch. The beautiful tile was covered with a strip of very worn red carpeting held in place with frayed duct tape. It looked awful, but the tile got very slick when it was wet, and no one wanted a tourist to fall down and sue.

"Don't try comin' back inside today," Claude warned Wayne. "You do, and your ass is mine."

Wayne looked around. He was really steamed. They'd made him put his toy back on the table, and now they were telling him he couldn't come back inside. He needed a way to express his anger.

Then he saw one of the small cannons flanking the Capitol entrance. The story was that the cannons had been used in both the Texas revolution and the Civil War, though the story might not have been true. Wayne didn't know the story, but he wouldn't have given much of a damn if he had known.

He pulled down his warm-ups, unzipped the zipper of the ragged jeans that he was wearing underneath, hauled out his penis, and urinated on the cannon.

The yellow stream sizzled against the cannon and then dripped onto the porch.

A man, a woman, and a little big-eyed girl of about five were walking up the steps.

"Look what that man's doing," the girl told her parents, pointing at Wayne. "He's peeing on the gun!"

"Oh my God," the woman said, covering the girl's eyes with a hand and hustling her past the disgusting spectacle.

"Goddamnit, that's it!" Claude said, grabbing his night-stick and going for Wayne.

Prince got to Claude and snatched the fat cop's arm from behind.

"You can't do that," Prince said. "You'd never work here again."

Claude, panting from having run two steps, lowered his

arm. "I guess you're right, but we can damn sure arrest him now."

Stan couldn't believe he was hearing correctly. "You couldn't arrest him for fondling himself in front of the tour groups and the guides, but you can arrest him for this?"

"That's right," Prince said. "You can do a lot of things around here, but you can't piss on state landmarks. You watch the son of a bitch, Claude. I'll go call the Austin police."

Wayne casually shook the last couple of drops off his penis and put it back where it belonged. He zipped up and pulled on his warm-ups.

It seemed to him that there was a reason why the cops would be sorry they were arresting him, that there was something pretty interesting that he could tell them if he wanted to, but he couldn't for the life of him remember what it was.

FOUR

Senator Samuel Wilkins had served in the legislature ten years now, and if there was one thing he knew, it was his constituency. There were plenty of men who got elected to office and forgot about the home folks, but Wilkins wasn't one of them. The ones who forgot were often not reelected, a fate that Wilkins did not intend for himself, even if it meant that he sometimes had to take a stand that was unpopular with the rest of his colleagues.

His position on the issues did not always represent his own thinking; on some of them it represented the position he thought the people who put him in office wanted him to take. He figured that if they elected him, the least he could do was represent them, no matter how dumb assed their views were or how it made him look.

Of course, in issues that they cared nothing about, he was free to be his own man. Or anybody else's man. That was why the lobbyists loved him.

A Texas legislator makes $7,200 a year, plus his per diem pay when the legislature is in session, and the voters so far had resisted all efforts to give their governmental representatives a raise. The lobbyists didn't mind that a bit. They were glad to help out. There were no restrictions on their giving, and they gave generously. In one recent session of the legislature, lobbyists had spent something over $1.8 million to influence votes, an average of more than $12,800 a day during the regular session. That came out to about $10,000 for each senator and representative.

Samuel Wilkins had not come to the Capitol a rich man, but he had determined to be one when he left. He was well on the way. Lobbyists paid for his meals. They paid for his vacations. They gave him presents. They even gave him money, everyone's favorite gift.

There was nothing unusual in that, not in Texas, a state where a processed poultry magnate could actually wander freely around on the floor of the legislature passing out checks for $10,000 to men who would soon be voting on an environmental bill that was going to affect his business. Some of the people who had taken the checks thought better of it when their actions were reported in the newspapers. But not all of them.

Wilkins saw nothing wrong with taking the money. As he told his aide Ron Matson, "They can't expect me to live on that piddlin' little old salary they give me, can they? Hell, even schoolteachers get more than that, and they don't get shit. And the law won't let me use my political contributions to live on. What do folks expect me to do? Starve?"

Matson had an opinion on that matter, but he felt it best to keep it to himself. After all, he had to eat, too. "You're right, Senator." He ran a hand through his brush-cut blond hair. "What can they expect?"

So Wilkins was every lobbyist's friend, as long as the issues did not affect his own district. On those points, he would take nothing, would not even let his secretary accept the flowers that were delivered to the Capitol with such regularity that florists all over the city rejoiced along with the tavern keepers when the legislature was due in session.

In sexual matters, Wilkins was equally circumspect. He had never accepted the proffered favors of any woman sponsored by a lobbyist, no matter how irresistible she might have seemed. A lobbyist might talk, and the people back in Wilkins's home district in east Texas wouldn't have understood a married man messing around with some other woman. Well, they would have understood, but they wouldn't have put up with it, especially since Wilkins's taste ran to younger women. Say, about twenty or twenty-one.

"Don't know why the voters wouldn't let a man get by with a little bit of strange," he had once told Matson while in his folksy mode. "Sometimes it seems like they think a man don't have a pecker. So I got to be careful."

Matson understood, not that he cared much of anything for women himself. Oh, they could be fun, no doubt about that, and he'd been fooling around with one fairly recently, but as far as he was concerned, men were better. He was currently carrying on two little affairs of the heart with other men, one of them a legislator to whom the newspapers liked to refer as a "rising young representative."

Matson liked to refer to him that way, too. Sometimes when they were together he would say, "My, you're certainly a *rising* young representative this evening, aren't you," at which the r.y.r. would swat Matson across his naked buttocks with the back of his hand or possibly that part of him which was rising, usually eliciting a squeal of pleasure. Matson was looking forward to the beginning of the new session, when the r.y.r. would be returning to town.

Matson's other dalliance was on the opposite end of the spectrum, a former Capitol tour guide who was now making it as a low-level coke dealer. His name was Todd Elton and he probably spent more time in the building now than when he had been employed there. Matson was afraid he had been a bit indiscreet on more than one occasion when he and Elton were tooting up. Good blow tended to loosen his tongue, in more ways than one. If Wilkins ever found out that Matson had given away any senatorial secrets, he would no doubt have Matson's giblets for a jockstrap, and the problem was that Matson couldn't really remember what he might have said on those occasions when he was high.

Nevertheless, he agreed with the senator as he was expected to do. "Yessir, you've got to be careful. There's no doubt about it."

"Well, I am," Wilkins said. "I'm a careful man. You know that, Ron."

"Yessir, I know that," Matson said, though he knew nothing of the sort. In fact, Wilkins was not so very careful at all. He took chances that Matson would never dream of taking, including consummating some of his affairs in the Capitol chapel on the fourth floor.

Wilkins was not alone in that practice, Matson knew. There were a great many people who had gone down on their knees in the chapel, and the great majority of them hadn't been praying. Still, it was a dangerous practice, and Matson would never have chanced it. He might get a little talky when he was high, but he didn't screw in public places. Well, not usually, anyhow.

Today, Ron was casing the pressroom, making sure that everything was ready for the senator's meeting with the members of the fourth estate, most of whom were already gathered there in the hopes that Wilkins would give them something they could use. Everyone expected him to announce his sponsorship of a bill to ban abortions in the state.

Abortion had been a topic that most legislators liked to discuss in public about as much as they liked to discuss their bowel functions. Most of them believed that the Supreme Court of the United States had done a terrible thing to them by throwing the issue back to the states, though most of them would at the same time have said that they would fight to the death to support states' rights. They had hoped the issue was moot, and here it was again, threatening them.

Wilkins, however, wasn't afraid to speak up. His constituents were as conservative as cavemen when it came to the right to life, and they expected him to be, too. He really didn't give much of a damn about the whole thing, but what his district wanted, his district got. It was an election year, after all.

Matson tapped on a mike and there was an echo in the room. The mikes were working, the press was buzzing, and everything was ready. Matson ushered his boss behind the podium.

Senator Wilkins was an impressive man. He looked nothing like the stereotyped Texan of editorial cartoons, though he was over six feet tall, and rangy. He was forty-six years old and in good shape thanks to a careful diet and a daily walk. He was wearing a conservatively cut gray suit that he had bought off the rack at Dillard's right there in Austin, a white shirt, and a dark tie. He had on black wing tips. When he was with Ron Matson or when he was politicking the district, he usually spoke with a folksy drawl, but when he met the press he showed the effects of the several speech classes he had taken in college, as well as ten years of singing bass in the church choir.

He went through his prepared speech quickly, announcing just what everyone had thought he would—that he would sponsor a bill in the session beginning the following Tuesday in which the provisions were that no one would be able to receive an abortion in Texas for any reason.

Then the questions began.

"Don't you realize that the pro-choice candidates carried every vote in the last election, not only in Texas but in the entire country?" a woman from one of the local TV stations asked.

Wilkins liked her. She was a young brunette with big knockers and he'd often wondered if he had a chance of getting her into bed. He thought it was a good possibility, but she was really a few years older than he would have liked. Too risky, besides. You never knew whom a reporter might talk to.

"I'll tell you," he said, looking righteous and thoughtful. "I know how the elections went, but that doesn't really matter to me. What matters to me is what's *right,* and murdering a baby just isn't right, no matter how you look at it."

"What if it was your own daughter who got raped by some escaped loony?" asked a reporter from one of the Houston papers.

Peckerwood shitass, Wilkins thought. He knew that the reporter was a notorious womanizer himself. Wilkins knew a lot of things like that.

"That's a hypothetical question, I suppose," Wilkins said, smiling. "Since my wife and I haven't been blessed with any children." And it's her damn fault, he wanted to add, but didn't. "I don't like to answer hypothetical questions. It's too much like responding to one of those 'have you stopped beating your wife' things."

"All right, then," the reporter said. "Let's put it another way. What if—God forbid—*you* got some woman pregnant. Some woman other than your wife. Wouldn't you urge her to have an abortion?"

Ron Matson felt his heart stop. He tried to remember what he might have said to Todd. And to decide if Todd would have betrayed him so quickly. He looked at Wilkins.

The senator was perfectly controlled. There wasn't even a bead of sweat on his forehead.

"That's another hypothetical question, I hope," he said. His eyes were hard as steel balls. "And quite a way out of line, I think. I hate to say it, but I'm afraid you representatives of the press are a lot more interested in stirring up a little controversy to sell papers than you are in the real issues, which in this case are life and death." He paused to let that sink in and then repeated it. "Life and death."

"But Senator Wilkins—" the reporter began.

"No more questions," Matson said, stepping to the podium. "I'll provide all of you with copies of the press release."

The reporters grumbled, but there wasn't much they could do. They began gathering up their materials to leave and Wilkins headed to the elevator. Matson wasn't far behind.

They went down to the first floor, where Wilkins's office was located just down the hall from the tour-guide desk. The first-floor offices were not prized as prime locations. They were much too accessible to the constituents, and most senators preferred to be located in the depths of the basement or somewhere on one of the higher floors where the voters would not be able to find them just by wandering in off the street.

Not Wilkins, however. He had in fact requested the office. He liked being where the voters could find him, liked having them drop in and chat.

But not today.

"Don't let anybody in, Suzimae," he told his secretary as he breezed by her desk on his way back to his own sanctum.

Suzimae looked at Matson, who simply shrugged at her and followed Wilkins, closing the door to the inner office behind him.

Wilkins sat in the high-backed leather chair behind his cherry-wood desk, took a couple of deep breaths, and stared at Matson, who thought he now knew what laser beams must feel like at close range. He had to resist the temptation to look behind him to see if the stare had burned through the office door the way it had through his head.

"All right, Ron," Wilkins said. His face was red. "What does that mother-rapin' son of a bitch know?"

"Nothing," Matson said, praying that he was right. "He

40

was just asking a question. You know how those reporters are. They always ask something like that. Haven't you ever seen them on TV when they're talking to a mother whose child has been mutilated by a pit bull? 'And how did you feel when you saw the animal's teeth sinking into your daughter's throat, Mrs. Smith?' " He knew he was babbling, but he couldn't stop himself. "Besides, how could he know anything? There's not anything for him to know. Is there?"

Wilkins puffed his cheeks and blew out a long breath. "No," he said after a minute. "There's nothing to know. After all these years, you'd think I wouldn't let myself get so worked up about some reporter. Those bastards just get to me now and then."

The steel band that was clamped around Matson's chest loosened a bit.

Wilkins tilted back in his chair and crossed his arms. "Who do we know that can hurt him?"

Matson thought a minute. Wilkins, like most politicians, had a well-deserved reputation for retaliation, and one thing that the senator had learned in his tenure in the Capitol was whom to squeeze and how to apply the pressure. No one crossed Wilkins and walked away unscathed.

The reporter could be a real problem, however. If you upset a reporter, he was likely to start digging in places you'd rather not have him dig and finding out things that were better left unfound. Matson had his own secrets to think of.

"I'm not sure it's such a good idea to hurt a reporter," Matson said.

"I didn't ask you what you thought about it, Goddamnit. I asked you who we knew."

Matson thought again, not caring whether Wilkins wanted him to or not. He wasn't going to be able to get out of this one easily, he decided. He was going to have to come up with a name.

"Hap Reatherford," he said finally. Reatherford was a lobbyist for the insurance industry, among others. He'd been a senator himself until he decided that there was even more money in working directly for the people who had it. "He's about the only one that would even think of tackling it."

"Get him," Wilkins said.

Matson reached for the phone on the front of the desk. "Suzimae, get me Hap Reatherford, please," he said. He tried to sound perfectly normal, but he couldn't keep a note of bitterness out of his voice. He was afraid that Wilkins was making a mistake. He was afraid it was a big one.

FIVE

Brian Lollard didn't care much about the Texas Capitol, even though he'd ridden the big yellow school bus for more than three hours to get there, along with the entire high school student body of Brookesmith, Texas.

He didn't care about the Confederate memorial that the bus had passed as it entered the Capitol grounds.

He didn't care about the twelve famous battles fought on Texas soil and memorialized in terrazzo on the floor of the south foyer, and he would not have cared even if he had known that the plans for the restoration of the Capitol called for the tile on the second, third, and fourth floors to be jackhammered up and replaced with the kind of encaustic tile that had been in the original building, in spite of the fact that the terrazzo was a work of art in itself and a part of the living heritage of the Capitol.

He didn't care about the huge paintings of the Battle of San Jacinto and the Battle of the Alamo that were displayed on the wall of the Senate chamber.

He didn't even care about getting a free road map of Texas at the Highway Department desk.

What he cared about was getting some tit off Rhonda Johnson.

She'd been sitting by him on the bus all the way from Brookesmith, but of course there was no opportunity to do anything then. For one thing, it was broad daylight; and for another thing, old Miss Goswick, the history, government, and English teacher and bus chaperon, had eyes like a hawk behind her rimless glasses and would have been on him like ugly on an ape if he'd made one false move.

It hadn't been easy on him, sitting there beside Rhonda and exercising his self-control. Rhonda had red hair, a sweet smile, and the biggest boobs in Brookesmith, Texas. Even in the heat of his desire to make a grab at her, Brian found it hard to believe she'd allowed him to sit beside her, since she was a cheerleader and the best-looking girl in school and he wasn't even on the football team. But as the ride went on it became clear that she had more than a passing interest in him.

You could always tell things like that by the way a girl looked at you, brushed your arm with hers when she fiddled with her hair, "accidentally" touched the back of your hand when she reached for her purse. Brian had been forced to squirm around in the seat a number of times so that a suddenly prominent portion of his anatomy wouldn't embarrass him, and his mind was going a mile a minute, plotting out ways to get Rhonda alone.

Almost as soon as they entered the Capitol, he seized his opportunity. Everyone had gathered in front of the tour desk, and Miss Goswick was issuing her instructions about the proper behavior in what she considered the sacred shrine of state government.

Brian and Rhonda were standing at the rear of the group, right at the head of the stairs to the basement, and when Miss Goswick turned her attention to the tour guide who had been assigned to the group, Brian grabbed Rhonda's hand and gave a tug.

She responded immediately, and in a second or two they were down the stairs and on the landing, out of sight of Miss Goswick and her snoopy eyes.

Rhonda pushed her shoulder into Brian's arm and smiled. "Where're you takin' me?" she said.

Brian had not released her hand. His groin was throbbing. "I thought we'd just look around a little on our own. We don't need a guide, do we?"

"I don't know. Do we?"

"Hell no. Let's see what's down these stairs."

They walked down to the snack area and found themselves surrounded by soft-drink dispensers, candy machines, and chattering tourists, all of which was a big disappointment to Brian, who had hoped to discover a nice quiet spot where he could make his move.

"This is kind of ugly," Rhonda said, looking around, and Brian had to agree. It didn't look anything like a state capitol building ought to look. The basement ceiling was just acoustical tile, and it was only a foot or so above his head, and in the other direction, there wasn't even any tile, just exposed pipes and wiring. The walls were covered with some kind of cheap paneling.

"They must have spent all the money decorating the upstairs," Brian said. "Want to look around?"

"Sure. What are we lookin' for?"

"I dunno." He couldn't very well tell her the truth, could he? "Just looking. Come on."

They started down the hallway to their left, passing under the security camera without even noticing it. No one noticed them, either.

"I wonder what's down there?" Brian said, pointing down a corridor that branched off the hall.

"Offices, looks like," Rhonda said. "See the signs?"

He could see the signs, all right, informing him of which legislators had a spot down there, but at least it looked a little more private than where they were.

"Let's go see," he said, and they turned to the right, following the hallway. They came to the offices, but there was no one in them. The legislators had not yet arrived in town for next week's session, and though their staffs were on the job, most of them were at an orientation meeting.

And then Brian saw the little room off to the side, the one with no door.

"Let's look in there," he said.

They did. It was the perfect place. There was nothing there but two trash hampers, there was no one in the hall, and the offices were closed.

Thank you, Lord, Brian thought.

"Did you say something?" Rhonda said, moving very close to him, so close that he could feel her breasts pushing on his shirt.

"Uh, no. I didn't." He put his arm around her and pulled her even closer. She looked up at him, and he moved to cover her mouth with his.

"There's a window," she said. "People are walking by."

Brian looked at the window. "They're not looking in here," he said. "You can't see anything but their legs."

"I guess you're right."

"Sure I'm right," Brian said, and at last he made his move.

The next few minutes were the best of Brian's life up to that point. He'd dated a few girls, taken them out in his car, a five-year-old Ford, driven in to Brownwood and bought them a pizza at the Pizza Hut, and even kissed a few of them, but he'd never gotten much past first base. He was doing a lot better than that now. If he died now, he would die happy.

Rhonda was panting and moving against him. Her blouse was untucked and the zipper on her pants was down. She was backed up to one of the trash hampers, braced against it, pushing herself against Brian.

Brian was working on the buttons of her blouse, and Rhonda was helping.

All in all, it was a whole hell of a lot better than seeing the dusty marble statues of Sam Houston and Stephen F. Austin in the south foyer.

It was, that is, until Rhonda lost her balance and made a grab for the hamper.

She missed, and her hand went inside it. The newspaper that it encountered did not support her, and her hand went past it until it met something else.

Something that felt pretty strange.

"Brian," she said. "I think—"

"I do, too, honey. I think I love you. I think—"

"It's not that, Brian," she said, pulling away from him. "I think there's something in there."

Brian's eyes were not exactly focused, and he reached out a hand to pull Rhonda back.

"It's just trash," he said. "C'm'ere."

"Wait a minute," Rhonda said. She did not have much curiosity in the normal course of things, but she wanted to see what she had touched. It felt really funny.

She pulled a handful of newspaper aside.

Then she started to scream.

Her screams were heard by Juana Lorca, who was halfway down the hall, on her way to pick up one of the hampers and begin her cleaning duties.

When he considered the events of that day later in his life, Brian Lollard often thought that a benevolent providence had saved him from real embarrassment by letting Rhonda find the body when she did. It would have been pretty humiliating to have been caught in the middle of a hot clinch by some Mexican house cleaner.

47

As it was, Rhonda managed to get her blouse tucked in and her pants zipped before Juana got there, and the protuberance that had been bothering Brian had instantly shriveled down to less than cumbersome proportions.

There was considerable confusion after that.

After Rhonda got her blouse in, she started screaming again, and Juana was screaming, and people were appearing from everywhere.

One of the first on the scene was Clinton Amory, the head of the custodial service, who seemed to pop out of the cheap paneling. He was about fifty years old, a little on the stocky side, and he looked to Brian like a man who took no pride in his appearance. His uniform was stained and dirty, his thin hair was unruly, and he had dandruff. The shoulders of his gray uniform were flecked with it on both sides. He had a toothpick dangling from the left side of his mouth.

"What the hell's all the noise about?" he said. He sounded as if he might be gargling rocks, and the toothpick danced up and down when he spoke.

"EEEEEEEEEEEEE," Juana said.

"Shut up," Amory said. "Jesus."

He looked at Brian and Rhonda, who had stopped screaming and started crying, her head against Brian's shoulder. "What're you kids doin' down here? Ain't you supposed to be on a tour of the buildin' or somethin'?"

"We were just looking around," Brian said, trying to keep his voice steady. "We didn't do anything."

"Sure you didn't." He looked at Juana. "That's why that bitch sounds like a runaway ambulance. You high school punks are all the same, always a pain in the ass."

"There's a dead woman in there," Brian said, pointing to the hamper.

"Huh?" Amory said. The toothpick stopped moving.

"A dead woman," Brian repeated. "In there."

Amory looked into the hamper, pulling out the crumpled newspaper sheets and throwing them on the floor.

There was a dead woman in there, all right.

The toothpick fell out of Amory's mouth. "Shit," he said.

It was quite awhile before Brian and Rhonda ever got back to the yellow school bus.

SIX

News of the murder spread through the building, as Sam Wilkins would have said in one of his folksy moments, "quicker than a cat can lick his ass."

Mrs. Stanton and Mrs. Tolbert heard it from a woman who heard it from a man who had been buying a Payday from one of the vending machines in the basement when the crime was discovered. The woman told them in passing as she was rushing out of the building, and she advised them to leave as well. There was a psychotic killer on the loose, and no woman was safe.

First being threatened with rape by a degenerate street person and having their exhibits tossed around like toys, and now this. Iradell Stanton had taken just about all she could stomach. She looked at Ethel Tolbert.

"The world is going to hell in a hand basket," she said.

Ethel agreed completely. "And even the state Capitol isn't safe for a woman anymore."

"What do you think we oughta do about it?" Iradell said.

Ethel looked across the hallway at the office with Senator

Wilkins's name on the pebbled glass door. "We ought to talk to one of our elected representatives and let him know exactly how the taxpayers feel about things."

"I think you're absolutely right." Iradell shoved aside the card table in front of her, making a space large enough for her to squeeze her thighs through if she turned sideways. "Let's go."

She led the way as the two marched to the senator's office. When they reached the door, she squared her shoulders and grabbed the handle. Just before she pulled open the door, she looked over her shoulder and saw Stan Donald at his post behind the guides' desk.

"You watch out for our exhibits," she called to him. "Anything happens to them, we're gonna hold you responsible. You hear?"

Stan said something or other to them, but Mrs. Stanton couldn't quite make it out. She assumed, however, that he was acknowledging his responsibility. He'd better. She opened the door to the senator's office and entered, followed closely by her cohort.

Suzimae Turner squinted at them through her fashionable big-lensed bifocal glasses when they entered. She didn't recall any appointments at that hour, but there was nothing unusual about people walking into the office to see the senator. He liked to have visitors.

"We want to see Senator Wilkins," Mrs. Stanton said.

"We know he's in there," Mrs. Tolbert added, looking toward the closed door behind Suzimae. "We saw him coming back from the press conference."

"I'll see if he's available," Suzimae said, picking up the intercom phone and speaking into it.

"He better be," Mrs. Stanton said. "He better not be too busy to see two of the voting public. He might find out what it's like to be out of a job when the next election rolls around."

"He'll see you right now," Suzimae said, hanging up the phone. "You can just go on in."

"Good thing," Mrs. Stanton said. "Come on, Ethel."

Senator Wilkins came around his big desk with open arms and a big smile. "Welcome, ladies," he said. "Won't you have a seat?"

He motioned them to two comfortable leather chairs that faced his desk before going back to his own chair. Suzimae had told him who his visitors were, and when they were seated he said, "I'm familiar with your good work, of course. To what do I owe the honor of this visit?" Though of course he had seen them in the halls, he didn't know the women personally, so he was using his speech-class voice.

Mrs. Stanton didn't mince words. "Murder," she said. "That's what you owe this visit to."

Wilkins's professional smile disappeared, to be replaced with a look of rueful sorrow. "Murder?" he said. "Of course. I understand perfectly. The murder of innocent children who are never given a chance in the world, who have no say-so about—"

"You don't understand diddly squat," Mrs. Stanton said. "I'm not talking about that kind of a murder."

Wilkins's face changed again. This time he didn't look rueful. He looked almost angry. "Then what kind *do* you mean?"

Ethel took over. "It's just horrible, Senator. There was a Mexican woman killed in the basement. Strangled to death. Someone found her in a trash hamper down there."

Wilkins sat up a little straighter in his chair, suddenly very attentive. "Strangled? Are you sure?"

"Sure we're sure," Iradell said. "We wouldn't make something like that up."

Wilkins picked up his phone. "Suzimae, there's been a woman murdered in this very building. I want to know about it. Right now."

Iradell and Ethel were impressed with Senator Wilkins's concern and forthright action.

"We want you to know, we don't think this kind of thing should happen right here in a state building," Mrs. Tolbert said. "It's bad enough when you read about something like that happening in Houston, but this is the Capitol!"

"I agree with you absolutely," Senator Wilkins said. He reached inside the coat of his suit and brought out a large white handkerchief. It was quite cool in the office, but the senator's forehead was damp with perspiration. He wiped it with the handkerchief and returned it to his coat pocket.

"Now if you two will excuse me," he said, standing, "I want to begin my own personal investigation into this matter. I know that you will want to return to your exhibits."

The two women stood, satisfied that Senator Wilkins was on the job. "We're certainly glad to see that at least one of the legislators is concerned about the welfare of the people," Mrs. Stanton said.

"Yes," Mrs. Tolbert said. "It just gives me a good feeling to see how you haven't lost touch with the voters who put you in office."

Wilkins was around the desk now, ushering them through the door. "I always have the best interests of the people at heart," he said.

When they were gone he sat back down and waited until he heard the outer door close firmly. Then he reached for his handkerchief and wiped his face again.

He put the handkerchief away and looked at his watch. *Five minutes,* he thought. That's how long he would give Suzimae to find out all she could. Exactly five minutes. Then he would give her a call.

Stan Donald had paid no attention to whatever it was Mrs. Stanton had yelled at him. He was no longer worried about either her or her exhibits. He was worried about getting through the day when all his guides could talk about was the murder. He knew it was going to be difficult keeping their minds on the job, but it had to be done.

They couldn't let the death of a menial laborer get in the way of the tours. The show had to go on. It would have been impossible to explain to the arriving visitors that all tours had been canceled because of a murder. They might have understood, intellectually, but deep down inside they would never have forgiven or forgotten. The next time their local representative, the one who had most likely arranged the tour for them, came up for reelection, they would vaguely recall something that they had against him, some nagging little thing that they might not be able to put a finger on but that they knew was important. When they didn't vote for him, it would be Stan's fault.

Stan didn't think he was there to save legislators' jobs, not really. There were many legislators that he didn't even like; if they lost their jobs, he wouldn't lose any sleep. But he did work for them, in a sense. So he tried to do what he could to keep the customers satisfied. He didn't want to lose his own job.

He had talked the matter over with Jane Kettler, and she had agreed that the tours had to go on. He had a brief meeting with the guides and asked them to refrain from mentioning the murder on their tours. A certain degree of professionalism was required. The guides could talk about the murder all they wanted to in their lounge, a long, narrow room that they used for relaxing and changing clothes, but they weren't to frighten the tourists.

Personally, Chrissy Allen wondered if there was a serial killer on the loose, and she confided her fears to Tanya Melton, one of the other guides.

"You can't really trust anyone," Chrissy said. "You're always reading about people killing people that they know. Even their families. They just lose their tempers, and you

54

can't tell what's going to set them off or what they'll do. I used to date a guy who liked scary movies, and there was a terrible one about a man who liked to strangle people, especially young girls." She lowered her voice. "And sometimes he even *ate* parts of them."

Tanya, a petite brunette with very white skin, very short hair, and very red lips, was not impressed. "You don't really think someone like that killed that woman, do you?" she said.

They were the only two in the lounge at the moment. The other guides were conducting tours or hanging around the desk, and Chrissy was glad of it. The lounge generally provided for no privacy at all. It was so narrow that there was hardly room to turn around, and there was usually someone asleep on the couch. As a general rule, it was no place for private conversations.

Chrissy fluffed her abundant blond hair. "It could have been somebody like that," she said. "That's just exactly the kind of nutzoid that would kill a woman in the basement of the Capitol building. He could've hidden down there somewhere and waited for her to come by. Then he just jumped out and grabbed her."

"Do you think he raped her?" Tanya said.

"Maybe," Chrissy said, though there had as yet been no medical examination as far as she knew. "It sounds like a sex murder to me. He may have done something even worse."

Tanya was going to ask what could be worse than being raped and murdered, but she changed her mind. She was afraid that Chrissy might actually tell her.

"Or it might be something else," Chrissy said, a shrewd look on her pretty face.

Tanya was surprised at the sudden change of direction, but not at Chrissy's shrewdness. Chrissy might look like a fluff brain but she was nobody's fool. *Well,* Tanya thought, *Chrissy was nobody's fool* all *the time.*

"What do you mean?" she said.

"Well, it was Ramona Gonzalez, after all."

"So what?" Tanya said. She didn't know Ramona.

"She liked to talk," Chrissy said.

Tanya wasn't tracking the conversation. "I don't get it. What did she talk about?"

"Everything. That's the trouble. You know what Ms. Kettler tells us."

Tanya knew. Ms. Kettler gave young people doing temporary work in the Capitol a packet of information. One item in the packet was a note that stressed discretion, and it mentioned a motto from World War II. Tanya didn't know much about that war. It had happened much too long ago to interest her very much. She was pretty sure that anyone who had fought in it would be dead by now, or at least terribly old and decrepit. Anyway, the note explained that there was a saying in those days about how "loose lips sink ships," and working in the Capitol was like that. Tanya knew that Ms. Kettler meant they weren't supposed to talk about anything they heard on their jobs. She had to admit that they did hear a lot of stuff that might be damaging to certain people.

Tanya remembered now that Ramona had been a gossip. "You mean she talked about stuff she shouldn't have talked about. Like maybe about some of the senators or representatives."

Chrissy nodded. "Like that."

"People like that wouldn't kill anyone," Tanya said. It was just inconceivable. "They're all pretty respectable. And they've got too much to lose."

Chrissy looked bitterly wise, an expression that Tanya had never seen Chrissy use before.

"Not if they don't get caught," Chrissy said.

"But what could make them do something like . . . like kill somebody?" Tanya said. "She would have had to talk about something that was just awful!"

Chrissy nodded. "That's right. Something just awful."

Tanya was really getting curious by that time. It was clear that Chrissy knew more than she was saying.

"Is it about someone I know?"

"Yeah. You know her as well as I do."

"Oh," Tanya said. "You mean about Senator—"

"Never mind," Chrissy said.

Tanya looked around the narrow room. "Yeah," she said. "I know what you mean."

Ron Matson was standing in front of Senator Wilkins's desk, the spot he generally referred to as the ass-kicking spot. He didn't refer to it that way in front of Wilkins, however.

What he was getting his ass kicked for this time was the murder. Senator Wilkins was considerably exercised about something, and he was taking it out on Ron, and after listening for a few minutes, Matson thought he had caught on to what was bothering Wilkins.

"Our sources didn't let us know about the murder, Ron," Wilkins said. "Everybody in the building heard before we got wind of it. Now just what the hell is going on around here when two women who are no better than vagrants can find out what's going on in the building before we do?"

Wilkins paused to see if he was getting through. He was, but he went on anyway.

"You see what I mean, Ron? I'm a *senator,* Goddamnit. I'm supposed to know about things like this *before* they happen, not three or four hours after every son of a bitch in Austin knows about them. I don't like it, Ron. I really don't."

Matson knew what he meant. He didn't like it either. Information—not to say gossip—was the essence of survival, for both himself and the senator.

"Somebody fucked up," he said.

"I know that, Ron," Wilkins said. His voice was quiet, and Matson knew that was not a good sign. "And it wasn't me. So what does that leave us with, Ron? Who fell down on the job?"

Matson wanted to say that it wasn't his fault, but he knew it wouldn't do any good. Wilkins had already made up his mind, so there was nothing to do but make the best of things.

"I did," he said.

"That's right, Ron. I'm glad you're a big enough man to admit it. Some wouldn't be. It isn't going to happen again, is it." There was no question mark at the end of his last sentence.

"No, sir," Matson said. "It won't happen again."

He sincerely hoped he wasn't lying. He liked his job, not just for the people it put him in touch with but because he liked the power it gave him. As a senator's aide, he was in a wonderful position to get things, to know things, that he would have gotten and known in no other way.

"Damn right, it's not," Wilkins said, and the ass kicking was over. Or almost over. "I want to know everything about it from now on," Wilkins said. "Everything. You know what I mean, Ron?"

Ron knew. He knew only too well. And he was beginning to get more than a little curious himself. Wasn't the senator just a little *too* interested? Maybe there was more going on here than Matson had first thought. He was going to find out everything, all right. Everything.

"Now, then," Wilkins said, satisfied that his aide had been properly chastised. "You sit down and tell me what you found out about that damn reporter from Hap Reatherford. You did find out, didn't you?"

"Yes, sir," Matson said, settling himself into one of the leather chairs. "I found out."

"Is it something we can use?"

"Maybe," Matson said.

"It better be," Wilkins said. "If Reatherford wants my vote a single time this session, it better be."

"He wants your vote," Matson said. "He said he'd be in touch."

Wilkins nodded. "I thought so," he said.

SEVEN

For Darrel Prince, the murder was at first a dream come true. He had always wanted to be a real cop, but the closest he could come was working for the Capitol police, which wasn't "real" by any stretch of Darrel's imagination.

He knew he was too good for what he was doing. He pictured himself as the lean Clint Eastwood of the Dirty Harry glory days, begging punks to make his day, but instead he spent his on-duty hours dealing with criminals no worse than Wayne the Wagger, and somehow rousting transients was not his idea of fighting bigtime crime.

Sure, there was something different every now and then. Petty theft in one of the offices, a lot of coke dealing right there in the building, the occasional homosexual encounter in the rest rooms, but those things were still not in Darrel's picture of what crime fighting was all about.

The thefts always turned out to have been committed by one of the janitorial staff, the coke dealers had to be handled with kid gloves since God knows who they were supplying, and the homosexuals were usually sent on their way with a mild reprimand unless they approached a kid, which happened about as often as the Houston Oilers went to the Super Bowl.

The dealing was a major crime, all right, and Darrel would have liked nothing better than to have been able to take his nightstick to some of the dope-peddling assholes that were in and out of the building day and night, but he couldn't. He couldn't because that wasn't the way things were done.

Darrel, of course, didn't know for sure who any of the buyers were. That was one secret that actually got kept in the Capitol. There were rumors, naturally, and the rumors named names. Some of the names that got named were attached to persons of considerable influence, but there was no hard evidence. No one wanted there to be any evidence. It could be dangerous to careers if it existed. Very dangerous. So Darrel was told to keep his nose out of things, and he did, though it galled him sorely. As far as he was concerned, dope was dope, and anyone who used it was a criminal. If he ever saw anyone using it, or if he had an eyewitness he could trust, he would bust the user even if it was the governor.

Murder, however, was different. It wasn't some kid gloves affair. It was the real thing, and Darrel Prince was in on it from the beginning. He had been the first one on the scene when Clinton Amory had notified the cops, he had cleared out the rubberneckers, he had begun the investigation.

This was what he had waited for all his life, what he was trained to do, what he knew he could do better than anyone would ever have imagined.

He was in charge.

For about five minutes.

Then his dream turned into a nightmare. Darrel's boss, the head of security for the Capitol, panicked. That was the way Darrel saw it, but of course the head would never have admitted it. His excuse for what he did was that there was a jurisdictional problem.

Bullshit is what that was, in Darrel's eyes. The head was a wuss, and that was that. Too damn scared to take on the responsibility for a full-scale investigation. Darrel would have taken responsibility in a minute, but now the head was screwing it up.

His problem, so he said, was that there was a lot involved here. What about the Austin city cops? What about the DPS, the ones in charge of the governor's safety? They had to be brought in.

What he did was go to the room next door to his own office and notify the Department of Public Safety. That was all it took.

Darrel Prince was off the case, back to chasing dick waggers and bag ladies, back to protecting crazy women who set up card tables to display model wombs. It was enough to make you puke.

What pissed Darrel off most of all when he thought about it was that Claude Hebert didn't even seem to mind that they were booted out of the action.

Claude didn't want any part of the murder case. He was perfectly happy to be sitting in his swivel chair, kicked back, feet on his desk, cleaning his fingernails with his pocketknife, and looking occasionally at the video monitors to show that he was still on the job of keeping the building safe for the tourists.

"Jesus Christ," Darrel said. "I wish you'd at least *try* to look like a cop, Claude. Can't you just try to play like you're interested in your fucking job?"

"What's bitin' your ass?" Claude said. He pared his left thumbnail carefully, inspected it critically, and brought his hand to his mouth to bite off a cuticle which he then spit on the floor.

Darrel didn't try to hide his disgust. "I'll tell you what's

61

biting my ass. What's biting my ass is having to spend my life with second-class cops like you." He gave a laugh that came out like a strangled snort. "Second class, hell. Tenth class, if that. Look at you, Claude. Jesus. You act like the worst thing that ever happened in this place is that somebody pissed on a cannon."

"Nothin' wrong with liking a little peace and quiet," Claude said, folding his knife. He had to stand up to put it back in his uniform pocket. "When somethin' like a murder comes along, I just happen to think that we ought to let the experts take care of it." He sat back down and put his feet up again.

"I don't get how you can just sit there," Darrel said. "I thought this might be a little personal with you."

Claude's feet slid off the desk and hit the floor as he straightened in his chair. "What the hell's that supposed to mean?"

"I thought you and Ramona had a little thing going," Darrel said. "You bragged about it enough."

Claude was a ladies' man, as hard as that might be to believe for anyone seeing him for the first time. He often said that he couldn't help it if he was irresistible. He attributed his success in amorous matters to his bulk. "Women like a man with muscles" was the way he put it, though Darrel thought anyone would be hard pressed to find the muscles underneath all the flab. His idea was that Claude owed his success to his persistence. Even a blind hog turned up an acorn now and then, and like that blind hog, Claude never quit. He had a proposition for every woman he met.

Whatever his secret was, Claude did have a number of conquests to his credit, and Ramona Gonzalez had merely been one of the latest.

His favorite rendezvous spot was the seventh level. He never used it at the regular hours, however. He used his privileged status as a cop to stay in the building after closing time, and he found the seventh level a fine and private place. For some women, he offered what he called his "private after-hours tour of the Capitol," which he claimed would let them into places the public never got to see. That wasn't true, but some women seemed to like the idea of sneaking around the building late at night after everyone was supposed to be gone.

Claude had never gotten caught with any of the women, since he always warned the night shift when he was going to be in the building late. They always left him to it. They might want a favor from him one day. But he had come very close to getting in trouble once, thanks to Clinton Amory.

Some member of a VIP tour of the dome, a tour that went up to the seventh level and beyond, had found a woman's diamond earring in the chapel and turned it in to Amory. He had recognized it immediately as the one reported missing by the wife of a prominent representative. He also had a strong suspicion that the wife had not been visiting that particular part of the Capitol on an official tour.

Amory was not fond of the legislators he had met, and he had met a lot of them. He thought they looked down their noses at him because he was nothing more than a glorified janitor, and he saw the earring as a perfect opportunity to strike back at the whole sorry bunch by humiliating the wife of one of the best known.

Though he knew that Claude had taken the woman on one of his "tours" not too long before the earring had been found, Amory did not say one word about his suspicions as to how the earring got to the generally off-limits seventh level. Amory was more malicious than that. He simply spread the word among his staff members that he had the earring, and he told them where it had been found. Before long, the word was all over the Capitol, and nearly everyone who heard it drew the inevitably appropriate conclusion.

Amory did not return the earring to its owner, either. He

made her come to him and personally identify it. And when she did, he asked her how it came to be where it had been found.

"Fuck you," she said, her face blazing, and snatched the earring from Amory's grubby hand.

"Nah," he said, under his breath, careful not to let her hear him. "Somebody fucked *you*."

And that somebody had been Claude Hebert. Darrel Prince knew the story, and he still found it hard to believe. The woman in question had been quite pretty, a stylish, svelte brunette that you wouldn't think would ever look twice at a slug like Claude Hebert. But she had. And she'd done a lot more than look.

So had Ramona Gonzalez, if Claude were to be believed, and Darrel saw no reason not to believe him, not considering his track record.

"I wish you'd just forget about me and Ramona," Claude said. "You could get me in a lot of trouble, Darrel. That's why I want to stay the hell out of this. What if somebody finds out about me and her? I might lose my job. They might even think I had something to do with killin' her."

"Well," Darrel said, "it's a thought."

Claude picked up a copy of *US* magazine, trying to look unconcerned. "If that's the way you feel, then, there's nothin' I can do about it. You got to remember, though, I'm a cop, too. I'm your brother in blue."

Brother's ass, Darrel thought. He wasn't a brother to anyone like Claude. "You don't have anything to hide, do you, Claude?" he said.

Claude looked at him over the top of the magazine and shook his head sadly. "I'm sorry you'd even think somethin' like that, Darrel. You oughta know better."

"Yeah," Darrel said. "I guess you're right. Let's forget about it, like you said."

"Fine with me," Claude told him. "Let the big boys handle this one."

"Yeah," Darrel said, but what he was thinking was that while the DPS might be in charge, there was no way they could keep him from doing a little poking around on his own. If he found the killer before they did, he'd be a hero, and he'd be on the way to some real police work with a real department.

And if Claude tried to get in his way, well, that would be just too damn bad for Claude.

Craig Shaw was part of the Houston *Chronicle*'s Austin bureau, and his job was to report on the legislative session. When he heard about the murder, he wasn't even interested in it.

What interested Shaw was the morning press conference conducted by Senator Sam Wilkins. Shaw had been the one to ask the question that really seemed to sting, the one about what Wilkins would do if he got some woman pregnant.

Shaw hadn't really thought much about the question before he asked it. It was pretty much a standard kind of thing. But Wilkins's reaction hadn't been standard. The senator had been much too upset, or so it seemed to Shaw, who was good at spotting anything unusual.

Shaw leaned back in his chair and looked out the apartment window. From where he sat he couldn't see much, just some oak trees and a little grass, but it looked good to him. He pulled a Winston from his pack and lit it with a silver Zippo. He took a deep drag and blew a smoke ring at the window.

Wilkins was hiding something. Shaw was sure of it. The question was whether Shaw should pursue the matter.

Shaw was ambitious, and a good scandal could be the making of him if he was the one to uncover it and get it on the front page first. It probably wouldn't mean a Pulitzer, nothing like that, but he could count on some state journalism awards, a good bit of prestige among his peers, and probably a fairly sizable raise to boot.

On the other hand, it wasn't a good idea to get a state senator angry with you, especially someone like Wilkins, who had the reputation of being a fearsome enemy.

But what the hell. It would be better than reporting strictly on the antics of the legislature, a bunch that the cartoonist for the rival paper usually depicted, and with good reason, in full clown makeup and costume.

The trouble was, Shaw didn't know much about Wilkins's personal life. For all he knew, the man might be a veritable saint. True, that would make him a most uncommon man among his fellow legislators, but stranger things had happened. Or at least Shaw supposed they had; he certainly couldn't think of any right off hand, however.

He thought the whole matter would be worth looking into. He wouldn't bother his editor with it, though. That would be premature. For now, he would go along with the program, doing what he'd been sent to Austin to do, and provide the routine stories that he could practically write in his sleep. But at the same time he would pursue a private investigation into Wilkins's life and habits. If he turned up something, then he would talk to the editor.

For now, he would have to be content with doing something on the murder. That would be expected, and it would be a sensation for a day or two. It would die out after that, Shaw supposed. They would probably find out the woman had been killed by a jealous lover, or by one of the transients who frequented the Capitol. There were plenty of those around who looked crazy enough to do anything.

Shaw thought he would approach the story by finding out what some of the Capitol employees were thinking about the murder, how it was affecting their attitude toward their jobs, whether they felt safe in the building.

Fortunately, he already had an informant in place, though

he couldn't get in touch with her at the moment. He would have to call after she got off work.

He crushed the Winston in a clear-glass ashtray and looked out at the oak trees. Wouldn't it be a hell of a thing if there were some connection between the dead woman and Senator Wilkins? That would be almost too good to be true.

Shaw smiled and lit another Winston. Hey, it could happen.

EIGHT

Upon the death of his father, Governor A. Michael Newton had inherited somewhere around twenty million dollars and had possessed just enough good sense to hire clever accountants and ingenious investment counselors.

He didn't have much use for people who didn't have the gumption to do likewise, so he therefore looked down upon nearly everyone: teachers, farmers, day laborers, office workers, reporters, truck drivers, fixed-income retirees, barbers, store clerks, waitresses, students, stock boys, police officers, pharmacists, and his own aides—virtually everyone, in short, who had gone to the polls and exercised his or her sacred right to vote and elected A. Michael Newton governor of the sovereign state of Texas.

He did like country-and-western singers, most of whom knew their own audiences well enough to avoid him, and college football players, most of whom liked him a lot, since in spite of the reputed cleanup of the Southwestern Conference, he could be counted on to drop a few bucks on them any time he showed up in the locker room after a game.

His theory was that giving money to the players was bad only if you gave it to the players at one particular school; so he gave it to all of them. Except for those dirty Arkansas Razorbacks, who in the first place weren't Texans and therefore didn't belong in the conference anyhow, and who in the second place had a Christer for a coach and were probably too dumb to take the money if he offered it to them, which he wouldn't do in the first place.

Arkansas had in fact shown where Razorback loyalties really lay by defecting to the Southeastern Conference, and A. Michael Newton thought that would be just fine. Good riddance to bad rubbish. The only bad thing about it would be if the Southwestern Conference tried to bring in Oklahoma as a replacement. The only thing worse than Arkies were Okies, and Newton had privately vowed that as long as he was governor there would never be another out-of-state school brought into the conference. That would be the greatest public service he could perform.

He had not run for governor because he wanted to serve the public, however. It had just seemed like a good idea at the time, especially to Mary Lee, his wife, who was tired of being pushed around by people with really old money. She was richer than most of them, but she never got invited to the really good parties.

Her husband was rich, but his money was tainted by the way it had been obtained. Newton's father had owned a dairy, and he had parlayed his once-small herd into a milk and ice cream empire. All his products had from the beginning featured a photo of little A. Michael wearing a crown. Beneath the picture was the slogan "Newton's Dairy Products—Fit for a King." The photo changed as A. Michael grew up, and by the time he graduated from college (it took him six years), he was one of the best-known people in the state. Old money people, however, did not necessarily take to someone whose greatest claim to fame was the fact that his

69

photo had been on milk cartons even before it became fashionable.

Still, Newton was very rich, had a face and name that everyone knew, and had managed to hang onto his money. If that didn't qualify him to be the governor of Texas, what did?

Once elected, after a campaign that consisted mostly of his smiling face on millions of dollars worth of astutely produced television advertisements (and of course the milk cartons), he had almost immediately enraged virtually every resident of the entire state, from the legislature on down.

Or up, depending on how you looked at things.

He had no rapport with the legislators, most of whom thought he was a Johnny-come-lately who knew nothing about politics and who had bought the election, but normally that wouldn't have mattered, even if it was true, which it was. It wasn't the first time there had been a governor like that.

It wouldn't have mattered because the governor really has little power in Texas unless there is a crisis or unless he chooses to create one.

A. Michael Newton created one. In fact, he was a virtual crisis-manufacturing center.

He vetoed everything that crossed his desk.

He seemed determined to throw the state into chaos, destroying its finances, its schools, its welfare system, and everything else.

He didn't really want to destroy anything, however. He just wanted to show who was the boss, and he thought that a series of strong vetoes was just the ticket for that.

Finally, one of his more intelligent aides told him that if he didn't try to get along better with the House and Senate and stop what he was doing, he was likely to get impeached. The voters were getting riled.

Impeachment didn't appeal to A. Michael at all, and things improved a little after that, but not enough. He became known to editorial writers for the state's newspapers as "the only governor we've got," the implication being that they would all have preferred another one. Naturally he wasn't the first governor they'd said that about. And God knows he wouldn't be the last.

So A. Michael didn't care about what the newspapers said. He didn't like editorial writers, either, or editors, or reporters, or even delivery boys. He did like a publisher or two, but they generally wouldn't have anything to do with him.

The fact was that aside from the football players, no one liked the governor very much at all, and there was some question as to how much the football players would have liked him if it hadn't been for his extreme generosity after games. It was enough to make a man lose his faith in human beings, or even to make him imagine that people might be out to get him.

Trey Buford, the aide who had convinced Newton to stop all the vetoes, was now trying to convince him that no one was trying to kill him.

"The hell they aren't," Newton said. He was a beefy man of fifty with a red bulldog's face and a thick shock of prematurely white hair which he kept long and often had to brush away from his forehead, a far cry from the nearly bald little A. Michael whose picture had begun appearing on milk cartons so many years before. He wore Ben Franklin bifocals for reading, and he liked to intimidate people by looking at them over the tops of the rims.

"They're out to get me, all right," he went on. "That woman just got in their way."

"That woman" was Ramona Gonzalez, whom Newton was certain had been killed only because the murderer couldn't get at Newton himself. Trey Buford was not having much luck in persuading Newton that such an idea was preposterous, but he kept right on trying.

"You may not know this, Trey," Newton said, "but there

71

are a lot of people out there who don't like me very much."

Trey Buford, known as the "subgov" because he now dealt much more with the day-to-day business of being governor than Newton did, was a lawyer who looked exactly like a used-car salesman, except shiftier. He had little, close-set eyes, and his dark hair, no matter how many times a week he washed it, always seemed to have an oily sheen. He wore only suits of natural fibers, but he had the knack of making them all look as if they were made of some kind of shiny polyester.

Those who got to know him, including many of the legislators, realized that he was actually much more thoughtful, honest, and interested in the public welfare than the governor himself. Most people trusted Buford and liked dealing with him.

He estimated that the number of people who disliked the governor now equaled roughly the population of the state, but it wouldn't have been politic to say so. He could be honest with the legislators, but he couldn't be completely honest with A. Michael Newton.

So, feigning shock and disbelief at the governor's words, what he said was "Who doesn't like you, Governor?"

Newton didn't even have to think about it. "There's the school teachers, for one bunch. I vetoed that pay-raise bill last session."

There was that, all right.

"I don't think teachers are the kind to go around killing people," Buford said. He looked out the window of the governor's mansion at the pink granite Capitol building across the street. "They staged a protest march, but I think that's about as far as they would go."

Newton remembered the march and the gathering on the Capitol grounds. "Maybe you're right. That march was good for them. They needed the exercise. But what about the state employees?" He peered at Buford over the rims of his glasses. "I vetoed their pay raise, too."

72

That was true.

"They weren't very happy, were they?" Buford said. "They threatened a work stoppage."

"Yeah," Newton said. "But they called it off when they realized that nobody would notice they'd stopped, the lazy bastards. I guess it wasn't them. What about the damn environmentalists?" Newton had vetoed a bill which would have set aside a large parcel of state land in the Big Thicket and made it into a new state park. "Didn't a bunch of them in California get bombed by their own bomb?"

"That was California," Buford said as if that explained everything. "Besides, I think some other group claimed credit for planting that bomb in the car. Look, Governor, let's face facts. The murder of a Hispanic housekeeper in the Capitol doesn't have anything to do with a plot against you. It was something else entirely."

"It might be a plot to make me look bad, then," Newton said. "I told that joke about Mexicans, remember? Shit, who would've thought that asshole would leave the mike open?"

Buford remembered. There had been a lot of work for the damage control boys after that one. "I don't really think anyone would deliberately go that far to make you look bad," he said. "That open mike was probably an accident."

"I don't believe that," Newton said, brushing back the hank of hair that drooped down over his forehead. "But making me look bad isn't what they're after. They want my ass dead."

"I don't see it," Buford said, shaking his head. "Everyone knows that you hardly ever go over to the Capitol. It has to be something else entirely."

"What is it then?" Newton said. "You tell me that. What exactly is it? You think somebody's going around killing Mexican housekeepers? You know better than that. That poor woman was probably a hero, that's what she was, giving up her life so that the bastards couldn't get to me."

Buford looked hard at the governor's face, wondering if the man was joking, but he appeared to be absolutely serious. His term in office had been harder on him than Buford would have guessed.

"It's really Mary Lee I'm worried about," Newton went on. "Me, I can stand the thought of some deranged son of a bitch on my trail. But it's going to kill Mary Lee. She just couldn't take it if something happened to me."

Buford didn't believe that for a minute. He thought Mary Lee would probably be much better off if Newton were out of the way. She would inherit his fortune and gain a lot of sympathy at the same time. She might even get invited to some of those parties she so wanted to attend but which were still closed to her even with her husband in the governor's mansion.

"Yes, sir," Buford lied. "It would be hard on her, all right. But nothing's going to happen to you, Governor. You can count on that."

Newton got out of the leather chair he had been sitting in and walked over to Buford. His face was even redder than usual, his jaw set. "How in the hell do you know that?" he said. "You haven't been listening to a word I've been saying, have you, Buford? Somebody's out to get me, and you're just sitting here on your ass, letting it happen. Well, I'm telling you right now you'd better do something about it. And you'd better do it mighty damn quick."

"You've got your own bodyguards, not to mention the DPS troopers stationed here," Buford said. "They can take care of everything."

"I don't want to hear about what I've got," Newton said. "I want to hear about what I'm *going* to get."

Buford knew there was no use to hold out any longer. The governor was convinced, and no one was going to change his mind. "I'll call the Rangers," he said.

Newton gave the look that was as close as he ever came to smiling. "Goddamn right you will," he said.

The Texas Rangers are now a part of the Department of Public Safety rather than an independent branch of Texas law enforcement, but much of the Ranger legend is still intact. Rangers are still regarded by most of the general public as superior to officers of any other enforcement group, and in many ways they are. They answer only to higher-ranking Rangers, and woe be it to any officer from another agency who gets in their way. The Ranger colonel is responsible only to the governor, and within the borders of Texas even members of the FBI walk softly around the Rangers.

The state issues the Rangers their standard weapons, a .357 Magnum revolver, a shotgun, and a rifle. A Ranger has to qualify with these weapons every three months, and while he can carry any other weapon of his own that he especially likes, he has to qualify with that one, too.

Rangers have to be sharp, intelligent men who can get their teeth into an investigation and see it through to the end, but they also have to *look* like Rangers. Most of them are over six feet tall and weigh over two hundred pounds.

Ray Hartnett met all the qualifications. He stood 6 feet 5 inches in his custom-made sharkskin boots and weighed in at 225 without them. He was an expert with the Magnum, could blow apart a pickup truck in five seconds with his Remington 870 pump and shred a regiment with his Colt AR-15.

He was forty-eight years old and appeared to be ten years younger, with the kind of craggy good looks that might have made anyone think he was a real lady-killer, but his looks were deceiving. He had married early, seen very soon that it was a mistake, and gone off to Vietnam. He figured his twenties were a lost cause, and for years he had concentrated mainly on his job. He used to have his moments of really wanting female companionship, but for years now he just hadn't been interested enough to pursue anyone. It was too time consuming.

For whatever reason, he had considerably less success with women than a mound of suet like Claude Hebert, who worked at seduction as if it were his vocation.

Hartnett was a college graduate who liked to read Fitzgerald in his off hours, which were few, and he was a man who did not suffer fools gladly.

He thought A. Michael Newton was a fool.

"Goddamnit, sir," he said to the colonel. "Excuse me, sir, but Goddamnit. I just don't think I want to work on this one. Give it to Whatley."

The colonel was just as big as Harnett, but he was nearly twenty years older and a little bit softer. Only a little bit, however, and his face firmed up and his voice got hard when he spoke.

"The governor asked for you personally, Ray, or at least Trey Buford did, and that's the same as if the governor did it himself, as you damn well know. Seems like you've got a reputation for being the best man we've got. Now whose fault is that?"

Hartnett started to say that it wasn't right to punish a man for doing his job right, but he thought better of it. "I don't mind working on the murder," he said. "I'd be glad to get into that part of it. But I don't want to have to deal with Governor Newton."

"Maybe you won't have to," the colonel said. "You might be able to get this thing taken care of without ever having to see him. But if he wants to talk to you, you have to go. He is the governor, you know."

Hartnett knew, but that didn't mean he had to like it. Nobody else in the state did. "He's got his own bodyguards, doesn't he?" he said.

"Sure he does. But he's not satisfied with that, from what

76

Buford says. He thinks that cleaning woman was killed by someone who was trying to get to him." The colonel held up a palm to stave off the protest he could see coming. "I know it sounds crazy. But he's the only—"

"—governor we've got," Hartnett finished. "Yeah. I know. Lucky us."

"The head of Capitol security has already gotten in touch with the DPS office in the building, and they've already called here, so they know you're going to be taking over the case. They're glad to be out of it. No problem there." The colonel didn't know about Darrel Prince. "I've arranged for you to meet with the coroner in two hours to get the results of the autopsy. The crime scene's already been gone over by the Capitol police, and the DPS man there had the lab men in. You'll be getting their findings, and you'll want to go look the scene over before it gets completely screwed up."

Hartnett nodded. He trusted the lab guys, but he figured that the Capitol police would have gone through the scene like a bunch of madwomen scattering shit. With them, it was mostly amateur night.

"What about witnesses?" he said.

"As far as we know, there weren't any. We don't have a time of death yet, but it must have happened fairly late. The dead woman, Ramona Gonzalez, lived with her cousin. She never went home last night, and she might have stayed in the building after it closed. You can bet nobody was around and nobody saw a thing."

That figured. No clues, no witnesses, and he was going to have to deal with the Capitol cops *and* the governor. It was going to be great.

"I guess I should go to the Capitol and look things over first, then check with the coroner," he said.

"That's fine," the colonel said. "I'll call the governor and tell him you're on the case."

"Thanks," Hartnett said.

NINE

Hap Reatherford looked like everyone's idea of a medieval monk. He was sixty-two years old, plump from his face to his feet, with ruddy cheeks and a haircut that from necessity rather than design resembled a tonsure thick with gray. He liked to think that he merely had a high forehead, which he regarded as a sure sign of intelligence. He had sparkling blue eyes with smile wrinkles at the corners, and a small mouth that might have seemed tight and pursey if he had not spread it in a smile anytime he thought anyone might be watching him.

All in all, he looked like everyone's favorite uncle, the one that is always called upon to play Santa and distribute the gifts at the Christmas party, the kind of man who takes little children on his knee and tells them stories that delight them and make them laugh with pleasure while he laughs along with them in their simple joy.

Which just went to show how deceiving looks could be.

Hap Reatherford was not one of the most successful lobby-ists in Austin because of his serene benignity. He was successful because he knew not only where most of the bodies were buried but who had buried them there. He knew the probable cause of death and the first names of all the relatives of the deceased. He knew which closets held the skeletons, and he knew whose flesh had once been stretched on the bones.

He was also successful because he was free with the money of his employers, who had plenty of it. He worked for both the insurance lobby and the real estate lobby, two of the biggest, richest, and most powerful in town. Through their political action groups he funneled plenty of cash to the legislators who could and would help him out. He was always ready to send a legislator who needed a short rest on a free vacation to the sunny beaches of Hawaii, a ski trip to Vail, a hunting excursion to the Rockies, or an all-important fact-finding mission to Switzerland or maybe the Italian Riviera.

Reatherford had been a legislator himself, and he knew how much little things like that meant to a fellow.

He had left the legislature seven years previously, having served two terms in the House and one in the Senate before he discovered that he could make even more money working directly for the lobbies than he could while working for them indirectly as an elected public servant.

It was a move he had never regretted. No longer did he have to go home to the dusty west Texas area that he had once nominally represented and go through the charade of earning a living between campaigns and legislative sessions. He could stay in Austin the year around in the two-level house he had bought on a semicircular street in Westlake Hills only a couple of hundred yards from Lake Austin, a beautiful, peaceful neighborhood where he had begun to live in the style to which he intended to remain accustomed for the rest of his years.

He was sitting on his couch, his stockinged feet up on the coffee table while he sipped his after-lunch wine. He'd had to stop most of his drinking a few years before, thanks to a meddlesome doctor who said it wasn't good for him and who had made him stop smoking cigars as well, but he was still allowed two glasses of wine a day. His palate was not discriminating, and his taste ran to white zinfandel. He even drank Texas wines now and then to show his loyalty to the state that had made him rich and happy.

The north wall of his house was made up of two sliding glass doors on either side of an enormous fireplace, and he was looking out one of the doors, over the tops of the trees, mostly denuded now in January, to the other side of the lake. The houses over there were newer and bigger even than his own, but he didn't mind. He had what he wanted.

He wondered, though, as he sipped the wine, exactly what it was that Sam Wilkins wanted. Scratch that. He knew *what* Wilkins wanted. He just wasn't sure *why* the senator wanted it.

Reatherford knew a little bit about Craig Shaw, the reporter that Ron Matson had called about, which wasn't surprising. Reatherford seemed to know a little bit about everyone. Shaw was harmless enough, for a reporter. He'd been in Austin for the previous session and had not distinguished himself by any excessive zeal. He'd turned in competent stories, but he hadn't come up with anything that had set the public's hearts to palpitating or the legislators' underarms to perspiring.

And yet now Sam Wilkins wanted Shaw punished. Something must have happened at the morning's press conference. Reatherford would have to find out what, but that would be easy. He had friends among the press corps. He would wait until he'd talked to one of them to decide about what he was going to do about Shaw.

Oh, he would do what Wilkins was asking, no doubt of that. Wilkins was a useful man to have on your side, and Shaw was vulnerable. Everyone was.

But there was more going on here than Reatherford knew

about, and he didn't like that. There might even be some real profit in this for him, some way to get even more leverage on Wilkins than he already had. Or if things were going bad, he would be able to separate himself from Wilkins before it was too late.

He swallowed the last of the wine regretfully, wishing there could have been just a sip or two more, set the glass on a wood-and-cork coaster, and thought about what he knew already.

He knew about all the political contributions the various PACs had made to Wilkins's campaign fund, for one thing. There really wasn't much in that unless you stopped to analyze it and ask the question of why someone who had run unopposed for the last three terms needed a campaign fund that ran well over seven figures. Then you might get somewhere.

Reatherford knew the answer to that question, thanks to a bit of research, the kind of research he did on most of the members of the legislature.

Part of the answer was that Wilkins needed the funds to pay rent to his wife, who held the mortgage on a fashionable house in Barton Hills. The fact was that she had never been there, preferring to live in the senator's home district, an arrangement that suited both her and Wilkins just fine.

It was also a fact that the rent payments went to pay the mortgage, and the final fact was that Wilkins in reality was using campaign funds to buy a house. While not exactly illegal—probably quite a few of the other legislators were doing something similar—these things were not exactly in keeping with the spirit of ethical behavior, either. Hap didn't blame Wilkins or any of the others; it was better than trying to live in some raggedy-ass hovel of the sort that you could pay for on thirty dollars per diem.

And of course Wilkins needed the money to pay himself when he hired himself to run his opponentless campaigns.

Since he considered himself an exceptionally skillful campaign manager, he naturally paid himself top dollar. You couldn't expect a good man to work for anything less.

And naturally Wilkins needed the money to pay for food and entertainment, though the voters might wonder how a man who ate most of his meals with lobbyists who were eager to pick up his checks managed to spend nearly five thousand dollars of his own money for food and entertainment during one session of the legislature.

Reatherford got off the couch and walked over to one of the sliding glass doors, the one on the left, to get a better view of the lake. The bright noonday sun was shining on the water, giving it a silvery gleam. *He really was going to have to get out his old fishing gear one of these days,* he thought. Get down there to the shore of the lake and try a few casts. He wondered where the hell that gear was. It had been years since he'd thought about it.

He shook his head, laughing silently at himself. Fishing, for God's sake. Next thing you knew, he'd be thinking about walking barefoot in the bluebonnets in the spring. It was a sure sign of old age when you started thinking about things like that.

Bluebonnets reminded him of Laura. God rest her soul. Two years ago next month. Women weren't supposed to have heart attacks, that's what he'd always thought, but the doctors told him that it wasn't all that unusual. At least it had been quick, not like so many people Reatherford knew, all of whom had lingered for months with various debilitating ailments that had killed them long before they officially died.

He remembered once right after the war, they were just kids, had just started dating, Laura had made him drive her nearly all the way to Waco just to look at the bluebonnets.

He shook off the thought. He was thinking things like that far too often lately, getting to be a sentimental fool. Old age creeping up on him, for damn sure. He had to cut it out. A good cigar was what he needed, help him keep his mind on the job at hand.

Which was Wilkins and why he wanted to get back at that reporter.

And then there was the murder. Reatherford didn't think that was anything serious, probably just some kind of lovers' quarrel, but you never could tell. He'd heard about it almost as soon as the body had been found, but that was several hours ago. He wondered what the developments had been.

He decided to give Jane Kettler a call.

It seemed to Jane that practically everyone in Austin was giving her a call, but that wasn't unusual. Some days were just like that.

Today was different only in the types of calls she was getting. Her calls normally came mostly from groups that wanted to tour the Capitol, from legislators who wanted to arrange meetings and press conferences, or from out-of-state visitors who wanted a special tour, but today she was getting calls from print and broadcast reporters every few minutes. Usually it was as if reporters didn't know that her office existed.

The fact that she didn't know any more than they did about the murder of Ramona Gonzalez was not important to them. She had been right there in the building, they said. Surely she had seen or heard *some*thing, or knew someone who had. Those calls, along with the ones from legislators who were hoping that the session might somehow be delayed by the murder, kept her busy all morning. She hadn't even had time to eat lunch.

That part, she didn't mind so much. Stan Donald had brought her an apple sometime around noon, and that was all she needed. It was as much as she had most other days. She hated to admit it even to herself, but she was getting to an age where she had to watch her weight or let it get out of hand, something that she hadn't had to worry about for nearly thirty years. It didn't seem quite fair to her, somehow, that she was having to worry about it now.

The phone call from Hap Reatherford was not surprising. She had known him for a long time, ever since her husband, Gerald Kettler, had been elected to his first term in the House. Reatherford had not been a lobbyist then, and he had taken a liking to the new representative from central Texas. He had become Gerald's mentor.

Later, when it became clear that Hap wasn't exactly the kind of man that Gerald could admire, the friendship had cooled, but there remained a bond between the two men.

"You can't help but like the sneaky son of a bitch" was the way Gerald had put it. "Even if you do know he's grabbing with both hands."

Gerald never grabbed for anything himself, and that was why he had never gotten rich. He didn't sell his vote, ever. He actually tried to be a full-time legislator and to live on his seventy-two-hundred-dollar-a-year salary. They would never have made it had Jane not taken a job of her own. She worked as a secretary, and while her earnings were slim, they were enough to keep the Kettlers solvent, or close to it.

Jane often remembered what her government professor at the University of Texas had said: "Elected officials are usually no better and no worse than the average citizen." This idea was comforting when she was thinking of someone like Gerald, but lately she wondered about the voters—and not just in Texas. Working with politicians, she had seen all kinds, but things seemed to be going downhill. Most people thought that money and TV—often the same thing—had corrupted the officeholders. Jane didn't know, but she was convinced that if all politicians had to write their own speeches, things just might improve. Then maybe people could tell what they were getting.

At any rate, the result of Gerald's integrity was that when he had died in a senseless car accident three years previously, killed by a drunken driver who crossed the center line going eighty-five, Jane had been left with nothing more than a few thousand dollars in life insurance and a lot of sympathetic friends, many of whom were people of influence in Austin. They had used their influence to get her the job she now held, and she was glad they had. It paid better than her secretarial position had, and she didn't think Gerald would have regarded it as an improper gift, considering the fact that she was pretty damn good at what she did, even if she did say so herself. There were plenty of other people who said so, too. She had a file drawer full of letters from legislators who were thanking her for saving their asses in one way or another or for making them look good to the home folks who came to the Capitol.

One of the influential people who had assisted her in getting the job was Hap Reatherford.

"How are you, Hap?" she said, glad of the excuse to talk to someone she knew for a while. She had been tired of the reporters ever since the first one called, and she had refused to take the last few calls.

"You know me, Jane," Hap said, his voice sounding bluff and hearty even over the phone. Jane wondered if he practiced at it. "Sound as a two-dollar watch."

"You never owned a two-dollar watch in your life," Jane said. She knew Hap's taste ran more to Rolexes.

"Sure I did, long time ago. Lots of things were different then, though. I caught myself thinking about Laura today."

Laura had been Jane's friend just as Gerald had been Hap's. She had seen Jane through the tough times after Gerald's death, and her own death had been almost as devastating to Jane as it had been to Hap.

"It'll be spring before long," Jane said. "Laura always liked the springtime."

"She surely did," Hap said. "Bluebonnets and all. Damn, Jane, it's hard to get old."

"Tell me about it."

Hap laughed. "Hell, woman, you don't know what *old* means. You aren't even fifty yet. You've got lots of good years left. Lots of 'em."

They went on in that vein for a few minutes. Jane knew that Hap would get to the point sooner or later. He hadn't called to reminisce about old times, but he'd been a lobbyist for so long he didn't know how to get to the point without a certain amount of bullshitting beforehand.

"What I called for, Jane," Hap said finally, his voice getting deeper as he got serious, "is that murder you had there today."

"Not you, too," she said.

"Reporters been bothering you?" Hap said. "I hope you didn't tell them anything." He didn't like reporters now any more than he had when he'd been in the legislature. If anything, he liked them less. They were always trying to expose some scandal or another that he wanted kept quiet, which was one reason he didn't mind helping Sam Wilkins out with Craig Shaw.

"I didn't know anything to tell them," Jane said.

"You sure? This is old Hap you're talking to, not some nosy newshound."

"I'm sure, Hap. The woman who was killed was a janitor, Ramona Gonzalez, and I hardly knew her. She was assigned to this floor, but she hadn't been working here very long."

"Was she young? Pretty?"

"That sounds like a sexist comment to me," Jane said.

Hap said that he was sorry. "I didn't mean to sound like that. I was just curious."

"Well, as it happens, she was both. About twenty-five, and very pretty. But I still don't see what difference it makes."

Hap tried to explain. "Seems to me that if she was an older woman, there'd be a different motive. Young ones get involved with all kinds of men, some of them pretty rough. I was thinking this could be some kind of lovers' quarrel thing. Older women don't have those kinds of problems."

"Tell me about it," Jane said.

Hap laughed. "That's what you said before. And like *I* said before, you've got a lot of good years left, Jane. There are plenty of men who'd like to see you come out of that shell you're in."

Jane hadn't realized she was in a shell. It was true, however, that after Gerald's death she had lost all interest in the opposite sex. At first it had been because she and Gerald had been really in love and she couldn't imagine herself ever feeling that way about another man. Then it had been the new job. Learning her way around the Capitol, learning the politics of the position, handling all the people she had to deal with—from part-time employees and dignitaries of all sorts to the most powerful of legislators and their people—had consumed all her time for more than a year.

She knew now that there could be other men in her life, and she could handle the job quite well, thank you, but for some reason she had established no relationships outside her work. That had not bothered her at all until lately, when she'd begun to think about what she was missing.

"Name one man," she said.

"How about me?" Hap said. "I'm old and worn out, but I'm a good provider."

Jane wondered if he were serious. It wasn't that she didn't like him. She did. But somehow he was not the kind of man she could relate to. She had not realized until that very moment, perhaps because she had never consciously thought about it, what kind of man that would be; but she knew he would have to be more of an idealist than Hap Reatherford.

"I don't think so, Hap," she said. "We've known each other for too long."

Hap understood what she meant, and he didn't mind. He'd been only half serious. "That's all right, Jane. An old dog like

87

me couldn't keep up with you anyhow." He paused. "You sure you don't know anything else about that killing?"

"I'm sure. But if I find out anything, I'll give you a call." She didn't mean it. She wasn't going to try to find out anything, though she would no doubt hear the usual run of the gossip. She had no intention of calling Hap when she did, however.

"I'll be waiting by the phone," Hap said. He didn't mean it, either. The murder didn't seem to have anything to do with him or the people he cared about. "You take care of yourself, now, you hear?"

"I will, Hap," Jane said.

When she hung up the phone, she thought about what she'd said. She always took care of herself, but she never really thought about herself and her own life. Everything she did was related to her job. When was the last time she'd taken a vacation? Two years ago? She seldom even took a day off.

She got up in the morning and came to work. She went home in the evening, watched the six o'clock news, read a book, and went to bed. Even on Sundays she often drove to the Capitol and spent a few hours in her office, going over the schedule for the coming week, updating her records, preventing problems before they arose.

No wonder she didn't have any friends outside the job. Without intending to, she had built a fence around herself and put up a NO TRESPASSING sign.

Hap was right about her age, too. Forty-seven wasn't old. She had a lot of good years left. She should make the most of them.

She wondered if she remembered how.

TEN

There was a story that the Capitol basement had been used as a stable in the building's early days, back in the latter part of the nineteenth century. Ray Hartnett didn't know whether that was true or not, but if it was, the basement would have been a much more interesting place then than it was now.

Then again, when you thought about it, what with all the legislative offices down there now, there probably hadn't been any more horseshit around even in the old days.

Darrel Prince showed Hartnett to the room where the murder had occurred. Hartnett knew Prince vaguely, had at least seen him around, and he had the impression that Prince was more capable than most of the other Capitol cops, who were generally a pretty slovenly lot in Hartnett's opinion. Certainly Prince was better than his buddy Claude Hebert, whom Hartnett regarded as about as useful as the tits on a boar hog. Hebert was lazy and sneaky, but even at that he wasn't much different from the other Capitol cops Hartnett had met. He'd damn sure never make it as a Ranger, but then neither would the rest of them. There wasn't a one of them that came close to looking like a Ranger, and that was the least of it.

The hallway leading to the small alcove where Ramona Gonzalez had died was roped off with yellow plastic. Ordinarily there would have been a number of workers in the offices, but they had been kept out while the investigation was going on. Hartnett figured they didn't mind.

There wasn't much to see in the alcove. Just the two hampers, the one where the body had been found and the other one, filled with wadded-up newspapers. There were several sheets of wadded newspaper on the floor, but there was no sign of any struggle, no sign that anything at all out of the ordinary had taken place in the small room.

Hartnett asked about the papers on the floor.

"The body was covered with them," Prince said. "Who-ever did it didn't really try very hard to hide the body, though. Maybe he was in a hurry. There were a lot more papers in the other hamper that he didn't use."

"What about the two kids that found the body? What did they know about it?"

"I interrogated them myself," Prince said, enjoying the use of police jargon. "They were scared shitless. They said they got separated from their tour group, but I think they sneaked down here for a little slap and tickle."

"No way they could have had anything to do with the murder?"

Prince shook his head. "They came in on a school bus this morning. Hadn't been here more than fifteen minutes before they found the body. Just about time for the boy to get to first base."

"Who else was down here before you got on the scene?" Hartnett said.

"Clinton Amory. He's the head janitor. Excuse me, head of the Capitol maintenance. And there was some Mexican woman. Juana Lorca. I think she might be the dead woman's cousin. She got here about the same time as Amory."

Hartnett made a mental note to talk to those two; then he

examined the hampers. "Why are these papers crumpled like this?" he said. "Who'd go to that much trouble to throw away newspapers?"

Prince hadn't thought about that. "I don't know. Maybe somebody unpacked something."

Hartnett took a sheet of paper and smoothed it until he could see the date. "This is yesterday's paper. Nobody had anything packed in this."

Prince couldn't see what the hell difference it made.

"Somebody wadded this paper up," Hartnett explained. "Whoever did it didn't do it for entertainment. I want to talk to the housekeeper who put these hampers here."

"That would probably be Juana," Prince said. "She'll still be on shift if she didn't go home. The way she was taking on, she might have left."

Hartnett dug down into the hamper from which he'd taken the paper, but there was nothing else in there. He brought up another sheet from near the bottom and examined it. It bore the same date as the one from the top.

He looked at the paper as if there might be something he could learn from it, though Prince was at a loss as to guess what that could be unless maybe it was the Southwestern Conference basketball standings.

"This paper has a kind of funny smell," Hartnett said, sniffing at it.

"It's been in a trash hamper," Prince pointed out. "It probably smells like trash."

"That's not exactly it." Hartnett stuck the paper under Prince's nose.

Prince sniffed. There was a sort of faintly familiar odor to the paper, not counting the distinctive smell of the paper and the ink, but he couldn't quite figure out what it was. "Garbage, maybe?" he said.

"Maybe," Hartnett said. "Would there be garbage in these hampers?"

"Shouldn't be. Maybe somebody wrapped his lunch in the newspaper yesterday."

"Maybe." It was a weak explanation, and Hartnett wasn't convinced. He held the paper up and looked at it as if it might contain the name of the killer. "I hope the lab crew took some of this with them."

"I think they did," Prince said, wondering why the indistinct odor that clung to the paper seemed almost to remind him of something that he couldn't quite call to mind. Maybe he could think of it later.

"What about your security cameras?" Hartnett said, changing the subject. "I thought these halls were monitored twenty-four hours a day."

"They are," Prince said. "We got tapes, too."

"Well, Jesus Christ," Hartnett said. "What are we wasting our time here for? We should be questioning whoever was on duty last night. Let's get hold of him. He must have seen whoever was down here."

"Uh, well," Prince said, not meeting Hartnett's eyes. "You know how it is sometimes."

"No," Hartnett said. "I don't know how it is sometimes. Why don't you tell me?"

Prince, nearly a foot shorter than Hartnett and at least seventy-five pounds lighter, was intimidated by the big Ranger. How could you explain to somebody like that about the fact that watching the damn monitors occasionally got so fucking boring that you just didn't watch them? You looked at a magazine or you shot the shit with whoever else was around or you watched a real TV. There was nothing for it but to tell the truth, though. He had to say it.

"So the officer on duty probably didn't see anyone at all," Hartnett said. "He was too busy catching up on the great books of the western world."

Prince swallowed. "Something like that, I guess."

"What about the tapes?" Hartnett said. "You do have the tapes, I guess."

Prince's mouth felt exceedingly dry. He swallowed again. Twice.

"You got something caught in your throat, Prince?" Hartnett said.

"It's not that. It's just, hell, I don't know, it's just that—"

"Goddamnit, Prince. Don't tell me you don't even have the tapes."

Prince didn't swallow, but he did look at the floor rather than at the Ranger. "We've got 'em, all right. That part of things was working fine."

"All right, then. So there's no problem. Let's go review the tapes."

"We can do that," Prince said. "But it won't do any good."

Hartnett stood a little straighter. It seemed to Prince that the Ranger's white Stetson was brushing the ceiling of the little room, and Prince looked out the air shaft window and wished he was outside under a tree.

"Tell me why it won't do any good," Hartnett said.

So Prince told him about the masking tape.

"Good God almighty," Hartnett said, looking up at the concrete ceiling of the alcove. "I don't suppose there's any way that whoever was on duty got a look at the guy who put the tape over the lens."

Prince admitted that there probably wasn't. No one had said anything about it.

"What about the other cameras?" Hartnett said. "Wouldn't they have gotten a shot of whoever put the masking tape over the lens?"

Prince didn't think so.

"Why not?" Hartnett said. He was resigned to getting bad news, but it didn't take the edge out of his question.

Prince explained how the other cameras were positioned.

"You can't have enough cameras to cover the whole Capitol, so you just have to cover certain areas. If the perp came down the stairs by the vending machines, he could slide along the wall, slap the tape over the camera lens, and that would be that."

Hartnett sighed. "Just for the hell of it, why don't you tell me what would have happened if one of your really alert officers had happened to notice last night that one of the cameras wasn't functioning? What would he have done then?"

"Well, he'd probably have checked it out. That's what happened this morning. Claude Hebert caught it almost as soon as we came on duty, and I came down here and found out what the trouble was."

"And you checked out the hallway, checked all the office doors, and then you looked in this room to see if there was anything going on. Right?"

Prince shook his head miserably. "No. I didn't do any of that."

Hartnett was trying not to lose his temper, but it wasn't easy. He could hardly believe the kind of shoddy police technique that he was hearing about.

"Then what the hell *did* you do?" he said.

"I pulled the tape off the lens," Prince said.

"Good," Hartnett said. "That way, if anyone ever did look at the monitor, he might see something. But I doubt, by God, that he'd know he was looking at a bulldog unless it bit him in the ass."

There wasn't much Prince could say to that. He kept his mouth shut, afraid of what he strongly suspected was coming next and hoping that he was wrong.

"All right," Hartnett said. He took a deep breath, held it, let it out. "Let's forget that. Nothing we can do about it now, is there? Where's the masking tape? Tape takes fingerprints like nobody's business."

Shit, Prince thought. He hadn't been wrong. For just the smallest part of a second he was tempted to lie, but he'd never been very good at that. Besides, he couldn't think of anything that would have sounded at all believable, much less convincing. Not to a man like Hartnett.

"I threw it away," he said. He seemed to shrink into his uniform, as if he thought Hartnett might be going to knock his head off.

Hartnett felt like doing exactly that, but he was prevented from doing so by the knowledge that it would have done him no good at all.

"You threw it away," he said. "I hope you're kidding me, Prince."

Prince wished the same thing. "I'm not kidding," he said.

Hartnett turned abruptly and walked out of the alcove. Prince started to follow him, but he thought better of it almost at once. Hartnett probably needed a few minutes to calm down, and Prince was more than willing to give him the time.

Hartnett needed more than time. He needed someone to hit, and he thought he might punch a fist through the paneling in the hall since he really couldn't justify hitting Prince. But while breaking the paneling might satisfy him, it might also break his hand.

He stood for a minute and thought about what he had. A murdered woman, that was what he had, and that was all. While there should have been videotapes of the killer, there was nothing. And there was nothing in the room where the woman had died, either. There was nothing to go on at all.

He hadn't asked for this. He'd even tried to get out of it, but the colonel hadn't let him. He hadn't been forced to talk to the governor yet, but that was coming. And what was he going to tell him?

"Well, Governor, there were plenty of clues, but your

Kapitol Kops threw them away." That ought to go over really well.

Shit. Maybe the coroner would have something more for him. The autopsy could at least establish the time of death, probably the manner of it. That would be something.

And maybe Clinton Amory and Juana Lorca could shed some light on things. He could talk to them before he checked with the coroner.

And there was one other thing. He turned back to the alcove where Ramona Gonzalez had died. Prince was still in there, looking out the little window.

"Where did you throw it?" Hartnett said.

Prince turned around. "Throw what?"

"The masking tape that you took off the camera lens. Where did you throw it?"

"In the trash," Prince said.

"I hope you can be just a little bit more specific than that," Hartnett said. "Like telling me exactly which trash can you threw it in."

Prince thought about it. "Yeah," he said. "I remember now."

"It's a good damn thing. Go find it."

"Huh?" Prince didn't quite get it.

"I said go and find it. Dig it out of the trash if you have to. I want that damn tape."

"It'll have my prints all over it," Prince said.

"I don't care. It might have some others, too. Get it."

"All right. I'll get it. But. . . ."

Hartnett felt himself starting to get angry again. He told himself to calm down, to breathe easier. "But what?" he said.

"But it won't do you any good. I, uh, I wadded it up."

"You wadded it up."

"Yeah. I sort of rolled it up in a ball, you know? Sticky side in. Just wadded it up."

"Sticky side in."

Prince's eyes pled for understanding. "I didn't know it was important," he said. "How was I supposed to know?"

Hartnett didn't trust himself to say anything. He turned his back and walked out of the room.

"I'll find it, though," Prince called after him. He didn't know if Hartnett could hear him. He could hear the big man's boot heels as they echoed off the concrete floor of the hallway like gunshots.

"I know exactly which trash I threw it in," Prince said. "I'll get it out and bring it to you."

The sound of the boot heels stopped. After a few seconds they started again. Hartnett didn't return.

"I'll get the damn tape," Prince said quietly, almost to himself. His plan to solve the crime on his own and be a hero wasn't getting off to a very good start.

After a while he left the room and went to dig through the trash for the masking tape.

ELEVEN

Hartnett disliked Clinton Amory on sight. He tried to tell himself that he wasn't prejudiced against people who looked like sloppy sleaze bags, but he couldn't make a satisfactory case. He had to resist the impulse to reach across Amory's desk and brush the dandruff off the man's shoulder after jerking the toothpick out of his mouth.

For his part, Amory didn't like Hartnett, either. He didn't like anyone who meddled in his business, and the death of Ramona Gonzalez was his business, or a portion of it, because there was more to Amory's livelihood than merely the Capitol custodial service.

He had a few interests on the side that he told no one about, least of all someone like Hartnett, who represented the law.

Amory was a minor-league blackmailer, though he preferred to think of what he did along those lines as a simple venture in private enterprise.

He worked on an admittedly small scale, but he nevertheless took in a tidy sum of cash money that no one from the Internal fucking Revenue would ever hear about.

He throve on the gossip that flowed through the Capitol like a muddy stream, and he blackmailed only those who had so much to lose that they didn't dare attack him. There were therefore many people that he would never have considered approaching with his sly, insinuating demands, just as a jackal would never dream of attacking a healthy lion.

He had never approached the woman who lost the earring, for example. It would not have been worth the risk. Her husband would have squashed Amory like a bug. But there were plenty of others, weaker and thus more vulnerable to Amory's special brand of intimidation.

While most of the people who worked in the building subscribed to Jane Kettler's dictum about loose lips and sunken ships and would never have contemplated making use of the things they heard in the course of their jobs, Amory listened avidly to everything and was quick to make use of it on those who were in no position to strike back, thanks mostly to the fact that they had more to lose than he did.

He had recovered from his shock at seeing Ramona's body in the canvas hamper, had replaced his dropped toothpick with another that made its way slowly from one side of his mouth to the other as he spoke, but he had only begun to grieve for his loss.

He had liked Ramona; she was all right for a Mexican, but he wasn't grieving for that reason. He was grieving because she had been one of the best sources of information that he had. She had enjoyed nosing around, finding things out, and she had never been hesitant to share with him. She had talked to everyone, of course, though not everyone had been as willing to listen to her as Amory had been.

He knew that, because he had other sources. He also knew that Ramona's tendency to gossip had not made her popular with most of those her work brought her into contact with, and he wondered if one of them could have disliked her enough to kill her.

He also wondered if she had found out something so dangerous that she had been killed for knowing it. He hoped that if she had, she hadn't told him about it. There were some things he just didn't want to know, and anything that could be that risky was one of them.

He had liked Ramona for another reason, too. She didn't mind putting out. That was what he'd heard anyhow, and he was counting on her putting out to him, as soon as he got something on her.

That was just the way his mind worked. He couldn't imagine anyone actually wanting to sleep with him. He'd never had a woman who hadn't been subtly coerced into his bed by his implications of what he knew or could tell about her if she didn't give in to his demands.

That coercion was a big part of his enjoyment. The sex was a fleeting pleasure, but the knowledge that what he knew gave him power over someone else was something that provided a pleasure that endured beyond the moment.

He wasn't going to tell the big asshole standing across the desk from him any of that, though. He didn't like lawmen, whether they were Rangers or just time-servers like Claude Hebert. They were likely to take a dim view of Amory's profitable little sideline.

He laced his fingers behind his head, leaned back in his chair, and looked up at Hartnett. He hadn't offered Hartnett a seat, and he didn't intend to.

"What can I do for you?" Amory said, the toothpick jiggling.

Hartnett knew that Amory was not as casual as he was trying to appear. No one was casual when a murder had been committed, not even a Texas Ranger, though he could appear just as nonchalant as Amory. He walked over to the door frame and leaned against it.

"You can tell me about Ramona Gonzalez," he said.

"She was all right, for a Mexican," Amory said. "Good worker. Not like some of them."

"You knew her strictly in a supervisory capacity, then?"

Amory wondered if Hartnett had been talking to someone. "Well, I guess you could say I knew her a little better than that," he said.

"How much better?"

Amory sat forward and put his hands on the scarred top of his desk. "What're you getting at?" he said.

Hartnett smiled. It wasn't a comforting smile. It wasn't intended to be. "Nothing," he said. "What did you think I was getting at?"

"Look, I know everybody who works for me," Amory said. "Some better than others. Me and Ramona were friends, sort of, you could say. We talked to each other on her coffee breaks, you know? Like that. But I didn't know her any better than just to talk to."

"So what kind of woman was she to talk to?" Hartnett said.

"She was OK. What the hell do you want me to say?"

"I want you to tell me about her. Who she talked to besides you, whether she was married, where she lived, and what she did after she got off work."

"Shit, I don't know," Amory said. "I don't know any of that stuff. Well, I do know she wasn't married. She was a good-looking woman, and maybe some of the guys around here tried to put the make on her. Those legislators and their assistants are about as horny as billygoats, you know?"

Hartnett knew. In Texas, sex and politics went together like black-eyed peas and cornbread. He was sure it was that way just about everywhere. But, unlike Amory, he acknowledged the number of women who now had jobs as legislators or who worked for them in important jobs. He couldn't easily imagine a woman legislator manipulating someone for sexual favors, much less killing her, but maybe he was just out of date about women and sex.

101

"No legislator would be seen with Ramona Gonzalez, though," Amory went on. "You can bet on that. They're too damn good for some Mexican woman, least they think they are."

Hartnett knew that, too.

"You got any names for me?" he said.

"Hell, no. We didn't know each other that well," Amory said. It wasn't exactly the truth, but he wasn't going to give away anything that he might later be able to turn to a profit.

Hartnett thought that Amory was probably lying, but he let it pass. Now wasn't the time to press it. He'd see Amory again. "What about her other friends? Besides you, I mean."

"Just Juana," Amory said. "And now and then she talked to some of those college girl guides. She liked everybody, but not everybody liked her."

"Why?"

Amory wished he hadn't said anything. "Well, she had sort of a reputation, you know?"

This time, Hartnett didn't know. "Suppose you tell me," he said.

"She was sort of a flirt and a gossip," Amory said.

"What did she gossip about?"

Amory took his toothpick out of his mouth and looked at it. The end was flat and wet. "You know. The usual stuff."

Again, Hartnett didn't know. "You'd better tell me," he said.

"Who was dating who, who was maybe smoking a joint in the ladies' room. That kind of thing."

Hartnett's first thought was the same as Amory's had been. That kind of gossip could possibly be dangerous, especially if you substituted the word *screwing* for *dating*.

"Why did a good-looking young woman who apparently knew English pretty well have such a low-level job?" Hartnett said. The more he found out about Ramona, the more he wondered about that.

Amory looked uneasy again. "Well, nobody but me knew it, of course. It's confidential. But Ramona was an ex-con."

Uh-oh, Hartnett thought. *A whole new mess.* "What had she done?" he said.

"She stole some money from a store where she worked right after she got out of high school. Didn't amount to much, and she was out on parole pretty quick. I like to try to help people get rehabilitated, and she liked the idea of working in the Capitol."

Hartnett began to suspect a nasty pattern. Maybe this murder involved real corruption.

"She talked to you specifically about the stuff she saw?" he said.

"Sometimes," Amory said, still looking at the toothpick.

"So you know everything that she knew."

Amory's head jerked up. "Hell, no! Don't say anything like that." He looked around his cubbyhole of an office, but there was no one there except for him and the Ranger. "She didn't tell me much of anything. She just liked to talk to me, that was all."

Hartnett straightened up and leaned away from the door frame. "I'd like to believe you, Amory. You seem like an all-right guy, and I'd hate to see you wind up like Ramona."

There was a fine sheen of perspiration on Amory's upper lip now, and he wiped it off with his thumb and forefinger. "I don't know why you'd say a thing like that," he said.

"Sure you do," Hartnett said. "If she got killed because of something she knew, the same thing could happen to someone else who knew the same thing."

"But I don't know anything like that," Amory said. "Not a damn thing."

Hartnett smiled and nodded. "I hope so, for your sake. I'm going to talk to some other people, but I'll be back to see you. If you think of anything that might help me before then, you let me know." He walked over to the desk and laid a white business card on it. "That number's always answered. They'll know where to reach me."

Amory looked at the card but didn't take it. "I don't know anything," he repeated. "Not a damn thing."

"Sure," Hartnett said. "See you later, Amory." He walked out of the office. He could feel Amory's eyes on his back all the way, and they felt stupid and sleazy.

Juana Lorca, a middle-aged woman whose hair was still jet black, wasn't much help. She was frightened of Hartnett, which didn't surprise him. The murder had upset her terribly, and that wasn't the only thing that hindered communication between them. The Texas Rangers didn't have a very good reputation with Hispanics, thanks to some things that had happened in the past. Some of the things had even happened within Hartnett's own lifetime, so he didn't really blame Juana too much. He knew it wouldn't do any good to tell her that he wasn't like that and that the Rangers didn't do things that way any longer.

In spite of the woman's reticence, however, he did learn that Ramona had been a little free with her favors, not that Juana had put it quite that way. In fact, she had tried to make it appear that Ramona was practically a saint, but Hartnett had pressed a little, saying that Clinton Amory had told him Ramona was more likely a slut than a virgin.

Sometimes a little lie like that could get the ball rolling, and it did with Juana. She leapt to Ramona's defense, saying that her cousin was very choosy about men, that she went with only the best of them.

"Very *guapo*. With money and good cars," Juana said.

But she couldn't, or wouldn't, give him any names, not even when he told her that this was a murder investigation and that she might be letting the killer of her cousin go free.

"I do not know their names," she said. "I swear it." She put her hand over her heart.

104

Hartnett wasn't sure he believed her, any more than he believed Amory, but he wasn't bothered by that fact. In a murder investigation, the one thing that you could count on every time was that nearly everyone would lie to you. At first. Sooner or later, someone would break down and tell the truth.

And Juana did confirm that Ramona had been fond of gossip, though Juana seemed to think that Ramona's talking was merely a harmless pastime.

"She liked everyone. She liked to talk to them to show she liked them," Juana said, but she had to admit that not everyone liked Ramona and that maybe, just maybe, she had talked a little too much.

And there was one other thing. He found out that Juana Lorca did not have a high opinion of her supervisor.

"He should not say those things about Ramona," she told Hartnett. "He told her that he was her friend, and he liked for her to tell him secrets."

"Secrets?"

"The things she knew. Not everyone would listen to her, but Mr. Amory would always like to hear. He liked to know bad things. He is not a nice man."

Hartnett found that very interesting, and slightly different from what Amory had told him.

All in all, Hartnett wasn't dissatisfied with what he had learned in his two interviews. It wasn't much, but now he had a place to start. He would talk to some of the other regular employees about Ramona, particularly several of the guides, who would probably know her because she apparently hung around the desk a lot. They might even be able to shed some light on her death. And of course they might be able to tell him whom she had been going out with and most likely going to bed with. Then he'd really have something.

But right now he had to go to see the coroner.

★   ★   ★

105

"How the hell do I know what trash can you threw the fucking tape in?" Claude Hebert said. "I don't see why you want it in the first place."

Darrel Prince explained why he wanted it.

Claude shook his head. "It won't be a damn bit of good to anybody if you wadded it up. The fingerprints would be on the sticky side, and most of them would be yours anyhow. But that won't matter, since you won't be able to pull the tape apart without messin' everything up anyway."

Prince knew all that. But he also knew that the Ranger wanted the tape. He'd just have to go scrounging through all the trash cans he might have passed until he found it. He wasn't looking forward to doing that, and it was clear that he wasn't going to get any help from Claude.

He decided to start down in the concession area. There were two big cans down there, and that was probably where he'd dumped the tape.

It was. He found it in the very first can he searched, down near the bottom, under wrappers off Peanutbutter Snickers and Hershey bars, under diet Coke and Dr Pepper cans, under Fritos' packages and the cellophane wrappings from cheese crackers.

He practically had to dive into the damn can to get the tape, but at least he got it.

He got something else, too. He got an idea.

While he was down there rummaging around like a raccoon in a trash pile, it came to him. You might say he inhaled it.

The odor of the trash can reminded him of the smell of the newspaper from the hamper, and it reminded him of something else, too.

Or some*one* else.

Wayne the Wagger. Old Wayne. The son of a bitch had slept in that hamper, under those newspapers. Prince wouldn't have thought Wayne was smart enough to come up

106

with an idea like that, but the more he thought about it, the more certain he was that Wayne had been in the hamper.

With that revelation came another. Wayne had killed Ramona Gonzalez.

It was so obvious that Prince wondered why he hadn't seen it at once. Wayne was a crazy man, and he liked to wag his dick in public. In other words, he was exactly the kind of person who'd kill a woman and dump her in the trash.

Prince held the piece of wadded tape carefully between two fingertips and backed his head out of the trash can. He wasn't going to get any more prints on the damn tape, that was for sure, not that it mattered now. He had the killer.

He stood up and looked around the concession area. No one there but a few tourists, watching him curiously as they drank their Pepsis. Little did they know that he had the clue that would break what he was already thinking of as The Capitol Murder.

He could hardly wait to tell Hartnett. The Ranger would give him a little respect then, by God.

As he started up the broad steps to the ground floor, however, Prince thought again about telling Hartnett. Why should he do that?

Why should Hartnett get any credit at all when Darrel Prince was the man who had solved the crime?

Why shouldn't Prince capture Wayne and get all the credit himself?

The answer to the last question was that there was no reason why Prince shouldn't be the hero, just the way he had planned it all along.

He bounded up the steps on his way to headquarters. When he got to the top, he nearly ran over Stan Donald, who was on his way down for a soft drink.

"What's all the excitement?" Stan said.

"I've got the guy who killed the Gonzalez woman," Darrel said.

Stan looked around. "Where?"

"I don't have him here," Prince said. "I mean I know who did it. It's just a matter of time."

"That's great police work," Stan said, sounding as if he meant it. "Who is it?"

"The Wagger," Prince said.

"You're kidding."

Prince felt his face getting red. "You think I'm wrong? Well, I'm not. I've got the proof."

Prince knew he was coming on a little strong, since he was well aware of the fact that his thinking a piece of newspaper smelled like Wayne wasn't exactly the kind of thing that would stand up in court. But damn it, he was right, and he didn't like for people like Donald, who didn't know a thing about police work or a cop's intuition, to question him.

"That's great, then," Stan said. "I'm sure you'll get some kind of commendation out of this, Darrel."

Prince was sure of it, too. Now all he had to do was get his hands on Wayne.

TWELVE

Getting his hands on Wayne was a lot easier for Prince to think about than to accomplish.

"You *what*?" he said into the telephone, an incredulous look spreading across his face. "You let the son of a bitch go?"

He was talking to the Austin police, who had released Wayne on his own recognizance several hours earlier.

"Yep," the booking sergeant said. "What you think, Prince? You think we got room here to hold somebody who pissed on a cannon? We got guys here should've been in Huntsville months ago, but the state can't take 'em off our hands 'cause the prison's filled to the limit. So we're filled *past* the limit. You send me a murderer, and I'll keep him, but don't be thinking the judge is gonna make us hold on to some man who pisses on a cannon."

Prince slammed down the phone, thinking that if the sergeant only knew the truth he wouldn't be so fucking sarcastic. Prince *had* sent them a killer, but they didn't know it. Of course he hadn't known it either, not when he sent him, but that was beside the point. They should have held onto Wayne as a matter of public safety. Who could say who—or what—he might piss on next?

"What's the trouble?" Claude Hebert said, laying aside a much-thumbed copy of *Spy* magazine and looking up at Prince. "You sound a little chapped."

Darrel had not told Claude about Wayne. He already regretted having told Stan Donald. The fewer people who knew, the better, for now. He didn't want anybody horning in on the credit.

"It's nothing," he said. He could catch up with the Wagger later. Wayne would probably be back to the Capitol that very night, looking for a warm place to sleep.

"Sounded like something to me," Claude said.

"Hell, it's just that the city cops let Wayne go. I thought we wouldn't have to worry about him for a few days, but he's already back on the loose. They said they didn't have room for him."

Claude wasn't interested in Wayne. He changed the subject. "What did that Ranger have to say? He have any ideas about the killing?"

"Sure. He thinks you did it."

"Don't say things like that." Claude sat up in his chair. "You shouldn't even joke about somethin' like that."

Claude seemed more upset than the situation warranted, and Prince couldn't resist the opportunity to needle him.

"Yeah, I told him that you'd been porking the Gonzalez woman. He was real interested."

"Jesus, Darrel. You didn't tell him that, did you?"

Claude was beginning to sweat heavily, and Darrel thought he smelled a little like Wayne.

"You can calm down," Darrel said. "I didn't tell him. I should have, though."

Claude's piggy face took on a hurt expression. "You ought not to get me worked up like that," he said.

"Yeah. Well, you ought not to go around putting it to all the women in the building."

Claude's hurt look changed to a porcine smirk. "You're just jealous."

There was a certain amount of truth in that, but Darrel poked a skinny finger into Claude's soft belly and said, "Not on your life."

There were three places where Ray Hartnett removed his Stetson: church, the Texas A&M University Memorial Student Center, which he visited about as often as he went to church, and the coroner's office. He was holding the hat in his lap now as he talked things over with Paul Benavides.

The coroner was a dapper little man with a Cesar Romero mustache and a cheerful smile. Only his sad brown eyes betrayed the fact that he was anything more than a lighthearted lightweight when it came to life and death.

He was explaining to Hartnett what he had learned from the autopsy.

"Strangled," he said. "The ligature marks indicate that something soft was used. Cloth. A handkerchief or scarf. There were no fibers left behind. Whoever did it stood behind her and strangled her. It didn't take long, and she didn't really have a chance to fight back. There was no skin under her fingernails, and there were no other marks on her. No bruises to indicate a struggle."

"He'd have to be strong, then," Hartnett said. "If there was no struggle, I guess she wasn't raped. Is that right?"

"Probably. But there had been sexual intercourse."

"Did you get the blood type from the semen?"

"We will. It's at the lab right now."

Hartnett nodded. That might help, if they could find someone to match the type to.

"Pubic hairs?"

"Three. They're at the lab, too."

"Any guesses?"

"I don't like to guess. But I'd say a white male. Brunette."

Hartnett thought that things were looking up. If there was no struggle, that meant Ramona Gonzalez had more than likely known the man who killed her. That narrowed the field. So did the hair color.

"What about the time of death?" Hartnett said.

"I can't be exact. Between midnight and two o'clock is as close as I can come."

That figured. The Capitol would have been closed, but there were plenty of ways to get in and out without being seen if you knew the building. Ramona would have known the building, and she might even have been able to obtain a key.

"All that's a big help," Hartnett said.

"That's not all," the coroner said, the sadness deepening in his eyes. No matter how many times he dealt with things like this, he never found it any easier.

"What else?" Hartnett said.

The coroner shook his head slowly. "She was six weeks pregnant," he said.

Senator Sam Wilkins talked to his wife every day between five and half-past five, as soon as Suzimae Turner had left for the day. Her last duty was to call Mrs. Wilkins and transfer the call to the senator's office. Then she turned off the lights in the outer office and went home.

He was hoping today that his wife had not heard the news about the murder, but she had.

"It's such a terrible thing," she said. "That poor young woman."

Wilkins could imagine her sitting on the couch, the TV remote in her hand. She would have pressed the mute button when the portable telephone rang, but he knew she would be running through the channels as she talked, not really listen-

112

ing to him—as usual—but instead watching the colors as the channels changed. If there was something that appealed to her she would stop switching and watch as alertly as if she could hear the words being spoken. They had been married a long time, twenty-five years. He knew her habits only too well.

"Yes," he said. "It was terrible."

"And it happened right in the building," she said.

She was a large, comfortable woman, and she would be wearing her old velour robe, shiny on the seat and elbows. She often didn't bother to get dressed these days. She stayed in bed until nearly noon, got up and had coffee and a sweet roll or two, and watched TV until the six o'clock news came on, at which time she would have a TV dinner and a bowl of Blue Bell ice cream. Then she would watch TV until midnight. It didn't really seem to matter too much what was on; she would watch anything that caught her interest.

"Right in the building," Wilkins said. Just talking about it made him sweat. The telephone felt slick in his hand. He got out his handkerchief and wiped his face. If his wife ever suspected that he had known the dead woman—

"I hope you're being careful," she said. "I don't like to think of you there in a building where people are getting killed. Do they know who did it yet?"

Wilkins put his handkerchief away. "No, but there was a Texas Ranger in the building today." Ron Matson had given him that little bit of information. "When the Rangers get involved, you can be sure that there'll be an arrest soon."

"I hope so," his wife said.

He imagined her face as the channels flipped past—MTV, local news, cartoons, old movies, evangelists. It was no wonder he got involved with other women. Anyone would understand why he had to do that.

Wouldn't they?

Yes, he told himself. They would. But what about Ramona Gonzalez? Would they understand that?

113

"—enough exercise?" his wife said.

"What was that?" Wilkins said. "I missed the first part."

"I said are you taking your pills and getting enough exercise?"

Wilkins had a mild heart condition for which the doctor had prescribed a blood thinner and moderate exercise. Wilkins took the pills. He didn't do the exercise.

"I certainly am," he lied. "Nothing like a good walk to begin the day."

"That's good," she said. "You take care of yourself and watch out when you're in that building."

"I will," he said. "And you take care of yourself, too."

"I will, dear. Good-bye."

"Good-bye," Wilkins said and hung up the phone. Jesus, he needed a woman.

Stan Donald needed a woman, too, but not a young one. He was not like Wilkins, though he did not disdain young women for the purpose of sex. That was about all they were good for, however, as far as he was concerned. What he really yearned for was a relationship with a mature woman, someone about forty-six or forty-seven, say.

Someone like Jane Kettler.

Or, why be coy about it, Jane Kettler herself.

He had made himself as indispensable to her as he could by being the most efficient tour-guide supervisor she could possibly want. He had tried to be her friend and confidant, though she was not an easy woman to know, and he thought he detected at least a small crack or two in her armor.

But up until now he had been afraid to approach her on the level he wanted to know her. He had no trouble with the young ones, though some of them were put off by his age. He knew that Chrissy was, for one. It was almost enough to make him laugh. He was no more than ten years older than Chrissy, but she thought of him as ancient. He, on the other hand, valued Jane Kettler for her experience, her wit, her knowledge of the world, all the things that Chrissy showed little promise of ever having.

Stan had no trouble getting dates among the guides, but the relationships he had with them were superficial, based on momentary needs and desires. They were no more to him than a tissue that he threw away after using.

He knew that Jane would eventually recognize his worth, however. She *had* to recognize it. Sooner or later, she was going to see just what kind of person he was. She was going to realize just how important he could be in her life. And when that happened, he was going to be ready. In fact, he was going to *make* it happen.

He picked up his telephone to make a call.

A. Michael Newton stood with his hands clasped behind his back and looked through the window, across the broad front lawn of the governor's mansion, across the top of the wrought-iron fence spiked with Texas stars that surrounded it. There was nothing much to see aside from the late afternoon traffic and the darkness gathering in shadows on the lawn.

"Have they caught that murderer yet?" he said.

"I don't believe so," Trey Buford said. "But the Rangers have put their best man on the job. Ray Hartnett. He's the one who caught that escaped convict who dressed like a woman. It was about nine or ten years ago, I think. You remember that incident?"

Newton remembered. "Incident" was a mild way of putting it. The convict, Bailey Peters, had escaped from the Ramsey I unit and made his way down to Angleton, where he'd entered a house, killed the woman who lived there, raped her after she was dead, and stolen her car. Along with the woman's purse, a dress and hat, and the .38 revolver she'd bought for protection only a month before. She had gotten to the gun and gotten it out of her nightstand, but when the time came to fire it, she hadn't been able to pull the trigger. Peters had no such inhibitions. He took the pistol from her and shot her in the face, turned her over, raped her from behind, put on the dress and hat, and drove away in the car.

He might have made it all the way to Mexico if he hadn't been stopped for having an expired license tag by a local cop. Even then, he might have gotten away if he hadn't panicked. It was dark and the cop was nearsighted in the first place. He would probably have issued a ticket without a second glance at the driver's license Peters showed him. Peters wasn't pretty, but neither had the woman been.

But while the cop was taking his first glance at the license, Peters pulled out the pistol and shot him in the chest. The backup the cop had called for drove up about that time, and Peters shot him, too. Both cops died on the scene. The score for Peters was three people with three shots. Not bad for a guy who'd hadn't been practicing on the firing range.

Hartnett had been a highway patrolman then. Before he died, the first cop somehow managed to get out a radio message that he'd been shot by a woman, and he even gave the make of the car and the license number.

Hartnett spotted the car a few minutes later and went after it, though it was being driven by a man. By then Peters had taken off the hat and ripped the dress down to his waist.

Peters headed for the country, down a road through a rice field, with Hartnett right behind. The con abandoned the car and took to the woods. Hartnett didn't wait for backup. He went right in after him and relentlessly trailed him through the woods for five hours that night before he finally caught up with him.

Peters was bedraggled and tired. He let Hartnett catch up with him, told him that he'd lost his weapon and that he surrendered.

Then he waited for Hartnett to relax and holster his own pistol.

Hartnett did what Peters expected, and the convict pulled the .38 from behind his back, ready to fire and make it four for four.

He had misjudged Hartnett, however. Hartnett hadn't relaxed at all, and before Peters could level the .38, Hartnett had pulled his own gun and shot Peters three times in the center of his chest. Any one of the shots would have been enough to kill the convict, but Hartnett was a man who liked to make sure of things.

It wasn't long after that well-publicized exploit that there was an opening on the Rangers, and Hartnett applied. He had the necessary experience, he was a member of the DPS, he was even sort of famous. He had more than the required college hours, and he did very well on the written test. There were eighty applicants for the position, but the other seventy-nine didn't stand a chance.

"You think he'll catch the murderer by tonight?" Newton said. "I don't want to get killed tonight."

"I don't think anyone would try anything here in the mansion," Buford said. He was getting a little worried about the governor's state of mind.

"What about those women's libbers?" Newton said. "I told that rape joke, you remember?"

Buford remembered. It had not been a pleasant few days around the mansion after that one.

"Maybe they've forgotten it by now," he said.

"I doubt it," Newton said. "Those women never forget anything."

"Maybe," Buford said. "But they aren't the kind to take the law into their own hands."

Newton appeared to think about it. "Maybe you're right," he said. "But what about the oyster fishermen? They're pretty tough."

That was true, Buford supposed. Newton had angered the oystermen with a remark to the effect that he'd just as soon swallow phlegm as an oyster and that in fact phlegm was probably better since it hadn't been sitting in a bay full of sewage and toxic waste. And to tell the truth, Newton hadn't said "phlegm." He'd said "snot."

"I'd expect that the oystermen are all too busy down on the coast to come up here and kill you," Buford said. "I think you're making too much of this whole thing."

Newton continued to look gloomy. "No way," he said. "They're out to get me, all right."

Buford had a sudden flash that Newton was going to be a one-term governor. The man was going to pieces. He should never have run for the office in the first place, and now he'd not only proved himself almost totally unfit for it, he was cracking up into the bargain. It was a miracle that he'd ever been elected, and he had almost no constituency left.

Naturally Buford didn't say any of that. He was thinking about his own position. He'd been offered a couple of jobs in private business lately. Maybe he should begin giving them serious consideration.

"Where are Jess and Marvin?" Newton said. Jess and Marvin were his personal bodyguards. "Why aren't they here?"

"They're here in the house," Buford said. "They were going to have a sandwich in the kitchen."

"I want them in the same room with me," Newton said. He pushed back his white hair. "I want them right here with me. You go get them."

"All right," Buford said, wondering where he'd written down the phone numbers of those guys who'd called him with job offers. "I'll get them right now."

PART TWO

PART TWO

THIRTEEN

The area of Austin's Sixth Street just to the east of Congress Avenue had once been an area of the city avoided by the city's more fastidious residents. It had been home to the kind of cheap appliance-rental stores that catered to people with little money and no credit at all, offices for insurance companies that dealt mostly in burial insurance for the black population, cheap bars, and a wino or two.

Then someone had decided that the area was "quaint," or could be if some of the buildings were restored and a different crowd could be attracted. Times were flush then, in the days when Austin was beginning its great spurt of growth that had ended in a frenzy of overbuilding and deserted office buildings, and before too long, the street boasted a new look, and different people were walking along it, even after dark. They were young, they were looking for fun, and they had money to spend. On the weekends, especially if the weather was nice, the crowds were sometimes so thick it was hard to drive down the street.

Now that the period of growth was over and depression,

or at least recession, had set in, the streets were not so crowded. They were roamed by teenage gang members, and a lot of the college crowd had found other places to go. The city had recently passed ordinances prohibiting open drinking on the street and establishing a curfew for those under seventeen as ways to get the respectable crowds back.

Ron Matson liked the crowds, and he was sorry they were gone. Part of the reason was the gangs and the fact that Sixth Street wasn't safe nowadays, and part of it was the crisp chill in the January air. Nevertheless, there were plenty of people out and about, more than enough to justify the presence of two good-looking young men who were without dates but who seemed to be searching for some beautiful women to take home for an evening of fun and games.

That was the way the two men were supposed to look, anyway. Matson and Todd Elton had worked out the system to give themselves the freedom to avoid the gay bars and mingle with the everyday crowds. If anyone noticed that they never picked up any women, no one seemed to mind.

Tonight they were in the Cannibal Club, surrounded by some of the college kids who hadn't gone home for the break and some of Austin's punk crowd, the latter group probably being attracted by the fact that Bouffant Jellyfish was playing in the Cannibal that night.

Ron and Todd were sitting at a table near the door, as far from the stage as they could get. They were not as fond of Bouffant Jellyfish as some of the others were, and they didn't want to be too near the dance floor, either. They wanted to be able to talk.

Todd was shorter than Matson, dark skinned, with black hair, black eyes that were hard as marbles, and a mouth that was thin-lipped as a snake's. He'd been doing coke deals for quite a while now, and with every month that passed the eyes grew harder. He was wearing Italian loafers, soft wool pants, a leather jacket, and a cotton shirt open at the neck to reveal

122

two gold necklaces and a paisley scarf. He looked exactly like what he was, and that was the only thing about him that bothered Ron; but since it excited Ron as much as it bothered him, he tried not to worry that anyone he knew would see him in the company of a coke dealer.

Todd was asking about the murder, a topic that seemed to hold a great deal of interest for him.

"No one knows anything yet," Matson said, pitching his voice so that it carried over the clash of the guitars but not so loud that it could be overheard at the next table. It wasn't a topic he was fond of.

"She's the one you told me about, isn't she?" Todd said. He drank his Lone Star from the bottle. He would have preferred white wine, but he didn't want to take the chance of looking effete. "The one the senator was screwing?"

"She's the one," Matson said, looking around to make sure no one had overheard. "God knows what he'll do if that comes out."

"She wasn't the only one," Elton said. "I don't see how the old buzzard gets away with it."

"Me neither. It's not as if it was a secret."

What Matson said was true. Sam Wilkins thought that his sex life was as secret as a Swiss bank account, but he was wrong in his assumption. Half the people who worked in the Capitol knew about his penchant for young women. The press knew, too, but Wilkins benefited from the fact that, in Texas at least, a man's private life was still pretty much his own business after he was elected. Up until then, however, anything he'd ever done was open for discussion.

And if he decided to run for governor, God help him. If he did that, all bets were off. Gubernatorial campaigns in Texas these days were as dirty as a mud bath in an east Texas hog wallow. And that was just in the primaries. In fact, A. Michael Newton was most likely the incumbent governor of Texas because during the campaign his handlers had kept him tightly muzzled and leashed and because his sex life was as clean as a compulsive's underdrawers.

"She *was* a cute little bitch, though," Elton said, looking at Ron over the rim of the beer bottle. "Wasn't she, Ron?"

Matson looked down at the table. He was also having a beer, and he looked at the rings of moisture left by the bottle. "That's been over for a long time, Todd."

"You just can't stay away from the pretty ones," Todd said with a wicked smile. He took a deep pull at his Lone Star. "It's going to get you in a lot of trouble one of these days." He put the bottle down on the table. "If it hasn't already. You really should leave the women alone, Ron."

The band came to the end of its tune, if that was the right word, and there was sporadic applause. Ron looked up and met Todd's eyes.

"There's no need to be crude," he said. "I told you that I had no interest in anyone but you now." He conveniently forgot about the young representative who would soon be returning to town for the session.

"I think it's funny, really," Todd said. "You and that old fart Wilkins both chasing after the same woman. If the newspapers would print half of what goes on in the Capitol, the people would march on the place with torches and gasoline, like something out of *Frankenstein*."

"It's not funny," Ron said. "The senator doesn't know about me, and I don't think I'd like for him to find out. Or anybody else, either. Do you know what I mean, Todd?"

Todd leaned back in his chair and pushed the beer bottle around on the table. "I know what you mean. But you can't hurt me. I know too much for anyone to let anything happen to me."

"Don't count on it," Ron said.

Todd smiled his thin-lipped smile. "You wouldn't want anything to happen to me, Ron. I know too much about you and your friends. I want to thank you for that last meeting you set up with your buddy Gene Watts, though."

Watts was the rising young representative. Ron didn't think Todd knew just how far Ron's friendship with Gene extended. He hoped not.

"It was profitable for you, then?" he said.

He didn't like the idea that Gene was doing coke, but when Gene had hinted around about making a connection, Ron had obliged him by giving him Todd's name. Gene had been in town for a few hours a couple of weeks previously, and he and Todd had met in the Capitol chapel to conduct their business.

Todd looked smug. "*Very* profitable. One of the biggest buys anyone's ever made from me."

That wouldn't take much, Ron thought. Todd was strictly small time, though in his business even small time was plenty profitable.

"You don't ever talk to anyone else about things like that, do you?" Todd said suddenly.

Three college students, two men and a woman, came through the door laughing and talking, giving Ron time to think of an answer, not that he really needed any time. The lie came quite easily.

"Of course not. Do you think I'm crazy?"

"No," Todd said. "I just know what you're like. Let the old sinus passages get a nice chemical massage and you sing like a bird. Or don't you remember some of the things you've told me from time to time?"

"Well, you're different. I can trust you."

"Of course you can, Ron, but what about that girl that was killed? Could you trust her?"

"I don't think I like the direction this conversation's taking, Todd." Ron pushed back his chair as if he were about to get up and leave.

Todd reached across the table and grabbed Ron's right

wrist and squeezed hard. Both men worked out at a local club, and both were strong, but Todd was the stronger. Ron, who had been halfway out of his chair, sat back down.

"You're hurting me, Todd."

"Good. That's what I wanted to do. There's no need for the two of us to fight. I was just saying that you didn't have to worry anymore, even if you did talk to her. She's dead, and that takes care of that."

"I hope you don't think I had anything to do with that," Ron said.

Todd smiled. "Now why would I think a thing like that?"

There was something in Todd's voice that bothered Ron. "Todd," he said.

"What?"

Ron looked at Todd's hard black eyes. "Never mind," he said.

"That's what I say. Never mind." Todd turned jolly. "Let bygones be gonebys. Want another beer?"

Ron didn't want another beer. Suddenly the music was so loud that it was about to split his head open. He wanted to get out of there.

"Sure," he said. "I'll buy."

When the telephone rang, Jane Kettler almost let the answering machine take it. On the third ring, however, just before the machine would automatically pick up, she decided to take it herself.

"Hi," Stan Donald said, and then rushed on before she could respond. "The reason I'm calling is, I thought you might like to go out to dinner with me tonight, that is if you haven't already made plans. We could go to El Rancho. I know you like Mexican food."

Jane didn't know what to say. She didn't want to hurt Stan's feelings, but she really didn't feel like going out. "Stan—" she began.

126

"I know you're probably tired," he said. "But I thought you and I ought to talk over the murder. I mean, we might come up with something that would help the police if we put our heads together."

"I don't think we know anything, Stan. I spoke to her occasionally, that's all."

"I know, but we've probably heard people say things that might be important. We should talk it over. Frankly, I'd like for you to tell me how to handle things in my area. I'd appreciate it."

Jane had never heard Stan talk quite like this, and she suddenly wondered just what was going on. "Stan, is there more to this than you're telling me?"

"What do you mean?"

Jane didn't know what she meant. It wasn't as if Stan were asking her for a date. Or was he?

"Stan—" she said.

"I won't keep you out too late. It'll take your mind off the job. We don't have to talk about the murder if you don't want to, but I'd like to discuss things."

"I don't really think—"

"Good. Don't think. Just say you'll go."

Jane laughed. "You're very persistent."

"That's right. I never give up. Say yes."

"Well, all right. I guess we should talk things over, and that's hard to do right now. But I have to warn you that when it comes to crime, I'm no Jessica Fletcher."

"I'll pick you up in about an hour," Stan said. "How's that?"

"That's fine."

Jane hung up, wondering if she had done the right thing. She was almost certain there was something in Stan's voice that she hadn't heard for a long time, that indefinable note that let a woman know that a man was interested in more than just talking to her.

127

She decided that she was being ridiculous. Stan Donald was young enough to be her son, practically, or he would have been if she had married and had a child while very young. He couldn't possibly be interested in her romantically. Could he? Well, could he? It was like something on one of those TV talk shows the guides talked about but that she had never seen herself, something that Phil Donahue or Oprah Winfrey would have on—"Younger Men Who Fall for Older Women."

She walked into her bedroom and looked at herself in the full-length mirror on the wall by the bed. *She looked pretty good for forty-seven,* she thought. Stomach still flat, thanks a lot more to good genes than to any exercise program, though she got plenty of walking around on her job in the Capitol. Face still firm, once again thanks to heredity, to the high cheekbones she got from her mother and not from any kind of cosmetic surgery. There was a good bit of gray in her brown hair around the temples, but there was nothing wrong with that. Plenty of people had gray hair.

Listen to yourself, Jane Kettler, she thought, smiling at her reflection. This afternoon you were feeling sorry for yourself, thinking that you'd never get out of your shell and meet another man, never have a chance at anything like that again, not even sure you wanted to, and here you are. You've got poor Stan Donald half seduced, and all he wants to do is have a little talk. He'd probably be scared to death if he had any idea of what you're thinking.

Nevertheless, she told herself, it wouldn't hurt to take a quick shower and change clothes. You never knew what might develop.

She laughed at herself as she stripped for the shower, but she noticed that there was a quaver in the laugh, an uncertainty. She wasn't even sure why she was laughing. And she wasn't sure she should be laughing at all.

★ ★ ★

Craig Shaw picked up Tanya Melton at her apartment. They were going for frozen yogurt. Tanya was watching her weight, and though Craig could see absolutely no reason for her to do so, he didn't say anything about it. She was a cheap date.

She was also his major spy in the Capitol. He'd met her last year when he first arrived in town and started taking her out. She was flattered that a reporter for a major Texas newspaper would be interested in her, and he never pressed her for information. He was content to pick up a few tidbits in conversation and use them when he saw fit.

This time was different. He was going to find out if she knew anything about Sam Wilkins, the more scurrilous the better. There had to be something, judging from the senator's reaction at the press conference, and Shaw was determined to find out what it was.

They were at Baskin-Robbins, a clean, well-lighted place on the drag, that stretch of Guadalupe Street that ran along the edge of the campus of the University of Texas, the place that gave drag-worms like Wayne their name because so many of them hung out there.

Tanya and Shaw were the only customers, it being January and no one else being interested in frozen dessert at that particular time. The counterman was sitting on a stool in the corner and reading a magazine, so they were free to talk.

Craig led into his subject by bringing up the murder, and he was surprised to find that Tanya knew the dead woman. He thought he might be able to get a fresh angle on the murder, so he let Tanya talk about that.

"She didn't follow the rules," Tanya said. "That was one thing."

"What rules?" Craig said. He wanted a cigarette badly, but Tanya didn't like for him to smoke.

"The unwritten rules," Tanya said.

She was wearing very red lipstick that was almost startling

129

with her pale skin. Shaw watched as she took a bite out of her low-fat vanilla yogurt.

"Which ones are those?" he said.

"Loose lips sink ships," Tanya said, thinking about what Chrissy had said. "We're not supposed to pass around gossip about our work," she explained.

"She talked too much, huh? Well, that's not so bad. Lots of people like to talk. How well did you know her?"

"Not so well. Chrissy knew her better than I did."

Shaw wasn't interested in Chrissy. "I don't guess she ever said anything about Senator Wilkins," he said.

Tanya looked at him. "I don't think I should say anything about that. You're a reporter, after all."

Shaw could almost feel his ears perk up. He forgot all about wanting a cigarette. "I wouldn't ever use anything you said," he lied. "You can tell me."

Wilkins was the man whose name Chrissy had been about to mention earlier. Tanya knew the story, all right, but she wasn't sure she wanted to discuss it.

"Off the record," Shaw said. "Trust me."

"Well," Tanya said. "Just be sure it's off the record."

"I'm sure."

"OK. The senator likes pretty young girls. I don't guess that's a secret."

"It's no secret," Shaw said. Then he smiled. "Don't tell me that this Ramona Gonzalez was one of the young women Senator Wilkins liked."

"Yes," Tanya said. "She sure was."

"Well, well, well," Shaw said. For some reason, he couldn't stop smiling. "Well, well, well."

FOURTEEN

El Rancho was crowded and noisy, as always. They had to wait for a table. Jane liked the food there, but like many who remembered the restaurant's old location on First Street, she thought the flavor of the food had changed subtly since the move to South Lamar. The flavor probably hadn't changed, however; it was much more likely that she had changed. Still, she couldn't help but think about the old days.

And that was one of the problems with being there with Stan. He wasn't part of the old days, and he could probably barely recall things that Jane took for granted that everyone not only knew about but had experienced.

He had still been in grade school during the sixties, and for him Vietnam was not even a memory. He had practically no idea who Humphrey Bogart was, and he had never driven down the road with the AM radio on and pushed the button that brought in some station that was playing "Love Me Tender" for the very first time. When the Beatles played on *The Ed Sullivan Show,* Stan had barely been old enough to talk.

Jane didn't know it, but her feelings about Stan were almost the reverse of Chrissy Allen's. To Chrissy, Stan was practically ancient; to Jane, he was practically a child.

Except that a child wouldn't be looking at her across the table the way Stan was, or talking to her about the things Stan was talking about, which were not related at all to the murder of Ramona Gonzalez or how it related to his job at the tour-guide service.

As they ate their Regular Dinners, hers with the *chili con queso* and his with the tamale, he was telling her that he had been wanting to call her for more than a year. That he had watched her when she didn't know that he was watching. That he cared about her in ways that she didn't realize.

Behind his thick glasses, his eyes were sincere, almost pleading. Jane glanced surreptitiously around them at all the other diners absorbed in their own dinners, their own noisy conversations sounding like a rumbling buzz above the clatter of tableware. The waiters wound their way among the tables carrying steaming platters loaded with shrimp à la Matt Martinez, with enchilada plates, orders of the Number One, guacamole salad, *pico de gallo,* tortillas. No one was paying any attention to Stan and Jane at all, though it seemed to her that at any moment there would be a sudden silence and everyone would turn and stare at them, intent on their every word.

Jane wanted to tell Stan that she was much too old for him, that he should be saying those things to some other, younger woman, that they should keep their relationship on a strictly professional basis.

Somehow, however, she couldn't tell him that. Every time she opened her mouth to protest, Stan would say something else about his devotion to her, about how hiding it for so long had torn him apart, about how he had to speak now or burst with longing.

And Jane had to admit he was getting to her. Maybe it was the conversation she'd had with Hap Reatherford and the fear of growing old and lonely, or maybe it was just hormones. Whatever it was, it was making her feel things that she hadn't felt—hadn't even really thought about feeling—for years.

It was almost scary.

Stan didn't touch her. He didn't even reach across the table and take her hand. He didn't pressure her that way. He just kept talking, pressing his case, trying to make her to see that he was serious.

She was convinced.

She believed.

Damn it, she even liked the way he was making her feel. She felt a warmth that started in her belly and spread downward and upward until it tingled through her entire body.

She didn't want to like it, but she did. She told herself that it was wrong to like it, but the telling didn't help. It felt good. It felt better than anything she'd experienced for more years than she cared to think about.

She put butter and salt on a tortilla and rolled it up and ate it with her beans and rice. She thought she should be watching things like the butter and maybe not even eating it, but that didn't keep her from enjoying the taste, which was terrific, any more than her telling herself that she shouldn't listen to Stan made any difference to her feelings, which were also terrific. After all, plenty of women over forty were having a great time, even having babies. Why should they have all the fun?

There was an easy answer to that one. They shouldn't. But could Jane make an emotional commitment after avoiding it for so long, especially to someone like Stan?

She thought she was going to get a chance to find out, but Stan abruptly changed the topic of his conversation.

"I know it's the wrong time to be talking about my feelings for you," he said. "I mean, considering what's happened and everything." His Regular Dinner was practically untouched, and he was toying with his fork. "It's really too bad about Ramona."

Jane realized with embarrassment that she had almost forgotten about Ramona and about why Stan had asked her out to dinner. But she still didn't exactly understand why Stan wanted to discuss the murder, and she told him so.

"It's just that I think we might know something. You know how much Ramona liked to talk, and how she noticed things. She might have known something she shouldn't have, something that was dangerous to her. And she might have told someone what it was."

He was right about Ramona's noticing things. Jane remembered the time the water fountain near the tour desk had been stolen. A man dressed in what appeared to be a company uniform came in, turned off the water at the fountain, loaded it on a dolly, and hauled it away. No one thought anything of it, though the fountain had been working perfectly and did not need repair. It was only later, when Stan was telling Jane about the incident, that they decided to call Clinton Amory and ask why the fountain had been removed.

Amory apparently had no idea what was going on. He said that he had not called anyone about the fountain, and neither had anyone else. After a little investigation, they found out that three fountains had been removed, never to be returned. Everyone who saw the man in the uniform assumed that he knew what he was doing and had a right to do it, so no one had really paid any attention to him, no one had paid any attention to his uniform, no one had thought to ask for his work order, no one had even stepped outside to look at his truck.

No one, that is, except for Ramona Gonzalez.

It was typical of her inquisitiveness, or nosiness, whichever one preferred to call it, that she had talked to the man. She had asked what he was doing, and she had even followed him outside to see what he was doing with the fountains.

When Darrel Prince was finally called in to see what could be done, he began questioning everyone who had been around the tour desk. Stan and Jane had both been there when the fountain was removed, but neither could remember much about the incident; however, they both thought of Ramona at the same time. She always seemed to know everything.

Sure enough, she knew what had happened to the fountains, too. She described the man accurately, and she also gave Prince the information that eventually led him to the man. When she followed him outside, she had seen that he was loading the fountains onto a U-Haul truck.

That was enough for Prince, who tracked down the rental and then brought in the local police, who located and arrested the man responsible for the theft. He had taken fountains from several businesses that same day and had already sold and installed most of them in other businesses.

"See, that's the kind of thing Ramona noticed," Stan said. "No one else paid any attention to that guy, but she did."

"So you think she might have noticed something else," Jane said. "Something that was really dangerous for her to have seen."

"That's right. And she might have told one of us about it."

The waiter interrupted them then to take their plates and to ask if they wanted a praline or sherbet for dessert. They both ordered the pineapple sherbet, and the waiter went away.

"But wouldn't we know it if she'd told us something like that?" Jane said.

"Not necessarily. She must not have known it herself. She didn't look afraid of anything the last time you saw her, did she?"

Jane thought about it. "No. She didn't."

"Did she ever really try to talk to you? She could be a real bother at the guide desk."

Jane really couldn't remember. She usually just tuned Ramona out. She tried to encourage everyone to avoid gossip, but Ramona just bubbled over with it. Jane had found that it was easier to ignore her than to stop her.

"She didn't say anything about anyone important?" Stan said.

"Certainly not. And why would it have to be someone important?"

"Because no one who didn't have a lot to lose would kill someone."

"Maybe there was another reason," Jane said. "Maybe she was molested."

"Or maybe someone who *wasn't* important had a lot to lose," Stan said.

The waiter returned with their sherbet, and they ate it in silence, trying to think of a reason why Ramona might have been murdered.

When Stan had finished, he put down his spoon. "I can't think of anything or anyone," he said. "Maybe you were right. I'll tell the guides not to discuss it at all with the public. But I'm glad you came to dinner with me."

"I'm glad, too," Jane said.

Hap Reatherford was rereading the story about the murder at the Capitol when something clicked in his head. It was just like a switch being thrown, and he felt like an old fool. He'd thought earlier that he was getting soft and sentimental, and now he was worried that it might be worse than that.

A year ago, he would have snapped to attention immediately upon reading the woman's name for the first time. Today, he'd read the article in the newspaper, heard the name on television at least three times, and then reread the article before anything dawned on him.

Jesus, was he getting Alzheimer's?

Ramona Gonzalez. He knew that name, and it was associated with someone else he knew very well, someone who wanted a favor from him.

It was a good thing he hadn't already granted that favor, though he'd said he would. Now he would have to postpone it. A lobbyist didn't always get all the respect he deserved from the press and the public. He damn sure couldn't afford to get mixed up in anything like murder.

Poor old Sam Wilkins. He had a wife who was about as interesting as a drive across Nebraska, and he had a weakness for pretty young things. Sam should know better, but there were plenty of men in the legislature who should know better about a lot of things.

Not all of them did, which was just fine with Hap, since he was one of the things they probably should have known better about, but there were times when not knowing better could lead to trouble.

One of those times was when a reporter got a bee in his bonnet and started causing trouble. That didn't happen too often in Texas, where it was still pretty much a politician's own business where he put his pecker, but there were exceptions. And one of the exceptions would surely be in the case of murder.

Hap walked over to one of the glass doors and looked out at the night sky. Austin was like a lot of places now. There was so much light from the city that you couldn't really see the stars. There were stars up there, but they showed only faintly these days.

He remembered the first time he had ever visited Austin. He had been only a kid then, and there were no streetlights. The dark city was lit by what the people called "artificial moons," some kind of ghostly blue lights that were strategically placed around town on high towers. There were plenty of places out in the hills, like the place he was now, where there were no houses or lights at all and the stars were like hard rhinestone chips that glittered and sparked. Now most of

137

the fake moons were gone, except for the ones that had been kept around for historical reasons, and you could hardly see the stars.

He shook his head. There he went again, drifting off into the past. Maybe it was time for him to see a doctor, have a checkup, make sure all the old plumbing was in good working order. It wouldn't do to keel over in the middle of making a deal one day.

He dragged his mind back to the business at hand. It was time to give Craig Shaw a call.

He went into the smallest of the house's three bedrooms, which he had converted into his office. There was a sturdy oak desk that he had found at a flea market, and on the desk there was a Rolodex that had every telephone number a good lobbyist was likely to need. He had a duplicate Rolodex at his office downtown. He was sure Shaw's number would be on one of the cards, and he was right. He picked up the red telephone and punched in the number.

An answering machine picked up on the second ring.

"This is Craig Shaw," it said. "I can't come to the phone right now, but if you'll leave a message at the tone, I'll return your call as soon as I can."

Reatherford didn't like talking to answering machines, but at the same time he thought that they were one of the great inventions of the twentieth century. There were times he didn't want to be within reach of a telephone, so he knew for a certainty that he would never have a cellular phone; but on the other hand, he didn't want to miss any calls. He had answering machines on all his own phones.

He left a message for Shaw, saying that he would like to have a conversation about "a matter of mutual interest," and left his number. That ought to do it.

He hoped that what he was thinking about Sam Wilkins wasn't true, but he'd been around Austin long enough not to bet against it.

In a way, it was really too bad. He'd been counting on Wilkins to support a number of bills and maybe even to author one or two. In return he might have been able to line up support for Wilkins's abortion bill, though probably not very much.

That bill was going to make things very tough on Wilkins if he had been involved with the Gonzalez woman in any way. A great many legislators already resented Wilkins's attempt to make them actually take a public stand on abortion, and the murder might very well give them the opportunity they were looking for to destroy his credibility, if not his career. If there was any blood in the water, the sharks would smell it. Or see it, or whatever the hell it was that sharks did. It wouldn't be pretty.

Yes, it was really too bad. Reatherford wondered who he was going to get to take Wilkins's place if worst came to worst. Well, he could worry about that after he talked to Shaw. And actually there was no need to worry. There was always someone who needed money, someone who had his hand out. It wouldn't take long to find him.

In fact, he wouldn't be surprised if someone came looking for him. Maybe several someones.

That wasn't to say that Sam had done anything wrong. It would be a mistake to think so at this stage of the game. Maybe he hadn't done anything at all, but sometimes that didn't matter. That old crap about a man being innocent until being proven guilty sounded fine when you said it in a speech or discussed it in a civics class, but that was about all.

In reality, a man—especially if he was a politician—was often convicted in the public mind at the least hint of trouble, and it looked as if trouble were about to land on Sam Wilkins like a ton of shit. It all depended on how deep his association with Ramona Gonzalez ran.

If their relationship amounted to no more than a flirtation, a little office slap and tickle, no more than that, Wilkins might get out of it clean. But if there were more to it, if, say, Wilkins had taken her to a motel, or if Wilkins's wife had found out something, there could be real trouble for the senator. He might still be innocent of murder, but it wouldn't matter. His political career would be over.

More than ever, Reatherford wondered what Shaw had asked at that press conference.

He hoped the reporter would call him back soon, or else he wasn't going to sleep worth a damn that night.

FIFTEEN

The norther with its heavy black clouds had rolled in very early, around five or half-past five, as if to prove that the previous day's almost springlike weather had been nothing more than a fluke. Lightning flickered through the clouds, turning them purple and gray as the wind pushed them swiftly toward the city.

The cold wind slashed across Town Lake and tore at Stan Donald's sweatsuit as he ran along the jogging and bike trail. Occasional drops of icy rain spattered the lenses of his glasses and blurred his vision.

He didn't mind. He had already run a mile, and his body was perspiring inside the sweats. He kept up a regular rhythm, pumping his arms and legs steadily. It was half-past six, and there were very few other runners out. It was too early and too dark, and the weather was keeping them inside.

That was fine with Stan. He had a lot on his mind, and he didn't need the distraction of having to watch for other runners. Or for the bikers. They were the worst. Even if they were all expert riders and careful into the bargain, it still bothered him to see one of them headed in his direction going thirty miles an hour on the narrow trail. Even worse was having one come up behind and zip by with barely an inch of clearance.

He didn't much like the people who ran with their dogs, either. It was all very well to assume that the dogs were trained and mannerly, but when they were huge beasts with gleaming white teeth, even the heaviest chain did not seem enough security to Stan, especially when the chain was being held by someone who appeared to weigh in at fifty pounds less than the dog.

He pounded over the bridge at Barton Creek, his feet echoing on the boards, and he wondered what Jane Kettler was doing this morning. He suspected that she had some kind of exercise routine, too; otherwise she wouldn't have been in such great shape. Maybe she rode a stationary bike or did some kind of aerobics.

He wondered if she were thinking about him. He hoped so. He had not pushed her last night, but he knew that what he had said made an impression on her. When he had taken her home—early because he said that he had some work to do at home—he had briefly considered asking if he could come in. She might have asked him to, but he didn't want to go too fast and make a mistake. He had waited too long to speak his mind to take any chances like that. He didn't want to scare her, and he had some other business to take care of anyway.

He thought about what she'd said as they stood outside her door in the crisp night.

"I've enjoyed the evening very much, Stan. More than I expected to."

"I had fun, too. I hope we can do it again."

She smiled. "I'm not sure that would be such a good idea."

He tried not to look hurt. "Why not?"

"Because we work together. Socializing off the job can sometimes cause complications."

"There wouldn't be any complications," he said. "I can keep the two things separate."

She looked doubtful. "That's not always as easy as it seems, Stan."

He liked hearing her say his name, but he didn't like what she was saying. "I know that. But wouldn't it be worth it to see what happened?"

"Maybe," she said. "I'll have to think about it. Give me a little time."

"Sure. I understand. But I'm right. You'll see."

"We can talk about it later, then. I'll see you tomorrow."

Thinking about it made him grin, his face tight in the cold wind. He passed a concrete marker beside the trail and glanced at his watch. He was maintaining his usual pace, just under eight minutes per mile. He thought he would cross the bridge at Lamar and turn around when he got to the other side of the lake. Then he would start back.

He thought about Jane again. He had almost ruined his chances with her, but things were going to be all right now that she could see how much he cared about her. She *should* be able to see it. He hadn't been able to think about anyone else for weeks now. She just had to see that, and if she did, he merely had to pursue his advantage.

He felt the sting of the rain in his face, the chill of the wind on his bare head. It felt just fine, but he could hardly wait to finish his run and get to work. Seeing Jane again was going to be the best part of the day.

Wayne the Wagger was not enjoying the cold wind and the occasional spatters of rain in the least. He would just as soon have stayed in jail as to have had to face the weather, but when he was released he had not even considered returning to the Capitol.

143

For one thing, he was angry with everyone there. They had betrayed him. He hadn't done anything bad, or anything *really* bad, and they had called the real cops on him and had him carted off to the jail. There hadn't been any need of that. Who cared if he pissed on a cannon or not? Those cannons had sat out in all kinds of weather for over a hundred years. Wayne was sure that if there was acid rain in Austin, it was a lot worse for the cannons than a little piss. They hadn't had to treat him like some kind of criminal.

There were more serious kinds of criminals in the Capitol, if they only knew about it. Wayne knew, but he couldn't quite remember just exactly what it was that he knew. It was bad, he was pretty sure of that, but just how bad and specifically who was involved in it wasn't quite clear.

He seemed to recall that it had something to do with a woman who worked there in the building and a man that Wayne had seen pretty often, but maybe that was all a dream. It felt like a dream by now, which was the way things often were with Wayne after a few hours passed. It wasn't always like that; some things he could remember quite clearly for days or even weeks at a time, but more often things faded out pretty quickly.

Anyhow, if what he knew about wasn't a dream, it definitely had something to do with sleeping, that much he was sure of, and that was another reason Wayne had avoided the Capitol last night. He connected sleeping there with the bad thing that had happened, whatever it was.

The sleeping had been good, though, except for that one thing that he couldn't quite remember. It had been warm and cozy, and he had been curled safely in the bottom of the hamper where no one could find him.

It was with a little jolt of surprise that he thought of the hamper. It had been the best place he'd ever found to sleep in the Capitol, and he'd forgotten all about it. Thinking about it now brought another scene into his mind, a woman's

144

contorted face, a man's hands tightening something around her neck, her feet kicking . . .

Wayne shut off the flow of thought, wondering why it was that he could never seem to remember the good stuff. It was always the bad things that popped into his mind.

Nevertheless, he was going to have to return to the Capitol. Spending last night outside hadn't been so bad, but when the wind and the clouds moved in, he knew that he was going to have to find a better shelter than the one he'd had in the alley behind the old downtown bus station. He had found a cardboard box, broken it apart, wrapped himself in it, and positioned himself between a utility pole and a dumpster. It was all right for one night, but the wind and the rain made it impractical for another one.

He didn't want to spend the day being wet and cold, either, and he was sure the weather wasn't going to improve. It was only going to get worse.

Getting back in the Capitol building wasn't going to be easy. He knew that the cops there would be looking for him. They had never liked him, and they would send him back to the jail if they got half a chance. He would have to sneak past them somehow.

He patted his cap to make sure that his aluminum foil was still there. It wouldn't stop the spy cameras from seeing him, but their rays wouldn't penetrate his skull. Besides, the foil helped to keep his head dry.

He shuffled through the entrance to the Capitol grounds. All the parking spaces inside the grounds were reserved for important people like legislators. The old guys who sat out in chairs and kept ordinary people from parking there hadn't taken up their positions yet, and Wayne wondered if they would bother today.

He had often envied those old guys because he thought they had the best jobs of anyone in Austin. All they had to do was sit in their chairs and watch the parking. They could do

145

whatever else they wanted to do—talk to friends, read books, listen to the radio. It was a great life, except for days like this one. He wouldn't want to be out there on a day like this, and he wouldn't blame them if they didn't, either.

There wasn't anyone trying to park there now, anyhow. It was too early. No one would be reporting for work for at least another hour, and the visitors wouldn't start until an hour after that. That would make it easier for Wayne in one way. There wouldn't be very many people around to see him and report him to the cops. In another way it would make things a little bit trickier. There wouldn't be any crowds for him to blend into.

It said something for the state of Wayne's mental powers that he considered himself to possess the ability to blend into a crowd. He was, if anything, dirtier and smellier than he had been the day before, and he was wearing the same filthy layers of clothing. He, however, considered himself perfectly normal in appearance.

He turned away from the front entrance and went around to the east side of the building. He'd seen a cat around there not long ago, and he figured that the cat was living somewhere in or under the building. If the cat could get in and out, maybe Wayne could do it, too.

The cat was nowhere in sight. The cops had probably offed it; that would be about their speed. He pictured fat Claude Hebert blasting the cat to smithereens with a soft-nosed Magnum bullet. They'd like to do that to Wayne, too, but he was too smart for them, or so he told himself.

Wayne went up on the east porch. There didn't appear to be any cops around. Maybe he could get in without them seeing him if he did it fast and slick. He avoided the automatic door and grabbed the big brass handle of one of the others. He pulled it open and looked down the long hall.

No one was looking for him. He could see somebody

down in the rotunda, but whoever it was wasn't looking in Wayne's direction.

He scooted through the door and down the hall, keeping to the side and ducking into the entrances of several offices on his way toward the basement stairs. He was careful not to squeak the rubber soles of his Keds on the slick terrazzo floor.

The men's room down in the basement was always good for a few hours of hiding. He could sit on one of the toilets for a good long time before anyone bothered him. The locks on all the stalls were broken, but the door to one of them stuck closed unless it was shoved hard, and nobody would open it if they thought the stall was occupied. All he had to do was get there before being seen. He was already feeling warmer, now that he was inside, and before long he would have a place to stay.

By the time he got to the stairs, he had recognized the small figure of Darrel Prince in the rotunda. Prince was trying to watch all four entrances, but he was being too methodical about it. He was looking south, then west, then north, then east. Wayne simply ducked into a doorway or behind a column every time Darrel looked north and then waited until it was time for him to look south again. When he did, Wayne would slink to another place of concealment.

Thinking that he was pretty damn clever, Wayne slipped down the stairs to the basement while Darrel was facing west. There was no one buying a snack or soft drink, but Wayne knew the cameras would be on down there, so he had to be careful.

Someone had been there earlier and left the sports section from the paper. Wayne picked it up and held it in front of his face as if he were reading it. With the paper keeping most of his upper body hidden, Wayne went down the west basement hall to the men's room.

He wrinkled his nose when he entered. He was unaware of his own odor, but he could smell the rest room's distinctive fragrance, a mingling of disinfectant, deodorizer, and piss. Wayne thought they might as well leave off the deodorizer. It smelled worse than the piss did, at least to him.

That was all right, though. He could put up with the smell. He was safe now. All he had to do was get into a stall and sit there until someone chased him away. If he was lucky that might be hours from now.

He chose one of the middle stalls and opened the door.

The dead man was sitting on the toilet with his pants down around his knees. He stared at Wayne with bulging eyes that looked as if they were about to roll down his darkly mottled face.

Wayne took a deep breath, started to scream, couldn't, and passed out.

Darrel Prince was sure that Wayne would be back to the Capitol. Prince had stayed in the building until it closed the previous night, but when Wayne hadn't showed up, Prince went home determined to return early the next morning. He wouldn't even file for overtime.

He'd gotten there at six o'clock and taken up his position in the rotunda. There had been several transients who'd tried to get in, and Darrel had taken a little pleasure in sending them on their way. Normally he wouldn't have done that, but this morning was different. Wayne hadn't shown up yet, but Prince could at least take some of his frustrations out on someone else.

Darrel had waited for an hour, watching all the entrances from his position in the rotunda, and Wayne still hadn't put in an appearance. Darrel thought for a minute that maybe Wayne had been run over by a truck or hauled off with the morning's trash. There had been a time when Darrel would have welcomed the news of such an event, would not have cared if Wayne's mangled body had turned up six weeks later

148

in the city dump, but this was not the time. Wayne had come to mean a lot to Darrel over the past twenty-four hours.

More than anything, he represented Darrel's ticket out of the Capitol and into the real police world. If he were the one to solve the murder, he would get press coverage that would make his name a household word in Austin and maybe around the state. His photo would be in the papers. He would be on television. The Austin police would beg him to join the force. Maybe even the Rangers would take him.

But none of those things would happen if he didn't capture Wayne. Where was the sorry fucker? It was almost as if Wayne were deliberately avoiding Darrel, deliberately trying to thwart his ambitions.

The longer Prince waited, the more frustrated he became. He began to understand the phrase "itchy trigger finger" for the first time. He thought if Wayne walked into the building just then, he would be asking for it. Just asking for it.

But Wayne didn't come in.

Lots of other people did. As it got closer and closer to eight o'clock, more and more people entered the building. Darrel knew most of them by sight; they were all people who worked there and had a legitimate reason for being there.

Down in the east hall, Frick and Frack were setting up their abortion exhibits again. Stan Donald was behind the tour desk. Claude Hebert had come in and asked what the hell was going on before heading into the office to read *People*.

Darrel hadn't told Claude a thing. He just kept looking for Wayne.

It was only around half-past eight that Darrel happened to consider that he might have somehow missed seeing Wayne come into the building.

He didn't see how that could be possible, since he knew that his own brain power was considerably larger than Wayne's. There was no way Wayne could have outsmarted him.

But what if Wayne had gotten lucky? What if by some

149

bizarre quirk of fate Wayne had come in one door while Darrel was looking at a different one? It could have happened, and if it had, Wayne could be prowling around the building at that very moment.

Darrel was torn. He didn't know whether to give up his vigil and begin a search or to keep his post.

He could have asked Claude for help, but to do so would have required him to tell Claude why he was so interested in Wayne, and Darrel wasn't going to do that. He didn't want Claude to get any of the credit. This was all Darrel's idea.

He found himself spinning from door to door faster and faster as if he were some kind of stupid top. That wouldn't do. He was going to make himself look foolish, and someone was sure to ask him what the hell was going on. And the tours were going to begin soon. He was going to have to try something else.

He supposed that he could search the building. Wayne wouldn't be there, but it would be better to be doing something productive than to be whirling around on his heels in the rotunda.

He thought he'd start with the basement men's room. That was one of Wayne's favorite hiding places.

SIXTEEN

Wayne could feel the cold tile under his cheek, and the stink of the men's room filled his nostrils.

He wondered why he was on the floor and why his head was hurting. He touched his forehead and felt a bump there. How had that happened?

Then he glanced to his right and saw the shiny shoes of the dead man. Memory returned, though he wished it hadn't. This time, it was all too clear.

Maybe the man sitting on the toilet wasn't really dead, Wayne told himself. Maybe he'd had just been surprised that someone had opened the door on him. Maybe that look on his face was nothing more than simple astonishment.

It wasn't like Wayne to burst into the stall like that, after all. He usually gave a quick glance to make sure that he wasn't intruding on anyone. Wayne didn't like to be bothered when he was on the toilet, and he thought that most people probably felt the same way. So he tried to be considerate of others.

But he'd been in a hurry, and it had been early, and he hadn't really thought about anyone being there. He'd just shoved the door open and looked right in.

He wished he hadn't, because it was obvious that the man was dead, all right. If he'd been merely surprised, he would have said something, and surely he would have moved. Surely his face wouldn't look as if it belonged to a badly made-up actor of some old horror movie of the kind Wayne had watched when he was younger and did things like that.

Wayne moved his head slightly. He could see a small, distorted reflection of his face in the toes of the man's shoes. He didn't look so good.

As far as Wayne could tell, the man hadn't moved at all. And he certainly hadn't made a sound.

And his face—well, Wayne wasn't going to look at that again.

Wayne pushed himself up off the floor, keeping his eyes on the man's feet. He got up and turned around to face the stall door, his back to the dead man.

"Excuse me," he said, just in case the guy was alive after all. It didn't hurt to be polite.

He opened the stall door. There was no one else in the men's room, so he stepped out.

Whack!

The stall door slammed shut behind Wayne, causing him to jump five feet forward.

"Jesus," he said as he stood there shaking.

He knew he had to get out of there quickly. He was going to be in real trouble if they caught him in the same room with a corpse. Pissing on a cannon was one thing, but he had a feeling that this would be a whole lot worse.

He thought about Claude killing the cat again. Or had that really happened? It didn't matter, really, whether it had happened or not. Claude wouldn't hesitate to kill Wayne if he found him in the men's room with a dead man.

He didn't stop to think about where he would go or about Darrel Prince keeping watch in the rotunda one floor above. He couldn't think about anything except getting out of there and finding another place to hide. He crossed the floor and reached for the door handle.

Darrel Prince was in the hallway outside when he heard the muffled sound of the slamming stall door.

There was someone in the men's room, all right, though it might not be the Wagger. On the other hand, it just might. Who else would be down there so early in the morning?

Just in case, he drew his sidearm as he moved forward.

The men's room door smacked into him as Wayne came racing out.

Prince staggered backward, his finger tightening on the trigger of his short-barreled .38.

The explosion echoed in the hallway, and the .38 slug tore through the wooden door of the men's room.

Prince banged into the wall behind him and slid down it as Wayne ran for the stairway, screaming.

"Yaaaaahhhhhhhhhhh!" Wayne yelled at the top of his lungs.

They were trying to kill him, just like they had killed the cat! They'd blow him apart and splatter his blood on the walls if he didn't get out of there!

Clinton Amory had just arrived at the bottom of the stairway on his way to his cubbyhole office. He was moving cautiously because he'd heard the gunshot, though he wasn't sure what it had been. He thought maybe a can of Coke had exploded or something.

Wayne ran right past him, ramming into him with his right shoulder and throwing him to the side, right into the big red and white Coke machine.

"Hey!" Amory yelled after him. "What the hell's going on down here?"

Darrel Prince got to his feet and went after Wayne. Amory saw him coming and moved out of the way. He didn't want to get run over by a crazy son of a bitch who was waving a pistol around.

"Stop!" Darrel yelled. "Stop or I'll shoot!"

Wayne paid him no attention at all. He was already on the landing and heading for the first floor.

Stan Donald and Chrissy Allen were behind the tour desk discussing the day's visitors with some of the other tour guides. They were talking mainly about a group of Future American Statesmen, high school students who had come to Austin for a session of mock government.

The tour guides despised the sessions. The students blocked the halls and stairways and interfered with the tours. Rick, one of the guides, had to sit in the Senate and keep an eye on them to be sure they didn't tear up the antique desks. He was offended by their immaturity and lack of decorum. Several of the boys had even thrown up in the hallway. Rick was sure that their nausea had been caused by the hideous flowered dresses all the girls wore, but Chrissy maintained that the effect was the result of the dance the students held the night before and at which they overindulged in alcoholic beverages.

The sound of the ruckus from below interrupted the discussion, and Stan came out from behind the desk to see what was going on. He heard Prince's yell, and then he saw Wayne charging up the stairs and went over to stop him if he could.

Wayne was not to be stopped. With a move that would have done an NFL wide receiver proud, he faked right, cut left, and sailed off down the east hallway. The move, though artful, caused Wayne's head to spin and threw him off balance. His arms were windmilling wildly, and he was barely in control of his momentum.

Mrs. Tolbert saw him coming. He was headed right for the card tables, and she had to make a split-second decision about what to do. It was either allow him to crash headlong into the exhibits or sacrifice her body by throwing herself in front of him.

Remembering Wayne's smell and general untidy appearance, she elected to sacrifice the exhibits, pulling back into a doorway in order to avoid the impending collision, but Mrs. Stanton had no such fear for her own person. She had seen Wayne at almost the same time Mrs. Tolbert had, and she had begun to move.

"Stop!" she said.

If she'd had a gun, as Darrel Prince did, she would probably have used it. Her ideas about the sanctity of life didn't extend to the life of people like Wayne, who had the misfortune to have already been born.

Not having a gun, however, she did the next best thing, hardly getting herself into a defensive postion, legs spread, arms crossed protectively on her ample breast, before Wayne collided with her.

He struck her with such force that her attempt to save the exhibits was a total failure. She flew up and backward and landed on her spine on top of one of the tables, which collapsed beneath her weight, the four legs splayed out to the sides, the womb and fetus that had been displayed on it clattering to the floor and skidding across the hallway.

By then Prince had reached the top of the stairs—and reached the tour desk.

"Stop!" he yelled, leveling his pistol, gripping it with both hands, and assuming the firing position. His eyes were glazed and hard.

Stan watched as if paralyzed, making no move to stop Darrel from shooting.

"Don't!" Chrissy yelled from the desk. "You'll hurt someone!"

In his frenzied desire to capture—or, what the hell, kill—Wayne, Darrel had forgotten the number-one rule of using the sidearm.

He'd forgotten the innocent bystanders, of which there were quite a few gathered at the east entrance, getting ready for the day's tour.

They were golden agers who had come into town the day before from Oklahoma on a church tour, and they all thought they were getting more than their money's worth from the trip they had signed on to take.

Some of them were wondering if the whole scene had not been staged for their entertainment or if maybe there was a movie being filmed in the building.

Some of them, convinced that they were seeing was only too real, hit the floor and put their hands over their heads. They crabbed into doorways to avoid the shots they were sure were about to come.

Wayne flew down the hallway, his Keds squeaking like a dozen tortured rats, and plowed into the oldsters who were still standing, bulling his way through them like a steroid-crazed linebacker on a red-dog blitz.

"Pee-you!" one white-haired man said, ducking to avoid a flying elbow to the head. "That fella smells worse than a longhorn steer."

They all turned to watch as Wayne smashed through the doors, across the porch, and out onto the Capitol grounds.

All the commotion had drawn Claude Hebert out of the cop shop. He had forgotten to put down his magazine, and he was carrying it tucked underneath his left arm.

"What's all the racket?" he said. "What've you got your pistol out for, Darrel?"

Prince looked at the sidearm as if he'd never seen it before and crammed it back into the holster. "It's that damn Wayne," he said. "The bastard got away."

"Well, hell," Claude said. "You don't have to shoot him just because he pissed on the cannon."

Prince shook his head angrily. "You just don't get it, do you, Claude?"

Claude admitted that he didn't get it.

"He was down there in the basement," Darrel said. "He was down there the night that girl was killed, too. He's the one that killed her, and I almost had him."

"I'll be damned," Claude said. "Old Wayne. Who'd have thought it. You sure, Darrel?"

"Yes, I'm sure. I had him, damn it." Darrel's dream was fading fast. He would never be a Texas Ranger. Hell, he couldn't even catch a feeb like Wayne the Wagger.

"You think we should notify the locals?" Claude said.

"Why?" Darrel said. "They'd just turn him loose if they caught him."

"Yeah, but if he killed that girl—"

"All right, all right. Go call them. But they'll never find him. He'll find a rat hole to hide in and won't come out for a month."

"You never know about Wayne," Claude said. "He might come right on back here."

Darrel didn't believe Wayne would be back that soon, but Claude had a point. Where else did Wayne have to go? What worried Prince, though, was how he was going to explain all this to Ray Hartnett. It wasn't going to be easy to do, not without making himself look bad. Maybe he could think of something before Hartnett came for that masking tape, but he doubted it. Shit. Why didn't things ever work out for him?

"You look like you need a cup of coffee," Claude said. "And if that was your pistol that I heard, you're gonna have to file a report."

Darrel had forgotten about that. Damn. Some days you couldn't do anything right.

It took Stan several minutes to get the tour group calmed down. He explained that a crime had been committed in the building the day before and that the police were just doing their job, possibly with a little too much enthusiasm, but doing their job nevertheless.

The Oklahomans took the incident in good spirits, for the most part. They didn't want Stan to think that a little gunplay could deter them from having a good time.

"Hell," the man with the white hair said, "we got football players at OU who do more shootin' than that in their dorm rooms."

Chrissy Allen stood at the tour desk and watched with admiration as Stan got things under control. She thought he was mature and calm, which was one of the benefits of being an older person. As for her, she could still feel her heart beating. She had been really scared when she saw the policeman waving the gun around. She didn't hear what he had said, and she still didn't know why he was after Wayne, not that he shouldn't have been. Wayne was really disgusting. She was, however, a little surprised that Stan showed no concern for Wayne. All he seemed to care about was getting things back in order.

"Young lady," Ethel Tolbert said. "Young lady, could you give us a hand here, please?"

Chrissy looked over to where Mrs. Stanton lay flat on her back, sprawled atop the crumpled card table. Mrs. Tolbert had hold of one of Mrs. Stanton's hands and was trying without much success to pull her to her feet.

Chrissy went across the hall and picked up the exhibits that had fallen to the floor. She thought they were revolting and didn't like touching them even if they were just models, but she thought she should help. She took them over to where the two women were still struggling.

"Well, don't just stand there gawking," Mrs. Stanton said. "Help me get up."

Chrissy didn't appreciate the woman's tone, but she set the exhibits down and reached to take Mrs. Stanton's free hand.

"All right," Mrs. Tolbert said. "Pull."

Chrissy pulled, and between the two of them they got the hefty Mrs. Stanton off the floor. Chrissy thought that Mrs. Stanton could do with a good diet and exercise program. People didn't have to be fat and out of shape just because they weren't young any longer. Look at Cher; she didn't let herself go like so many older women did. But what could you expect from a woman who wore polyester pants like Mrs. Stanton's?

"That's the last straw," Mrs. Stanton said after she brushed herself off. "I'm going to file an official complaint."

"Who will you file it with?" Chrissy said.

She was genuinely curious. She didn't know there was a complaint department, though Stan fielded his share of problems just by virtue of being visible. All she knew about were the books for visitors' comments. The books were located in the House, the Senate, and the governor's reception room, and for the most part they didn't ever get any complaints in them. Some people might say the building was dirty, but mostly they wrote things like "beautiful" or "great tour." Once some fan of *In Living Color* wrote what had become everyone's favorite: "two snaps up."

Mrs. Stanton hadn't thought about where the complaint department was, either, but the answer came to her. "Senator Wilkins. He'll put a stop to these outrages. Come with me, Ethel."

The two women marched across the hall toward the senator's office as Stan brought the tour group to meet Chrissy. It was completely recovered from the excitement, and before it even got into the rotunda one of its members had asked the first dumb question of the day.

"It is true," a woman said, "that the ten-gallon Stetson is really the state hat of Texas?"

"No," Chrissy said, thinking that she'd heard that one at least five times before. Where did people get their ideas? "That's not true at all. We have a state bird and a state flower, but we don't have a state hat."

159

"Hey," someone else said when they got into the rotunda, "what're all these pictures of old men doin' here? Where's all the Miss Americas?"

Chrissy sighed. It was going to be another long day.

Jane Kettler left for work later than usual. She had been too involved in sorting out her thoughts about the night before to get ready on time.

Her main problem was that she didn't know exactly how to approach Stan when she got to the Capitol, or how to react when he approached her. She was afraid that it was going to be an extremely awkward meeting, that too much had been said for them to continue in their normal working relationship.

One minute she would think that was bad, and the next minute she would think the opposite. She had not been this confused in years, and she didn't like the feeling.

At the same time, she *did* like the feeling. She found herself humming an old tune by The Platters as she got dressed. "Enchanted," that was the name of it. She had not thought of the song in twenty years, but here she was, humming it. She remembered a phrase from her college psych class so many years before—"cognitive dissonance." If she remembered correctly, that was exactly what she was experiencing.

But cognitive dissonance or not, something was definitely happening to her.

She hoped it was good.

Wayne had no such problems. He knew that what was happening to him wasn't good at all. He was on the run from the Kapitol Kops, he was cold, his clothes were wet, and he was trembling.

But he wasn't trembling because he was cold and wet.

He was trembling because now that he had stopped behind

the old bus station and caught his breath, the face of the dead man had jumped back into his mind.

The bad part about that was not how the face looked, though that was certainly bad enough. Its staring eyes that bugged out of the head, its horrible color, its slightly opened mouth filled with the purple tongue—those were things that Wayne wanted to scrub out of his head, but they weren't the really bad part about it all.

For once, Wayne's memory was functioning almost normally, and he didn't like it. He thought about something that somebody had told him back in the sixties about how reality was for people who couldn't face drugs.

Right now, he could have used some drugs, because reality sucked. But drugs were hard to find these days, or the good ones were. Now all anybody wanted to push was coke, and he couldn't afford that, didn't even like it. If he couldn't get smoke, he would take pills. Practically any pills. They went down smoothly, and they didn't rot your nasal passages.

If he had some pills, they might have helped him forget the face.

And the bad part about the face was that he was sure it belonged to someone he knew.

Another horrible thought came to him.

That makes two.

He knew the man he'd seen in the dream, if it had been a dream, the one who'd killed the woman.

And he knew the dead man.

Damn, he thought, shivering in the rain. *This is turning out to be a really rotten day.*

SEVENTEEN

Interstate Highway 35 divides Austin neatly into east and west. On the west are the downtown, the Capitol, the University of Texas, and the old, established homes. Still farther to the west are the newer homes, and in the hills the homes are elaborate and expensive.

To the east is everything else, and Ray Hartnett was starting his day in East Austin, looking for the house where Ramona Gonzalez had lived.

He knew he wouldn't be welcome there, for the same reason that Juana Lorca had been so reticent with him the previous day, but he had to try to interview the family. There was always the chance that Ramona had said something to them about her pregnancy, though there was a lot less of a chance that the family would tell him anything about it.

He located the small wood-frame house on a narrow street filled with similar houses. Some of them had yards fenced with pickets, while other yards were fenced with hog wire strung between rough cedar posts. In front of one house was an old Ford with rotting tires and a license tag that had expired three years before. Behind one of the hog-wire fences a dog bristled and barked. It wasn't wearing a collar or vaccination tag.

Hartnett stopped his car in front of the Lorca house and got out. The wind hit him and whipped his jacket around his hips. It also nearly took his hat off. He put a hand on top of it to hold it down. He had put a plastic rain cover on the hat to protect it from the drops of cold water that were spattering down.

There was no gate on the short sidewalk leading to the porch of the house, just an opening in the fence. Hartnett walked through the opening, stepped up on the porch, and knocked on the door. He knew that someone was home; he could hear people talking inside.

The talking stopped at the sound of his knock, and the door was eventually opened by a short woman with graying hair. Her eyes were black and sad. A hefty orange tabby wound between her ankles.

"Are you Mrs. Lorca?" Hartnett said, thinking that the woman might be Juana's mother.

"I am Mrs. Gonzalez," the woman said.

"Ramona's mother?"

"Yes."

Hartnett had not realized that the mother was also living in the house with Juana Lorca. "I'd like to talk with you about your daughter if I could," he said. He knew that she wouldn't refuse to let him come in. She might not talk to him, but she would never be so impolite as to turn him away from the door. He showed her his identification.

"Please," she said, standing aside to allow him to pass by her and into the room. The cat hid itself behind her, and Hartnett went in.

The floor of the room was bare and clean. There was a worn couch in front of a coffee table. A vase of cut flowers sat on the table. Someone must have sent the flowers in memory of Ramona. There was a wooden rocker and an old ColorTrak TV set that was tuned in to Phil Donahue. Phil's face was a sickly green. The sound on the set was turned off. Or maybe it just didn't work.

Hartnett hated situations like this. He had never figured out exactly what the right words were, and he had about decided that was because there weren't any right words.

"Please," Mrs. Gonzalez said, indicating the chair.

Hartnett sat down awkwardly and took off his hat. He looked through the door leading out of the room and saw a group of silent brown faces. The rest of the family, including Juana Lorca, was in the kitchen. Uncles, aunts, cousins, brothers, sisters. Hartnett didn't try to count them all. They watched him without speaking.

He turned to Mrs. Gonzalez. "I'm sorry for your trouble. I have to ask you a few questions," he said.

Mrs. Gonzalez sat on the couch and looked at him with those black eyes. She didn't say anything, just sat and waited for him to speak. She wasn't going to make things easy.

He didn't blame her. Her daughter had been murdered and the body hadn't even been released from the morgue. Why should she make things easy?

He began by asking about Ramona's friends. Mrs. Gonzalez didn't seem to know much about them, or else she wasn't saying. All he could really get out of her was that everyone liked Ramona. He knew that wasn't true. After all, someone had killed her.

He worked the questions around to men.

"Ramona liked men," Mrs. Gonzalez said, the sadness in her eyes deepening.

Hartnett thought he might finally be onto something. "Were there any men that she liked more than others?" he said.

Mrs. Gonzalez couldn't say. The men Ramona liked were

164

not the boys she had grown up with, and she never brought any of her men friends home.

"Why not?" Hartnett said, and then was immediately sorry when Mrs. Gonzalez looked silently around the room where they were sitting and shrugged.

"Do you know the names of any of them?" Hartnett said.

Mrs. Gonzalez didn't know that, either. All she knew was that Ramona's men friends were mostly Anglo and mostly much better off financially than Ramona was.

The cat was still winding itself between Mrs. Gonzalez's legs. It stopped long enough to look at Hartnett for a second and then continued.

Hartnett ignored the cat and kept his eyes on Mrs. Gonzalez's face. He wasn't going to risk a glance into the kitchen when he asked his next question. "Did she ever mention that she might be thinking about having a baby?"

Mrs. Gonzalez sat up a little straighter in her chair. "What do you mean to say?"

That was what he got for trying to be evasive. There was just no way around saying what he meant, so he said it. "I mean that your daughter was pregnant."

"No," Mrs. Gonzalez said. Her face was set in hard lines. "That is not true. Ramona did like the men, but she was a good girl. She went to mass. She went to confession."

Going to confession and actually confessing were two different things, but Hartnett didn't say that. He said, "I'm sorry, Mrs. Gonzalez, but it's true. Ramona was going to have a baby." He could feel all the eyes in the other room focused on him, but he didn't turn.

Mrs. Gonzalez thought about what he had said for a while. "Then whoever killed my daughter also killed my grandchild," she said finally.

"That's right," Hartnett said. "Now you can see why I want to know the names of her men friends."

165

"If I knew who did this thing, I would tell you. But I do not know the names."

The cat seemed to have made up its mind about Hartnett. It left the shelter of Mrs. Gonzalez's legs and walked over to the Ranger. Then it jumped up in his lap and started purring. Hartnett didn't especially like cats, but he let it sit there.

"Did she have any pictures of them?" Hartnett said.

"No," Mrs. Gonzalez said. "She shared a room with her sister. I would know if there were pictures."

"Could I see the room?"

Mrs. Gonzalez got up. "Yes. You come with me."

Hartnett set the cat on the floor and followed Mrs. Gonzalez. He could feel the people in the kitchen watching him.

The room was small but clean. There were red curtains on the window and red spreads on the twin beds. There was an old wooden dresser with a knob missing from the top drawer. There were pictures on the wall, but they were posters of Gloria Estefan and the Miami Sound Machine and Little Joe y la Familia. Between them there was a crucifix with rosary beads hanging from it. There were no pictures on top of the dresser at all, just a hand mirror, two combs, and two brushes.

"You can look in the drawers," Mrs. Gonzalez said.

Hartnett didn't bother. He knew that he wouldn't find anything. Ramona didn't seem to be the sentimental type when it came to men.

"Mama?" someone said from the doorway.

Hartnett turned. There was a girl standing there, about fifteen, with dark hair and eyes.

"What, Rosa?" Mrs. Gonzalez said.

"I saw some of the men when they came for Ramona in their cars. I could tell this policeman who they were if I saw them or saw their pictures."

"Thank you," Hartnett said. He meant it. He hadn't thought he would get any help at all, but this was at least something. He might be able to take the girl to the Capitol

166

and let her look around. "I appreciate your help. Later on, I might want you to look at some men for me. If your mother agrees."

"If it will help get the man who killed Ramona, I agree," Mrs. Gonzalez said.

When Hartnett left a few minutes later, he had not learned anything more, but he was not as depressed about things as he had been. There was always a chance that Ramona's sister could help. It was a small chance, but it was better than nothing.

"It's the big oil companies, isn't it? They're out to get me." A. Michael Newton stared at his breakfast croissant with the blueberry jelly oozing out the sides. "It's because of what I said about the oil spill."

Trey Buford buttered a piece of whole wheat toast. Maybe the governor had a point. Or it could be the environmental groups that the governor had suspected earlier, since Newton had the uncanny ability to infuriate both sides in almost any situation.

When a supertanker had ruptured off the Texas gulf coast, he'd made a statement to the newspapers in which he said that in his opinion the oil companies that did business in the gulf should all have to put up a ten-million-dollar bond with the state, the bond to be forfeited whenever there was a spill that reached the state's beaches. The forfeit would be paid directly to the state of Texas, and it would not apply to the cost of cleaning up the spill. The oil company responsible for the mess would still have to pay for that.

The environmentalists thought that was a fine idea until one of the reporters asked Newton what he thought about the effects of the spill on the beaches.

"Well," he said, "those people go down there and rub suntan oil all over themselves, and it washes right off in the water when they swim. Then they complain when a little oil

167

comes on shore from some ship. I don't know what their problem is. Oil's oil, right?"

It had made a nice headline: OIL'S OIL, RIGHT? Buford still dreamed about it sometimes.

"I don't think Jess and Marvin are going to let some oil company hit man sneak through," Buford said. "Isn't that right, boys?"

Jess and Marvin nodded. They couldn't talk because their mouths were full of eggs and toast and bacon and grits, all shoveled in at approximately the same time.

Buford had trouble telling which one was Jess and which one was Marvin. They had both played tackle for some Southwestern Conference team or another, they both weighed in at around 275, and they both had little piggy eyes set in faces that were composed of pink granite slabs, just like the Capitol building. Their heads seemed to rest directly on their broad shoulders, though Buford supposed they must have necks of some kind. Neither of them was impressively intelligent.

"See, Governor?" Buford said. "The boys won't let anyone hurt you." He'd given up on trying to tell Newton that there wasn't anyone after him. It wasn't doing any good.

"I hope they won't," Newton said. "We pay you boys pretty good, don't we?"

The boys nodded again, their jaws working up and down on the huge mouthfuls of food they were chewing.

One of them decided to answer orally, but he couldn't get the words out. Little bits of egg and bacon dribbled off his lips and onto the front of his shirt.

"Never mind," Newton said. "But I think we'll give you a little raise anyhow. We can do that, can't we, Trey?"

Buford nodded. He supposed they could. There was always a little money around for things like that.

Jess and Marvin looked pleased. Their little piggy eyes glistened with happiness. Of course that might simply have

168

been because there was so much food still on the table for them to eat.

"Good," Newton said. He finally took a bite of his croissant, but he didn't look nearly as happy as Jess and Marvin did.

Suzimae Turner had bad news for Mrs. Stanton and Mrs. Tolbert. "The senator has asked that he not be disturbed for the rest of the morning," she said when the two women came in through the hall door.

"But we're the voting public," Mrs. Stanton said. "He has to talk to us. We want to file a complaint."

Suzimae got out a piece of note paper and a ballpoint pen. "I can make a note of your complaint and give it to the senator later," she said.

"We don't want you to make any notes," Mrs. Stanton said. "We've been attacked again, and we want something done about it. We were told that man was in jail, and he was back here this morning, trying to assault us. We want to see the senator about it."

She eyed the closed door to the senator's private office as if she might just make a run around the end of Suzimae's desk and go in without permission. "What's wrong with the senator, anyway?" she said. "He's always ready to talk to the voting public."

Suzimae didn't know the answer to the question Mrs. Stanton was asking. In fact, she was rather curious about it herself. It had all started when Clinton Amory, the head of the maintenance staff, had come in first thing that morning and asked to see Senator Wilkins.

The senator hadn't been exactly cheerful, but as soon as Amory had left the office, the senator had come out, wiping his face with his handkerchief and asking her to take all his calls, cancel all his appointments, and to keep everyone out of his office. Nothing like that had ever happened before, and Susimae wondered what on earth was the matter.

169

She didn't like Clinton Amory. He looked dirty to her, as if he didn't bathe more than once a week, and she didn't like the way he looked at her, as if he knew some dirty secret about her and as if he would love to whisper that dirty secret in her ear. Or someone's ear.

Of course, as a good secretary, she would never tell any of that to Mrs. Tolbert and Mrs. Stanton. Or to anyone else. She had a position of trust, and she never abused that trust.

"The senator isn't feeling very well today," she said. "He has migraines, you know."

Mrs. Tolbert and Mrs. Stanton didn't know. No one knew, since Suzimae had made up the migraine on the spur of the moment. She hoped the senator wouldn't mind.

"Well, then," Mrs. Stanton said.

"We understand, of course," Mrs. Tolbert said.

"But we'll be back tomorrow," Mrs. Stanton said. "You tell the senator that."

"I surely will," Suzimae said, making a note on her pad. "You can count on me."

"I hope so," Mrs. Stanton said. "That man broke one of our tables."

Mrs. Tolbert thought that wasn't the exact truth, but she didn't think it was worth mentioning. They went back outside to see if the table could be fixed.

The dead man was still sitting in the stall in the basement men's room, his pants still down around his legs.

As was the custom, everyone not in as big a hurry as Wayne the Wagger discreetly looked beneath the doors before choosing a stall. So no one bothered the dead man.

No one except for the white-haired man from the Oklahoma tour group who sat in the stall next door.

Son of a gun, he thought. *It smells like that fella in the next stall's got a real problem.*

It wasn't any of his business, he knew, and the man next

door might not want to be bothered, but on the other hand it was a fella's Christian duty to help out his fellow man if there was something wrong. He tapped on the dividing wall with his knuckle.

"You all right in there, fella?"

The dead man, naturally enough, didn't say a word.

That didn't bother the white-haired man. "Well, nothin' to be ashamed of. You might wanta try some of that Parapectolin, though. You can get it without a prescription, but you gotta sign the book for it. Works real good when you got the runs. Me, my problem used to be the opposite, but I started in takin' that Metamucil ever' day. Let me tell you, boy, that stuff keeps you regular as an eight-day clock."

The dead man remained silent, and the white-haired man finished what he'd come to do. Then he flushed and left, thinking about the nice conversation he'd had with the man in the neighboring stall. You never could tell when you were going to meet somebody interesting. Those Texans weren't near as bad as most people said they were. Real polite and nice when you got to know 'em.

EIGHTEEN

When Senator Wilkins heard the outer office door close he let himself relax slightly. Not much. He was not sure he would ever relax completely again, and he was not sure he could face those two women, not now, maybe not ever again. Not considering what they represented. Not considering what Clinton Amory had threatened him with earlier.

How did Amory know? That was what Wilkins would have liked to find out. He might be able to keep Amory quiet, but what if there were others who knew? And there must be. Good Lord, Amory was nothing more than a glorified janitor. If he knew, everyone must know.

Wilkins put his head in his hands and leaned his elbows on his desk. This was by far the worst thing that had ever happened to him in the course of his political career.

Here he was, a respected member of the Texas Senate, about to sponsor a bill that would make abortions illegal.

Here he was, a champion of the right to life.

And here he was, guilty of having made a woman pregnant

and having tried to persuade her to have an abortion. Worse yet, from the point of view of most female voters, the woman was not even his wife. Worse even than that, from the same point of view, she was young enough to be his daughter.

And somehow Amory had found out about all of it.

Wilkins shuddered. He had been an idiot to think that he was being discreet in his affairs. He had always been contemptuous of legislators—representatives, mostly—who were stupid enough to go to parties like "Speaker's Night" at the Broken Spoke. The young kids who worked at the Capitol liked to go because it was free. The girls giggled about dancing with the "old men," but a few of them occasionally drank too much and gave the gossip mills grind on the next day. Wilkins regarded such public goings-on as beneath men like him. Now, however, it appeared that his personal life was the common gossip of the Capitol building. If it was, then there was nothing he could do except throw himself on the mercy of the electorate and his wife. He didn't think that there would be much comfort in either place.

He looked at the photocopied pages on his desk. Everyone called the political articles copied from the Texas press "the clippings," though the official title was *Legislative Clipping Service*. He had thumbed through it earlier, but there was no mention of his indiscretions or of the murder. It was too soon for that.

If, however, his personal life was still a secret from nearly everyone, if Amory was the only one to know, then Wilkins would have to do something. He was a practical man, and he believed strongly in a few words that he had once heard attributed to Benjamin Franklin, another practical man: A sin well hidden is half forgiven.

One way or another, then, Amory would have to be taken care of.

Wilkins lowered his hands and looked at the frosted-glass

173

back of his office door. After a couple of minutes, he buzzed Suzimae Turner.

"Send in Mr. Matson," he said. "I have some things to discuss with him."

Hap Reatherford and Craig Shaw were sitting in Reatherford's kitchen at the butcher-block table, having breakfast. The bacon was crisp, the orange juice was fresh, the melon was cold, the coffee was hot, and Shaw was wondering just what the heck was going on.

He had responded to the message on his answering machine late the previous evening, and Reatherford had issued the invitation.

"We need to meet somewhere private," Reatherford said. "Somewhere that the word won't get all over town."

"There's not any place like that in Austin," Shaw said. "The town's not that big."

"You could come to my house," Reatherford said, and so Shaw had agreed. He was interested to find out what one of the slickest lobbyists in town had to say to him.

It took awhile for Reatherford to get around to the actual subject. He smiled and chatted, but there were no sensitive issues brought up. They talked about the upcoming session, about the concerns that would surely arise, and about Senator Wilkins's bill on abortion.

"The senator had a press conference yesterday," Reatherford said, taking a sip of the coffee. "I believe you were there." His eyes sparkled as if at some private joke.

"That's right," Shaw said, thinking that they were probably about to get to the point. "I was there. He didn't say very much, though."

"You must have said something, however," Reatherford said. "Something that annoyed the senator."

"Maybe," Shaw said. "Why would that be of interest to you?"

174

Reatherford set down his coffee cup. "It's of more interest to *you*. Senator Wilkins asked me to do something about you." Reatherford had decided to reveal that much. He believed it would be necessary to get Shaw's cooperation.

"Do what, exactly?" Shaw said. The coffee was excellent. There was just a hint of cinnamon in it.

"The implication was that something to damage your credibility would be very much appreciated. Can you tell me why he would ask something like that?"

Shaw decided to play along. Why not? He might find out something he could use. He had a feeling, however, that he had already found out more from Tanya than Reatherford knew.

"Do you mind if I smoke?" Shaw said, bringing out his pack of Winstons. There was something about a cigarette with coffee at breakfast, something that had broken Shaw every time he had ever tried to quit smoking.

"Not at all," Reatherford said. "Let me get you an ashtray."

Though Reatherford himself couldn't smoke, he was around many people who did. He didn't actually like the idea of breathing their secondhand smoke since he couldn't generate any of his own, but he wasn't about to say that. He didn't want to offend anyone who might be of use to him, and he kept several heavy glass ashtrays in one of the cabinets in the kitchen. He got one out and set it on the table.

Shaw had already brought out his Zippo and set fire to a Winston. He tapped it on the edge of the ashtray.

"Could you have done it?" he said.

"Done what?" Hap said.

"Damaged my credibility." Shaw took a drag on the cigarette. "I'm just curious."

"Of course I could have done it. I still might do it. It all depends."

"Depends on what?" Shaw said. Grayish-white smoke wreathed his face.

"On how much we can do for one another. I'm sure you understand that."

Shaw understood, all right, and he believed that Reatherford could do any damage he chose to do. "I don't suppose you'd tell me how."

"Of course not. But I could do it." Reatherford smiled. He seemed to Shaw never to stop smiling. "You probably don't like lobbyists very much, do you?"

Shaw took a deep drag on the cigarette and let the smoke out slowly. "Not very much," he said.

"We do perform some useful functions, you know."

Shaw had to smile at that. "I'm sure you do. You make the legislators very happy, for one thing."

Reatherford agreed. "And we make sure that they're well informed on the issues. That's a very important function of lobbyists."

"I bet," Shaw said.

In a sense, though, what Reatherford said was true. Lobbyists made very sure that legislators were provided with all the information the lobby wanted them to have on every issue. Any other information, however, had to be obtained from somewhere else.

"But that's neither here nor there," Reatherford said. "What matters is what we can do for one another. It's a simple trade-off. You help me out, I help you out."

"How do you help me?"

"I don't damage your credibility with your readers and your editor."

"Oh."

"Yes. So what did you ask at that press conference?"

"I asked Wilkins, purely hypothetically of course, if he would recommend an abortion to a woman he got pregnant, assuming that woman wasn't his wife."

176

Reatherford didn't say anything. He picked up a slice of bacon and bit off half of it.

"That's all there was to it," Shaw said. "If you're waiting for more, there isn't any."

"I wasn't waiting," Reatherford said. "I was just thinking."

"About what?" Shaw crushed out his cigarette and got out another one.

"What if the hypothetical pregnant woman was murdered? What then?"

Shaw covered his surprise by lighting the Winston. Reatherford might know more about things than it had first appeared.

"About this hypothetical pregnant woman," Shaw said. "Do you have a name?"

"I have a source downtown," Reatherford said. "He called me this morning. Ramona Gonzalez was pregnant."

"Uh-oh," Shaw said. "You know how Wilkins is about young women?"

"I know," Reatherford said, shaking his tonsured head. "It's an unfortunate situation."

"It's more than that," Shaw said.

"I was afraid it might be," Reatherford said, but he was still smiling.

"Yeah. One of the young women Wilkins liked was Ramona Gonzalez."

"Can you prove that?" Reatherford said. He knew it was true, but he would not say so.

"I don't think I'll have to. I have an unnamed source who will vouch for it." Shaw didn't know for sure that Tanya would vouch for anything if he told her it was for publication, even if he promised to protect her completely. But Reatherford didn't know that.

"That's really too bad," Reatherford said. "I was hoping that Senator Wilkins and I could continue our mutually satisfactory relationship. Under the circumstances, I don't think that will be possible."

"There ought to be plenty of other guys in the Capitol who're willing to go on the take," Shaw said.

Reatherford finally stopped smiling. "That's a rather offensive thing to say to your host."

"Yeah, I guess it is. Sorry about that." Shaw didn't look sorry.

"I'm sure you are. Well, you've told me something I needed to know, so I'll forgive you."

"What about my credibility?"

Reatherford smiled again. "You'll have to damage that yourself. I'd be careful how I handled this story if I were you."

"Don't worry about that. I'll be careful. My paper has some very picky lawyers. I'll probably wind up writing something about 'a rumored connection between the dead woman and a powerful state senator' and hope that smokes him out."

"That might do it." Reatherford put his hand on the silver pot that sat in the middle of the table. "Or it might not. Would you like some more coffee?"

Shaw knew that the meeting was over. He stubbed out his cigarette. "No thanks. Will we be seeing each other again?"

"That depends," Reatherford said.

Shaw pushed back his chair and stood up. "On what?"

Reatherford stood up as well. "On whether we need one another again," he said.

Stan Donald was polishing his glasses with a clean white handkerchief when Jane Kettler came through the east door. He folded his handkerchief and shoved it into his back pocket. He put on the glasses as she walked toward the tour desk.

"Good morning," he said when she got there.

She smiled tentatively. "Good morning." She looked at

Mrs. Stanton and Mrs. Tolbert, who were trying to stabilize the legs of the table that Mrs. Stanton had fallen on. "What's been going on here?"

"Why don't I explain in your office?" Stan said.

Jane wasn't sure she wanted to be alone with him, but she wasn't sure she didn't want to be. "All right," she said. "Come around in a few minutes. She needed time to manufacture an errand for Zach Venner if the assistant was around.

In a few minutes Stan walked into her outer office. Zach was just leaving, but Stan stopped to talk to him about the hulabaloo stirred up by the murder. When Zach went on his way, Stan went into Jane's inner office.

"They think Wayne killed Ramona Gonzalez," he said when the door closed behind him.

"What?" Jane said. She had expected him to talk about something else entirely. She didn't know whether to be glad or sorry that he hadn't.

"Wayne. The Wagger. Darrel Prince tried to shoot him this morning. He says Wayne killed Ramona Gonzalez."

Jane sat behind her desk and slipped out of her Nikes and into her uniform shoes. "That's ridiculous," she said.

"It's not ridiculous. Prince thinks Wayne was down in the basement that night. And Wayne's crazy, all right."

"He wouldn't kill anyone. Not Wayne. He's just not the type." Jane found it hard to believe that Stan could think of Wayne as a murderer.

"Who is the type?" Stan said.

Jane had to admit that she didn't know.

"Prince is a policeman, as much as we hate to admit it," Stan said. "He knows more than we do about that kind of thing."

"Maybe," Jane said. She still wasn't convinced about Wayne. She wasn't even convinced that Prince knew more than she did about anything. After all, Claude Hebert was a policeman, too, and she suspected that his IQ wasn't much bigger than his belt size.

"Well, anyway, Prince seems pretty sure. He chased Wayne up out of the basement, and Wayne ran down Mrs. Stanton."

"And Prince was going to shoot Wayne? Right here in the Capitol?"

"He was aiming his pistol. I thought some of the tourists were going to have a heart attack."

"Then I think Prince is the crazy one," Jane said. "He's probably more dangerous than Wayne."

"Do you think *I'm* dangerous?" Stan said.

"I . . . what do you mean?"

"I mean would you go out with me again? Have dinner? Talk about things?"

Jane felt a flush creeping slowly up her neck. "I don't know, Stan. I'm still not sure that it's a good idea. We have a working relationship that's very important to getting things done around here. We shouldn't jeopardize that. We both need our jobs."

Stan stepped around her desk and put a hand on her shoulder. She looked up at him and he bent down and kissed her gently on the lips.

Jane felt her face growing hot. "Don't," she said. "Not here. Not in the office."

"Where, then?"

"We can talk about it later. You go and see what's going on in your department. Right now." She tried to look stern and schoolteacherish, but she wasn't at all sure she was bringing it off.

Stan smiled. "All right. But we *will* talk about it later, won't we?"

"Yes. Yes. Now go on out there."

He went, but he was still smiling. And after the door closed, Jane was smiling, too.

★ ★ ★

The dead man was not smiling.

He was not doing much of anything. He was just sitting still and quiet, occupying space.

The white-haired man was long gone, and no one else had come in to sit in the stall near the dead man. No one looked in on him to see if he was all right.

A roach crawled out from somewhere in the wall behind the toilet and moved silently along the tile. He came to the dead man's shoe and crawled up and over its shiny surface.

Down the line, a toilet flushed and the stall door slammed. Someone turned on the water in a basin and washed his hands.

The dead man took no notice, but the roach scuttled back to wherever it had come from. It was too noisy out there for it.

The dead man didn't see the roach go.

NINETEEN

Todd Elton thought he'd go down to the Capitol and do a little business. The legislature wasn't in session, true, but there were plenty of other state employees who liked to see him coming.

Todd lived in an old house just off Thirty-second Street, not too far from the university campus. It was an unpretentious house in a quiet neighborhood, shaded by tall oak trees. Comfortable and homey, nothing flashy about it. It suited Todd perfectly. He believed in a low profile. No need in calling attention to the fact that his income was considerably more per month than the legislators were paid per year.

Candy man, that's what he was, just like in the old song. Not the one by Sammy Davis, Jr. That one sucked. The one by Roy Orbison. He brought a little happiness into the drab lives of others, and they paid him well for the service.

He stood in his boxer shorts looking out the bedroom window at the leaves blowing across his lawn in the rain. He slapped his flat stomach. "I'm your candy man," he said to no one in particular. There was no one there to hear him.

Ron Matson would have been there if things had taken their intended course the previous evening, but they had quarreled too long and too hard about Ron's talkativeness and his relationship with Ramona Gonzalez.

It was too bad about Ron, Todd thought. He would have been much better off if he had stayed away from all women, and especially Ramona. She talked even more than Ron did, as Todd had reason to know. He heard a lot of things in his line of work, but he kept them to himself, and he had little patience for those who didn't do likewise.

The Gonzalez bitch had been a threat to him, but she wouldn't bother him now. He wondered just how old Senator Wilkins was feeling about that. Probably pretty damn bad. Todd hoped so. It would serve the old bastard right, fooling around with a woman less than half his age. He had never liked Wilkins, whom he thought of as an old hypocrite, but then he felt that way about most of the legislators. Even the younger ones had something to hide, or the ones that dealt with Todd did.

The cold rain blew out of the cold gray sky and spattered against the windowpane; the wind drove the dead leaves across the lawn.

All in all, Todd thought, it was shaping up to be a nice day.

Ray Hartnett sometimes thought he'd seen and heard it all, but every time he thought that, something came along to prove that he was wrong.

"Run through it one more time for me," he told Darrel Prince. They were sitting in the cop shop, Claude Hebert having been sent out to patrol the building so that their conversation could be private.

"Well, that's the tape you asked for," Prince said, pointing to the dirty wad of masking tape that lay on the desk where Hartnett was sitting. "I found it in the trash can where I threw it."

183

Hartnett looked at the lump of tape. He could tell it was going to be of no use to anyone, though he would send it to the lab just in case. "And the trash can is where you got your big idea," he said.

Prince looked offended. "I had it before then. I knew that paper smelled funny from the beginning. I just couldn't remember what it smelled like."

"But you did remember."

"Yeah. It smelled like Wayne. He slept in that hamper. I'd bet on it."

"And he killed Ramona Gonzalez."

"Sure he did. He was there. He's a sex maniac. He did it." To Prince the logic was clear.

It wasn't so clear to Hartnett. From what Prince had told him, Wayne was an exhibitionist, and exhibitionists rarely got any pleasure from other kinds of sexual activity. That's why they wanted everyone to think they were so proud of their private parts. They were trying to convince others, and themselves at the same time, that they possessed potent sexual weapons, when in reality those weapons would fire only blanks or wouldn't fire at all. Exhibitionists didn't have sexual relations with women and then kill them. It just didn't work that way, not in Hartnett's experience.

But Wayne just might have been in the hamper. If he wasn't the killer, he might have seen something.

"So you decided to kill him," Hartnett said.

Prince had the grace to look embarrassed. "I got a little crazy. My sidearm went off accidentally when Wayne pushed the door of the men's room in my face."

Hartnett leaned back in his chair. "Of course the big question is why you didn't tell me about Wayne yesterday. You did find the tape yesterday, didn't you?"

Prince admitted that he had, but he didn't say anything else.

"You wanted to be a hero, right?" Hartnett said after a while.

"I guess that was it," Prince said. "You don't know what it's like, trying to be a cop in a place like this. No one likes you. No one appreciates what you're trying to do. It's like they think more of the assholes that you're trying to protect them from than they think of you."

"It's that way everywhere," Hartnett said.

"That's easy for you to say. You're a Ranger."

Hartnett stood up. "That doesn't make any difference. Let me tell you something, Prince. You just have to do your job, and do it right. That's the only satisfaction there is."

"I'm doing the best I can."

Hartnett figured Prince was telling the truth, which was too bad. "If Wayne comes back here, I don't want any shooting," he said. "I want you to hold him and give me a call."

"He might not be back," Prince said.

"Did you call the locals?"

"Claude did. They'll let us know if they pick him up."

"All right," Hartnett said, thinking that there was nothing else he could do about Wayne at the moment. "I have a few more people to talk to here. I'll check back with you before I leave."

Prince watched Hartnett's back as the Ranger left the office, listened as the sound of his boot heels receded down the corridor outside.

Prince hadn't told Hartnett the whole truth. He did think Wayne would be back. He'd thought about it and decided that Claude was right. It wasn't as if the Wagger had a home. And when he came back, Darrel Prince would be waiting for him.

Hartnett thought that Jane Kettler was a good-looking woman, smart, and almost totally devoid of bullshit, the kind of woman he sometimes fantasized about meeting outside his line of work, on those rare occasions when he allowed himself to think about such things at all.

Jane thought almost the same thing about Hartnett, and that confused her more than ever as far as her feelings about Stan Donald went. She wished that Hap Reatherford had never called her and started her thinking about men again. It was as if some button had been pushed inside her, changing her life suddenly and completely.

She had gotten along perfectly well on her own for years, and now there was a very young man interested in her, while at the same time she was finding herself attracted to a perfect stranger. And a Texas Ranger at that.

She wondered whether she should read a book about menopause. Maybe that was what was happening to her.

"I'm sorry," she said, having missed most of what Hartnett was saying. "Would you go over the last part again?"

"I was just asking if Ramona Gonzalez ever talked to you or to anyone in your office about the men she dated. I've heard that she liked to talk."

"There's an unwritten policy against passing along gossip in the Capitol," Jane said, feeling entirely too prim for her own good. "And I try to impress the wisdom of that policy on all the young people who work in the offices."

"I didn't say that you or anyone else passed it along," Hartnett told her. "That doesn't mean nobody listened to it, though."

"Well," Jane said.

Hartnett liked the way she looked when she said it, with a little half smile that she probably didn't even know she had. He knew she wasn't married, but he'd bet she was going out with two or three guys.

"I don't want to hurt anyone, or even intimidate them," he said. "Just find out if Ramona told them anything that could have caused her murder."

"Have you talked to Darrel Prince? He thinks he knows who killed her."

"Darrel Prince is an idiot," Hartnett said, surprising himself.

Jane laughed. "Yes, he is, isn't he? But he's probably the best cop they've got here."

"So you don't think he has the right man?"

"No. Wayne would never do anything like that."

Just as Hartnett had thought. She was smart.

"Ramona never really talked to me very much," she said. "Just an occasional remark about the cleaning or about something related to her job. She liked to talk to people, though. I know she occasionally bothered people in some of the offices. She used to get crushes on some of the more prominent men, and I think she embarrassed the Speaker once at a reception. But I don't think she made anyone mad enough to kill her."

"But she never mentioned any of this to you?" Hartnett said.

"Never. She might have talked to some of the tour guides, though. They're more her age."

"You don't look so old," Hartnett said, and he was sorry the minute the words came out. They didn't sound the way he had meant them to sound.

Jane smiled. She didn't mind the way Hartnett had put things. She knew what he meant. "Thanks. But Ramona wouldn't have thought that way. You should talk to some of the tour guides. There should be some of them at the desk right now, or they might be in the lounge if they aren't leading a tour. Stan Donald can show you where the lounge is."

"All right," Hartnett said. "Thanks for your help."

"Anytime," Jane said, and Hartnett sincerely hoped that he would have an excuse to talk to her again.

He left her office and walked back to the tour desk. There

were no guides there at the moment, so he asked Stan Donald to show him where the lounge was located. He thought Donald was a little hostile toward him and wondered why, until a shocking thought occurred to him. *The bastard's jealous. He doesn't want me talking to his boss.* Could that really be it? Donald had to be at least ten years younger than Jane, but then she was very attractive. Hartnett wondered just exactly what was going on between the two of them, but he decided that it was none of his business. Not yet, at any rate.

Suzimae Turner couldn't understand it. She couldn't locate Ron Matson anywhere, and he was supposed to be there.

The senator was furious, and Suzimae didn't blame him. It wasn't like Ron to be so irresponsible. He was usually the first one into the office every morning and the last one to leave every night. He was never sick, had never missed a day for any reason for as long as Suzimae could remember.

She had tried calling his apartment, but all she got was the answering machine with its recorded message. She didn't know who his close friends were, or she would have called them. He never talked much about his friends.

She thought about calling the police and asking them to check Ron's apartment, but that would be silly. Ron wasn't likely to have injured himself and be too hurt to get to the phone. He was a very careful person.

Maybe he was working on something to do with the upcoming session, going around and visiting some of the other senators' aides and lining up votes for Senator Wilkins's bill. Maybe that was it. Suzimae hoped so. She didn't like for bad things to happen to people she knew.

She thought she might try calling some of the other offices. Maybe someone had seen Ron that morning. He should have checked in, but maybe he was too busy.

She picked up the phone just as Craig Shaw walked through the door.

★　★　★

The lounge seemed to shrink when Ray Hartnett walked inside.

He's really big, Chrissy thought. *I wonder if he works out?*

Stan introduced Hartnett to Tanya and Chrissy, the only guides in the lounge, and told them what the Ranger wanted to talk to them about. Then he left Hartnett on his own.

Tanya and Chrissy looked at one another and then at Hartnett, who immediately decided that they knew something. He didn't want to scare them, however, so he tried to put them at their ease as best he could by asking about their job and how they liked it.

"It's all right," Tanya said with a shrug. "We don't get paid a lot, but we have time to study if we're stationed somewhere like the reception rooms."

"We're not really here for the money," Chrissy said. "We're here to get experience in dealing with people and to learn about our state government."

Her little speech sounded to Hartnett as if it were something she might have written on her application form, but he didn't mind. "I suppose you see all kinds of people," he said. "I was just talking to the police about someone named Wayne."

"Wayne likes Chrissy," Tanya said.

Chrissy did not smile. "Yes, we all know who Wayne is," she said.

"Are you afraid of him?" Hartnett said.

Both girls laughed. "Afraid of Wayne?" Chrissy said. "You must be joking."

"You don't think he might be involved in the murder, then?"

The two girls looked at one another again.

"Not Wayne," Tanya said. "He's weird, but he's harmless. Did one of those cops tell you he had something to do with it?"

189

Hartnett admitted that one of the cops might have mentioned it.

"That's about how smart they are," Tanya said.

"I suppose that Wayne wasn't Ramona's type," Hartnett said.

"No," Tanya said. "Wayne's not anybody's type."

"She did like men, though, didn't she?" Hartnett said. "I didn't hear that from the police," he added.

"I don't really think we should talk about that," Chrissy said. "We aren't supposed to gossip."

Hartnett looked at her. She was pretty, and she was probably reasonably intelligent. But she didn't know the facts of life.

"This is a murder investigation," he said. "Ramona Gonzalez is dead, and she was most likely killed by someone in this building. If you know anything—and I mean anything—that might help in finding her killer, you're morally obligated to tell me about it. And that means repeating gossip if you have to."

Chrissy looked at Tanya, who was looking down at the floor. Tanya wasn't going to help her friend out of this one.

"Well," Chrissy said. She stopped and looked at Tanya again, but Tanya didn't look up. "Well, Ramona talked to us sometimes about the men she dated."

"Did she tell you who they were?"

"Sometimes," Chrissy said. "Not always."

"Why not always?"

"Because she said we might know them too well. I think she was just bragging, but I don't know for sure."

Hartnett didn't know either. "What were some of the names she did tell you?"

"Claude Hebert," Chrissy said. "She went out with him."

"Not *out*, exactly," Tanya said, apparently deciding to help Chrissy a little bit after all in order to keep the facts straight.

Ramona hadn't really dated Hebert. "She got one of Claude's famous after-hours tours."

"You'd better explain that," Hartnett said.

"Do you know Claude?" Tanya said.

"I've met him."

"Well, you probably think he's a pig, and I guess he is, but he's got something that women seem to like."

Chrissy drew a sharp breath and looked shocked. Hartnett didn't blame her. It was hard for him to believe, too.

"Some women," Tanya said. "Not me and Chrissy. But he's got a kind of a reputation."

Funny, Prince didn't mention that, Hartnett thought. "Who else?" he said.

"Ron Matson," Tanya said. "That's Senator Wilkins's chief aide. That was kind of a surprise. We thought Ron was gay. We've seen him with men a lot of the time. One of them's a coke runner."

"Who would that be?" Hartnett said. If drugs were involved, that could change the whole picture.

"A guy named Todd Elton. He used to work here as a guide, and later he worked in the House."

That wouldn't look good for Wilkins if it came out. Hartnett would have to be careful how he handled it, but he would definitely investigate Matson and Elton.

"Was there anyone else?" he said.

"Senator Wilkins," Tanya said. She might as well bring him into it; she'd already told Craig Shaw. "I don't think he knew about Ron, though. Senator Wilkins likes young girls."

Hartnett had heard that rumor about Wilkins, but he'd never really believed it. You heard a lot of things like that about legislators. "Are you sure about that one?" he said.

"We're sure," Tanya said. "She's not the only one."

Something in the way she said it made Hartnett ask his next question. "Did either one of you—?"

"No way!" Chrissy said. "He's just so . . . old."

"But it was someone you knew?"

"It was Sandy Harrelson," Tanya said, since Chrissy apparently didn't want to discuss it. "She used to work here. As a guide."

"She didn't really want to date Senator Wilkins," Chrissy said. "She thought it was about getting a job or something when she graduated." Chrissy did not mention the fact that wanting a good job after college graduation was the one thing that all Capitol guides had in common. "That's what she said, anyway."

"How did the dating happen, then?" Hartnett said. "Did she tell you?"

"It was Ron Matson that asked her," Tanya said. "He told her the senator had seen her in the hallway and wanted to talk to her about working for him."

"That was the really sneaky part," Chrissy said. "She thought maybe he wanted to tell her she was doing a good job or like that. But that wasn't what he wanted."

"It sure wasn't," Tanya said. "He wouldn't get what he wanted from *me,* let me tell you."

"But he got it from Sandy?" Hartnett said.

There was silence in the long, narrow room.

"It's all right," Hartnett said. "It's part of the investigation."

"Well, then, OK," Tanya said. "He got it. But not then. It was later."

"He pressured her," Chrissy said. "He threatened her about her job."

"That's not the worst part," Tanya said.

"What's that, then?" Hartnett said.

"He got her pregnant," Tanya said. "And then he got her to have an abortion."

Well, Hartnett thought, *these two are certainly getting experience in dealing with people and learning a lot about their state government.*

192

TWENTY

Craig Shaw had never been an outstanding political reporter because he was a cynic. He did not really believe he could make a difference, no matter what he told in his stories.

After all, he lived in Texas, the state that proved incorrect the old adage about the people getting the government they deserved. The people of Texas often got even worse government than they deserved.

In recent memory they had suffered a governor who, during his tenure in office, had been deeply and thoroughly involved in a football recruiting scandal of massive proportions at his alma mater. When the scandal was uncovered in all its sordid detail and the governor was asked about the incorrect statements—not to call them outright lies—that he had uttered with regard to his school's activities, his reply was that he hadn't seen any Bibles in the room where he was being questioned.

That same governor had been forced to call the legislature into special session a record six times one year in an attempt to get it to come up with an education finance bill that would satisfy the courts and at the same time live up to his own desire for no new taxes; only the judge's threat of placing school financing under the jurisdiction of a court-appointed master finally brought the two sides together and resulted in the passage of a bill that satisfied no one in particular, including the governor, who finally did what everyone knew he would have to do all along and agreed to a tax increase. And then a judge declared that bill unconstitutional.

To Shaw, the governor's office wasn't the only problem. To him the legislature seemed composed mostly of self-seeking officeholders who cared little for the people they represented. For example, for the protection of all motorists, it had passed, in the early eighties, a law requiring all drivers to have automobile liability insurance. But it had only recently passed a law requiring anyone to show proof of insurance before receiving either a license to drive or an automobile license tag. Therefore something like 40 percent of the accidents in the state involved uninsured drivers, and the insured drivers were paying the price for all of them. The uninsured drivers paid a small fine when caught, and that was all.

One reason there were so many uninsured drivers was the incredibly high cost of automobile insurance, but the legislature would never do anything to regulate that cost. The insurance lobby would never have stood for it.

And the legislature would never enact a no-fault insurance bill. The trial lawyers' lobby was too powerful.

Despite the legislature's lack of action on anything significant, it could throw enormous amounts of energy into pseudoevents such as making one of its members "Governor for a Day," with bands playing, choirs singing, and citizens being shown a high old time.

And then there was the "ghost voting" that went on in every legislative session. Unless a roll-call vote was requested by one of the members, voting was done by the members pressing a button on their desks. There were filmed records of one member sitting in his own seat and pressing the buttons on three other desks, all vacant: the one behind him and the ones on either side of him. All without leaving his own chair. And of course there was also the filmed record of a member's child visiting the floor and going around to vacant desks and pushing a few of the buttons on one vote.

And from what Shaw had seen of other states and even D.C., the system was just as bad everywere. Or worse.

It was pretty distressing when you thought about it, but even more distressing to Shaw was that despite the fact that all these things were widely reported and commented on, the same old faces turned up in the legislature year after year after year. If you were an incumbent, there was hardly any necessity for you to run a campaign. You were virtually a cinch to win office again and again.

Maybe the people *did* get the government they deserved after all.

Craig Shaw thought about all that as he drove back to town from his visit with Hap Reatherford, a visit that had shown him one more thing to be cynical about. Here was the lobbyist who for years had lined Sam Wilkins's pockets and curried his favor and who was taking the opportunity to distance himself from Wilkins before the shit hit the fan. It wasn't even a matter of "What have you done for me lately?" It was simply a matter of leaving a supposed friend in the lurch.

Maybe that was why Shaw was going to talk to Wilkins. He couldn't say for sure, but maybe he was just tired of all the hypocrisy. Maybe he could, for once, write a story that would make a difference. Maybe his cynicism had made him no better than the people that he believed were perverting the process of government. He might not be able to make a difference, but it was time to find out.

There were two ways to go about it. He could take the approach that he was giving Wilkins a chance to tell his side of things before the story was distorted by rumor and innuendo. Or he could write a story that exposed the whole seamy side of life in the Capitol: the sex, the drugs, the under-the-table deals that the public really hadn't heard about before.

As he sat there across the desk from Senator Wilkins, he was trying to make up his mind about which story it would be.

"Your secretary told me you had a headache," he said.

The senator didn't look too good, that was for sure. There were worry wrinkles in his face that Shaw would have sworn hadn't been there the day before, and his off-the-rack suit hung on him as if he had lost several pounds overnight.

"I'm fine," Wilkins said, waving off Shaw's concern. "I took a couple of aspirin."

"I hope you don't mind talking to me."

Wilkins attempted a hearty smile that was a sad parody of his true politician's beam. "Always glad to speak with a member of the press," he said.

"I just wanted to clarify something I asked you about yesterday," Shaw said.

Wilkins leaned back in his chair, trying to pretend that he was completely at ease in spite of having the look of a man whose digestive system had stopped working sometime several months previously.

"Ron Matson usually handles those clarifications," he said.

"I know. But I couldn't see Ron. Your secretary says he hasn't been in today. Anyway, I wanted to talk to you personally about this." He had made up his mind about the approach he was going to use. "I think you're going to have some hard questions to answer fairly soon, and the rumors are going to be vicious even before that. I wanted to give you the opportunity to get your side of things on the record."

"My side of things?" Wilkins said. "On the record?"

"I want our whole conversation to be on the record," Shaw said. "I want that understood from the beginning."

Wilkins began to perspire heavily. He brought out his

handkerchief and wiped his face. "And what, may I ask, is this conversation to be about?"

"You," Shaw said. "You and Ramona Gonzalez."

Wilkins looked as if he might throw up. "Ramona Gonzalez?" he said.

"You knew her very well, didn't you," Shaw said. It wasn't a question.

Wilkins looked at his damp handkerchief, then folded it carefully. "Yes," he said. "Yes, I knew her."

Shaw didn't trust tape recorders. He had a small notebook that he now flipped open. "Just how well did you know her?" he said.

Todd Elton strolled through the west entrance of the Capitol as if he owned the building. In one sense, he did, or rather he owned a number of the people in it.

He brushed the raindrops off his London Fog raincoat and onto the floor. He didn't care if someone followed him in and slipped in the water. It was no skin off his dick.

He walked down the quiet hallway, a little disappointed with the calm atmosphere. He had expected an air of excitement, what with the session coming up, but there seemed to be nothing out of the ordinary going on.

Before leaving home, he had made a couple of calls to his regulars and set up appointments in the chapel, but he hadn't run into any traffic on the way, and he'd found a parking place almost immediately. So he had arrived twenty minutes early and more or less at loose ends. There wasn't really anyone there who wanted to talk to him in public, and he sure didn't want to go on the tour.

He thought he'd drop by the tour desk, however, and have a chat with Stan Donald. Stan didn't like him any more than anyone else did, but Stan felt obligated to talk to him. Being a former tour guide had its advantages, though Todd couldn't push it very far. Jane Kettler, for example, wouldn't give him the time of day. He was sure someone had told her something about him, but he knew she would keep her mouth shut. She didn't pass along gossip.

Todd had thought of himself as the superstar of the tour guides during his time of service. He always spiced up the lecture when he could, which meant whenever Stan Donald wasn't watching him and checking up.

He liked to give the tourists what they wanted, unlike the squares who preferred to tell the truth. When questioned, he had told any number of groups that, yes, indeed, the stories they had heard about the crack in the floor of the rotunda were absolutely true. The crack was caused by a man falling from the winding stairway that led to the tip top of the building where the Goddess of Liberty was perched.

The man hadn't been a painter in Todd's version of the story, however. He was a college fraternity pledge who had been sent to climb to the top of the stairs and bring back a picture to prove he'd done so. He'd leaned too far out while focusing his camera and fallen all the way down.

"But would you believe it?" Todd would always say. "The camera landed on top of his body somehow and wasn't even damaged. The fraternity sent another pledge to steal it from the morgue, and they had the pictures developed. They're hanging in the front hall of the frat house even as we speak."

It was a good story, and it always got a good reaction. It also made a lot of people want him to reveal the name of the fraternity.

"I can't do that." His voice would grow low and confidential as he spoke, and he would look over his shoulder as if expecting some stranger to be lurking nearby to overhear him. "Frankly, I've been threatened several times for even telling the story. If I gave out the name, well, who knows what they might do to me?"

There might be one or two skeptics in the group, but

nearly everyone who heard the story believed it. And most of the other stories he told, too. Let's face it. He had the gift.

Of course, Stan Donald had never liked him, and his telling the stories didn't help any, but that didn't matter. By the time they were getting ready to fire him for absenteeism, among other offenses, he'd found other work. Much better-paying work. And it was even easier than being a tour guide.

To be a tour guide, you had to meet certain standards, and you had to keep to those standards to hold onto your job. Todd had been able to fool Stan at first, but not for long, so he was glad he had been able to find something else.

He had dropped out of school one semester short of graduation and devoted himself to his career. It was much better than looking for a real job. It was even better than graduate school.

You had to be hard sometimes in his new line of endeavor, but he could be hard. He'd proved that often enough. Just ask the ones who'd crossed him. If you could find them.

He crossed the rotunda as one of the tours was beginning. He looked up to the second floor and saw another one of the guides up there, trying to talk, smile, and at the same time help someone in a wheelchair. He wondered how he'd stood it as long as he had.

He walked through the rotunda and saw Stan behind the tour desk. "Hi-ho, Stanio," he said.

Stan looked up. He didn't seem pleased. "Hello, Todd."

"What's shakin', buddy?" Todd said.

"Nothing," Stan said. "So why don't you go on back where you came from?"

"Is that any way to talk to an old friend?" Todd said.

"I'm not your friend."

"Sure you are. I used to work for you."

"That doesn't make us friends."

"You're really hostile, Stan. You know that? You oughta take a few days off. Get laid. Or for that matter, stay here and

199

take a few days off at the same time. I could help you do that, if you know what I mean. It's even better than getting laid."

"Get out of here," Stan said.

"You never did like me much, did you?" Todd said. "You were always afraid of me because I was smarter than you and I knew too much."

"I'm not afraid of you. I never was."

"Bullshit. You were afraid of me because I know how you feel about the Kettler cow."

Stan's face grew red. "You shut your Goddamned mouth."

Todd stepped closer to Stan and flicked a forefinger into his chest. "I don't work here any more, Stanio. You can't tell me what to do or say. I think I'll go into Kettler's office and tell her a few things about her white-haired boy."

Stan shoved Todd away from the desk. "You won't tell anyone anything."

"Who's going to stop me?" Todd said, shoving back.

"There's a Texas Ranger in the lounge right now," Stan said. "I wonder if he might not like to talk to you. Maybe we could look through your pockets and see if you have anything he'd be interested in seeing." He reached out as if to put his hand inside one of the pockets of Todd's coat.

Todd knocked the hand aside. "Get away from me before I slap the shit out of you," he said. "You can't scare me with that Ranger crap."

"Maybe not," Stan said, looking over Todd's shoulder. "But here he comes now."

Todd didn't really believe that Stan was looking at anyone, but just to be sure he turned to look. When he saw Hartnett coming out of the lounge, his attitude suddenly changed. He had no desire to have a conversation with the law, not at the present time. Not ever, for that matter.

"It's been great hashing over old times with you," he said, turning to Stan. "We'll talk again one of these days." He walked rapidly across the hallway and trotted up the stairs without looking back.

Stan watched him go. He thought he was going to have to do something about Todd, who had the potential to become a dangerous nuisance. Stan certainly didn't want him talking to Jane, or to anyone else, and he was relieved to see that the Ranger had taken no notice of their conversation. For a second, Stan thought about following Todd, but he knew that there was nothing he could do about the drug dealer at the present time, not without causing some awkward questions from Jane.

He would have to deal with Todd some other time.

Hartnett was more observant than Stan thought, but he didn't know that the byplay at the tour desk had anything to do with him. He also had no idea that the man leaving in rather a hurry was Todd Elton, the very man he was going to ask Stan Donald about.

Stan was very surprised when Hartnett stopped at the desk and said, "Do you know someone named Todd Elton?"

"That was him who just left," Stan said, pointing toward the stairs. "What's he got to do with this?"

"I was told that he and Ron Matson are close friends. I wanted to have a talk with him."

"Oh." Stan wasn't quite sure what was going on, but it didn't sound too good for Todd, whatever it was. And that was just fine with Stan in one way, but he didn't really care for the idea of the Ranger conversing with Todd. "There are a few other things you should probably know about Todd," he said.

"I heard about one of them," Hartnett said. "About the dope. Is it true?"

"It's true," Stan said. "He might be here today for that very reason."

"Just what's his situation?"

"What do you mean?"

"I mean, is he a dealer, a user, a runner, what?"

"Yes," Stan said.

"Yes?"

"He's all of those. I don't think he does very much on his own, but he's worked a deal or two, according to what I've heard. He does very well for himself."

"And he's a user?"

"Not a heavy one. Or at least not as far as I know. But I'm sure he's a user."

"How do you know?"

"Let's just say I've heard it around."

Donald seemed to know a hell of a lot about Todd Elton, Hartnett thought, but then nearly everyone around here knew a lot about one or another of his fellow workers.

"Do you know where he was headed?" he said.

"No. He didn't seem too eager to talk to me when he saw you coming out of the lounge. I guess a Texas Ranger wouldn't be one of his favorite people, so he left pretty fast. He could be anywhere in the building."

"I think I might take a look around, then," Hartnett said. "If he comes back by here, try to keep him occupied until I get back."

"All right," Stan said. He hadn't liked Hartnett earlier; he didn't like any big good-looking man who talked in private to Jane Kettler. But he was beginning to think that the Ranger might be useful to have around after all, at least if he could be used against Todd. "Todd likes to talk. If he comes back, I shouldn't have any trouble keeping him here at the desk."

"Good," Hartnett said. "You do that." He crossed the hallway and started up the stairs.

TWENTY-ONE

The Cowboy thought of himself as one of the world's great country-and-western singers, although he was, temporarily and unfortunately, between engagements. He had been between engagements, by his own estimation, for about twenty-five years, ever since the time he had been hooted into silence at Threadgill's when he tried to pick and sing "Wildwood Flower" in the style of the Carter family. The singing, he had always told himself, was fine, though the picking had been a little off. He had always told himself that it was the picking that the crowd had objected to. Or maybe they hadn't liked the fact that he was black. The Cowboy was sure that in spite of Charley Pride, there was still a lot of prejudice against black men who sang country songs.

Since that time at Threadgill's he had been more or less, usually more, on the bum. He was, to be accurate, one of Wayne the Wagger's ilk, a transient who had succeeded in making the Capitol his home, or what passed for his home. He didn't stay there all the time, but he was there as often as he could be and for as long as he could get away with.

In all seasons he wore his cowboy getup, which consisted of a stained and greasy ten-gallon felt hat with a scaling rattlesnake band, several layers of Western shirts and jeans, and boots whose heels were so worn down that they were hardly heels at all. He also had a hand-tooled leather belt that had his name on the back. "Cowboy," it said in letters that had once been red but had long since faded back to the color of the original leather.

The Cowboy was a man of regular habits. He slept regular hours, he ate at the same time every day if he had something to eat, and he liked for his bowels to move with the same regularity that governed the rest of his life.

He also liked to use the same stall in the basement men's room.

It really bothered him that there was someone already there. Didn't everyone know that stall belonged to the Cowboy at this particular time of the day? It didn't matter that all the other stalls were vacant. The Cowboy wanted *his* stall, and he wanted the intruder out of it.

Nevertheless, he could be patient when he had to be, or that's what he told himself. How long could it take the guy to finish up, anyway?

The Cowboy stood by the men's room door and leaned against the wall, trying to relax and tell himself that he could wait. He glanced around the room trying to amuse himself by counting the hypodermic syringes that he could see near the wastebasket and wondering who had thrown them there so carelessly. He told himself that the man in his stall would have to finish pretty soon.

Except that he didn't.

The Cowboy didn't have a watch, but he had developed a fairly accurate sense of time over the years. He had been leaning on the wall for nearly ten minutes when his irritability overcame his small supply of patience.

He walked over to the stall and rattled the door. "C'mon, c'mon," he said. "Give somebody else a chance."

The man in the stall didn't answer. That bothered the Cowboy. It wasn't polite to ignore someone who was talking to you.

"You better shit or get off the pot, buddy," he said. "This is the Cowboy talking to you. You're in my stall, and I need to get in there."

There was still no answer. The Cowboy didn't like that. This time he didn't rattle the door. He pounded on it, making it jump in the frame.

"Hurry it up, fella. Are you gonna come outta there, or what?"

The Cowboy's face was getting even darker than its usual Hershey chocolate color, and he could feel his chest tightening. That was never a good sign. He didn't like to fight. It always got him in trouble, but there were times when he just couldn't help himself.

Once more there was no reply from the stall.

"All right, Goddamnit," the Cowboy said. He stepped back from the stall door, raised his right foot, and kicked as hard as he could with his booted foot.

The stall door snapped open and flew back. The edge hit the dead man in the knees.

"Shit, fella, you don't look so good," the Cowboy said, his anger changing to sympathy as soon as he saw the dead man's face. "You need some help?"

The dead man didn't answer. The blow from the door had caused him to tilt slightly forward, and as he began to lean farther and farther, he started to topple slowly off the toilet, like something from a slow-motion film.

As the dead man moved, the Cowboy got a better look at his face. *Goddamn,* he thought. *That sumbitch don't need help. He's dead as a mackerel.*

As soon as he completed the thought, the Cowboy's survival instinct kicked in, and he realized that he didn't need to move his bowels after all. In fact, they had suddenly locked right up on him.

There were much more important things in his life right then than taking a shit.

He needed to get out of the men's room and put as much distance between himself and the Capitol as he could before someone else came across the dead man and tried to say the Cowboy had something to do with whatever had happened.

It was a good plan, but it didn't work.

Before the Cowboy got the stall door closed, three little boys between the ages of four and eight came charging into the men's room, their father right behind them.

The first boy skidded to a stop, his shoe soles squeaking on the floor. He pointed toward the dead man. "Look at that man on the floor, Daddy," he yelled. "What's wrong with him?"

Even then the Cowboy might have gotten away, but Claude Hebert was meandering down the hallway on his way back to the cop shop, having received word on the two-way radio from Darrel that the Ranger was gone. The Cowboy stampeded the man and the three kids and got past them to the door, but he couldn't stampede Claude.

"What the hell's goin' on here?" Claude said, grabbing a handful of the Cowboy's outermost shirt as the Cowboy caromed off Claude's stomach and tried to get by him on the rebound.

"Slow down, Cowboy," Claude said, tightening his grip on the shirt. "You're liable to hurt somebody, runnin' around like a chicken with its head cut off. Just hold on till we get this mess all straightened out."

He propelled the Cowboy into the men's room ahead of him. "What seems to be the trouble here, sir?" he said to the boys' father, who was now gaping at the dead man lying half in and half out of the stall.

The boys were looking too, but unlike their father they hadn't quite figured things out.

"What's the matter with that man?" one of the boys said. "He looks funny down there on the floor."

"Uh-oh," Claude said. "Looks like you done got yourself in a real mess, Cowboy. Another dead body. That Texas Ranger is gonna love this."

He got his radio off his belt and called Darrel Prince.

Todd Elton wasn't around for all the excitement.

After leaving Stan at the tour desk, Todd went up to the second floor, crossed over to the west stairway, trotted down, and walked calmly down the hall and out the west doors.

"Ladies and gentlemen," he said as he opened the doors and the cold, damp air hit him in the face, "Todd Elton has left the fucking building."

He walked rapidly down the steps and across the Capitol grounds. By the time the Cowboy was beating on the stall door, Todd had reached his car; and by the time Claude shoved the Cowboy back into the men's room, Todd was cruising through the rain-washed streets on his way home.

He hated to miss his meetings, but his clients would understand when he called them to explain why he hadn't been there at the appointed time. They didn't want to get mixed up with the Texas Rangers any more than Todd did. They may have wanted it even less. Some of them had more to lose. A hell of a lot more.

Missing the appointments didn't really matter too much to Todd. He could meet his clients some other time. They might get a little shaky, might find themselves breaking out in a sweat at odd hours or dropping a ballpoint from trembling fingers after scrawling something almost unrecognizable on a sheet of paper, but, hey, that wasn't Todd's problem. They'd just have to deal with it as best they could.

The candy man had troubles of his own.

Clinton Amory heard about the dead man before anyone else, just as he heard about most things. He sidled down the side of the hallway and poked his head through the open door to see just what was going on.

He saw the backs of a number of gawkers who had by now crowded into the room, and looking between their legs he got a glimpse of the dead man.

Although the dead man's face was contorted and discolored, Amory knew who it was at once.

He almost swallowed his toothpick when the realization hit him. His first thought was that he had let Senator Wilkins off the hook far too easily, but there was a ready remedy for that mistake.

He headed for the stairs, shoving through the crowd that was gathering. He had to talk to Wilkins before someone else got there with the news.

If indeed it *was* news to Wilkins.

Amory's mouth twisted into a crooked grin. If it was news, if it was just a coincidence, the senator was certainly having a run of bad luck lately. That was too bad for the senator, but it didn't bother Amory any. It was good for business.

He entered the senator's office. Suzimae Turner hung up the phone and looked at him.

"Senator Wilkins in?" Amory said.

"He has a visitor from the press right now," Suzimae said.

Amory didn't like the idea of being seen by a reporter. "Maybe I can come back later," he said.

He didn't like that, either, but he was pretty sure the senator wouldn't go anywhere before seeing him. "You tell him I'll be by."

"All right," Suzimae said. Then as Amory turned to leave, she said, "Have you seen Mr. Matson today, by any chance?"

Amory stopped and turned slowly back. "Why are you

208

asking me that?" he said. The toothpick jittered from left to right across his mouth.

Suzimae looked at the telephone. "He hasn't come in this morning. I've been trying to locate him, but no one seems to know where he is. It isn't like him not to be here, especially with the session getting so close."

"Why do you think I might've seen him?"

Suzimae sensed something in Amory's tone. "I'm sure I don't know," she said. "You go into a lot of different parts of the building because of your job, and I thought you might have seen Ron."

"I've seen him all right," Amory said.

"Oh, good. Where is he?"

"He's in the men's room in the basement."

Suzimae looked concerned. "I hope he's not sick."

"He's not sick," Amory said.

"Well, then. Would you tell him to please come to the office? The senator wants to talk to him."

"I could tell him, I guess," Amory said, enjoying himself. Knowing things that someone else didn't know always tickled him. "I don't think he's going to be doing any talking to the senator, though."

"Why not? Is there something wrong?"

"You could say that," Amory told her.

Suzimae was getting impatient. "Well, what is it, then? You said he wasn't sick."

"He's not sick," Amory said. His toothpick stood up almost straight when he grinned. "He's dead."

Jane Kettler was working on a report, carefully entering data into her desktop computer and wishing for a full-time secretary, when the row broke out in the basement. She wasn't aware of anything at first, but when several guides and messengers came into the outer office and began talking to Zach in loud voices, she became curious. She got up to see what was going on just as Stan knocked on her door.

"What's the matter?" Jane said as he stepped inside.

"There's a dead man in the basement men's room," Stan said.

"A dead man? In the men's room?"

"It's Ron Matson," he said.

Jane sank back in her chair. The news was almost too much for her. "What happened?" she said. She hoped that Stan would tell her that Ron had suffered a heart attack or some other kind of natural death, though she didn't really believe he would. Ron was too young for something natural.

"He was strangled," Stan said.

"Just like Ramona," Jane said. "I can't believe this is happening."

Stan walked over beside her and put a hand on her shoulder. "Don't let it get to you. It doesn't have anything to do with us. That Ranger will find out who did it."

Jane could tell that Stan didn't believe the Ranger would do any such thing. He was just trying to make her feel better.

But he wasn't succeeding. She didn't feel a bit better. If anything she felt much worse. One death, one murder, that was something that could be explained, maybe even something that could be understood.

Jealousy, lust, a pretty young woman. It was just like a bad movie. Stupid, but understandable.

But Ron Matson? A senator's chief aide? How could that be explained? Was there a connection between the two deaths? And if there was, what was it?

Jane's mind started worrying at the problem in a way that it hadn't before. She was beginning to believe that there was some sinister undercurrent flowing through the Capitol that she had never been aware of.

"Is there something wrong?" Stan said.

Jane looked at him. "Something wrong? You're damn

right there's something wrong. This is the second time some-one's been murdered in two days. I'd say that something was wrong, wouldn't you?"

"I didn't mean it that way," Stan said, taking his hand from her shoulder. "I just meant—"

"I know what you meant. I'm sorry I snapped at you."

She wasn't really sorry. She thought he should be taking things more seriously. She thought *she* should be taking things more seriously. After all, it had been Stan who had asked her out last night to discuss the problem one murder had caused. Now there were two. And, although she recognized the weaknesses of the people she worked with, she couldn't help thinking of them as family.

"Why don't you go see if you can find out some more about what happened to Ron?" she told Stan. "I need a little time by myself right now."

"Sure," Stan said, eager to please. "I'll talk to the cops. They ought to know something."

Jane doubted it, but she suddenly wanted Stan out of the office. The warmth that she had felt for him last night was still there, but there was something else, too. She didn't quite know what it was yet, and that was another thing she needed to think about.

When the door closed, Jane turned her chair around to face the window that looked out over the Capitol grounds. The rain was much harder now than it had been when she came to work. The gray sky drooped down over the city and gave the day a gloomy cover. There was no one walking up the long walk in front of the Capitol. The drivers on Congress Avenue had turned their car lights on.

Jane thought about what she and Stan had discussed in El Rancho the previous evening. Ramona, of course, and the way she liked to talk. Stan thought Ramona might have said something to Jane, and Ray Hartnett had thought the same thing.

211

Jane was sure that Ramona had said nothing, or nothing that really mattered. She and Jane didn't do much talking. But that didn't mean that Jane hadn't heard certain gossip that was going around. She hadn't mentioned it to either Ray or Stan because she still believed, just as she always had, that gossip should not be repeated for any reason. That was one of the principles with which she indoctrinated everyone who came to work for her, and she was firm in her resolve to set a good example by never gossiping herself.

Now she was beginning to wonder whether it might not be wise to relax her rule. Even if she did, the gossip she heard might be hard to recall. She'd developed the habit of letting it go in one ear and out the other. She had too many other things to think about to keep idle talk in her head.

There were a lot of people who worked in the Capitol who thought that her job was mostly public relations, and in a sense they were right. But they didn't realize the amount of time she had to spend on the phone, or writing letters and memos, or talking to senators and representatives and their staff members to help them in organizing press conferences, meetings, and events for their constituents and visiting dignitaries. She had to keep up with the agendas and bills and filing dates during the session, which was about to begin. She was busy with things like that almost all the time; there were days when she never even had time to leave her desk between the time she arrived in the morning and the time she left for home in the late afternoon.

Nevertheless, some of the things she heard stuck with her, and if she tried, she could remember them. She started thinking about Ramona Gonzalez and Ron Matson.

It wasn't long before lots of things were coming back to her.

TWENTY-TWO

Counting from the outside, the third layer of Wayne the Wagger's upper garments consisted of a fashionable plastic garbage bag. If it hadn't been for the bag, Wayne would have been colder and wetter than he was, which was already colder and wetter than he wanted to be.

The problem he faced was that he couldn't go back to the Capitol to get warm and dry, not now. They really had a hard-on for him there, and sooner or later they were going to find the dead man.

That wouldn't cheer them up any, and it wouldn't make them think any the better of Wayne.

So Wayne had to find somewhere else to spend the day. He wanted somewhere that he could get out of the rain, and he wanted somewhere that he wouldn't be too conspicuous. He had a feeling that if the Kapitol Kops were going to shoot at him, they might have called in the city boys to help them, so he had to stay out of their way, too.

There was one place he could go that might suit his needs, and that was the university area. He had spent a lot of time there, years before. He had even enrolled for classes now and then, though he couldn't remember now just how many he'd actually completed. He was pretty sure he'd finished one or two, but he couldn't recall which ones.

Thinking of the classes he'd taken, however briefly he had been enrolled, gave him a momentary scare. They had his name on their records at the university, stored in their computers where they could get it anytime they wanted it. They could call it up and look at his grades and whatever other information they had on him.

Wayne shuddered and touched his cap. Feeling the aluminum foil crackle inside it reassured him. They might have his grades, but they couldn't get inside his head. It would be all right for him to go on out there. He could take cover on the drag, maybe in front of the Co-op, or maybe down below street level in whatever building that was they'd built where the old Y used to be. There would be plenty of other drag-worms there, and no one would give him a second look.

After dark, he could go back to the Capitol. They'd have forgotten all about him by then.

Darrel Prince hadn't forgotten about Wayne. In fact, the Wagger was the first thing he thought of when he saw Ron Matson's body.

"Son of a bitch," he said. "No wonder Wayne was in such a big hurry to get the hell out of here this morning."

He wished he had checked out the men's room then, but he didn't say so. Maybe if he didn't mention it, no one else would say anything about it.

Claude had gotten the crowd under control and out of the area and the DPS technicians were on the way to do their investigation of the crime scene, but Darrel could see some things for himself. It didn't take a trained eye to note that Ron Matson had been strangled, but this time the murder weapon, if that was the proper term, was still in place. Darrel could see the ends of a paisley tie drooping on Matson's back. The rest of the tie was embedded in Matson's neck.

It was now more urgent than ever that they catch up with Wayne. It looked as if the Wagger had a second murder to explain, and it appeared more obvious than ever to Darrel that Wayne was indeed the murderer they were looking for, even if no one else had realized that fact.

Mrs. Tolbert and Mrs. Stanton hadn't forgotten about Wayne, either, and the news of the second murder was too much for them. They began packing up their exhibits as soon as they heard about it.

They could tell that there was no need for them to be located where they were, not any more. Although they didn't associate the murders with a lack of reverence for life in the Capitol, they were nervous about their own safety. They didn't even think about going to Senator Wilkins's office to complain this time. They didn't want to make the poor man's headache worse.

They didn't mind complaining to Ray Hartnett, however, when they spotted him coming down the stairs.

Hartnett had not been able to find Todd Elton on any of the three floors he'd searched, and he had come to the conclusion either that Todd was better at hiding than Hartnett was at finding, or that Todd had skipped out. He could find Elton later, however. Now he wanted to talk to Jane Kettler again; he still needed to find out about Sandy Harrelson.

Mrs. Stanton and Mrs. Tolbert accosted him before he made it to the tour desk.

"You're the representative of law and order," Mrs. Stanton said. "You've got to do something about these murders. It's a sin and a shame when two decent women can't present a harmless and tasteful exhibit about the sanctity of life in the halls of the state Capitol building without having murders done all around them."

Hartnett didn't know what they were talking about. Two young men, obviously guides, were standing by the tour desk, talking to Tanya and Crissy, and he looked over to them for help.

"Somebody found a dead man in the men's room," one of the young men said. "Just a few minutes ago."

"You see?" Mrs. Stanton said. "Another murder. Mrs. Tolbert and I will be taking our exhibit elsewhere until these sacred hallways have been made safe for the citizens of Texas once more!"

Mrs. Tolbert didn't say anything, but she was nodding vigorously.

"What's going on?" Hartnett said, directing his question to Tanya. "Who's been killed?"

"No one knows. One of the cleaning ladies just came by and said that someone was dead. Stan's gone in to tell Ms. Kettler about it."

Clinton Amory came out of Wilkins's office in time to hear Hartnett's question and the answer. "I can tell you who it was they found in the men's room," he said, getting another little zip from being the first one to know. "It was Ron Matson. Senator Wilkins's aide."

"Oh my God," Chrissy said, looking at Tanya. "We were just talking about him to Mr. Hartnett a little bit ago."

Hartnett would have preferred not to have Amory know that, especially when he saw the way Amory smiled at the information.

"You see?" Mrs. Stanton said. "No one's safe. No one." She and Mrs. Tolbert returned to getting their exhibits off the tables as Stan Donald emerged from Jane Kettler's office.

"Did you find Todd?" he asked Hartnett.

"No. He didn't come back here?"

"I didn't see him." He looked at Tanya and Chrissy, but they shook their heads. "Are you going to investigate this new murder?" he asked Hartnett.

Hartnett didn't know, but it seemed more than likely that the murder of Ron Matson and the murder of Ramona Gonzalez were connected. Hartnett didn't believe in coincidence. So he was pretty sure he would be working on both murders.

"Probably," he said. "I'd better go down there and see what I can find out."

He left the tour desk and Amory followed him downstairs. Hartnett stopped on the landing and turned to him. "Didn't I see you come out of Senator Wilkins's office?" he said.

Amory nodded, working his toothpick up and down. "Yeah," he said. "That's right."

"What were you doing in there?" Hartnett said.

Amory looked over at the shiny wooden stair railing as if he might be thinking about polishing it. "I went up to tell him about the murder," he said. "Somebody had to do it."

"And it might as well be you, right?"

"Yeah. It might as well be. Why not?"

"No reason," Hartnett said, and started down the stairs.

The concession area was crowded with talkative and excited tourists, most of whom were trying to find out something about the murder. Hartnett made his way through them, turned to the right, and went to the men's room.

Darrel Prince and Claude Hebert were outside, having succeeded in sealing the room off for the crime-scene investigators. They had the Cowboy with them, but they were both satisfied that he'd had nothing to do with Ron Matson's death. They introduced him to Hartnett.

"Was there anyone else in there when you found the body?" Hartnett said.

The Cowboy shook his head. "No sir, just me and him. I usually come in about this time of day to do my business, and he was in my stall. I waited a little while, but he wouldn't come out. Wouldn't say anything, either. So I kind of opened the stall—"

"Broke the sucker open," Claude said. "I checked it."

"OK, so I guess I got a little rough. I needed to take a shit. Anyway, that's when he fell on the floor."

"Did you see anyone leaving when you came?" Hartnett said.

"Nope. That's why I like it down here. It's kinda private."

Hartnett talked to the Cowboy for a few more minutes, but it was obvious that the Cowboy didn't know any more than he had told. Nevertheless, Hartnett told Prince and Hebert to hold on to him for the investigators. Then he went into the men's room to have a look.

Neither Hebert nor Prince tried to stop Hartnett as he ducked under the plastic ribbon they had strung across the men's room door. As far as they were concerned, he could do whatever he wanted to.

Hartnett looked inside the stall first, but there was nothing to see in there. Then he looked at the body. It was lying where it had fallen, swollen face turned to the side. Matson was halfway up on his knees, as if he were trying to crawl away from the stall and not quite making it. His pants were down around his ankles; his bare ass stuck up in the air. He'd been dead for quite a while.

Hartnett knelt down and looked at the tie, which might be their best clue. If they could trace where it was bought. If the clerk remembered selling it. If there were fingerprints on it.

He wondered if silk would take prints. Maybe not, but then again the lab boys could do wonders these days.

He stood up and walked back over to Hebert and Prince, ducking under the ribbon again.

"All right," he said. "Now tell me why no one saw anything on the security camera this time."

Darrel and Claude looked at one another.

"Son of a bitch," Darrel said after a second.

They could see the camera from where they stood, and they all stared at it, even the Cowboy, as if it could tell them something.

"There's no masking tape this time," Darrel said.

"There'll be traces of it," Hartnett said. He was guessing, but he had to be right. "This time the killer took it with him after he did his job." He could see how it could be done if you stood in the right spot. "You won't have him on video this time, either."

He thought about that for a minute. "Did you tell anyone about that tape?" he asked Darrel.

"Just Claude," Darrel said.

"That shot you fired this morning," Hartnett said. "Where was Wayne when you fired it?"

Prince turned red. "Coming out of the men's room," he said.

"This one?"

"Yeah, that's right. This one."

"And now we have another dead man."

Prince didn't trust himself to say anything. He just nodded.

"And Wayne got away again," Hartnett said.

Prince nodded again.

"It's just as well," Hartnett said. "Wayne's a little peculiar, all right, and I can see how you might think he would kill Ramona Gonzalez. But why would he want to kill a senator's aide?"

"It's the same thing," Prince said. "Don't you see it? It's the same thing."

"How could it be the same thing?" Hartnett said. "You told me the Gonzalez murder was a sex crime."

"So is this one. Don't you get it?"

Hartnett didn't get it.

"Tell him, Claude. Hell, everybody knows, except maybe the senator."

"Yeah, tell me, Claude," Hartnett said. "What is it that everybody knows?"

Claude licked his fat lips. "Ever'body knows," he said, "that Ron Matson's a queer."

Not everyone knew.

Suzimae Turner didn't know, and of course the senator didn't know. He would never have kept Ron on his staff if he had entertained the least suspicion. The voters back home wouldn't have stood for it.

So not everyone knew about Ron when Suzimae burst into the senator's private office, interrupting his interview with Craig Shaw.

Suzimae was crying, and she had taken off her bifocals to wipe her eyes with a tissue.

Wilkins's head jerked up when she came through the door, and Shaw turned to see what was going on.

"What's the matter, Suzimae?" Wilkins said, momentarily forgetting his own problems at the sight of Suzimae in tears. He'd never seen her cry before.

"It's Mr. Matson," Suzimae said. "Somebody's killed him in the men's room."

Craig Shaw was watching the senator's face when she said it and saw Wilkins's face crumple like a cardboard box left out in the rain overnight. All definition, all trace of personality left it, and for just a moment there was nothing more behind the eyes than there was in a dark, empty room.

Shaw had never thought he'd feel sorry for a politician, but he did, for as long as the moment lasted.

Then Wilkins pulled himself together. Shaw could tell that it required a tremendous effort, and he had to admire the man for being able to find the strength necessary to do it.

He'd never thought he'd admire a politician, either. This was turning out to be quite a day.

But he was still a reporter. "Would you care to make a statement, Senator?" he said. "Do you think there could be a connection between this murder and the murder of Ramona Gonzalez?"

Shaw had already confronted Wilkins with the fact that it

was well known around the Capitol that the senator had consorted with Ramona and that she had been pregnant.

Wilkins had denied knowing the woman at all and asked Shaw for his proof, which of course Shaw had not been able to produce. *It might be possible for Wilkins to brazen it out,* Shaw thought, but the murder of Matson was going to make it much more difficult. Matson was the man who knew all the senator's secrets, and people were going to wonder if he had not known more than was good for him.

That was what Shaw was wondering.

"Mr. Matson was a fine young man," Wilkins said, standing up and resting his clenched hands on the desk. "He was a credit to our state and to the people of my district. I hope that the law will be swift in bringing down the malefactor responsible for his death. You can print that." He straightened and folded his arms.

"That's nothing but boilerplate," Shaw said. "Give me a break, Senator."

"I have nothing further to say to you," Wilkins said, completely in control now. "Suzimae, show Mr. Shaw out. We have to do what we can for Ron. We'll have to call his family. I'm sure Mr. Shaw can understand that."

Shaw didn't want to leave, but he knew he wasn't going to get any more information from the senator that day. Still, he gave it a try. "What about our earlier conversation?" he said. "What about Ramona Gonzalez?"

"I have nothing further to say on that matter, either. I was, of course, very sorry to hear of the young woman's death. I'm sure she was a valued employee of the state, though I hardly knew her myself."

That was going to be it, then. Shaw was sure he'd almost had the man on the point of revealing something important before the secretary had burst in. Why the hell couldn't Matson have gotten himself killed somewhere else?

Nevertheless, Shaw had a story, of sorts. It was based so far on a conversation with a lobbyist and a tour guide, but it could be written that way, the senator's affair with Gonzalez hinted at with reference to "sources close to the investigation who asked not to be identified." Then the murder of Matson could be brought in and a lot of other vague hints thrown around.

It wasn't going to be Pulitzer material, nothing like that, but it was going to be good enough to make the readers curious and whet their appetites for more.

The editor would be happy, too. There was nothing like the mixture of sex, politics, and murder to get the paper's circulation up.

Shaw seemed to be the only reporter on top of the story, so it was all his, at least for a little while. Now all he had to do was stay one step ahead of everyone else.

Well, why not? He was right in the building, and there was another dead body downstairs. What was he waiting for?

"So you're not going to comment further?" he said to Wilkins.

"Not until I have made a complete investigation of the facts. Then I will make whatever comments I feel to be appropriate. Naturally, the death of my chief aide is a great tragedy, both personal and political. But there are other things to be considered. The session will begin next week, no matter what has happened here today, and I intend to do the job that the voters sent me to Austin to do."

Shaw marveled at Wilkins's ability to turn on the bullshit, especially considering the circumstances. A few minutes ago, the senator had been sagging to the canvas, ready to drop for the count. Now he was bouncing back, doing the old rope a dope, floating like a butterfly if not stinging like a bee.

For an instant there, Shaw had thought Wilkins was just going to collapse and lie there, but it hadn't happened. From somewhere he'd gotten the strength to put himself back in the match.

"All right, then," Shaw said. "If that's the way you want to play it. But I have to say that the paper will be running my story, regardless of your unwillingness to confirm the rumors that have been reported to me."

"Then you will have to face the consequences," Wilkins said. "Now if you'll please excuse me, I have some arrangements that I have to make. Miss Turner?"

Suzimae had been standing by sniffing into her tissue while all this was going on, but now she stuffed it into a pocket of her dress and opened the office door.

Shaw went out. "I can get the other door myself," he said.

Wilkins watched him until he had left the office. Then he sat back down. "In view of the circumstances, you may take the rest of the day off, Suzimae," he said.

"Yes, sir. Isn't there something that we can do? It just seems so terrible."

"It is terrible, and there will be a lot to do later. For now, we want to avoid all contact with the press and with anyone else. Switch all our calls to the machine."

Wilkins never liked to use the answering machine and in fact generally did so only after hours. But these were extraordinary circumstances.

"Yes, sir," Suzimae said. "I'll be in tomorrow, though."

"That's fine," Wilkins said. "I'll get in touch with Ron's family personally and find out about the arrangements."

"Yes, sir." Suzimae gathered up her purse and coat and left the office.

Wilkins sat at his desk and looked out at the rain.

TWENTY-THREE

Hartnett could hardly miss the look that Stan Donald gave him as he passed by the younger man on his way down the hall to Jane Kettler's office. It was clear to him that Donald didn't like him one little bit.

Hartnett didn't care. He was just doing his job, and if Donald didn't like it, that was too damn bad.

The outer office was empty when Hartnett got there, but he tapped on the inner door and stepped in when Jane responded to his knock.

She looked up when he entered. "Oh," she said. "I didn't think I'd be seeing you again so soon."

"I guess this is your lucky day," Hartnett said, immediately hating himself. It sounded incredibly stupid, even to him. He never said things like that. "I didn't mean that, not with another murder in the building. I just—"

Jane smiled. "Never mind. I'm glad you came back. I've been doing some thinking ever since Stan told me that Ron Matson had been strangled. I think there are a few things I should tell you."

Hartnett looked around for a seat. There was nothing except for a straight-backed chair of lacquered wood near the door.

"I keep that to discourage visitors," Jane said. "I have a lot of work to do, most days. I can't afford to have people hanging around talking."

"I hope you don't want to discourage me," Hartnett said. Then he wondered what the hell was the matter with him. It was as if he were reading dialogue written for someone else. "I didn't mean that the way it sounded. I meant—"

"Do you spend a lot of your time apologizing?" Jane said.

Hartnett smiled ruefully. "Not usually. Hardly ever, in fact."

"I didn't think so. You're not very good at it."

"I know. It's just—"

"Never mind." It was as if she didn't want to go into his reasons. "Let me tell you what I've been thinking about."

She started to explain her policy on gossip, but Hartnett interrupted her. "I know about that. Those two guides I talked to, Tanya and Chrissy, they told me. I had a little trouble getting anything out of them."

Jane was pleased to see that some of her preaching had actually sunk in. Stan probably warned them often. "What did they tell you?"

Hartnett gave her a brief summary.

"Oh, my," Jane said. "I didn't know about Sandy. I mean, I'd heard rumors about her seeing Wilkins, but nothing at all about her being pregnant. My God. Were they sure?"

"Pretty sure. But I need to hear it from her. Do you know where she is now?"

"Just a minute." Jane accessed the files in her computer. "Goldthwaite, Texas," she said.

"Is that her home?"

"I don't know. She has a job at the county courthouse there."

"Maybe someone owed the senator a favor," Hartnett said. "I guess I'll have to drive down there."

"There are a few more things you should know," Jane said. "Ramona saw quite a few men, as I'm sure you've heard."

"I've heard."

"Well, one of them was Senator Wilkins, as Tanya told you. But another one was Ron Matson."

"Are you sure about that?"

"No. It's just one of the rumors I've heard. Why?"

"The cops seem to think that Matson's sexual orientation was a little different from that."

"I never heard that. You know how cops are. If a man ever admits to having seen a foreign film or doesn't chew tobacco, they think—"

She looked at Hartnett and felt herself blushing. "Now I'm the one who didn't mean something the way it sounded," she said.

"I saw a foreign film once," he said. "*Fistful of Dollars.* Made in Spain. I don't chew tobacco, though."

"I'm sorry. I—"

Hartnett smiled. "Never mind. Why don't we just say that cops aren't the only people who're guilty of stereotyping and let it go at that?"

"Sounds good to me." Jane couldn't believe she was so flustered. She wished she knew what was happening to her. "But what about Ron Matson?"

"Who's to say he didn't swing both ways? Did you know him very well?"

"Not well at all. He was in and out of Senator Wilkins's office a lot, and I occasionally saw him in the hallway, but he didn't often stop to talk with me." She thought about it. "There is one other thing, though."

"What?"

"He was pretty friendly with a young man who used to work as a guide. Stan had to let him go because he didn't take

226

the job seriously, but I still see him around the building now and then. I think he's a coke runner, to tell the truth."

"Todd Elton," Hartnett said.

Jane was surprised. "That's the one. How did you know about him?"

"Just a hunch. We cops have them all the time."

"I said I was sorry about that."

"Right. What else do you know about Elton?"

"Well, for one thing he supposedly shared the sexual orientation the cops implied for Ron."

"How do you know?" Hartnett said.

"Some of the guides told me. The girls. Todd never approached anyone, if that's what you mean."

"What about Stan Donald?" ·

"Stan?" Jane tried to hide her surprise. "Why would Todd approach Stan?"

"Stan's a good-looking young guy. Why not?"

"But Stan's not gay!"

"You sound pretty sure of that."

"He dates quite a bit," Jane said, too quickly she was afraid, though Hartnett didn't seem to notice. "I think he's even dated a few of the guides."

She realized that she was telling the truth, though Stan had not dated anyone recently, not that she was aware of. She thought she knew the reason for that.

"He is quite attractive," she added, for some reason.

"I don't think he likes me very much," Hartnett said.

Jane blushed again. She hoped that Hartnett didn't notice. "I can't imagine why," she said. "You seem quite nice."

"For a cop," Hartnett said, and Jane laughed. "Listen," Hartnett went on, "it's almost time for lunch. I know it's raining, but why don't we go somewhere for a quick bite?"

He couldn't believe he'd said it. He hadn't asked a woman to eat lunch, or to do anything else, with him in years. Besides, he was in the middle of a murder investigation. He

227

didn't have time to go running off for lunch with a woman he hardly knew.

Jane didn't know what to say. For a moment she just sat there.

"I know you have a lot of work to do," Hartnett said, getting to his feet. "I'll just—"

"No," Jane said. "Wait. I'd love to go with you." It was true, though she wasn't sure why. Texas Rangers weren't generally high on her list of favorite people. Nor were people who wore boots and cowboy hats.

There she went, stereotyping people again. This Texas Ranger wasn't exactly what she had expected. It was time she started trying to change some of her misconceptions about people, and lunch would be a good time to start.

She worried briefly about what Stan would say, but she told herself that he would understand. It was just part of an investigatory interview, after all. A question-and-answer session that was moving from one location to another. That was all there was to it, wasn't it?

"Just let me get my coat and my umbrella," she said.

Stan Donald watched them go with a murderous look.

"What's the matter, Stan?" Tanya said. She was looking forward to her own lunch hour in a few minutes, when she would slip away to join Craig Shaw, who had waved at her on his way to the basement. "You look like you just swallowed something that tasted really bad."

"It's nothing," Stan said. "I don't feel very well today. I think it's something I ate."

"Well, don't forget that Ms. Kettler won't be around to deal with the press for a while. There're going to be reporters all over this place in a little while, I bet."

She had a point. Two murders in two days would have the local paper and the television stations out in force. Well, Stan could handle that. Just route them downstairs and let them worry about keeping out of one another's way. That part of it wasn't his problem.

The Ranger was his problem, though. Maybe going to lunch was a standard interrogation technique, but Stan doubted it. And he didn't like it, not one little bit. After all this time, he was making real progress with Jane, and now the Ranger had to meddle in. It wouldn't have been so bad if she'd gone to lunch with someone else. Even a senator would have been better than a Ranger.

Stan was sorry now for some of the things he'd said to Jane. He'd thought their relationship had developed to the point that he could trust her, but now he had to wonder.

It just wasn't fair.

Governor A. Michael Newton, wearing pajamas and a silk lounging robe, lay on his bed and watched the raindrops slide down the window. He had been there ever since the news of the second murder reached the governor's mansion.

As soon as he heard about Ron Matson's death, he arranged for his private jet to take his wife to Dallas to visit her mother, called his three most trusted men together, and barricaded himself in the bedroom.

Jess sat in a chair in front of the door, his coat off, a 9mm automatic in his shoulder holster. He was reading a *Spiderman* comic book.

Marvin was by the window, looking out over the lawn to make sure that no one was trying to slip through the shrubbery and into the house. An Uzi, looking almost like a child's toy, dangled from his left hand.

Trey Buford, who was very uncomfortable with all this open display of weaponry, was sitting by the bed trying to talk sense to the governor.

He wasn't doing much good. Newton wasn't in the mood to listen to sense.

"It's the agriculture commissioner, isn't it?" Newton said.

"I knew that son of a bitch was out to get me, but I never thought he'd go this far."

"I don't really think that Kyle Landry is trying to kill anyone," Buford said.

In fact, Agriculture Commissioner Landry was one of the least likely murderers Buford could think of. The commissioner was a fiery campaigner and a man who fought tooth and nail for the things he believed in. But only in the political sense. In all other ways, Laundry was quite mild mannered.

"I didn't mean he was trying it personally," Newton said. "Son of a bitch wouldn't have the balls. But he'd hire a hit man. He could afford it, all right, and that'd be just his style. Get someone else to do his dirty work."

One thing Newton resented about Landry, Buford knew, was that Landry was almost as rich as Newton was. A lot of the state's farmers resented that, too. They thought that Landry was a man whose background was not fitting for the office he held, and they had been trying to oust him for years.

The main reason for their opposition, however, was not Landry's wealth but his strong stand against insecticides that were harmful both to man and to the environment.

A great many of the farmers didn't want to hear about things like that. They just wanted the damn bugs to stay off their crops and to hell with human or environmental consequences. It didn't matter that Landry had miles of scientific data to prove that insects quickly became resistant to insecticides and that crops averaged about the same no matter whether insecticides were used or not.

Some of the farmers didn't want to hear *that,* either. They wanted Landry's ass out of office.

They couldn't get him out, however. Somehow, he kept on getting elected, even in the year the farm lobby ran ten different candidates against him in the hopes he'd get lost in the crowd.

There were now rumors that the lobby was trying to get

a former quarterback for the Dallas Cowboys, who was not a farmer by any stretch of the imagination, to run against Landry in the next election. Because Kyle Landry had the same last name as the only head coach the Cowboys ever fired, there were those who thought a race between the quarterback and Landry would be one of the more entertaining in the state's history. So far, however, the possibility of such a campaign had not advanced beyond the rumor stage.

Governor Newton's part in all this was that he had taken the farmers' side, though not because he agreed with them. He just didn't like Landry, maybe because of the money, maybe for other reasons.

But whatever it was, he had made enemies of a lot of people when he tried to get the agriculture commissioner's job changed from an elected position to an appointed one.

He had the wholehearted support of the farmers, but the scheme hadn't worked, and Newton had only made things worse by his reply to a reporter who had asked him about the pesticide issue.

"I don't know what people are so worried about pesticides for," Newton said. "They're all going to die of something or other anyhow, sooner or later."

Buford often thought that it was lucky Newton had not counted on his sensitivity to get him elected governor in the first place.

"That man that was killed, Ron Matson," Buford said. "He didn't look a thing like you, Governor. And he was killed in the basement men's room in the Capitol. Have you ever even been in that men's room?"

Newton turned his head on the pillow so that he could see Buford better. "What difference does that make?"

Buford took a deep breath and let it out slowly. He looked at Jess and Marvin. They had taken no interest in the conversation. Jess was still reading the comic book, his lips moving slowly. Marvin was still staring out the window, though Bu-

231

ford knew there was nothing to see out there other than wet grass and trees.

"There was a woman killed, then a man," Buford said. "Neither one of them had any connection with you that anyone can see. I think you're worrying yourself needlessly about this. I think you should get up, get dressed, and make some kind of statement to the media about the murders. Let the people of the state know that their governor is on the job and concerned about state employees, that he's doing everything he can to ensure their safety, and that he's ready and waiting for the session that starts next week."

"It could be the state employees, all right," Newton said, turning his face to the ceiling and ignoring everything that Buford had said except the one thing that suited his obsession. "They haven't gotten a raise since I've been in office, have they?"

"No," Buford said. "They haven't."

"What about that Ranger? Have you talked to him today? Is he on the job?"

"I haven't talked to him," Buford said. "But he's on the job. You can count on the Rangers."

It was probably a good thing that A. Michael Newton could not see Ray Hartnett at that moment, since the Ranger's devotion to his job was in serious jeopardy. He was much more interested in Jane Kettler, for the time being, than he was in finding out who had killed Ron Matson.

Hartnett was surprised at himself. He had never before let someone distract him from an investigation, but he was sure that his distraction was only a temporary aberration. Right after lunch, he told himself, he would be back on the job.

They were at a small restaurant a few blocks down Congress Avenue from the Capitol, having walked there in the rain, both of them crowded under Jane's small red umbrella. They knew they would most likely not be able to find a parking place any nearer to the restaurant than where their cars already were, so the walk seemed like a good idea. It wasn't raining very hard.

As they walked, Hartnett found it very disturbing to be so close to a woman, though not disturbing in an unpleasant way. He wondered why he hadn't tried to get close to one sooner, and he thought that he was guilty of letting his job take over his life. Maybe he should do something about that. Or maybe he already had.

Jane was, if anything, more confused than Hartnett. She found that she liked him very much, but at the same time she found herself thinking about Stan. She had known it was a terrible mistake to get involved with someone at work, and now she was finding out a new reason why. Stan was going to be very hurt if she ditched him for a Texas Ranger.

She smiled at the thought. How could she ditch someone whom she really had established no relationship with? They had gone out and had Mexican food, for God's sake. What did that mean? That they were engaged?

And how could she ditch Stan for Ray when they hadn't even done so much as have dinner? She really was getting crazy in her old age.

Not that she was old. Far from it. Still a few years away from fifty, and fifty was not old these days. There were lots of sexy women who were even older than fifty. Why did she keep thinking about things like that?

The inside of the restaurant was "rustic," with rough wooden floors and walls. It was crowded, loud, and very warm, almost steamy after the weather outside. Jane shook her umbrella, folded it, and looked around for a place to sit.

"Why don't we just go through the line?" Hartnett said. "Soup and a salad sounds good to me, and I like the cornbread here."

"I like the cornbread, too," Jane said.

They got trays and served themselves cafeteria style, and

before too long they were seated at a table surrounded on all sides by other talking, gesturing, chewing diners.

It was not exactly an intimate situation, but it did give them a kind of privacy. There was not much likelihood that anyone at another table could hear what they were discussing. Hartnett, trying to keep things on a professional plane, brought up Sandy Harrelson again.

"She was a quiet girl," Jane said. "But very pretty. I thought for a while that Stan was interested in her, but then I heard that she was involved with Senator Wilkins."

Hartnett buttered his cornbread. "That's not going to do the senator any good if it comes out. If he really got her pregnant and got her to have an abortion, his credibility is going to be zero."

"Yes, especially since he's supposed to be pushing that anti-abortion bill in this session. And now Ron Matson's been killed. I'd say the opposition will be delighted."

"How well do you know Wilkins?"

Jane dipped into her soup. Steam rose up out of the bowl. The soup was still too hot to eat. She didn't want to burn her mouth. "In my job I have to deal with all the senators. I knew him as well as any of them."

"What does that mean?" Hartnett said. He took a bite of his cornbread.

"He's an honest man, after his fashion. Why?" She didn't feel much like explaining just what that fashion was, but Hartnett seemed to know what she meant.

"I know he represents his district well. But I was wondering if he could be involved in these murders. First Ramona Gonzalez, a woman he's fooling around with on the sly, then his aide. There has to be a connection."

"Are you saying he killed them?"

"No. I was just wondering what you thought."

"I don't know. I don't like to think anyone I know could

234

do something like that. The man's a state senator, after all. He has so much to lose."

"He's also a married man. That didn't stop him from going out with young women and getting at least one of them pregnant, maybe two of them."

Jane nodded. "I know you're right. I just don't like to think of things like that. I guess in your line of work you have to, though."

"You won't hold that against me, will you?" Hartnett said, wondering why the second it was out of his mouth.

Jane smiled. "No," she said. "I won't."

"Good," Hartnett said. "How about some warm gingerbread for dessert?"

"Fine," Jane said. She liked the gingerbread, too.

TWENTY-FOUR

Craig Shaw wasn't getting anywhere questioning Claude and Darrel until the Cowboy spoke up. The cops had let the reporter look at the crime scene and the body, but they weren't very forthcoming about anything that had happened.

The Cowboy, meanwhile, had remembered why he came to the men's room in the first place, and he was having difficulty standing still. He shifted from one leg to the other, but the cops didn't pay him any attention.

"Hey," he said. "I got to go in there and use the toilet. How about it?"

"You should've thought about that sooner," Darrel said. "Now you'll just have to wait until the locals take you off our hands."

"Hey, man, what the hell? You can't turn me over to them guys. I didn't do anything."

"What are they holding you for?" Shaw said.

"You don't have to talk to this man," Darrel said.

"You a reporter?" the Cowboy said.

Shaw nodded.

236

"Well, I'm getting a bum rap here. I'm a country and western singer. All I wanted was to take a shit, and now they won't let me in there. That's against the Constitution. Besides, these two let the killer get away. They shot at him, but they missed."

"What's he talking about?" Shaw said, looking at Claude and Darrel.

"Don't look at me," Claude said. "I didn't shoot at anybody."

Asshole, Darrel thought.

"I guess that leaves you then," Shaw told Darrel. "Want to tell me what's going on?"

"A suspect was fleeing the scene," Darrel said. "I drew my sidearm, and it discharged accidentally." That was what he'd put on the report, anyway. "The suspect escaped, and the local police were notified."

"Was this 'suspect' identified?" Shaw said.

"We know him, all right," Darrel said. "He's a transient, like the Cowboy here."

"Hey, I ain't no transient. I'm a singer. I'm just between engagements right now."

"Sure you are," Claude said. "And that's why you live on the streets. You better just shut up, Cowboy."

The Cowboy shut up, but not because Claude told him to. He shut up because his feelings were hurt. One of these days he'd hear from Nashville, cut a hit, and then those stupid cops would be calling him and begging him for an autograph or a free ticket to his next show, which they damn sure wouldn't get. He'd be bigger than Charley Pride ever thought about. Then those damn cops'd be sorry for the way they'd treated him.

"So you're expecting an arrest at any time," Shaw said to Prince. "What about any connection between this murder and the murder of Ramona Gonzalez? Is it possible that the same person is guilty of both?"

"That's my theory," Darrel said. "The same man was in the building when Ms. Gonzalez was killed."

If he couldn't catch the Wagger, which he hadn't given up on doing by any means, he could at least get his name in the paper and claim credit for being the first to suspect Wayne as long as the Cowboy had blurted out about the firing of the pistol.

The Ranger didn't think Wayne was the guilty one, but Darrel was still betting on him. The Ranger would also probably not appreciate it one bit that Darrel had told the reporter about Wayne, but that was tough shit. If the Ranger wanted to get his say-so in the news, he should have been there.

"I don't suppose you want to reveal the suspect's name?" Shaw said.

"I don't know his name," Prince said. "Not his real name."

"What about a photo?"

"I doubt he's had any taken in a long time, if ever. If we don't get him soon, we can have a drawing made, though."

Shaw wanted to ask more, but at that point the crime-scene investigating team arrived, followed shortly by the TV news teams and the local reporters. Craig left the two Capitol policemen to them and went to interview the boys who had entered the men's room as the Cowboy was leaving it. Good human interest.

After that, he thought he could slip off with Tanya for a quick lunch and then he would write his story.

But what kind of story would he write? The fleeing suspect was a new wrinkle, and while Shaw couldn't rid himself of the idea that Senator Wilkins was somehow involved in things, he didn't want to go too far and open himself up to a libel suit, not that the paper's lawyers would ever let it go that far.

He decided that it might be best to hedge his bet at first by mentioning the suspect while implying that there was also a relationship of some unspecified kind between Ramona Gonzalez and Senator Wilkins. That would be enough, until he got some more solid information.

Maybe Tanya would have some more to tell him.

Todd Elton ate a simple lunch: tuna out of the can, lettuce, whole wheat bread. He believed in taking care of himself, not eating too much fat or sugar, getting good nutrition. He did worry a little bit about the dolphins getting themselves caught with the tuna as he took a bite. He thought a public-spirited person such as himself should think about things like that, though he didn't let it hinder his appetite.

After lunch he called his clients back and explained what had happened earlier. Everyone understood. He told them that he would meet them that night in the members' lounge in the House about an hour before the Capitol closed. They were all respected citizens who had a right to be there then.

Then he called the tour desk and asked to speak with Stan Donald. There was some unfinished business there, thanks to that Texas Ranger who had interrupted them that morning.

"I'm glad you called," Stan said. "I'm afraid I didn't treat you very well earlier."

"That's exactly what I was calling about. I don't like being pushed around."

"I said I was sorry. Look, maybe we could have a drink or something."

Todd was surprised but gratified. "That's a thought. I've got some business in the building tonight, but why don't we go out later? Talk over old times, have a few laughs."

Stan sounded a bit reluctant, as if he hadn't really expected Todd to take him up on his invitation. "Well, I guess we could do that."

Todd wasn't about to let him off the hook. "Sure we can. You aren't ashamed to be seen with a professional man, are you?"

Stan didn't say anything.

"I know you're supposed to be a fucking boy scout," Todd said. "But you and I have a few things to talk over."

"What things?"

"I'll tell you when I see you. How about nine o'clock, at the tour desk?"

"All right. I guess."

"You know it is. I'll meet you there."

Todd hung up thinking how easy it all was. Before long, he was going to have Stan Donald off his case.

Permanently.

Ray Hartnett kept Jane Kettler at lunch longer than he had intended, mainly because they had begun talking about a lot of things that did not relate at all to the investigation of the two murders.

He found out that she liked old movies, chocolate, and watching baseball on TV. He told her that he liked some of the same things, though chocolate didn't appeal to him. He was allergic to it.

"You do know who Humphrey Bogart is, though, don't you?" she said.

"Are you kidding me? I've seen *The Big Sleep* twenty times. When I was a kid, I wanted to be Philip Marlowe."

"Well?" she said.

"Being a Texas Ranger's not quite the same thing." Hartnett thought about that for a second. "It's even better," he said. "I liked John Wayne, too. He played a Ranger in *The Comancheros*."

"Kris Kristofferson played a Ranger, too," Jane said. "In some TV movie with Willie Nelson."

"TV movies aren't like the real thing," Hartnett said. "They'd never make something like *Casablanca* for TV. Or if they did, they'd screw it up."

"Casablanca," Jane said. "You know, you're all right, for

240

a cop. Do you know who Paul Anka is? And I don't mean the Paul Anka who sang 'Having My Baby,' either."

"You mean the one who sang 'You Are My Destiny' and 'Lonely Boy?' "

"You know who he is, all right. How old are you, Ray?"

It was the first time she had called him by his given name. "Forty-eight," he said.

"Just—" Jane stopped herself. She had been about to say "just right."

" 'Just' what?" Hartnett said.

"Just about the same age I am."

"I'd never have guessed." Jesus, how corny could he get? Well, what the hell? He'd just have to make the best of it. "Does that make a difference?"

"I don't know," Jane said. And she didn't. She was getting more confused than ever. She was going to have to have a talk with Stan. Maybe that would clear things up.

Or maybe it wouldn't.

When they got back to the Capitol, Hartnett did not go back to Jane's office. He went directly to see Senator Wilkins.

There was no one in the outer office, so Hartnett went on back to the inner door and knocked.

"Who's there?" Wilkins called.

"Ray Hartnett, Texas Rangers. I have to talk to you, Senator."

There was a short silence. "Very well," Wilkins said finally. "Come in."

Hartnett opened the door. Wilkins was sitting at his desk. There was no one else in the room.

"I'm sorry if this is a bad time, Senator," Hartnett said. "I suspect that you know why I'm here."

"I'm sure it's about Ron's death, Mr. Hartnett," Wilkins said. "Won't you have a seat?"

Wilkins's chairs were large, comfortable, and covered in red leather. Hartnett sat down.

"It's about more than Matson," Hartnett said when he had settled himself. "It's also about Ramona Gonzalez. And about a young woman named Sandy Harrelson."

Although the mention of Ramona did not seem to affect Wilkins, the name of Sandy Harrelson startled him. "You know about her?"

"Yes," Hartnett said. "I know about her."

"She's all right, isn't she?"

"As far as I know, she is," Hartnett said. "But you have to admit that knowing you hasn't been very healthy lately."

Wilkins sighed and sank back in his chair. "I'm well aware of that," he said.

"Were you and Matson aware that Ramona Gonzalez was pregnant?" Hartnett said, hoping to keep Wilkins off balance, keep him from assuming the "I am a state senator, and even you can't fuck with me" pose that many lawmakers would have adopted almost immediately in dealing with a lawman, even with a Texas Ranger.

"My God, no. I wasn't. I can't speak for Ron."

Neither can he, Hartnett thought. "Did you know that Matson had been seeing Ramona Gonzalez?" he said.

"No. No. Are you certain about that? I never—what are you trying to do to me, sir? What are you saying these things for?"

"I'm saying them because they're true, and they're part of a murder investigation in which you're about to become involved very deeply."

Wilkins pulled out his handkerchief and wiped his face. "Are you saying, then, that I'm a suspect?" He put the handkerchief away.

"Let's just say that you might have had what you thought was good reason to kill both of them. You managed to keep Sandy Harrelson quiet, maybe by getting her a good job in local government, but what about Ramona Gonzalez? What if she wouldn't be bought off? Maybe you could say your aide was the one who got her pregnant, and now that he's been killed there'd be no one to testify against you. You might even be able to pull it off, if the Harrelson woman didn't come forward as a character witness against you."

Hartnett didn't really believe that Wilkins didn't know about Matson and Gonzalez, and the scenario he had outlined was certainly a possibility. He wondered just how Wilkins would respond to it. It wouldn't be the first time that someone had resorted to murder to keep his secret life from becoming known to everyone.

For a time, Wilkins didn't respond at all. He just sat at his desk staring at his hands, which rested in front of him. Then he picked up a piece of paper and held it up so that Hartnett could see it.

"Do you know what this is?" Wilkins said.

"No," Hartnett said. "It just looks like a piece of paper to me."

Wilkins almost smiled. "It's that, of course. And it's a lot more. It's something I wrote, Mr. Hartnett, and if I may say so, I never wrote anything that came harder."

"Does it have anything to do with the murders?" Hartnett found himself wondering if Wilkins had actually written a confession. It would certainly make things easier if he had. The governor would be very happy. Hartnett would probably even get a commendation.

"You can wipe that pleased look off your face," Wilkins said. "It's not what you seem to think it is."

"What is it then?"

"It's my letter of resignation from office," Wilkins said. He put the paper down. "I'm hoping that you, and others like you, will let me leave with some small shred of dignity."

"Others like me?" Hartnett couldn't think of anyone else who would have been questioning the senator. Prince and

Hebert wouldn't have the nerve. Maybe he meant the news-papers. "Who are you talking about?"

"Have you ever met the head of our maintenance service?" Wilkins said. "A glorified janitor, but he has an elevated sense of his own importance."

"Clinton Amory," Hartnett said. He didn't like it at all that Wilkins was comparing him with the likes of Amory.

"That's the man," Wilkins said.

"All right. What about him?"

Wilkins closed his eyes and pinched the bridge of his nose. Then he looked at Hartnett. "Amory came to my office early this morning. He knew about my . . . relationship with Miss Gonzalez. He threatened to go to the press if I didn't show my . . . appreciation for him."

"Blackmail?" Hartnett said.

"I wouldn't put it that strongly. He didn't ask for money or anything else, not exactly. He just said that his birthday was just around the corner. That he would appreciate a nice gift."

"What did you tell him?"

"I told him that I'd think about it."

Hartnett snorted in disgust.

"I know," Wilkins said. "I was weak, scared. I shouldn't have done it."

"Damn right you shouldn't."

"It's even worse than I've told you. Amory came back, only a few minutes ago. He said something about what you were saying, that Ron had also been seeing Ramona. Then he said that he really was looking forward to his birthday. That money was always an appropriate gift."

"I'll have a little talk with Amory," Hartnett said.

"I suspect that there will be others," Wilkins said. "They won't be after money, but they'll be after my ass."

"So that's why you wrote the letter."

"That is correct."

"It won't make any difference," Hartnett said. "Not to the

244

investigation. You're a part of it now, whether you like it or not. I'm surprised the reporters haven't been to see you already."

"Oh, they have. I just didn't answer the door."

"I can do something about Amory. But not about the reporters. And not about your involvement. You were involved with both the victims. You're a natural suspect."

"I'm a senator," Wilkins said.

"That doesn't make any difference," Hartnett said. "I could be wrong, but I don't think the people hold their elected representatives in very high regard these days. They're not going to cut you any slack."

Especially when it comes out that you're a world-class hypocrite, Hartnett added to himself, though he knew better than to say it aloud.

"I have a feeling you could be right," Wilkins said. "That's why I'm resigning. I don't want to tarnish the office any more than I have. And I'd appreciate it if you didn't mention anything about Sandra Harrelson. She married a fine young man in Goldthwaite, and they're expecting a baby in a few months, I'm told. I'm sure being reminded of me would be the worst thing that could happen to her. And to her marriage."

Hartnett had to give the man credit. He was making a clever move; he might even be sincere. Either way, he was going to be able to get whatever public sympathy existed.

"How much of what you've told me does the press know?" Wilkins said.

"Probably not very much," Hartnett said.

"And how much do they have to know?"

Hartnett gave it some thought. "That all depends. I'm not going to tell them anything, if that's what you mean. They'll have to find it out on their own."

"Do you know a reporter named Craig Shaw?"

"No," Hartnett said.

"He's been here today, too. He came before I found out about Ron's death. He already knows about my involvement with Miss Gonzalez, though I denied it to him. He might be able to find out the rest."

"But by the time he does, you will have resigned?"

"Correct."

"That won't change what I'm looking for. I think you're doing the right thing, but it won't help you one bit if you're guilty of those murders."

"I didn't kill anyone," Wilkins said.

Hartnett almost believed him, but then he remembered that Wilkins was a politician.

" 'Read my lips,' " Hartnett said.

"That has nothing to do with my actions," Wilkins said.

"It seems a lot the same to me. Say one thing, but do another."

"I can understand your feeling that way. You have a perfect right. But I didn't kill anyone."

Hartnett would have felt better if Wilkins were not behaving so reasonably. He'd been off balance at first, but then he'd gathered himself and now he was in complete control again. It was a good ability for a politician to have.

"I'm not saying you did kill anyone," Hartnett told him. "I'm just saying that your letter won't influence the way the investigation is carried out."

"I wouldn't expect it to. I only hope that you haven't made up your mind already about my guilt."

"I haven't done that," Hartnett said.

"Very well. I suppose that I can't ask for more. Is there anything I can tell you that might help my case?"

"For one thing, you could tell me where you were last night and the night before."

"I'm afraid that won't help me much. I was at home. Alone. I called my wife early, then watched television until about half-past ten. I always go to bed after the local news."

"I was hoping you'd have a better alibi than that."

"As I said, not much help."

"All right then," Hartnett said. "You can tell me who else would have a motive for killing Ron Matson."

"No one," Wilkins said. "He wasn't the kind to make enemies. He was friendly with everyone."

"Did you know that he was rumored to be homosexual?"

"Jesus Christ, no." Wilkins looked involuntarily at the letter he had written.

"I don't know that it's true," Hartnett said. "I've heard that he might have been involved with a man named Todd Elton."

"I don't believe I've heard of Elton. Did he ever work in the Capitol?"

"Are you sure you never had any dealings with him?" Hartnett had chosen the word "dealings" deliberately, but it didn't seem to strike a chord with the senator.

"No, I didn't know him. Ron never mentioned him. Surely it's not true about the two of them."

"That's something I'll find out," Hartnett said. "Along with the rest of it."

"I hope you do," Wilkins said. "I really hope you do."

Hartnett stayed with the senator for a few minutes longer, asking about Ramona Gonzalez, but he didn't learn anything of value. It appeared that Wilkins was either really innocent or an expert at hiding his true feelings. If Wilkins had been anything other than a politician, Hartnett probably would have eliminated him as a suspect then and there.

"Thank you for your help, Senator," Hartnett said, rising from the red-leather chair. "I'll go have a little talk with Amory now."

"Thank you. And I hope you'll catch whoever is responsible for these horrible murders."

"I will," Hartnett said. "Trust me."

After the Ranger left the office, Wilkins looked for a long time at the letter he had composed.

He knew that he had not told the whole truth in the letter, though he had admitted to indiscretions with women. He knew that he had been less than honest in his association with Hap Reatherford as well, but he hadn't mentioned that.

He had thought that taking the money and allowing himself to be swayed on issues that were of no seeming consequence to his own district was doing no harm to anyone, but now he saw his rationalization as the worst form of self-deception.

Or maybe he was wrong. Maybe there were things that were worse.

He took out his handkerchief and wiped his forehead. Then he looked at the handkerchief for a second or two before folding it and replacing it in his jacket pocket.

There was no easy way out of the mess he was in, but the letter might be the best for everyone. It might even get him off the hook.

Suzimae could type it in the morning. Until then, he had done all he could.

TWENTY-FIVE

Amory didn't have a toothpick in his mouth. Hartnett almost didn't recognize him.

"Hello, Amory," he said, standing in the doorway of the small office. "I hear you've been busy today."

"Yeah, I'm busy all the time." Amory wasn't going to be intimidated by some damn lawman, even if he was a Texas Ranger. "What's the trouble?"

"You are," Hartnett said.

Amory reached into his pocket and came out with a toothpick that he stuck between his teeth. "Huh?" he said. "I don't get it."

"You've been to see Senator Wilkins today, haven't you?"

"Yeah. So what?" Amory's mind was racing. Surely the senator wouldn't have the nerve to tell the Ranger what Amory had talked to him about.

"He says you put the squeeze on him. Offered to keep quiet about what you knew if he'd play along, give you a little something."

Fucking Wilkins, Amory thought. It just went to show that you couldn't trust a politician.

Amory removed his toothpick and tried to look innocent. "He must've been kidding. I just said my birthday was coming along. Sometimes the senators like to remember us outstanding supervisors here when it's a birthday or something like that."

"Just a simple misunderstanding, is that what you're telling me?" Hartnett said.

"You got it. A misunderstanding. That's what it was."

"Sure it was. And I'm Tom Cruise." Hartnett stepped across the small room and leaned down, placing his hands on Amory's desk and putting his face close to the other man's. "You're a fucking liar, Amory. You're lying about what you said to Wilkins, and you lied to me earlier about what Ramona Gonzalez had discussed with you. And I'm pretty sure you're not an 'outstanding supervisor.' You're just a cheap crook."

Amory pulled back as far as he could, which was only about an inch before his chair hit the wall behind him. "Hey, wait a minute. I didn't do anything wrong."

"The hell you didn't. You think it's all right to lie to a Texas Ranger?"

"Maybe I remembered some stuff after you left," Amory said. "Yeah. That's it. I remembered it after you left. I would've told you if you'd come back by."

Hartnett straightened up. "Sure you would. That's why you went to talk to Wilkins. Because I hadn't come back by and you didn't know where to find me."

"I just thought the senator might appreciate it if he knew I had some information he could use. That's all it was." Amory smiled a crooked smile and replaced his toothpick, convinced that he was going to get by again.

"Right," Hartnett said. "You know, Amory, I wouldn't be surprised if you weren't the one who killed those two."

Amory grabbed the toothpick and pulled it out again.

"Wait just a damn minute. You can't talk to me like that. I never killed anybody."

"Maybe not. But the dead woman was found in a hamper that you would have known about. She seems to have been fairly promiscuous. Maybe you were fooling around with her, too, and got jealous of Wilkins and Matson. So you killed her."

"Bullshit. Nothing like that ever happened."

"If it did, I'll find out. She probably told Matson about you, so you knew you had to get rid of him, too. Otherwise he might have gone to the police."

"Goddamnit, you can't say things like that! You make it sound like I'm really the one that killed them. I didn't have anything to do with it!"

"We'll see. If I were you, I wouldn't be going around to anyone making insinuations about what you know about the murders, though. You could get yourself in even worse trouble than you're in already."

"I'm not in trouble! I—"

"You're in trouble, all right, whether you know it or not. Can you prove your whereabouts for the last two nights?"

"Hell, yes, I can. I was at home."

"Who else was there?"

"My wife," Amory said, slipping the toothpick back between his teeth. "She'll tell you."

"You don't really think her testimony will mean a thing, do you? Like you said, she's your wife. Is there anyone else who can back up her testimony?"

"No, but—"

"So there you are, in deep shit. I'd be very careful if I were you, Amory. Very careful." Hartnett turned abruptly and left the office. When he was outside, he looked back and said, "I'll be seeing you again, Amory. Don't go and do anything stupid."

Hartnett walked away down the hall.

Amory's toothpick was quivering as if it had a life of its own.

Craig Shaw was disappointed in his lunch with Tanya.

Not in the food. They had driven to the Dirty's near the UT campus. Dirty's was a tradition in Austin, as well as having the best burgers in town, the old-fashioned kind.

So the food wasn't the disappointment. The disappointment was that Tanya didn't have much more to tell him, though she did mention being interviewed by the Texas Ranger. And she mentioned Sandy Harrelson.

"You didn't tell me about her last night," Shaw said.

"Well, I didn't think that had anything to do with the murder," Tanya said.

"It might, or it might not," Shaw said. "But it shows a behavior pattern that Wilkins's constituents wouldn't be happy with, to say the least. You're sure he tried to get her to have an abortion?"

"That's what Sandy said. He paid for it, and she went to San Antonio and had one. She didn't want anything to connect her to him."

"You wouldn't happen to know where she's living now, would you?"

"No, but I think Chrissy might have her address. I think Sandy's married now, though, and she doesn't want her husband to find out about the abortion."

Shaw took the last bite of his burger and wiped his mouth with a napkin. "I may need her address later," he said. "She might tell me something."

The story was getting better. Senator Wilkins might deny knowing Ramona Gonzalez, but here was one thing he might not be able to get out of. If only Sandy Harrelson would confirm what Tanya had told Shaw, the paper would be much more likely to allow the references to Wilkins and

Gonzalez, even if the information was supported only by unnamed sources.

Shaw smiled and lit up a Winston. Wilkins was going to be in deep shit.

Wayne the Wagger was snuggled up in the doorway of the University Baptist Church.

The norther had blown through, taking the rain with it and leaving behind a brilliant clear blue sky and plenty of sun. The only trouble was that the temperature was still dropping—it had to be into the middle thirties by now—and the wind was still whipping along about twenty-five or thirty miles an hour. Bits of paper scratched down the sidewalk and occasionally blew into the doorway.

The wind wasn't bothering Wayne too much at the moment, however. He was fairly well protected by the side of the doorway and by all the layers of clothing he was wearing, especially the fashionable plastic garbage bag.

He was worried about the coming night, though. If the sky stayed clear, and it almost certainly would, it was going to get really cold, probably drop down into the twenties. He was going to have to get back to the Capitol.

He wasn't worried about getting picked up by the cops, not any longer. No one had shown any interest in him since his arrival in the doorway, and by now he couldn't really remember why anyone would be looking for him in the first place.

It had something to do with a rest room, but that was about all he could recall. He thought hard about it, and two faces came back to him, but he couldn't remember which was the dead man and which was the other one.

The other one. He didn't want to think about that one at all. He was the one who had done something really bad.

What the bad thing was, exactly, Wayne couldn't quite pin down, but it was so scary that just thinking about whatever it was made Wayne need to take a piss, and he couldn't do that, not until he got back to the Capitol. The church wasn't open, so he couldn't go in there, and there weren't any public rest rooms around that he knew about.

He could just whip out right there, he supposed, cold as it was, but then he thought about the cannon. Better to stay zipped up. People got really mad at you when you pissed out in public these days.

Wayne leaned back against the church door and closed his eyes. Soon, in spite of the cold, he was dreaming about the old days, the days when the drag had been crowded with long-haired men and women who would share their drugs and their friendship with someone like Wayne. When he had been a part of things instead of just someone that people treated like a piece of trash that the wind blew into their path on the street. Things had been a lot better then for Wayne, a lot better.

But that had been a long time ago.

Jane Kettler was at her desk trying to get some work done. It wasn't easy. She kept thinking about how much she liked Ray Hartnett, and about Stan. She couldn't get her feelings sorted out. It was almost like being back in high school again.

On the one hand, Stan was young, attractive, intelligent, and obviously very interested in her. It was really quite flattering when she thought about it, considering all the young women who must be dying to go out with someone like Stan. In fact, she knew that he had gone out with quite a few of them, though not for some time now. It flattered her to think that he had dropped them because of his interest in her.

On the other hand, there was Ray Hartnett, more mature, more her age, and a very nice, very interesting, man. There was more to his appeal than that, too, she realized. There was something about him that she liked, something that was almost indefinable. It was an air he had, an air of almost old-fashioned integrity, as if he were somehow incorruptible. In that way, he reminded her of her husband, and she couldn't quite make up her mind whether that was good or bad. She didn't want to be taking old memories to bed with her when—

She shook her head and looked down at the paperwork scattered on her desk. What on earth could she possibly be thinking about? Now she had poor Ray practically seduced and in her bedroom, all because they'd had lunch together. Maybe someone had been slipping some kind of hormone pills in her drinking water.

Not that taking him to bed was such a bad idea. She hadn't slept with a man in so long that she'd almost forgotten what it was like.

She shook her head. That was a lie. She remembered, all right. She just didn't like to torture herself with thinking about it. Maybe she wouldn't be good at it now, though. Maybe she never had been good. What would a young man, Stan, say, want with an old woman who wasn't any good in bed?

Good Lord, she was doing it again. This time with Stan. It was going to be very crowded in her bedroom if this kept up.

She smiled. Time to get to work. It was just possible that she wouldn't see either one of them again in any capacity other than on the job or as part of a criminal investigation. She was going to have to get a grip on her runaway imagination and buckle down. Damn that Hap Reatherford, anyway. This was all his fault.

She sorted through her papers until she found the ones she was looking for, requests from lawmakers to use the pressrooms next week after the session got started. She was going to have to work out a schedule that would make everyone happy, which was of course impossible. It was just the thing to take her mind off men.

★   ★   ★

Ray Hartnett drove to his house, which was in Barton Hills, not far from Zilker Park. It was time for him to sit down and go over what he knew so far, see if he could make sense of any of it.

He liked to think of investigations as being like a jigsaw puzzle that had been dumped out onto a table. All the pieces were there, but some of them were upside down, some of them were hidden under others, and some of them were so much alike that you couldn't tell them apart. You had to go through them all, turn them over, look at each one individually, and then begin trying to fit them together.

Hartnett parked in the narrow drive, got out, and let himself in the front door of the house. He was seldom home, and when he was, he kept pretty much to himself. He didn't know any of his neighbors by their first names, and he doubted that they had any idea of what he did for a living.

That was just fine with him, or it had been up until today. For a long time now, he had been content to let his job dominate his life and not to think about the possibility that things could ever be any other way.

But talking to Jane Kettler had changed that. For the first time in quite a while he had begun wondering about what it would be like to get to know someone better, to have someone to talk to about his work and about the inconsequential things he never discussed with anyone, like the movies he had seen or the old records he could remember. And maybe he could find some new things to do and other music to listen to. The fact of the matter was that he had talked more about himself to Jane Kettler at lunch than he had told anyone else in years. And he felt good for having done so.

Maybe he was just getting old. He could be having some sort of midlife crisis, he supposed. He'd heard about such things, even witnessed one or two.

One supposedly happily married man of near fifty he had known in his DPS days had disappeared one night after getting off patrol, just gotten in his car and driven away. His wife had called the next day, looking for him. He'd never arrived at home.

He'd turned up a few months later in Fort Worth, living with a twenty-year-old community college dropout with bad teeth and big mammaries. It wasn't a case of amnesia or anything like that. It was just a case of someone having grown tired of his old life and wanting to try out something different.

The man had eventually repented, left the dropout, gone back to his wife, and tried to set things straight. Hartnett never heard how things had worked out.

He went into his bedroom and changed out of his Western-cut suit into jeans and a soft flannel shirt. He had to be comfortable to do this part of his investigation.

After he had changed, he went into the kitchen, opened his refrigerator, and got out the milk. Then he got a glass from the cabinet and filled it. There was nothing like a little milk and cookies to get the old thought processes going. He put the milk carton back in the refrigerator, then got a half-full package of Oreos from the cabinet and took it and the glass of milk over to his Formica-topped table.

He left the kitchen for a moment and came back with several pieces of blank typing paper and a pencil. Sometimes it helped to jot things down. That way he could keep everything straight, without trying to remember everything at once.

He started out by writing down the names of the obvious suspects, Wayne and Wilkins first. He didn't really believe Wayne could be the guilty one, but Wilkins was still a good possibility.

The senator appeared to be genuinely sorry about the deaths, but he was a good actor, and he wanted to save his ass. The letter of resignation was proof enough of that, if indeed it was a letter of resignation. Hartnett realized with a start that he hadn't even asked to see it. If he was getting to the point where he was actually willing to take a politician's word for something, maybe he was getting too soft for law enforcement work.

At any rate, Wilkins was still a prime suspect. Ramona Gonzalez could have threatened to let everyone know just who the father of her unborn child was unless the senator got a divorce and married her. That would be ample motive for murder right there. And if Ron Matson had been involved with her as well, her death might have moved him to make some remark to the senator about going public with his knowledge of Wilkins's affair with the dead woman. That would have given Wilkins the reason for murdering his aide.

No question about it, Wilkins was a top suspect.

So was Amory, though blackmailers usually didn't have the guts for anything involving physical action. They got their kicks in other ways. Nevertheless, the little scenario Hartnett had put together for Amory's benefit could come close to the truth, and Amory could very easily be the man Hartnett was looking for.

Then there was Claude Hebert. The guides had said that he had been involved with Ramona to some extent, a fact that Darrel Prince had neglected to mention. And Prince had said something else, something about the masking tape. The only person he had mentioned it to was Claude, so that would explain why it had been removed the second time rather than being left on the camera, not even Claude being dumb enough to make the same mistake twice, or at least not after having been warned about it.

Of course it was possible that the killer had thought of it himself, without prompting, so the missing tape wasn't that much help. It did seem to provide a positive link between the two killings, however. Not only had both victims been strangled, but tape had been placed over the cameras each time.

Or so Hartnett thought. He would have to check with the

crime-scene investigators to be sure, and to find out what else they may have located.

He needed to check with the coroner, too. The other clues were the pubic hair and the semen. By now, the semen should have provided a blood type, and the pubic hair would have given some more definite ideas about its owner's ethnicity and hair color than Hartnett had gotten the day before.

That all sounded fine, but the truth was that such clues were no good at all unless you had a suspect to match them to. By themselves they meant nothing at all. For example, if the blood type happened to show that the perpetrator of the crime had type O-positive blood, it would merely place him in the majority of the male population of the United States. Matching the blood type wasn't going to be enough. That's where the pubic hair would help, adding another link to the chain of evidence.

And then there was the tie. Something might come of that, though Hartnett doubted it. If the tie were a very recent purchase and if there were some identifying marks on it, such as a brand name, the chances would be better, but the tie wasn't anything to rely on. It might even be *Matson's* tie.

Hartnett took a big swallow of milk and ate two Oreos. It looked as if he were going to need all the energy he could get for this one.

He tried to think of other suspects. There might well be some. If Ramona Gonzalez had been romantically entangled with four men, there might have been another one. Or several others, whose names Hartnett hadn't discovered yet. Hadn't the guides hinted at that very possibility?

Hartnett wrote the word *others* on his paper and followed it with a question mark.

He stared at the paper for a minute as if that might make one of the names leap out at him, but none did.

He sighed, took another swallow of milk, and ate another cookie.

The next step was to try to establish a sequence of events as he knew them. After that he'd try to verify them and then try to fill in any blanks that were left.

He hoped he had enough cookies.

PART THREE

TWENTY-SIX

Just after five o'clock Stan Donald went into Jane Kettler's office. Zach had already left for the day, and Stan stood quietly until Jane looked up from the computer monitor.

"Hello, Stan," she said, glancing at the digital clock on her desk. "I didn't realize it was getting so late."

"I guess you had a lot of catching up to do, what with your long lunch hour," Stan said.

Jane pushed herself away from the monitor. "You sound a little upset." She found that she was secretly pleased and was a little ashamed of herself for the feeling.

"I'm not upset," Stan said. "If you want to go out with a Texas Ranger and have a long lunch date with him, I'm sure it's none of my business."

"It wasn't a date," Jane said. "He was questioning me about people who could be connected with the murders."

She felt a bit deceitful, but there was no use to upset Stan further. She was almost sure that she wouldn't be having lunch with Ray again, though she knew that she wouldn't mind if he asked her. In fact, she would jump at the chance.

"You can call it what you want." Stan's posture was rigid. "I saw the way he looked at you."

There was no question about it: Stan was jealous.

"I think you're overreacting," Jane said. "I hardly know the man."

"You don't have to know someone to feel that way about them."

"Well, I'm sure that Mr. Hartnett doesn't feel 'that way' about me. He only wanted to ask some questions, and he thought that I might feel more free to answer if we got out of the building."

"What did you tell him?"

"There wasn't much I could say. I didn't know Ron Matson that well, and Ramona didn't really talk to me." She wasn't going to go into what had been said about Senator Wilkins. Stan probably knew most of it already, but there was no need for him to discuss that information with the other tour guides.

"Did you say anything about me?"

"Of course not. I just mentioned that you told me about Ron's murder, but my personal life wasn't a part of the discussion."

Stan seemed to relax a little, though not much. "I'm glad to see that you consider me a part of your personal life."

Jane realized that what he said was true. She was already thinking of him as more important in her life than someone she dealt with only at work.

"I was hoping that we could get together again," Stan said. "Maybe tonight."

"Well, I don't know—"

"Why not? Do you have a date with the Texas Ranger?"

"You don't have to be that way, Stan. My only connection with Mr. Hartnett has to do with his murder investigation."

"Then why can't you go out with me tonight? I think we

need to talk, get a few things settled between us." His eyes behind his glasses were very sincere. "OK?"

Jane didn't have to think about it for very long. Maybe seeing Stan again so soon was a good idea; maybe it would help her clarify her feelings about him.

"All right," she said. "What time?"

"I have to do a few things first, and I have to meet someone here a little later. Could we have a late dinner? About ten?"

"That sounds fine to me. Will you pick me up?"

"Why don't you come by here? I'll meet you at the tour desk and then we can decide where to go."

That was fine with Jane. She was looking forward to a long, hot bath, and the Capitol was as good a place as any to meet Stan, being more or less centrally located.

"That's settled, then," Stan said. "I'll see you about ten."

When he went out, he seemed in a much better mood than he had been in when he entered. He was young, handsome, and reliable, so what difference did it make that he'd never seen *The Comancheros* except maybe on television and that he probably had never even heard of Paul Anka?

It did make a difference, however, and Jane knew that it did. She hoped that seeing him tonight would help her make up her mind about him one way or the other.

She was almost certain that Ray Hartnett was interested in her. She could still tell about things like that, though she was long out of practice, but he hadn't asked to see her again, hadn't even hinted at wanting to do so.

But then he was involved in investigating a murder. She couldn't expect him to drop everything and start spending his time with her. That would be foolish. Maybe after everything was taken care of, he would give her a call.

By then, however, it might be too late. She might be too committed to Stan Donald.

Well, a lot of things depended on what happened later that night. She would just have to see how things worked out. She turned back to her computer and got busy. She had to finish her work and get home. She had a big evening ahead of her.

Sam Wilkins called his wife at one minute after five. If writing the letter had been one of the hardest things he had ever done, the call was even harder.

"They're going to be saying some terrible things about me," he told his wife.

Her reply was distant and muted. It was almost as if she hadn't heard anything he told her. It was certainly as if she didn't care, and Wilkins realized that in fact she *didn't*. She had stopped caring about him years before, at just about the same time he had stopped caring about her.

"I can start practicing law again," he said. "I still have plenty of supporters. We won't suffer any."

He didn't really know whether that was the truth. A man's supporters had a way of disappearing on him when the going got tough. Still, a pretty good lawyer could always make a living, and he had been a pretty good lawyer before he got mixed up in politics.

"I'll be releasing the letter tomorrow," he said. "You'll be getting a lot of calls. Just turn on the machine and don't answer any of them."

She told him that she'd gotten a few calls already, but that she'd just said "no comment." She didn't have any idea what was going on, and she didn't want to know. She just wanted to be left alone.

Suddenly Wilkins realized that he didn't want to leave Austin. He never wanted to go home again to share the same house with his wife. He hadn't shared anything but space with her for years anyway. He wondered if he could open a practice in Austin.

Then he thought about Hap Reatherford. Now there was a man who had it made. Some of the same people who hired Reatherford might be interested in having another man around the Capitol, a man who knew the ins and outs of the legislative process, a man who knew all the senators and most of the House members by their first names.

A man like Sam Wilkins.

It was an idea well worth considering. Everything depended on how cleanly he could get out of the mess he was in. He'd been able to get rid of the newspaperman thanks to the interruption provided by Ron's death, and that Ranger had been fairly easy on him, but he couldn't expect that kind of treatment to continue.

"I've got to go now," he told his wife. "Got a lot of things to tend to."

His wife hardly seemed to notice when he hung up the phone.

The story of the second murder in the Capitol was in all the state's afternoon papers and one of the leads on nearly every television station's six o'clock news.

It set phones to ringing all over the city of Austin. Wilkins had unplugged his own phone by that time, but Hap Reatherford had not. He hadn't been expecting any calls, though news of Ron Matson's death had certainly been of keen interest to him.

He was of the opinion that things certainly looked bleak for Sam Wilkins, and he was more than ever glad that he had decided to sever his ties with the senator. It was all a very nasty mess, and Reatherford didn't want to be mixed up in it. Lobbyists didn't enjoy the best of reputations in any case, and being associated in any way with a man who was going to be tied in to a murder investigation—make that *two* murder investigations—would be enough to make Reatherford about as welcome as a leper on the legislative floors.

Well, it would unless there was some way he could use such an association to his advantage, and there didn't seem to be much of a possibility of that.

He was only mildly surprised to find that his caller was a young representative, Gene Watts, who had been Ron Matson's close friend. Reatherford had done a couple of minor deals with the man, and in the process had uncovered several things about him, including his affair with Matson and his drug use. Things like that were always useful to know.

"I hope I'm not disturbing you, calling you at home," the young man said.

"No, no," Reatherford said. "Not at all. What can I do for you?" He rubbed a hand across the top of his head. He thought he already knew what Watts wanted.

"I suppose you've heard about Ron Matson?"

"Yes," Reatherford said. "I've heard."

"Well, not very many people know this, but Ron was a very close friend of mine."

"So I've heard," Reatherford said.

"You have? I wasn't aware—well, never mind. What I'm calling for is that if my name gets brought into things by way of a murder investigation, it could be really bad for my career."

"It could, at that," Reatherford agreed. He wasn't surprised that the representative's thoughts were only for himself and that nothing was being said about the dead man. A man had to look out for number one.

"I wouldn't want to be involved if there were some way around it," the representative said, "and I know that you have a lot of influence. . . ." Watts let the sentence dangle.

Reatherford knew what Watts wanted, but he wasn't going to make any promises he couldn't keep. "Where are you calling from?" he said.

Watts told him. "It was on the news here just now," he said. "I couldn't believe it."

"You haven't been to Austin lately, then?"

"Well, not since a week or so ago. Surely you don't think that I—"

"Just checking," Reatherford said.

Watts's tone changed. "If you don't want to help me, just say so."

"I'll do what I can," Reatherford told him. "As you mentioned, I do have a little influence, but that doesn't mean that I can keep your name from coming up in the course of an investigation. If the law finds out about you and Matson, I'm not going to be able to do much. And I can't promise that I'll be able to keep your name out of the papers."

"I know all that. But there must be something you can do."

Reatherford gave it some thought. "There are always things that can be done to counter rumors. If there aren't any hard facts available." What he wanted to know was how well Watts had covered his tracks.

"There aren't any facts. I can promise you that."

"Then I'll do what I can. You'll have to make a few other promises, however."

"What kind of promises?"

"Nothing that would compromise you," Reatherford said. He wouldn't have to ask for anything like that. Watts would be easy to control from now on. He might even run for the Senate one day and take the place on Reatherford's payroll that Sam Wilkins had occupied until only a few hours before. In the meantime, a strong ally in the House was nothing to sneeze at. "But you will have to clean up your act considerably."

"What do you mean?"

"Drugs," Reatherford said. "There have been some disturbing stories about you and drugs."

"My God. Are you sure?" Watts thought that part of his life was as well kept a secret as his relationship with Ron Matson.

"I'm sure. And it wouldn't be a good idea to go looking

269

for a replacement for Matson in your affections, either. Sooner or later that kind of thing is going to hurt you."

"You're right, of course," Watts said.

Sincerity fairly oozed out of the telephone Reatherford was holding. He wiped his hand on his pants.

"I'll be far more careful from now on," his caller said. "But you will help me?"

"I'll do what I can," Reatherford said.

After he hung up, he thought about the young representative. It was a damn shame, but the man just had too many liabilities ever to amount to much in politics. He would never rise to the heights of even someone like Wilkins. It was a wonder he had gotten this far.

Nevertheless, Reatherford decided that he would actually try to help him. He wouldn't put himself out, but you never could tell. Maybe after this scare the young man would fool him, would really straighten up, get married and have children. It had happened before. More than once.

If it happened again, Reatherford wouldn't be sorry. He could use someone like Watts.

If Watts didn't change, well, Reatherford would keep his involvement to a minimum. When the time came to do so, if it did, he could cut loose from the man just as easily as he had cut loose from Sam Wilkins.

There was always someone else coming along.

By seven o'clock the wind had dropped, and the temperature had fallen just as Wayne had guessed it would. It was just about as dark as it was going to get, and Wayne thought it was time for him to head back to the Capitol.

He had left the church doorway at around five, moving down the drag from one place to another, never lingering long at any one spot.

He was cold, and he was hungry. He hadn't eaten all day, and his stomach was growling and churning around. He

270

thought he'd better find something to eat, so he started back toward downtown with the intention of rummaging around in the trash dumpsters around a pizza place or two. Cold pizza wasn't too bad, and lots of people never finished their pies. Most of them didn't like the crust, but Wayne thought that was the best part of all.

He needed to use the rest room really bad, too. His bladder felt like it was about to explode. He could take care of that easily enough, now that it was dark, but he still had to find a rest room pretty soon. He wasn't sure he wanted to use the one in the Capitol basement, but he figured he'd have to. Most businesses wouldn't let him use theirs, and there were some things you really didn't want to do in an alley, not even a dark one. He'd just have to wait. It shouldn't be hard. He'd waited before.

Claude Hebert was at home, getting ready for his big date.

He didn't think it was such a good idea, giving one of his private tours of the upper floors right after the two murders, but the woman had insisted. It seemed that the idea of the murders just made things that much more exciting to her, and Claude wanted her excited. That was the way he liked them.

Her name was Laurie, and she worked at the souvenir stand, standing behind the desk near the Capitol's north entrance and selling Texas mementoes to the tourists. She wasn't much more than twenty-five, and she had red hair and freckles.

Claude was partial to freckles, and he'd struck up a conversation with her a couple of weeks before. That's the way he liked to operate, get to know them, chat them up, and then work his way around to mentioning that he had keys to the upper floors.

"Nobody's allowed up there these days," he said. That wasn't the exact truth, since VIP tours were still conducted up there, but Claude didn't have an especially high regard for the truth. "There's always a way to see the sights, though, if you know the right people."

"What's up there that's worth seeing?" Laurie said, as if she didn't care. But Claude could tell she was curious.

"Well, for one thing there's those windin' stairs 'way up high there," he said. "You can see 'em from the rotunda if you tilt your head back."

"I've seen them. They don't look like such a big deal to me."

"Yeah, maybe they don't from down here, but can you imagine lookin' down from there at the star on the floor? Kind of makes the bottom drop out of your stomach."

"That doesn't sound like much fun," she said, her hand straying to Claude's baton. A lot of 'em liked the baton. "Will you be armed if we go up there? I might be scared."

Claude swelled his chest, which reduced the size of his stomach only marginally, and looked at her hand. "I'll be armed all right. Don't you worry about that."

"Will we get to go all the way to the top?"

That was something they all wanted to know. "Nope. Can't do that. Too dangerous. Those stairs kinda tilt out, you know? Wouldn't want to fall."

"Well, what else could we see? Besides the star on the floor?" She made a circle of her thumb and forefinger and slid the circle down the baton.

"There's a place up there, pretty high up, that we can walk out on a balcony and see the city," Claude said. "Best view in Austin, and it's really pretty at night, the lights and all."

"But wouldn't we get cold?" She slid her fingers slowly up and off the baton.

Claude smiled. "Honey, when you're around me, you don't ever have to worry about gettin' cold. Old Claude can take care of that part of things, don't you worry none about that."

"I guess it would be all right, then. If you're sure we won't get into any trouble."

"No way," Claude said. "I happen to know the cops."

He took his baton off his belt and gave it a little twirl. Laurie caught the end of it and slid her hand down it.

"I guess you do," she said.

Yessiree, Claude thought as he combed his hair in front of the bathroom mirror. He winked at his reflection. *You dog, you,* he thought.

He was going to give little Laurie a night she would never forget.

TWENTY-SEVEN

Darrel Prince was getting ready to return to the Capitol, too. He was positive that because of the cold weather Wayne would try to sneak back into the building that night. And when Wayne tried it, Darrel would be waiting for him.

Wayne had already managed to get past Darrel once, but if that happened again, Darrell had a backup plan. He was going to search the building.

It wouldn't be as hard as it sounded, since Darrel really didn't have to search the whole place. There were too many places that Wayne couldn't go without a key; Darrel didn't have to worry about those. And because he didn't have a key, Wayne couldn't get to the upper floors, either, or at least Darrel didn't think he could. So the number of hiding places was limited.

Darrel would check in with the cops on duty, then station himself in the rotunda. He'd keep watch till about ten o'clock. If Wayne hadn't shown by that time, the search would begin. There were several little nooks and crannies where Wayne had hidden in the past, and of course Darrel would make sure to check out the alcove where Ramona Gonzalez had been killed. He wouldn't put it past Wayne to try hiding there again.

If Wayne didn't show up and couldn't be found, Darrel wouldn't have wasted anything but time, and he had plenty of that. He had been married once, but his wife had left him for a piano tuner, something that had baffled Darrel for years. A piano tuner? What could a Goddamn piano tuner offer a woman?

Since that time Darrel had spent his evenings watching television and reading Western novels. He had read every novel in the Longarm and Trailsman series, as well as everything Louis L'Amour had ever written. He longed for the good old days when men were men and could shoot anybody they damn well pleased.

Clinton Amory wasn't going anywhere. He rarely did except on his league bowling night, the one night of the week he could get out of the house without his old lady tagging along with him.

He was in a bad mood. He was still pissed off because of the way that damn Ranger had talked to him. It wasn't only the *way* the Ranger had talked to him, either. It was what he had implied. The son of a bitch had made it pretty clear that Amory had better keep out of Wilkins's sight and not ask him for anything. That probably went for everybody in the whole damn place. What did that Ranger have to come nosing around for, anyhow?

And as if that weren't enough, Amory found out when he got home that his old lady had fixed a Frito chili pie for supper.

Amory hated Frito chili pie.

And to top things off, the TV set was on the blink. The picture kept sliding sideways, and no matter how many times

Amory hit the top of the set with his fist, his preferred repair method, the picture didn't improve.

"I been sayin' for three years we needed a new set," his old lady said. "But you won't listen to me. I might as well be talkin' to a fence post as to you."

"Shut the fuck up," Amory said, that being one of his favorite endearments.

"You didn't eat hardly any of the Frito pie. Did you have a bad time at work today?"

"You saw the news, didn't you?" Amory said. "Even with the picture sideways like that you must've heard what happened."

"It's just awful. Those two poor young people, killed like that. You knew them, didn't you, Clint?"

"Nah," Amory said.

"I thought you knew everybody there. You tell me all the time how you know—"

"Goddamnit, I don't mean I know every single person in the whole fucking building."

"But what about that woman? Ramona what's 'er name? I think I've heard you talk about her before. You said something once about—"

"Just shut the fuck up, will you? I never said a word about that woman, and I never want to hear you say that again. You understand what I'm saying to you?"

"Sure, Clint. But—"

Amory got up off the low-slung couch he was sitting on and walked slowly over to his wife. He put a hand on her chest and shoved her. She stumbled backward and hit the wall.

It wasn't a very sturdy wall. As far as that went, it wasn't a very sturdy house, and Mrs. Amory was a sizable woman.

When she hit the wall the entire room seemed to shake.

"I said, do you understand what I'm saying to you?"

276

"Sure, Clint. Sure. I understand. You don't have to worry about me. I got it."

"Good," Amory said, turning back to his television set. When he looked at it, he saw that the picture had straightened up. In fact, it was better than it had been for weeks. He sat down on the couch and reached in his pocket for a toothpick. By God, the next time the set went on the blink, he'd sure as hell know how to fix it.

He dug around in his molars for a minute and then started chewing on the toothpick. Maybe today wasn't a total loss after all.

It was getting late. Ray Hartnett had drunk most of the milk and eaten all the Oreos, but he still hadn't finished doing his paperwork.

The more things he wrote down, the less sense everything seemed to make.

Sam Wilkins was a man with years of public service behind him and a hell of a lot to lose. If he was going to kill someone, wouldn't he be too smart to do it in the Capitol building?

In fact, wouldn't he be too smart to do it himself at all? Wouldn't he find someone to do it for him?

Then there was Claude Hebert. Hartnett wondered about him. He was a man who, as a cop, would know his way around the Capitol better even than a senator. He would know about the placement of the TV cameras and be able to get his tape over them without being scanned. He had a reputation with women.

Suppose that Ramona had gotten tired of him and told him to take a hike. Claude wouldn't like being talked to like that, and he might have given her one last ride before killing her.

Ron Matson could have found out about Claude and Ramona and confronted the cop with what he knew. Claude might have asked Matson to meet him in the men's room and then killed him. It was a possibility.

But the more Hartnett thought about it, the better he liked someone else as the killer. Todd Elton. The man was a drug dealer on some kind of minor scale, and his motive was the same as Wilkins's in a sense.

He could have found out that Ron Matson was a bisexual and was having a fling with Ramona Gonzalez. He could have killed Ramona for revenge, raping her first to prove something or other to both himself and to Matson.

Maybe it didn't even have to be a matter of revenge. He could have looked on the murder as a way of saving his relationship with Matson.

Then when Elton confronted his lover and told Matson what he had done, Matson had not appreciated the favor. Maybe he had panicked, threatened to go to the police. So Elton had to kill him, too.

The second killing had been in the Capitol basement men's room, a place that had in the past been the scene of more than one homosexual encounter. Elton's murder of Matson there might have had a message in it.

It all seemed to fit, and Hartnett thought it fit the facts as he now knew them as well as anything, unless of course there was a wild card, someone Hartnett had not met or had no reason to suspect.

He thought about the other possibilities.

Amory? Too much the blackmailer.

Prince? Not likely. Too much the straight-arrow cop.

Wayne the Wagger. Least likely of all.

Someone else, say, some enemy of Wilkins who wanted to destroy the senator and was crazy enough to use the murders of two other people to do it? That seemed hardly more likely than Wayne.

It was Elton, all right. Had to be.

Hartnett went over his carefully written notes one more time, just to see if he had missed anything. He had written down everything he could remember of what had been said to him in all his interviews, and of course he had written down all he had said and done as well.

As he read over the notes, there was something about them that bothered him, but he couldn't quite say what it was. It seemed to him that there was something he had missed, something obvious that would give him the killer, but he couldn't quite figure it out.

It was an irritating feeling, and to counter it he decided to do something. He'd been sitting too long.

It wouldn't do to eat supper. He was still a little hungry, but the Oreos had contained enough calories for a week. There were other more productive things he could do, and two of those were at the top of his list.

One was a visit to Todd Elton. That would come first.

The other was something that he should have done that afternoon, and maybe it was what was worrying him about his notes. He should have reviewed the videotapes of the previous evening, and he should have talked to the night-duty officers about whom they might have seen in the building.

Maybe they had seen one of the suspects, or maybe they had seen someone else, someone who had no reason to be there.

Well, it would be simple to talk to them now. Considering the time, they would be well into their shift, which meant that they had probably already drunk eight cups of coffee each. He could drop by Todd Elton's place, wherever that was, and then swing back by the Capitol and have a talk with the cops.

He located Elton's address easily. He was in the phone book, and his neighborhood wasn't that far from the Capitol building. That was convenient.

As he looked in his bedroom closet for a coat, Hartnett thought about Jane Kettler. He wished he had asked her to have dinner with him, but right now he couldn't afford that kind of involvement. After he got this case wrapped up, and he didn't doubt for a second that he would do that, he might ask her out. He'd have time then.

Hartnett found an old down-lined jacket in the closet. It was bulky but warm. As he shrugged into the jacket, he couldn't help wondering what Jane was doing that evening.

He put the thought out of his mind. It was distracting, and that was exactly the reason he didn't want to let anyone into his life. Emotion affected your concentration. He couldn't help thinking that he ought to go over his notes one more time. If his mind weren't clouded by thoughts of Jane Kettler, he might find what he was looking for.

Oh, well, he thought. *It was probably nothing.*

Jane Kettler was ready for dinner, though it was still too early for her meeting with Stan Donald. She was bored with television and didn't want to start reading a book that she would soon have to put down. She decided that she might as well drive back to the Capitol and wait for Stan there. She could do a little work in her office while she waited.

The night drive up Congress Avenue was much quieter than the one she made every morning, especially on a cold night in midweek. There had been a time when the downtown area would have been bustling even then, when the two movie theaters would have been showing the latest Hollywood hits and the large department stores would be open to catch the late shoppers, but those days were long gone. There was a lot more light now, but there wasn't any life.

Neither of the two theaters had shown a movie for years, and most of the department stores had closed their doors and moved to the shopping malls.

Jane thought that was a real shame, especially the part about the movie theaters. They were the kind of place that no one built anymore, and they even had balconies. She was pretty certain that Stan Donald had never been to a theater with a balcony. There had even been a song called "Sittin' in the

Balcony" when she was a teenager, a song by Eddie Cochran, a rock star who had died young. Stan Donald most likely wouldn't know about him, either.

She found herself thinking about Ray Hartnett again and wondering if he had ever taken a girl to a theater and sat with her in the balcony, or if he had ever heard of Eddie Cochran.

And then she wondered what difference it made. So she and Ray had a lot more in common than she and Stan on the surface. So what? The things they had in common were mostly the result of their having grown up at a particular time and having shared the things that everyone who grew up at that time remembered.

She and Stan shared other things. They shared a common job interest. They shared. . . .

She couldn't think of anything else. They both liked the Regular Dinner at El Rancho, but that hardly counted. Besides, she liked the *chili con queso* with hers, and he got the tamale.

What could she and Stan talk about?

Current events?

Sometimes she wondered just how much people of Stan's age really kept up with what was going on in the world. He knew much more about the way the state government really worked than most people of any age, thanks to his job, but did he really know anything about national and international goings-on? Jane read the newspapers and news magazines carefully because she believed that everything that happened in the world affected everything else. But did Stan believe that or even care?

The seventies?

Stan would have been aware of some of the things that had gone on then, but he would still have been pretty young. Too young, really, to watch reruns of *The Bob Newhart Show* and have a sneaky feeling that Bob, Emily, and their friends

281

dressed and looked better than the way people dressed and looked now.

The eighties?

That would be Stan's decade, the "me generation." Jane didn't think she wanted to talk about the eighties at all.

But none of that would really matter if she and Stan were in love.

She thought that she detected the symptoms of love, or at least infatuation, in Stan, but she was afraid they were sadly missing in herself. She was flattered by his interest, and she was delighted to discover herself responding to that interest. It was as if she were waking up after a long winter's hibernation. But that was about as far as it went.

So what did love or infatuation matter? They didn't have to talk at all. Talking wasn't what she was really thinking about, was it?

As she drove into the Capitol grounds, she admitted to herself that she wasn't thinking about talking at all. She was really thinking about nonverbal communication, and she had a feeling that Stan would be very good at that sort of thing.

Ray Hartnett probably wouldn't. He was big and no doubt clumsy, the kind who wouldn't be able to express his feelings even if he would admit to having any, and she didn't think he would.

She was stereotyping again, she knew, and she should long ago have learned better than to do that. Ray had even pointed out that flaw in her character to her at lunch.

She decided simply to put him out of her mind. She would concentrate on Stan, see what developed this evening. She might not care one way or another about Ray Hartnett after spending another evening with Stan.

She parked in her usual spot and got out of the car. She had been driving with the heater on high, and stepping out into the freezing air was like being suddenly wrapped in ice cubes.

She shivered and headed for the Capitol as fast as she could in her medium-heeled shoes.

There were hardly any other cars around. There wouldn't be any tourists in the building on a night like this, not in the middle of the week. Only the night staff would be around, which was fine with Jane. She could get her work done with no interruptions.

Then she would meet Stan, see what happened between them. As she entered the building, she found that she was tingling with anticipation.

Or maybe it was just the cold.

TWENTY-EIGHT

Hartnett parked on the street in front of Todd Elton's house and got out of the car. The cold nipped at his face and hands and he could feel it even through the heavy denim jeans, but the puffy down jacket kept his upper body warm.

The house was dark, and there was no car in the driveway. The garage was closed, however, so the car could be inside. And Elton could be watching television in a back room.

The doorbell button glowed in the darkness, and Hartnett walked up and pushed it. He heard the muffled ding dong echo through the house, but there was no other sound.

He waited a second and tried the bell again, and after receiving no response, he knocked on the door.

"Damn," he said aloud when there was still no answer. He had been hoping to catch Elton at home and off guard, but he'd obviously missed him. He would have to try again early in the morning, maybe about the time Elton was waking up. That was always a good time to catch people, before their mental gears were all meshing.

He stuck his hands in the jacket's slash pockets and walked back to the car. It was time to visit the Capitol.

*   *   *

North of the Capitol was where the construction work for the extension was going on. There would be a large new addition to the building, all of it underground and connected to the original building by walkways. There would be offices for the legislators, and even a parking garage.

Wayne the Wagger lurked around the construction site for as long as he could. He figured the best time to go back inside would be fairly late, but not *too* late. He thought that there was a good reason for trying to make his entrance about ten o'clock, but he couldn't remember what the good reason was. Maybe that was when all the cops took a coffee break.

What a laugh, Wayne thought. That's all the cops did was take coffee breaks and eat doughnuts. Their whole job was just one long coffee break as far as he could tell, except when they were trying to shoot the ass off harmless people like Wayne.

Wayne was worried that someone would be watching for him. Despite the trickiness of his memory, he could still vividly recall that Prince had tried to kill him that morning. In Wayne's version of the event, the firing of the pistol was in no way accidental.

So Wayne was very careful. He slipped like a shadow around the construction area to the west side of the Capitol and went through the doors on that side.

Sure enough, there was Darrel Prince in the rotunda just as he had been that morning, but once more Wayne avoided him by the simple expedient of sidling along the sides of the corridor, slipping into doorways when Darrel turned in his direction, and scrambling down the stairs when he got to them.

He didn't want to go down into the basement, but that was where the closest rest room was located. Wayne had taken care of his bursting bladder at the construction site, thinking happily about his own contribution to the future of the state's most prominent building, but his intestines had begun their peristaltic movements now, and he had to get to a toilet or embarrass himself.

He made it to the rest room unseen and in moments had gained blessed relief. He didn't bother to wash his hands; he seldom did. He scooted out of the rest room and up the stairs, headed for the chapel.

He didn't want to be downstairs any longer than he had to. It seemed to Wayne that every time he had been in the basement lately, something bad had happened. He wasn't going back down there again any time soon, unless of course it was to relieve himself when he couldn't get to any other rest room. The basement was an unlucky place as far as he was concerned.

There were plenty of places he could hide out on the upper floors, and if he was lucky no one would find him there.

The chapel would be a good hideout, for example. He thought he might get away with secluding himself underneath the altar. If the cops swept the place, they might not be so careful as to check back there. Then after they left he could come out of hiding, get in the pew, and sleep there. It wasn't great, but it was better than the floor; at least there was a cushion on the pew. He'd gotten away with sleeping there once or twice in the past, or anyway he thought he had. It seemed like such a good idea that surely he'd tried it before.

What the hell. If he hadn't tried it before, he'd try it now. All they could do was throw him out.

If they didn't shoot him first.

Todd Elton, having concluded his last delivery of the evening, was filled with the satisfaction of a job well done.

Another soul made happy, he thought as the woman left the chapel. Todd looked around at the small room. There was not room inside for more than three or four people to sit comfortably, but meetings were not the chapel's purpose. It was there for the private meditations of those who needed a moment of restful quiet.

Since there was no one else around at the moment, Todd decided that a small sample of his own wares would not be out of place. He reached into the pocket of his stone-washed jeans and brought out a lip-balm tube. Removing the top of the tube, he tapped out a small quantity of white powder onto the crystal of his Rolex.

He deftly replaced the top of the tube with one hand, brought his wrist up to his nose, stopped his left nostril, and inhaled the powder with his right. The left nostril was a little more difficult, but Todd had become adroit through practice.

He put the tube back into his pocket and licked the watch crystal, running his tongue over his gums.

Damn! but he felt good. He sat for a minute in the pew, feeling the powder change to fire as it shot through him. All around him the quiet grew and grew. In front of him the stained-glass window glowed with a fire of its own, and the stone wall to his left seemed to soften into something less than stone.

He didn't look to his right, where the other wall was lined with photographs of typical Texas scenes. He thought the photos spoiled the whole mood of the room. He didn't know what wildflowers and things like that had to do with religion, and he could never understand why the pictures were hung in the chapel.

Todd enjoyed the quiet of the room, but he didn't particularly like sitting in there alone. He didn't like being anywhere alone for that matter, not even when he was full of Bolivian power. Besides, it was time for his meeting with Stan. He got up and started to leave when Wayne came in through the door.

"Shit," Todd said when he got a whiff of Wayne, whose distinctive odor had not been improved by his day in the rain. If anything the reverse was true, as it might be in the case of an old wet dog, and though Wayne had long since dried off, he retained a certain unsophisticated *je ne sais quoi*.

The narrow aisle to the right of the pew where Todd was standing was not big enough for the two of them to pass by one another either comfortably, or even uncomfortably, and Todd had no desire to come into contact with Wayne if he could avoid it.

As for Wayne, he wasn't to be stopped once that he had made up his mind. He was going to the front of the chapel, and Todd might as well not have been there for all the heed Wayne paid him. As soon as Wayne saw that there was someone else in the chapel and that the someone else was not a cop, he lowered his head to avoid all eye contact and strode forward.

Wrinkling his nose, Todd stepped into the pew and waited for Wayne to pass by him. If he noticed that Wayne failed to kneel at the bench but went behind the altar and slipped underneath it instead, Todd paid no attention. He had encountered any number of street people in his visits to the Capitol, and he had a pretty good idea what Wayne was doing there. Todd didn't give a damn.

As soon as Wayne passed him, Todd got up to leave again, and once again the door at the rear of the chapel opened. This time it admitted Stan Donald.

Todd was surprised. "I thought you were going to meet me at the tour desk."

"I was," Stan said. "But. . . . " He stopped and looked around the dimly lit room. "What's that awful smell?"

Todd looked up, then down. "What smell?"

"Don't tell me you don't smell anything," Stan said.

"Not me," Todd said. He sniffed an armpit. "I took a bath just last Saturday. Honest."

"That's not funny, Todd."

"Hey, it was free, though. What're you doing up here, Stan?"

"I saw you come in the building," Stan said, deciding to forget about the smell. "You didn't stop by and say hello."

"Gee, Stan, I didn't know you cared."

"I don't, actually," Stan said.

"So let me ask you one more time, then. Why're you here now? Why not wait at the desk?"

"I wanted to talk to you about some things. I thought you might be on the way up here to do a little business, and this is more private than the tour desk."

"I thought we were going to have a drink."

"I didn't mean tonight. I have a date in about an hour."

Todd didn't really care. As far as he was concerned, Stan had played right into his hands.

"A date?" he said. "Well, that's all right. But I'm glad you have time to talk. I've been wanting to talk to you, too."

"What about?" Stan said.

"You first."

"Murder," Stan said.

Todd took a deep breath. Little Bolivian generals were standing at attention in all his blood cells. "You son of a bitch," he said.

"I guess so," Stan said, putting a hand in his jacket pocket. "But I know all about it. I know you killed Ramona and Ron."

"You're losing it," Todd said. "As a matter of fact, you're crazy as hell."

"Maybe so," Stan said. "But I'm the one with the gun."

He brought his hand out of his pocket, and he was holding a small-caliber automatic pistol.

Jane was getting restless.

That was unusual for her, as she really liked her work and all that it involved. She liked the challenge of trying to fit everything into a tight schedule, she liked the difficult job of

289

trying to keep everyone happy with assigned times and places, and she even liked doing the paperwork.

Most of the time.

In fact, if anyone had asked her earlier in the week, even three days ago, she would have said that she enjoyed it all the time, and she would have relished the thought of some quiet time in her office to do some of the things she hadn't had time for previously.

But now things were different. She had too much on her mind. She kept thinking about Stan and Ray and the differences between them and wondering what she should do. She even found herself wondering if she should try keeping both of them on the string for a while until she decided for sure which of them she preferred.

The more she thought about that idea, the better she liked it. Why should she commit herself to one of them when both of them were available?

She looked at her watch. She still had forty-five minutes before it would be time to meet Stan. She began to go through the stack of accumulated work on her desk. A reminder to check on the dome tour sign caught her eye.

The sign stood on the fourth floor, at the foot of the stairs leading to the dome. On one side it said DOME TOURS CONDUCTED BY CAPITOL POLICE DAILY—TOURS BEGIN HERE. On the other side were the words DOME TOURS TEMPORARILY CANCELED BY CAPITOL POLICE DUE TO MAINTENANCE OR INCLEMENT WEATHER.

For months the sign had been supposed to say only dome tours temporarily canceled because of all the construction going on, but pranksters kept turning it around, and tourists, eager to take the tour, lined up and waited futilely, sometimes for nearly an hour. When they realized that there wasn't going to be a tour after all, their anger was equaled only by that of the tour guides who had to take the abuse heaped on them by the irate tourists.

Stan had complained about the sign earlier in the week, and Jane had asked the police to move it, to put it away somewhere until the dome was opened again. She doubted the police had done anything with the sign because of the excitement over the murders, so she decided to check it out herself before the problem occurred again. Also, a trip upstairs would give her something to do besides sit.

She did not expect there would be many people around, not at this hour, not on a night when the Capitol was practically deserted except for the transients who were hoping to find a warm place to cuddle up and sleep.

She hoped they all found what they were looking for. There was no real reason why they couldn't sleep in the Capitol, except that they were repulsive to the tourists and a lot of the workers. And of course if they were allowed to stay, their numbers would increase drastically. She had heard that New York's Grand Central Station was filled with the homeless every night and that they had to be driven out every morning.

There was something horrible and sad about it all, and Jane wished that she had some kind of answer to the problem.

Obviously she didn't. She couldn't solve her own simple dilemma, much less find a solution to a problem that was apparently baffling the local and state governments all over the country, not to mention the big boys in D.C., who as far as she knew, instead of spending money on people like Wayne the Wagger, were still sending massive amounts of foreign aid to countries whose soldiers might be shooting at Americans somewhere tomorrow.

When she left her office, she saw Darrel Prince standing in the rotunda. She walked down to ask what he was doing there.

"Surveillance," he said.

"Who are you surveilling?" she said.

"It's a police matter," Darrel told her.

Jane caught on then. "It's Wayne, isn't it? You're looking for Wayne."

Darrel ignored her, focusing his attention on the front doors.

"You can't possibly think that Wayne had anything to do with those murders," Jane said. She wanted to add something like, Not even you can be that stupid, but she didn't.

"It's a police matter," Darrel repeated. "You should move along."

Jane started to say something about the sign and stopped herself. If she stayed there much longer, she might take a swing at him. She turned back and went up the stairs. She hoped Wayne would find another place to spend the night.

Darrel watched her go. He didn't really like her very much. Thought she was smarter than he was, but she was wrong about that.

He was going to show her.

He was going to show them all.

Wayne could not believe what he was hearing.

He curled into a ball under the altar and put his hands over his ears, but it didn't help. He could still hear the two men, and they were still talking about the murders.

Wayne didn't want to hear that shit. He didn't want to hear it at all. And there was something else that worried him. Something about one of the voices.

He had to get out of there.

He uncoiled himself, clambered to his feet, and slithered from beneath the altar like an oiled snake.

"What the hell?" Stan said, barely jumping out of the way in time as Wayne jumped up and came barreling down the aisle and charged out the door.

Todd tried to take advantage of the distraction by jumping over the top of the pew and grabbing Stan's arm, but Stan got over his momentary startlement and clipped Todd in the side of the head with the butt of the pistol.

Todd slumped across the pew. A line of blood ran from his temple to his cheek.

"That Goddamn Wayne," Stan said. "He's nothing but trouble. Stand up, Todd."

Todd stood up, bracing himself with a hand on the pew back. "What're you doing, Stan? What's going on here?"

"I thought I told you that," Stan said.

"The murders," Todd said. "You're trying to be a hero or something. Is that it?"

"That's right."

"So you're making a citizen's arrest?" Todd said.

"I guess you could call it that if you wanted to."

Todd shook his head, then stopped when he realized that it was hurting him. "I can't believe this shit," he said.

"Why not?" Stan said. "It seems simple enough to me."

"You don't get it, do you?" Todd said. "I was the one who was going to accuse *you* of the murders. I thought *you* killed Ramona and Ron."

"You're kidding."

"Oh, no. No. I was going to get you off my case by telling you that if you didn't leave me alone, I'd tell the cops about you."

"And you called *me* crazy," Stan said, keeping the pistol leveled at Todd's chest. "Why would I want to kill anyone?"

"Hell, I don't know," Todd said. "You did screw around with Ramona a few times, though."

"How'd you know that?"

"Ron told me. You know how Ron talks."

"Yeah, he does. Did."

"Right. Anyway, now that we're through accusing each other, why don't we get that drink?" Having the gun pointed at him, Todd was rapidly getting over the effects of the coke he'd ingested, and he needed bucking up.

293

"I don't think so," Stan said. The pistol did not waver. And then Jane walked in.

Ray Hartnett had parked his car and started toward the Capitol when he noticed that a car was parked in the place reserved for Jane Kettler, the one marked CHIEF ADMINISTRATOR. He wondered whether she was working late or whether someone who wanted to get close to the building had simply parked in the reserved spot.

He entered the building and saw Darrel Prince, still on watch.

"You working two shifts?" Hartnett said.

"I'm watching for Wayne," Prince said. "He'll be back here tonight. It's too cold for him to stay outside, and he doesn't know of anywhere else to go."

"I don't think Wayne had a thing to do with any of this," Hartnett said. "Unless he's a witness to something."

"Fine," Prince said. "I'll get him as a witness. I bet his prints are all over that hamper. Maybe both of them."

Hartnett hadn't gotten a report from the crime-scene investigators yet, but he would probably have one by the next day. He didn't think the canvas of the hampers would take very good prints, however, and the frame was too small to have anything other than a partial on it, if that much.

"We'll see," he said. "Have you seen Ms. Kettler here tonight?"

"Yeah. She went up the stairs just a minute ago." Prince gave a thin-faced leer.

"Is there something else you need to tell me about that?" Hartnett said.

"Well, that fella who runs the guide desk went up just ahead of her. I guess you know what they say goes on in the chapel up there."

"That doesn't mean that either one of them is there."

"Yeah. Right. Sure. Whatever you say."

Hartnett wasn't interested in discussing the topic any further. If Jane had a clandestine meeting with Stan, it wasn't any of Hartnett's business. Or so he told himself.

"What about the videotapes from last night?" he said. "Did anyone check them?"

"Not that I know of," Prince said. "Somebody checked the camera, though, and there was masking tape over the lens for sure."

"But nobody noticed that," Hartnett said.

"I'm not on duty at night. I couldn't say."

"Who *was* on duty?"

"Cal Lexington and Tommy Tankersley, I think."

"Are they on duty tonight?"

"Yeah. They should be in the headquarters."

"I'll have a talk with them, then," Hartnett said.

"You don't have to worry," Prince said. "There won't be anybody getting strangled in the men's room tonight."

Hartnett hoped not. He was tired of bodies turning up in the Capitol. He thought about that morning when he had found out from Chrissy and Tanya about the murder of Ron Matson.

Then he thought about something else, which led him to still another thought.

"Is there anyone else on the upper floors?" he said.

"I don't keep up with everyone who comes in here," Prince said. "I'm looking for Wayne."

"You must have noticed whether there's been a lot of traffic in here tonight, though."

"There hasn't. Hardly anybody's been in. Too damn cold out there." He didn't mention Claude, though he knew about the after-hours tour. Claude couldn't keep from bragging about it. But that wasn't any of the Ranger's damn business.

"I'd better get up there," Hartnett said. He turned and trotted for the stairs.

He wished he hadn't worn his boots. They were warm, but they were hell for running. He hoped he'd make it in time.

TWENTY-NINE

Hartnett made it to the second floor just as Wayne came flailing down from the third.

Wayne saw the Ranger and tried to stop, his Keds shrieking loudly on the marble floor, but his headlong momentum was too great and he smashed into Hartnett, who had put his arms up in an attempt to ward Wayne off.

The two of them went down in a tangle on the floor, Hartnett landing on his rear and sliding back about two feet.

Wayne struggled frantically to separate himself from the Ranger and escape, and Hartnett, who had gotten a good whiff of the Wagger, was tempted to let him go.

But he didn't. He had a few things to ask him. He got to his feet and pulled Wayne up with him.

"Hello, Wayne," he said.

Wayne stared at Hartnett vacantly, trying to give the impression that his battery was a long way short of a full charge, an impression that happened to correspond pretty closely to the actual facts.

Hartnett shook him a little. "It's not polite to stare, Wayne. Say hello."

Wayne continued to stare.

"All right, Wayne. If that's the way you want it. I guess I'll have to take you downstairs and turn you over to Darrel."

"No," Wayne said, shaking his head violently, his eyes showing a lot more life. "Not him."

"I didn't think you'd like that. Now, tell me why you were in such a hurry."

Wayne stopped shaking his head and lapsed back into his vacant stare.

"I don't think Darrel likes you very much," Hartnett said. "He thinks you're a murderer."

"Hey, man. I never killed nobody."

"I don't think you did, but I can't convince Darrel unless you help me out. Why were you in such a hurry?"

Wayne looked over his shoulder. "There's a guy up there in the chapel. He's got a gun."

"What guy?"

"I didn't get a good look at him," Wayne said, not mentioning the somehow-familiar voice. "There's another guy, too."

"Did you get a look at that one?"

"Yeah."

"You're not very talkative, Wayne. Who was he?"

"He's a dealer," Wayne said. "I can't remember his name."

"Todd Elton?"

The name jolted Wayne's faulty memory. "Hey, right. That's the one. I guess I did know him."

"But he doesn't have the gun?"

"No, it's the other one."

"That wouldn't be Stan Donald, the director of the tour service, would it?"

"Hey, man, if you know all the answers, why're you asking all these questions?" Wayne said.

"Was Ms. Kettler in the chapel?"

That was a question that gave Wayne no trouble. "No, but she was headed that way. I nearly ran into her before you got in my way."

"Thanks, Wayne," Hartnett said. "That's all I needed to know." He let Wayne go and started up the stairs.

Wayne couldn't believe that the Ranger had let him go. He'd thought that he'd be taken to Darrel Prince for sure, but he'd had a reprieve. Now all he had to do was find somewhere to sleep, and he thought he'd better do that on this floor. No use in taking a chance with Darrel.

He started to look around.

Just as Jane reached the landing between the third and fourth floors, Wayne the Wagger had flown by her like a jet-propelled chicken. He was obviously running from someone, and she felt sure that an extra policeman or two must have been stationed upstairs because of the murders.

She climbed the rest of the way to the fourth floor and headed for the sign, which was not far from the chapel. Sure enough, the sign was facing the wrong way. She started to turn it in the right direction when she heard voices from the chapel. Wondering who was in there at that hour of the night, she decided to take a look.

She was quite surprised when she saw Stan and Todd. "What on earth is going on here?" Jane said. "What are you two standing there like that for? What's the matter with Todd's head?"

Then she saw the pistol in Stan's hand.

"Stan, is that a gun?" she said, thinking immediately that she'd just asked the stupidest question of the year. *Of course* it was a gun.

Stan was obviously stunned to see Jane standing there. He opened his mouth like a fish, but he didn't say anything.

"It's a gun, all right," Todd said, putting his hand to his

head and bringing it down to look at the blood on his fingers. "He uses it to hit people with."

"I don't understand," Jane said.

"I wish you hadn't come up here," Stan said, recovering from his surprise. "I told you I'd meet you at ten."

"I came early to catch up on some paperwork," she said. She ran a hand through her hair. "I needed a break, so I thought I'd come up and check on the dome tour sign. I certainly didn't expect to find you here holding a gun on Todd."

"Me neither," Todd said. "I think he's crazy."

"Just shut up," Stan told him. "Don't ever say that." He paused for a second to let that sink in. "Todd's the killer," he said to Jane.

"What? Are you sure?"

"He's not sure of anything. He's crazy."

Stan stepped close to Todd and jabbed the pistol into his breastbone. Hard.

"Jesus," Todd said, staggering and sucking in a sharp breath. "That hurt, Stan."

"I told you to shut up," Stan said. Light flashed off his glasses, hiding his eyes. "Now we'll have to decide what to do with you."

"Can't we turn him over to the police?" Jane said. "Darrel Prince is downstairs. He can take over now."

Stan laughed. "You call Darrel Prince the police?"

Jane saw his point. "Maybe not, but he's as close as we've got," she said.

"We don't need him, anyway," Stan said. "Todd's confessed, and now he's going to commit suicide."

"What?" Todd and Jane said together.

"You heard me," Stan said. "It's too bad you had to come up here, Jane, but both of you will have to come with me now."

"Come with you, my ass," Todd said. "I'm not going anywhere."

"Sure you are. Otherwise, I'll shoot you."

"You're cr—"

Stan stuck the pistol in Todd's mouth. "I told you to shut up, Todd. I won't warn you again."

Todd nodded slightly, his eyes big.

Stan removed the pistol. Todd's upper lip was bleeding where the pistol's sight had cut it.

"Stan," Jane said.

"Let's go," Stan said. "You two first." He gestured toward the door with his pistol.

Jane's head was spinning. She couldn't figure out what was happening, but she knew it was all wrong. She didn't move.

"Don't you see, Jane?" Stan said. "If we turn him over to Darrel Prince, there won't be any justice done. He'll get off some way. That's how things work. We'll have to do this ourselves."

"Stan, we're not the law. We can't—"

"Sure we can. He killed Ramona because his lover boy was sleeping with her. Then he killed his lover boy. I know it, but I can't prove it. So we'll have to help the law along a little."

"But that's crazy," Jane said. "You're angry and confused, Stan." Jane was confused, too, but she was also frightened. She had never seen anyone behave like Stan was doing now. He seemed to be a completely different person from the one she had known, and she wanted somehow to calm him.

"Don't you start," Stan said. "Just get out of here. Now!"

Jane started toward the door, still trying to figure out what was going on.

"Now you, Todd," Stan said, and Todd followed along. Stan walked behind them with the pistol.

★   ★   ★

300

The stairways leading to the upper floors of the Capitol were behind locked doors, but that didn't make much difference if you had a key.

Claude Hebert had a key that he had used an hour or so earlier, and he and Laurie had spent a lot of that time outside the building on the high balcony that looked out over the city.

It was a bright, clear night, and the view was just as fine as Claude had promised it would be. Laurie was delighted, and she kept locating different landmarks to point out.

The cold weather, as far as Claude was concerned, was an added bonus. Thanks to his excess poundage, he was thoroughly insulated, and he thought the cold was by far preferable to the heat of a Texas summer or even the milder weather of spring.

Besides, the cold encouraged Laurie to snuggle up to him in order to warm herself and allowed Claude to whisper to her things about how cute she was, how much he liked the sound of her voice, and how her freckles turned him on.

Men had a hard time understanding Claude's appeal, but women never did. A good part of it came from the fact that Claude, when he was alone with a woman, was a silver-tongued devil, quick with compliments and flattery that were always genuine. He was never crude, the way he was when he was with other men. He was always completely sincere.

After a while, Laurie had seen enough and wanted to go back inside and get warm. She didn't really want to go any higher up in the building, however.

That suited Claude just fine. He had a few plans for her once they were in the building. He had a place already fixed up, a place that he'd long ago swept clean of the dead birds and bird shit that cluttered the upper levels. He'd supplied the place earlier that day with a couple of blankets and a six-pack of wine coolers packed in ice in a Styrofoam container.

The best part of the private tour was about to begin.

★ ★ ★

After leaving the chapel, Todd and Jane walked hesitantly up a stairway that ended in a locked door. Stan followed them, holding the pistol pointed at their backs.

When they got to the door, Stan took a key out of his left-hand pants pocket. As the head of the tour guides, he, like Claude, had keys to the locks.

"Catch," he said, tossing the key to Todd.

Todd was caught by surprise, but he snatched the key out of the air. "What's this?" he said.

"Open the door," Stan said, waving the pistol at him.

"What? Why?"

"We're going on up," Stan told him. "Open it."

Todd put the key in the lock and turned it. Then he opened the door.

"Go on through," Stan said. "You first, Jane. Then Todd."

Jane considered breaking away. She couldn't believe that Stan would shoot her, and even if he would, she felt like taking the chance. However, she was stopped by a strange reluctance to leave Todd alone. She knew that whatever Stan had planned for him, it would not be pleasant.

So she followed Todd through the door. Stan came through next and locked the door behind him.

Ray Hartnett reached the chapel, but there was no one there. He looked around, but the room was too small for anyone to really hide in. He went back out and looked around. There was a standing exhibit of photographs depicting the Capitol at various stages of its history, but nothing else. Then he heard a door slam somewhere above him.

He jogged around the corner to the stairway, which was flanked by large photo exhibits of the 1901, 1903, and 1905 legislatures. He didn't waste any time looking at the pictures.

In front of the stairs was a sign saying something about the dome tours, but he ignored it and went up the stairs.

He tried the knob of the door when he got to the top, but the door was locked. He pounded on it. "Jane!" he said. "Are you in there?"

Jane heard his yell just as Stan was about to force her and Todd through the stairway door on the next floor. She turned and said, "Ray!"

"That's enough," Stan said. "Keep your mouth shut and keep going."

Jane didn't move. "That's Ray Hartnett. He's a Texas Ranger. You can't find a better representative of the law than that. We can turn Todd over to him."

"I'm sorry, but it's too late. Move it." Stan shoved Todd in the back, pushing him into Jane. "And don't yell again," he said when she opened her mouth. "I don't want any interference from you or from your Texas Ranger."

"What's all the noise?" Laurie said. "I thought you told me no one would bother us up here."

Claude had indeed told her that. He had cleared his little late-night "tour" with the officers on duty, and no one else would be walking around on the upper levels at that hour.

"Well?" Laurie said.

Claude looked at the wine cooler he was holding. It was beaded with icy water, hadn't even been opened yet.

"Don't you think you ought to see what's going on?" Laurie said.

Claude didn't want to see what was going on. He wanted to sit down on the blankets with Laurie, drink a couple of wine coolers, and see what Laurie looked like with her blouse off. He thought for sure she'd have a scattering of freckles across her breasts.

But that would have to wait. He was a police officer, after all, even if he was off duty. Besides, he wouldn't put it past that damn Tankersley to be slipping around and trying to get a little free show. That would be just like the bastard.

"You stay here," Claude said. "I'll see if I can find out something."

Laurie reached over and touched his baton. "You hurry back now, you hear?"

"Don't you worry about that," Claude said. "This won't take a minute."

He walked off in the direction of the sound. It was not dark on that level, thanks to the fact that the Capitol's double dome was well lit at night and some of the light filtered into most parts of the building, but Claude turned on his flashlight to chase away some of the shadows.

He went down to the sixth level, but there was no one there. However, he could definitely hear someone down on five now. He went over to the stairway.

It was the light that Stan saw first, shining under the door. "Who's that?" he said.

No one answered him, but Claude opened the door and came onto the floor with them. He didn't bother to shine his light on them. They were in the dim light from the dome, and he could see them just fine.

"What the hell are you all doin' up here?" Claude said. "Nobody's supposed to be up here unless it's because of official business."

"We're just taking an after-hours tour," Stan said. "Ms. Kettler's trying to get these floors opened to the tour again, like they used to be, and we're checking them out."

"Bullshit," Todd said. "He's got some stupid idea that I'm a murderer. I don't know what that has to do with us being here, but it's the truth."

"Is that right, Ms. Kettler?" Claude said, looking at Jane. He didn't know what was going on, but he thought he could trust her to tell him.

"No," Jane said. "Not all of it's right. Stan's not telling the

304

truth." For some reason she couldn't quite bring herself to say that he was lying. "He's got a gun."

Stan had been holding the pistol down by his side. Now he brought it up where Claude could see it.

"You aren't supposed to be carrying a sidearm," Claude said. He identified the weapon as a .25 automatic, though he didn't know the maker's name. "You better let me have it."

"Sure," Stan said.

He shot Claude in the right eye.

THIRTY

It had been Stan Donald all along.

Hartnett didn't know why, but he knew he was right as soon as he heard the shot.

Tanya and Chrissy had told him that no one knew who had been killed in the men's room, but Stan had been in Jane's office at that very instant, telling her not only who had been killed but how the murder had been committed.

Tanya and Chrissy had also said that Ramona told them about going out with some other men, at least one of whose names she wouldn't tell because they knew him too well.

Stan Donald.

Had to be.

And now he was up there somewhere with Jane and someone had just fired a shot.

It was a hell of a time for him to have left his own pistol in the car, but there was no time for him to go back and get it now.

There was a red fire extinguisher hanging on the wall behind the standing exhibit near the chapel. Hartnett ran back down the stairs and took the extinguisher off the wall, carried it back up, and hefted it over his head. Then he brought it crashing down on the doorknob, breaking it off and shattering the lock.

Destroying state property, he thought as he set down the fire extinguisher and shoved open the door. *I wonder what the penalty is for that?*

When Claude Hebert's head hit the floor, it sounded like the cracking of a very large hard-boiled egg, but the sound didn't bother Claude. He was already beyond being bothered, dead before he hit, and there was a ragged red hole where his eye had been. Dark blood ran out of the socket and down the side of his face into his hair.

"Oh, Jesus," Todd said. "Jesus, oh, Jesus." He didn't say it very loud. He wanted a hit of coke more than he had ever wanted anything in his whole life.

Jane didn't say anything. She couldn't say anything. It was as if someone had cut her vocal cords.

Stan was not interested in Claude. He had heard the smashing of the doorknob, and he turned to watch the stairway. He hadn't thought to lock the other door behind them.

When Hartnett came through the doorway, Stan snapped off a shot. The bullet went over the Ranger's head and *pinged* off the wall behind him.

Hartnett ducked back inside the doorway. He wished again for his pistol, but all he had was the fire extinguisher that he had carried with him. He had come to the Capitol to talk to the cops about the videotapes. Who needed a pistol for that? He'd never thought he'd be tangling with a killer.

And it was obvious that Stan was indeed a killer. Hartnett had glimpsed the body of Claude Hebert lying on the cold floor.

He had seen Jane, too, so Donald had her with him. He

also had someone else, a man whom Hartnett didn't recognize.

Hartnett heard noises and risked a look around the door frame. Donald was urging Jane and the other man through the door that led to the stairs going up to the next level. Hartnett waited until Donald had closed the door, and then he went after them.

Laurie heard them coming onto the seventh level, but she thought it was Claude coming back. She got up off the blanket and went to ask him what was going on.

But of course it wasn't Claude that she saw.

"Who're you?" she said. "Where's Claude?" She peered at them in the dim light, but she didn't recognize them.

"Claude had to rest for a minute," Stan said, bringing up the pistol.

For Jane the moment was like something from a slow-motion movie. She saw the woman standing there, she saw Stan's arm coming up, and then she was moving toward him about as fast as a swimmer in Jell-O.

Somehow she got to Stan before he pulled the trigger. Then time stopped stretching out like a rubber band and everything started happening at once, very fast, as if the movie had switched from slow motion to the speeded-up action of a Buster Keaton.

Jane jumped for Stan, clawing for the hand that held the pistol.

She missed the hand but got the arm, her weight forcing it down, and the gun went off.

The bullet hit the floor in front of Stan's right foot and screamed off at an oblique angle. Jane held onto his arm, trying to drag him to the floor.

Laurie didn't know what was going on, but she knew that she had nearly been shot, and she was scared. She started to scream.

Todd Elton watched Stan and Jane struggling for only a split second before his instinct for survival kicked in. He didn't give a damn about either one of them, and he cared even less than that about the woman standing in front of them holding her hands to her face and screaming like an actress auditioning for a B-grade horror film. Let them get it all straightened out if they could.

As for him, he was getting the hell out of there.

He turned and ran for the stairway.

Hartnett heard the shot, heard the screaming. Both things added to his sense of urgency.

The locked door in front of him was different from the others he had come through. The top half was pebbled glass, and he slammed the fire extinguisher into it.

The glass shattered and flew out of the frame. It splintered again on the hard floor on the opposite side of the door. Hartnett cleaned the frame of the jagged remnants with the fire extinguisher.

Todd Elton skidded to a stop just in time to avoid Hartnett as the Ranger came through the opening in top of the door. Todd looked around for a place to hide, but there was nowhere to go.

It didn't matter. Hartnett wasn't interested in Todd. He was focused on the figures struggling on the floor near the next stairway.

Stan heard the falling glass and knew what it meant. He hated to have to hit Jane, but there was nothing else to do now. All his plans were coming apart, but he thought there was still a chance for him if he could just get away from the Ranger.

He made a fist with his free hand and clubbed Jane in the temple. As her grip on his arm relaxed, he twisted around and fired at Hartnett.

This time he got lucky.

The bullet hit the fire extinguisher and ricocheted off into Hartnett's left shoulder. Hartnett suddenly lost all feeling in his left arm. He dropped the fire extinguisher, which hit the floor with a clanging roll. Then he stumbled and fell.

Stan looked for Todd, hoping to have a chance to shoot him, too, but he was not in time. Todd had climbed through the window opening and scooted away down the stairs.

Stan turned to Laurie, who had stopped screaming. She was simply standing there in front of him, her hands pressed to her mouth. Tears ran down her face.

"Get out of the way," Stan said.

Laurie didn't move.

Stan motioned with the gun. "I said get out of the way." He didn't want to kill her anymore. It just wasn't necessary, and he wanted to save his bullets. He hadn't brought along a second clip.

This time his message got through. Laurie moved aside while Stan took Jane's arm and dragged her to her feet.

"Can you hear me?" he said to Jane.

Jane nodded without speaking. The nodding hurt her head.

"We're going on upstairs now," Stan said. He started forward, tugging at her arm. She stumbled along beside him.

Stan didn't bother to lock the door behind him. He didn't think it would make any difference this time.

"What the hell is all that noise?" Tommy Tankersley said. He was standing in the rotunda shooting the breeze with Darrel Prince, whom he'd seen when he started to make the rounds of the first floor.

Tankersley was a big man, much taller and wider than Prince, and he was black, which made him unusual among the Capitol police.

"Sounds like it came from upstairs," Darrel said. "There's a Texas Ranger up there, and so's Ms. Kettler."

310

"I guess we better see what the hell's going on, then," Tankersley said, pulling up on his belt. In addition to being tall and wide, he had a large stomach and had trouble keeping his pants up. "It might have something to do with the murders."

Darrel didn't think so, since he was sure that Wayne, the perpetrator of the murders, wasn't in the building, but they had to check it out. "Right," he said. "Let's go." He turned toward the east stair.

"Hell, I don't mean to walk up those damn stairs," Tankersley said. "Let's get the elevator."

He called in his location and destination on his radio, then ambled across the rotunda toward the front entrance. The elevator was located in the entranceway. Prince followed. If Tankersley didn't want to walk, it didn't make any difference to Darrel.

If they had taken the stairs, they might have run into Todd Elton, but as it was they missed him completely.

Todd hit the first floor at a dead run, having set a new unofficial speed record for descending the Capitol stairs, but he didn't stop to catch his breath.

He didn't stop to visit the cop shop and tell anyone what was going on, either. He didn't believe in getting involved. He'd seen a T-shirt once that said something like KILL 'EM ALL AND LET GOD SORT 'EM OUT. At the moment, those were his sentiments exactly. He headed for the doors.

When he got outside, he was surprised when the cold hit him. Only then did he realize that he had been sweating heavily. Now he felt like he was bathing in ice water.

The feeling didn't even slow him down. Within fifteen minutes he was inside his house, packing his bags.

Hartnett shook his head to clear it and looked around. It seemed darker than it had, but he could still see. His shoulder hurt like hell.

There was a girl kneeling beside him.

"Where's Claude?" she said.

His first thought had been to send her for the cops, but her question changed his mind. If she was a friend of Claude's, there was no need for her to see what was down there. Surely the cops would hear all the noise and come to investigate.

"Claude's downstairs," he said. "But you'd better wait here until someone comes. Where did Stan Donald go?"

"The one with the gun?"

Hartnett nodded.

"Upstairs," Laurie said. "He had the woman with him."

"That's what I was afraid of." Hartnett stood up. He felt light-headed at first, as if he might fall again, but he stood still for a few seconds and then he was all right.

"Are you going after them?" Laurie said.

"Yes," Hartnett said.

"I didn't mean for things to work out like this, Jane," Stan was saying as he pulled Jane along. "It wasn't supposed to be like this at all."

Jane had been numbed at first by the blow to her head, but she was thinking clearly now, as clearly as she ever had in her life. She even thought she knew more or less what Stan was talking about.

"Where are we going?" she said.

"Up there," Stan said, pointing with the pistol toward the winding iron staircase that led high above them.

"I don't think I want to go up there, Stan."

"I know. I don't want to go either. But we have to, now. I'm sorry."

They were at the stairs now. "You first," he said, jabbing the pistol in her back when she hesitated. She started up the stairs.

"Why, Stan?" Jane said. She thought of the way he had

kissed her on her lips earlier that day and had to resist the urge
to wipe the back of her hand across her mouth.

"Why what?" he said. "Don't slow down!" He pushed her
with his hand.

"Why did you kill Ramona and Ron?" Jane said, continu-
ing to climb. "I don't understand."

"I had to," he said. "I want you to know that. It wasn't
because I liked it or anything."

"I'm sure you didn't," Jane said, forcing herself not to look
down. She was afraid of what she'd see. The stairs seemed not
to go straight up but instead to lean outward at a dangerous
angle.

"Well, I didn't. But Ramona was threatening to tell people
about us. She talked too much, that was her trouble. Why
couldn't she be like the others?"

"What others?" Jane said. She continued to climb the
twisting stairs, but she slowed as much as she dared.

"All the others," Stan said. "The ones I dated while I was
waiting for you to notice me. They never meant anything to
me. Nothing at all. You were the only one I ever really cared
about. I want you to know that."

"So you killed her for *talking*?"

"No," Stan said. "Of course not. I killed her because she
got pregnant. She told me she was careful, but she wasn't. She
lied."

He sounded quite resentful, Jane thought, as if the whole thing
were Ramona's fault. The part of her mind that was keeping
her sane because it was detached from events, the part that
was somewhere up above, watching all this as if it were a play
or a movie, concluded that, ironically enough, Stan's position
on pregnancy was similar to that of Mrs. Stanton and Mrs.
Tolbert. She didn't mention that, however. She didn't think
it was the right time for a philosophical discussion.

"She was going to tell people she was pregnant and that the
baby was mine," Stan said. "I didn't want that. That would

313

have ruined my chances with you. I'd been waiting so long, and things were finally starting to work out. She could have said the baby was someone else's, but she wouldn't do that. I tried to tell her, but she wouldn't listen."

Jane had stopped, and he jabbed her again. "You might as well go on. Your boyfriend won't be coming. I took care of that."

Jane felt her heart rise into her throat. "What do you mean?"

"Never mind. Just go on."

Jane went on.

"Nobody here," Tankersley said after he and Darrel had made the rounds of the second floor. "Guess we might as well go on up."

They hadn't heard anything else, but Darrel didn't argue. "Sure. Why not?" He'd about given up on finding Wayne anyway.

They went back to the elevator.

Hartnett's arm was bleeding slightly, and every time he moved he felt as if someone were jabbing a red-hot hat pin into his shoulder muscle.

From where he stood just inside the doorway on the seventh level he could see Stan and Jane up the circular staircase. He knew he should wait for the cops to show up, but maybe they weren't coming after all. They should have been there by now, considering all the noise. Darrel, in the rotunda, should have heard it if no one else had.

Hartnett knew better than to depend on Darrel. If anyone did anything, Hartnett would have to do it himself.

The trouble with that thought was that Hartnett didn't have any idea of what he could possibly do.

★ ★ ★

314

Jane didn't know what to do either, other than to keep Stan talking.

"It's partly Chrissy's fault," he was saying. "If Darrel Prince had just gone ahead and shot Wayne, it would have been all over. Wayne could have taken the blame for everything. But Chrissy yelled at Darrel before he could shoot."

"Why Ron?" Jane said. "Why kill him?"

"He talked as much as Ramona, and he had been going out with her. If she even hinted to him that she was pregnant by me, he would have told everyone. I met him in the basement and took care of that."

Jane had a horrible thought. "That must have been right after we went to El Rancho." She might not ever eat a Regular Dinner again, even if she got out of this mess.

"I called Ron when I got home," Stan said. "I told him that I needed to talk to him. I could tell you liked me after we talked at El Rancho. You liked me a lot. I couldn't take any chances about Ron. You can see that."

"I can't see it at all," Jane said. "You must be cr—"

"Don't say that," Stan said. "I really don't like it when you say things like that."

Jane stopped where she was and turned around. She looked at Stan, who was very close, only two steps below her. He seemed quite young and sincere, but the light from the dome glinted off his glasses, making it look as if his eyes were flashing crazily at her.

"You don't like it because it's true," she said. "You were even going to kill Todd Elton."

"Of course," Stan said. "He was the perfect suspect. He was Ron's lover. If he committed suicide, it would look like he was guilty of the murders and had killed himself out of remorse. A lovers' quarrel. Now he's ruined everything."

"He was right, though," Jane said. "You're crazy."

"Stop it!" Stan said, bringing up the pistol. He drew back

315

his arm as if he might hit her, but he stopped himself and took a deep breath.

"I wish you still loved me," he said.

"Still loved you?" Jane said. "You're wrong about that. I never loved you, Stan. I was flattered by your interest, and I liked you because I thought you were nice and did your job well." She shook her head and half smiled. "I guess you did your job well, but you aren't very nice."

"I haven't changed," he said.

"Maybe not. I was just wrong about you. It's not the first time I've been wrong, though. And it won't be the last."

"It might be," Stan said.

"No it won't. You're not going to kill me."

"Oh, yes I am," Stan said. "I've been thinking, and I have it all figured out. We're going to commit suicide, just like Todd was."

"What?"

"Two lovers, plunging to their deaths. It's not what I hoped for, but I can't think of any other way for this to end."

"Not me, buster," Jane said, swinging her fist at Stan's face.

"Jesus Christ," Tankersley said.

He and Darrel were looking down at the body of Claude Hebert.

"Call for backup," Darrel said. "The Wagger's on the loose up here! Get a SWAT team!"

Tankersley reached for his radio to make the call.

When Jane swung at Stan, Hartnett moved onto the floor and started up the stairway. It looked like this would be Hartnett's only chance to do anything. Stan was as about as distracted as he was likely to get.

Hartnett just hoped he could get to them before Jane got hurt.

He didn't give a damn about Stan.

THIRTY-ONE

Stan snapped his head back and jerked the pistol up, firing a shot that whanged twice off the metal stairs. Off balance, he slipped down two steps, scraping his shins and crying out in pain and rage.

Jane didn't think she could get by him, so the only way to go was up. She turned and started ascending the stairs.

She didn't get far. Stan's hand closed around her ankle and jerked her to a stop. She kicked viciously at his fingers, trying to free herself, but he did not let go. He was much stronger than she would have thought. His fingers bit into her ankle like iron.

Stan pulled himself to his feet, then released Jane's ankle. He walked up the steps that separated them, the pistol pointed at her face.

"If you do anything like that again, I'll have to shoot you," he said. "I'd really hate to do that. It would spoil things."

Jane didn't really care if she spoiled things. She swung at him again.

Stan ducked and Jane's momentum carried her halfway around and twisted her over the outside stair rail.

She hung there, bent at the waist, looking down for the first time. For a moment the rotunda seemed to spin beneath her, but then things locked into place and she could see the star on the floor so far below her that it was smaller than a star in the sky, as if she were looking at it through the wrong end of a telescope.

Then the telescope suddenly reversed itself and her stomach did flip-flops as the star suddenly rushed toward her. She could see it clearly now, even down to the speckles in the terrazzo, and she could see the crack that spread across the floor.

She felt Stan's hands on her hips. "If you want to go first, that's fine with me," he said. "I thought we could go together, but maybe this is the best way."

He lifted her slightly and her stomach did its trick again. She tried to close her eyes, but she could not. She found she was horribly fascinated with the height, with the sight of the very hard floor, with the thought of that crack. She thought about the story of the man who fell, the story that the tour guides weren't permitted to tell.

I guess now we'll find out if a falling body really could make a crack like that, she thought, and she almost laughed.

Tankersley and Prince heard the shot that clanged on the iron stairs. Both men had their sidearms out.

"Where the hell is that SWAT team?" Darrel said. "Somebody ought to be here by now."

"I don't know," Tankersley said. "You think we oughta go on up, see what's happening up there?"

Darrel didn't like the idea. He had no idea of what was happening, but he was beginning to have serious doubts that Wayne the Wagger was the cause of it. Strangling was one thing. Shooting a cop in the eye was another. He didn't think Wayne's hand was steady enough for that.

But what the hell. This was still Darrel's big chance. He

could capture a killer. Or maybe it would be even better than that. Maybe he would get a shot at the bastard and kill him, even if it wasn't Wayne.

He got a tighter grip on his pistol. "Let's go," he said.

Hartnett knew he wasn't going to be able to make it in time. The twisting stairs were too steep, his shoulder hurt too much, and things were happening much too fast.

That son-of-a-bitch Stan was going to throw Jane over the stair rail and there wasn't a damn thing Hartnett could do about it.

Well, there was one thing. He could yell.

"Hold it right there, Donald!" he said.

Too late.

Stan flipped Jane over the rail and started after Hartnett.

Darrel didn't shoot Laurie, but it was a close call. He had the pistol lined up on her head when Tankersley stopped him.

"Hold on, Prince," Tankersley said. "It's just a girl."

Darrel didn't lower his gun. He was going for the head if he had to shoot. They couldn't wear a bulletproof vest on their heads.

"Girls can kill people," he said.

"I didn't kill anyone!" Laurie said. "There's a man with a gun in there, though." She pointed to the door. "He shot a man."

"We know he shot a man," Tankersley said. "We saw him."

"You saw him shoot someone?" Laurie said.

"No, Goddamnit," Darrel said. "We saw the dead man."

"The man's not dead," Laurie said. "He's in there, too. And there's a woman."

"Shit," Tankersley said. "In where?"

Laurie pointed to the door again. "In there."

"To that circular stair," Darrel said. "The one you can see

from the rotunda if you look up. You wanta check it out?"

"All right," Tankersley said.

"What about her?" Darrel said. He was still pointing his pistol at Laurie.

"She's OK," Tankersley said. He looked at Laurie. "You stay here, Miss."

"Don't worry," Laurie said. "I'm not going anywhere."

Jane had not done skin-a-cat since grade school. She hadn't even thought about it since then. But now she had done it again.

As Stan flipped her, she grabbed a thin iron balustrade in each hand and got a death grip. Now she hung outside the rail, her back to the stairs. It seemed as if the star on the floor down below was miles below her feet.

It's only an optical illusion, she told herself. *I'm really only a few inches off the seventh level.*

She looked down at her feet.

She saw the star. Nothing separated her from it but what looked like two miles of air.

She swallowed hard. Her hands were sweating and she was losing her grip on the balustrade. She wished that she was a size two and weighed only eighty pounds.

Above her head Stan's pistol cracked.

Hartnett stumbled down several steps, trying to put the stairs between Stan and himself. "Hang on!" he yelled to Jane. He hoped she could do it. It was a miracle that she hadn't already plunged down to the first floor.

Stan clattered down the steps after Hartnett, firing again.

Hartnett was wondering how many rounds had been fired when Prince and Tankersley came on the scene.

Prince's pistol boomed and a bullet shrieked off the stairs near Hartnett's ear.

Hartnett turned and saw Prince. "Stop shooting, you fucking idiot!" he yelled. "It's me. Ray Hartnett!"

Prince had not paid a great deal of attention to who might be on the stairs, and he'd completely forgotten about Hartnett's having told him that he was going upstairs.

Prince lowered his pistol, and Stan shot him in the leg.

Darrel screamed. Tankersley grabbed him by the shoulders and dragged him back through the doorway.

"It's your turn now, Hartnett," Stan said. "I thought I got you before, but you're not going to spoil this now." He started down the stairs after the Ranger.

Jane knew she couldn't hold on much longer, so she thought she might as well try to save herself. It didn't appear that anyone else was going to do it.

If she could just let go with one hand for a split second, she could spin around and grab hold again. She'd still be hanging there in space, but she would be facing the stairs. It was worth a try.

She closed her eyes, took a few deep breaths, and let go with her right hand.

She didn't exactly spin around, but she didn't fall. Her left wrist scraped painfully against the iron as she turned slowly around. Finally her right hand grasped the balustrade, but it slipped immediately, and her left hand almost lost its grip. She slapped wildly with her right and when it touched the balustrade, she grabbed it tightly.

This time she held on.

Her arms were trembling, and she was sweating heavily. She knew she couldn't just hang there.

She kicked her shoes off, not looking to see where they fell and willing her ears not to listen for the sound of their hitting.

She swung her left leg up, trying to hook her heel on the stairs. It took her three times, but on the third she was satisfied that she had a firm hold. She started to pull herself up.

★ ★ ★

Stan walked slowly down the stairs, pointing the gun, forcing Hartnett down before him.

"You should never have started coming around here," Stan said. "I was afraid you'd catch on to me when Jane said that she told you about Ron. I should have been more careful, but I never expected her to mention to anyone that I told her he was the one who was dead. You've known since then, haven't you?"

Hartnett didn't say anything. He was trying to keep at least one of the iron stairs between himself and Stan, but sooner or later he was going to have to stand his ground and try to take the pistol away. Stan might shoot him again, but he could survive if he wasn't hit in a vital spot. He hoped the cops didn't come back in and start shooting. They were even more dangerous than Stan.

Jane heaved herself over the stair rail and sat on the steps, panting. She was never going to climb another stair as long as she lived. From now on it was going to be elevators all the way.

She would have liked to sit there for an hour or two catching her breath, but she didn't have time. Ray Hartnett was almost to the bottom of the stairs, and when he got there Stan was sure to shoot him.

In her stockinged feet she slipped down the stairs as quietly as a cat.

Hartnett saw her coming. He was tempted to warn her off, but he didn't say a thing. He hadn't done such a great job himself so far, and she'd already survived getting thrown off the stairs.

What else could happen?

When Jane was as close as she could get without being seen, she threw herself on Stan's back. Stan was off balance and fell forward, pulling Jane along with him. They caromed around a curve in the stair and piled into Hartnett, who couldn't get out of the way in time.

All three of them slid around the last of the rail and onto the floor in a heap of thrashing arms and legs.

There was a hand over Hartnett's face, but he heard the gun hit the floor as it left Stan's hand. The trouble was that Hartnett couldn't decide which of the bodies twitching around on top of him belonged to Stan and which to Jane, something he thought he would have been able to figure out under less stressful circumstances.

The hat pin that had been jabbing his shoulder had been replaced by a jackhammer.

Someone had hold of his head and was banging it against the floor. He hoped it was Stan.

Suddenly the weight on top of Hartnett lightened and Stan stopped the head banging.

"Now get off him, Stan," Hartnett heard Jane say.

Hartnett twisted his head around and saw her standing about ten feet away. She was holding the .25 automatic in both hands and pointing it at Stan, who was sitting on top of Hartnett with his hands on both sides of Hartnett's head.

"You wouldn't shoot me, Jane," Stan said. "I know how you feel about me. Besides, you don't know anything about guns." He started pounding Hartnett's head on the floor again.

"Maybe not," Jane said. "But I know how to pull a trigger."

Stan paid her no attention. He took Hartnett's hair in one hand in order to continue beating the Ranger's head on the floor. With his other hand he bashed the shoulder wound.

"Stop it!" Jane said.

Stan didn't stop it.

Jane pulled the trigger.

There was a flat *crack* and the pistol jumped slightly in Jane's hand.

Stan let go of Hartnett's hair and tried to stand up. Blood pumped out of his throat. He looked at Jane in disbelief.

"You—" he said. The word gurgled in his mouth and he pitched forward across Hartnett.

Hartnett shoved Stan off with his good arm, but he couldn't get up. He couldn't quite focus his eyes, either, but he thought he saw Jane kneeling beside him.

"Are you all right?" she said.

"Sure," Hartnett said.

Then he passed out.

THIRTY-TWO

"Are you sure?" Governor A. Michael Newton pushed his hair back from his bulldog face as he spoke into the telephone. "There's no mistake about that?"

He listened for a short while longer, then hung up, shaking his head. "No one was trying to kill me," he told Trey Buford.

"I know," Buford said. He had taken the call from the Rangers himself. Newton hadn't even wanted to touch the phone until Buford told him what the call was about.

"I can't believe it," Newton said. "I thought for sure someone was out to get me."

Jess and Marvin didn't have any comment. They were eating a midnight snack of meatball sandwiches that the kitchen had sent up for them. Marvin had dribbled sauce on the front of his shirt.

"No one was out to get you," Buford said. "You've got to get that idea out of your head."

"I guess I do," Newton said, getting out of bed. "I don't know why I offend so many people. Hell, it's not as if I got to be governor to make people mad."

"It might be because you don't think before you speak," Buford said. He'd been wanting to tell the governor that for a long time, but he hadn't thought it would do any good.

"What do you mean?" Newton said.

"I mean you just weren't cut out for making off-the-cuff remarks. You need to have everything scripted. There are a lot of people on your payroll who are good with words. You ought to give them a chance to earn their money."

Newton pushed up his glasses. "I guess you think I ought to listen to the people I pay to advise me, too."

"It wouldn't be a bad idea," Buford said.

"I'll give it a thought," Newton said. "I wonder if the kitchen would send up one of those sandwiches for me?"

"You're the governor," Buford said.

"I am, at that. Call 'em up, Trey. Tell 'em the governor's hungry."

"Have 'em send up some milk," Jess said. "I've finished mine off."

Newton looked at him. "I hate milk," he said.

Hartnett was propped up in the hospital bed. He had a head-ache and his shoulder still hurt, but not as much as it had. He suspected that some of the pills he'd taken had been pain-killers.

Jane Kettler sat in a chair beside the bed. She'd brought in a bouquet of red carnations. Hartnett wished he'd shaved.

"It was nice of you to stop by," he said. "Aren't you supposed to be at work?"

"I didn't want to go in at all this morning," Jane said. She didn't look any the worse for her night's experience. In fact, to Hartnett she looked better than ever. "It's going to be a real hassle, what with the tour guides not having a director and every legislator and reporter in the state calling. I even had to disconnect my telephone at home last night. I got tired of listening to my message on the answering machine."

"But you're going in to work anyway?"

"Of course. I have a job to do."

"I appreciate the job you did last night. Did you ever think about entering law enforcement?"

Jane laughed. "Hardly ever," she said.

"It took a lot of guts to pull that trigger."

"I wasn't sure I could do it," Jane said. She was no longer laughing. "But I'm glad I did. I think Stan planned to kill me all along, maybe blame it on Todd. Otherwise he wouldn't have asked me to meet him at the Capitol."

"What happened after I fainted?" Hartnett said.

"I wouldn't call it fainting."

"Whatever. I was sure Prince would come in there and gun us all down."

"You were already down."

"Whatever."

"They did come charging in with a SWAT team right after I . . . shot Stan. I think that by then even Darrel had pretty much figured things out. Before it was all over, he was staggering round and taking all the credit for catching up with 'the Capitol killer,' as he was calling Stan by then."

Hartnett grinned. "This isn't going to do my reputation as a lawman much good."

"You caught on before anyone else," Jane said.

"Too late, though."

"Not entirely."

"Maybe not." Hartnett leaned back against the pillow. "Would you consider going out with me sometime? Maybe for dinner?"

Jane smiled. "As long as it's not Mexican food," she said.

Hap Reatherford heard the news on an early broadcast. *I'll be damned,* he thought. Wilkins didn't have a thing to do with any of the killings. Maybe it had been a little premature to ditch him. As soon as he had breakfast, he'd have to give the senator a call, see how he was doing.

You never knew when you'd need a friend.

Wilkins heard the same news broadcast and thanked God that he hadn't mailed his letter of resignation yet.

He smiled broadly as he lathered his face to shave. There was no reason to mail it now. He was in the clear, for the most part. The murders had nothing to do with him, and if he could keep the girl in Goldthwaite under wraps, no one could touch him.

He thought he might have to talk to Hap Reatherford again about that nosy reporter, but even if the reporter printed what he suspected and put in plenty of innuendo, everything was going to be temporarily overshadowed by the murders and the dramatic events of the previous evening. If the story on the radio was right, Jane Kettler was going to be the talk of the town for weeks to come. Maybe there would even be a movie about her. She was quite an attractive woman, really.

Too bad, he thought, *that she isn't a little younger.*

Wayne the Wagger turned over and yawned. After all the excitement the night before, he had sneaked back into the chapel and curled up on a pew to sleep.

No one had bothered him. Everyone was too busy elsewhere to be interested in checking out the chapel.

Wayne didn't know what time it was. The stained-glass window at the front of the room was charged with color, but that didn't mean anything. It was lighted artificially.

Wayne was pretty sure it was morning, though. Maybe everything was still in an uproar and no one would be cleaning in the chapel today. Wayne wasn't quite sure what had gone on, but he had gotten a look at one of the dead men before they hauled him out of the Capitol late last night.

He hadn't been wearing his glasses, but it was the bad one, the one that had killed the woman in the basement. Wayne remembered having seen him in the chapel earlier, but he hadn't really recognized him then.

That thought made Wayne sit up with a jerk and look around.

There was no one in the chapel but him, however, and he soon relaxed.

The colors in the window caught his eye again, and he stared at them until they began to run together, swirling him up and away into a red and blue and gold memory of what the world had once been for him.

Then he stretched, yawned, lay down in the pew, and floated away in a dream, back to those long-lost times.